'He wasn't v

'What would yo
could be measu
jagged spear of l_____ across his
angry face. Unconsciously, Amelia held her
breath.

'Go home, Mrs Cummings,' he warned.
'Before you're struck by lightning.'

'I don't need your advice, Mr Tanner,' she
countered. 'I can take care of myself.'

'Then do it,' Ross stated darkly. ''Cause I sure
as hell won't.'

Dear Reader

We welcome back Gail Mallin who offers DEBT OF HONOUR set against the brooding backdrop of the Lake District, and in DEVIL-MAY-DARE Mary Nichols gives us Lydia, who walks a tightrope of possible disgrace. Our American offerings are STARDUST AND WHIRLWINDS by Pamela Litton set in Texas 1873, and AUTUMN ROSE by Louisa Rawlings gives us seventeenth-century France. Happy New Year!

The Editor

Pamela Litton grew up in West Texas, where she used to spin adventure stories for her friends and her to act out. A voracious reader then and now, Pamela's love for history, romance and adventure caused her to once more begin making up adventures of her own, this time in the form of novels.

Pamela now lives in San Antonio, Texas, with her two sons and her husband of twenty years, whom she describes as a 'hero'. She is a self-proclaimed home-maker and a full-time writer.

STARDUST AND WHIRLWINDS

Pamela Litton

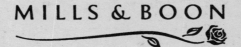

MILLS & BOON LIMITED
ETON HOUSE, 18-24 PARADISE ROAD
RICHMOND, SURREY TW9 1SR

Originally published by
Harlequin Historicals 1991

First published in Great Britain 1994
by Mills & Boon Limited

© Pamela Litton 1991

Australian copyright 1994
Philippine copyright 1994
This edition 1994

ISBN 0 263 78328 6

Set in Times Roman 10 on 10¼ pt.
04-9401-98766 C

Made and printed in Great Britain

Prologue

June 1869

Blue, scarlet and gold flames soared into the black sapphire night. Crackling and hissing, the fire writhed and twisted on an orange-hot mound of embers. On three sides of the blaze, steep, jagged walls of red earth formed a curving backdrop of glowing copper. Huge shadows, like ghostly demons, danced across the earthen stage. From the canyon floor the sounds of heartbreaking weeping and bloodcurdling screams drifted upward on the smoke and cinders to be captured by the wind and scattered onto the vast, empty plain, the Llano Estacado.

Ross Tanner stood alone on a high precipice above the deep canyon. His eyes narrowed against the smoke and cinders that rose from the crack in the flat plain to swirl around him.

"¡Dios!" he cursed, his voice little more than a rasping whisper. "This is the edge of hell."

The acrid smoke clouded his thoughts with gut-grinding memories. His throat corded as he watched a howling, half-naked Indian wrench a squalling toddler from its begging mother's arms. Unconsciously Ross scraped his arm across his nose and mouth to clear away the sour stench of the Indian's sweating skin, a foulness that haunted his dreams to this day. When another member of the large war party bashed the wailing woman's head with his war club, Ross closed his eyes and saw his mother's bloody face. The last and only memory he had of her.

Slow, deep anger sizzled against the icy contempt that had numbed his soul for so many years. In silent torment he watched half of the war-painted savages mount their ponies, their booty of four struggling children securely tied to the lead ponies. With barbarous cries of jubilation they rode off into the darkness waving their feathered lances. The remaining Indians fell on the women with renewed furor, tearing away their clothing and throwing them down into the red dust. One slender reed of a girl looked no older than thirteen. Rage exploded through Ross, leaving emptiness in its wake.

"Es verdad, mi amigo."

Ross whirled around at the soft-spoken words. The small campfire and the muttering among the men sitting around it pulled his thoughts from the horror in the valley. Ross shook his head. "What?"

The tall New Mexican standing behind him shrugged his broad shoulders, bare under the leather vest he wore. He notched his chin upward, indicating the scene behind Ross. "You are right. This place is hell. Hell for the children who must forget who they are, hell for their mothers who cannot. *Los comancheros* call this valley El Valle de las lágrimas, the Valley of Tears."

Armando Fierro joined Ross on the lip of the canyon. They turned to look down on the scene below, now clouded in a red mist of dust.

Mando muttered, *"Por Dios,* it is that." He took a long pull from an earthenware jug and winced as the fiery *aguardiente* burned down his throat. "Let us leave this place. We can do nothing. *Los comancheros* are *loco* with whiskey and blood. We are too late to trade for those poor souls." Mando crossed himself and started to leave, until he saw the dangerous glint in Ross's eyes. Mando knew trouble brewed as he saw fury sweeping away his companion's usual expression of catlike indifference. He wished Ross had not found him this night.

Sweat rolled off Ross despite the cool night breeze. Not much of what Mando had said reached him. He couldn't take his eyes from the bloody dolls the Indians tormented in the glaring circle of firelight. Tears stung his amber eyes.

After throwing down another swig of *aguardiente,* Mando grabbed Ross's arm, turning him away from the unholy scene, and shoved the jug into his chest. "This will help. It is a fine friend on a night like this."

Ross jerked the jug from Mando and threw it into the emptiness behind him. With a scowling glare, he jerked his arm free and strode toward their tethered horses. Resolution hardened his broad mouth into a tight grimace that deepened the curved lines bracketing it.

Mando quickly caught up with him and grasped his shoulders in a viselike grip. "I told you, *mi hermano,* there is nothing to be done."

"The hell you say." Ross shoved the tall New Mexican away from him. "I'm through trading with them. We've got to kill them."

"No!" Mando commanded. "We fight with them against the *americanos* as we always have. We cannot raise our guns against them."

A long agonized scream echoed up from the canyon. Ross swallowed the bile rising in his throat. "God forgive me, but I'm glad your mother is dead. She would die of shame to see you a part of this."

Mando struck like a coiled snake, his hard fist catching Ross on the jaw. Ross staggered back a step, then returned the blow with lightning speed, sending the *comanchero* leader skidding into the red, powdery dirt. Before Ross could take two steps toward the fallen man, pistols cleared leather, rifles cocked and a long-bladed knife stuck the ground between his feet. Ross lifted his hands cautiously from the gun strapped low on his hip.

Scattered behind Mando, eleven bandoliered men trained their weapons at Ross. Mando quickly signaled them to put away their guns. With deliberate slowness, they obeyed his silent order. Ross lowered his hands and let out his breath in a long sigh. He warily scanned the men's glowering faces, their features contorted into fierce evil masks in the flick-ering light of the campfire. His gaze fell to Mando where he lay in a dusty firelit aura, his shoulders propped up with his arms. Ross tried to hate the man, but he had loved the boy too much.

With a lithe, graceful movement, Mando rolled to his feet and stood a good two inches above Ross. "You think be-cause I am a greaser—" Mando ground out the slur "—those screams do not shred my soul?" He swayed slightly, but his shining onyx eyes bore into Ross's. "Has living with the *tejanos* made you forget my father called you 'son'?"

"I'll never forget the man who saved me from becoming a savage like those in the canyon!" Ross's hands balled into hard fists. "We will always be brothers," he grated. Turning his back on Mando, Ross raised his head to the heavens, heavens Don Alphonso had taught him to read like a dia-mond-studded map. The strict Spanish don had raised them to value honor above all. He turned to face Mando, his voice a double-edged knife. "I haven't forgotten what your father taught us, but have you, Mando?"

Mando raised his strong jaw proudly. His gaze locked with Ross's. "My father taught me to survive. Our women and children go hungry. The greedy *americanos* are creep-ing into our land, taking all they see, killing the buffalo un-til nothing is left for us or the Comanche. There is plenty for all, but the *americanos* are never satisfied."

"There is no honor in killing women and children."

"Perhaps not, but honor alone can't stop a thief or fill an empty belly."

Ross clamped his jaw against any further arguments. They would do no good. He swallowed the painful loneli-ness closing his throat. Whatever Mando told himself, it wouldn't work for him. He was finished here.

Ross silently saddled his horse and, without a backward glance, rode slowly into the cool summer night, away from the only family he claimed, away from the dying fire in the canyon. He thought of riding into the valley alone, but he'd be damned if he'd risk his neck for any more lost causes. The women were probably either dead or gone by now.

After he had passed the edge of the campfire's glow, Mando's voice, harsh and guttural, reached him through the night. "Ross Tanner!" The Anglo name was as a curse on Mando's chiseled lips. "The *americanos* want too much. We will fight with the Comanche, as we always have, the only way we can. Where do you stand?"

Mando listened to the receding hoofbeats grow weaker until only the wind whispered back to him. Let Ross think the worst; maybe it would make his choice easier. Grabbing up a new jug, he followed Ross's steps until a curtain of darkness dropped behind him. Staring at the dark, broken hills, he uncorked the jug and poured down a long swallow, then scraped the back of his hand across his mouth. *"Vaya con Dios, mi hermano,"* he called, his voice blending into the blowing wind.

Mando stumbled back to his men, who had gathered again at the campfire. He studied the face of each renegade who rode with him, and remembered better days, better companions. Mando threw his head back and filled the awful night with bitter laughter. His black, shoulder-length hair lifted in the night wind and reflected flashes of orange firelight; his dark skin glowed bronze. His men soon joined him, their laughter drowning out the tormented echoes from the canyon.

Ross reined his horse to a halt. He thought he heard Mando calling him. He twisted around and listened closely to the roar of the wind in his ears. Laughter. Could that be laughter? "Oh, God, Mando." He wanted to hurt. He wanted to feel something. He waited for the pain. Nothing.

Ross shifted around and touched his spurs to his big black's flanks. The horse headed south toward the Conchos. Ross started to turn him west toward New Mexico, then let the reins go slack. Nothing was left for him there, now that the old man was gone, and Mando was lost. Nothing waited for him in Texas, either, but hard feelings from a family who wished a Comanche's knife or a bluebelly's bullet had fin-

ished him. Ross shrugged. That wasn't important. He didn't
give a damn about them, either.

Ross spurred his horse into an easy, ground-covering
canter. It didn't much matter where he went as long as he
kept going.

Chapter One

Spring 1873

"As whirlwinds in the south pass through; so it cometh from the desert, from a terrible land." Amelia Cummings stared at the opened Bible in her hands. Her scalp tingled with premonition as she reread the ominous passage she had turned to by chance. A jagged chunk of cold dread settled heavily in her stomach. It was as though God had tapped her shoulder and warned, "Whirlwinds wait in a terrible land."

She tried to dispel the ridiculous notion. Desert, indeed! Texas was no desert. In the past days of traveling, she had seen rolling green hills and tall trees from the stagecoach window. They had certainly crossed enough rivers on the journey south and west from the end of the rail line at Sherman. The little verse in Isaiah catching her eye was a coincidence, nothing more. Still, she couldn't quite shake the chill of those words.

"Are you feeling well, Mrs. Cummings? You look a little sickly."

Amelia looked up quickly to meet the direct gaze of her fellow stagecoach passenger. She slammed the Bible's black leather covers together with a thump and pushed the holy book across the leather-cushioned seat. Taking a calming breath, she answered, "I—I'm fine, thank you, Mr. Carter. It must be this heat." To illustrate her point, Amelia dashed

up a square paper fan proclaiming the merits of the Nimitz
Hotel of Fredricksburg, Texas, and madly fanned her face.

"It is a mite warm for early spring," Haywood Carter
drawled. "That's one thing about Texas. Weather's full of
surprises. Out where you're headed . . . you said your husband has a dry-goods store in Santa Angela, there by Fort
Concho?" At Amelia's nod, he went on, "Out there, it can
be so cold and wet it'll make your bones ache, or so hot and
dry a man could near bake."

Amelia abruptly halted her brisk fanning. "A desert?"
Her eyes darted an accusing glare toward the Bible, jostling
against the wooden side of the big Concord coach, before
she brought her attention to the older man sitting across
from her.

Mr. Carter nodded his broad-brimmed, gray felt hat dipping over his eyes. "Yes, ma'am, a desert of sorts. Mighty
dry out there at times. Of course, it ain't as dry and mean as
the Llano, that bein' a real desert. Not too far from your
new home, either."

Amelia cast a troubled look at the white-mustached man.
First that verse, now deserts? Though her hands felt clammy
inside her black kid gloves, she steadied her voice to reply,
"I don't recall my husband mentioning any nearby desert in
his letters."

"Take my word for it. It's there. Some call it the Staked
Plains. The Mexes call it the Llano Estacado. Comanches
call it home."

Amelia studied Mr. Carter. Could he be trying to frighten
her, a newcomer, a Yankee? Her clipped Ohio accent had
produced several rebuffs on her journey south. His no-
nonsense grandfatherly face disclosed a man of strong
character. Someone she could trust. She glanced apprehensively at the Bible again. The comfort her mother's parting
gift had provided on this long journey from Ohio to Texas
had suddenly vanished. Slowly she brought the fan in motion again and turned her attention to the scenery passing
swiftly by the broad window. Mr. Carter's talk of deserts
and Comanches unsettled her. "It must be a..." She paused

searching for the correct words, then she knew. "A terrible land," she finished with flat finality.

Mr. Carter pulled his Colt revolver from its holster at his hip and checked the chamber, a precaution not lost on Amelia. "Yes, ma'am." He holstered the Colt with practiced ease. "But the land ain't half as bad as the men it breeds. Red ones, brown ones, even white ones, it don't matter. They're all spawns of the devil, specially those gun-running *comancheros.*"

Amelia shot Mr. Carter a startled glance, her heart skipping a beat at his choice of words. He nodded silently confirming his harsh testament. Amelia turned her attention back to the rushing landscape beyond the window. Her husband, Devin, had never mentioned any of this in his letters to her over the past year. Perhaps that was why he had never sent for her. He should have told her.

When Amelia made no further comments, Haywood Carter picked up the newspaper folded beside him, but from beneath his shaggy white brows, he watched the young woman across from him. A pretty little thing, he mused, with that smooth white skin and dark hair. He liked her eyes best, though. A nice blue, not so light they looked cold, not so dark they looked hard. They revealed everything she was thinking. Those eyes made a man feel comfortable until he noticed her mouth. Her lips were full and shapely, almost pouty, though they usually wore a smile. Her mouth made a man imagine all kinds of things, even things he oughta be too old to remember.

Mr. Carter rattled the paper open and tried to read. Despite his efforts to concentrate on a story about the governor's tussles with the army, he wondered what had made her eyes cloud up the way they had and her cheeks get all chalky. He'd bet a ten-dollar gold piece against a Yankee greenback she didn't have any idea what to expect once she reached Santa Angela.

Amelia tried to dismiss the dark wings of impending doom spreading inside her. All her doubts, all her parents' warnings spilled into the glaring light of second thoughts. She thought they had been neatly folded, packed away deep inside her, and the locks fastened tightly. She had hoped that particular baggage would have gotten lost on the journey to Texas. Instead that Bible verse had scattered all the old fears haphazardly through her mind. Amelia's small hands drew up into tight fists. She would just have to gather them up and cram them back where they belonged. Somewhere so hidden they would never bother her again.

It wasn't an easy task. It hadn't been an easy task in Ohio surrounded by the blanketing love and comfort of her parents' home, where she had lived while waiting for Devin to send for her. It hadn't been easy when she had insisted she was joining her husband in Texas, when she had argued it didn't matter that he hadn't sent for her, when she had begged her father for traveling money.

Now, inside the swaying, hot, stagecoach, seated across from a heavily armed man who claimed to be a newspaper reporter and gazing out at the vast empty reaches of land, the task of putting her fears and doubts to rest seemed impossible. Pictures muddled her thoughts. Pictures of her mother and younger sister, Libby, huddled together at the train depot, tears streaming down their faces as they said their goodbyes. Pictures of her papa blustering about his good friend General Sherman assuring him of her safety from Indians; yet his eyes had misted and his ruddy cheeks had looked pale. Amelia quickly passed a hand across her own eyes. With a determination she was surprised to find within herself, she fought the panic threatening to overwhelm her.

Devin did love her. He just had to love her. When they were together again, things would be different, better. Her parents wouldn't be just down the street, but thousands of miles away. Too far ever to interfere again. And with love to sustain them, it wouldn't matter if they must live in a terrible land, or even a desert. Ohio had been a wilderness when her parents had moved there. They had survived and built a comfortable life together with the same business Devin was starting, a mercantile. When she reached Santa Angela everything would be fine. She would make it work.

The words sounded good to her bludgeoned confidence, even after the hundredth repetition, and she smiled with a certain satisfaction. She had taken hold of her life despite the obstacles she'd faced. Whatever desert whirlwinds waited, she could hang on tight to that.

"Kickapoo Springs up ahead," the stage driver called out, startling Amelia. She noticed the interior of the coach had grown dark and a little cooler. Night was falling.

"Won't be long now," Mr. Carter said, giving up on reading his paper. "Next to the last stop for you. After Kickapoo Springs there's ten more miles to Lipan Springs, then only nineteen more to Concho Station."

"That's certainly good news," Amelia replied. Despite all the problems that might await her, Amelia felt her heart quicken. By tomorrow morning she would be in Concho Station. Devin waited for her there. Her long journey was almost over.

The driver cracked his whip and swore at the horses. Without slowing its breakneck speed, the coach rattled and bounced its way toward the setting sun. Amelia couldn't make much out of the kaleidoscope of scrub-covered hills and scattered groves of trees in the gathering dusk. Perhaps what she didn't see was as important as what she saw. They hadn't passed another human being since yesterday. Didn't anyone live out here in this part of Texas?

The coach raced into the small stage station of Kickapoo Springs and halted with a squeal of brakes and great clouds of dust. In a moment, the coach door swung open and the now cursing master of the reins gave her a tobacco-stained smile as he gently assisted her to the ground. Mr. Carter stepped down beside her with a loud creaking of the leather straps that cradled the heavy coach and joined the men gathered by the steaming, blowing team.

Amelia's legs cramped and almost buckled after the long ride in the stage. It took a moment for the swaying landscape to right itself—even longer for her stomach to realize it had. Coffee, she thought; she needed a cup of coffee to settle her nerves and her queasy stomach. Tea would be better, but she doubted they would have any.

As she started out toward the station manager's small house, she noticed that all the men working to change the team were careful to keep their rifles nearby. From his vantage point on top of the coach the soldier riding shotgun peered into the darkness surrounding the station. It seemed a strange way to live, always on guard, expecting trouble. She supposed it was something to which she would have to grow accustomed.

A short, smiling man approached her on his way from the corral to the coach. Amelia assumed he was the station manager from the way the young man gave orders to the others. He gestured toward the house as he passed by and said, "Ma'am, go on in. Supper's on the stove. The place is a little messy. We got in a new herd of horses and didn't get to clean up after the last passengers."

Amelia thanked the man, but she doubted she would be able to eat anything. She still tasted the sour gravy from her last meal. A cup of coffee and some fresh air were all she needed.

The station manager's house was constructed with logs vertically lashed together and mud used as mortar between the cracks. She had seen several like it along the way. Mr. Carter had called them picket houses. She imagined it would be awful to live in one. Probably drafty and impossible to clean.

When Amelia entered the low-ceilinged building she was assaulted by a nauseous mix of pungent odors. Quickly raising her handkerchief to her nose, she surveyed the interior of the primitive hut, hoping to find brewing coffee. Instead a pall of smoke redolent with rancid grease and sour onions hung over a stove in a corner. A preview of what supper might be? Amelia wrinkled her nose at that thought and turned to leave, but a couple of mongrel dogs sprang up from the dirt floor. Their growls and raised hackles were warning enough. She backed against a long trestle table, toppling a stack of tin plates covered with dried food and congealed grease and sending a cloud of angry flies buzzing upward toward the two smoking coal-oil lamps swaying from the rafters.

Amelia's stomach heaved. She feared she would retch right there in the middle of the room. With no regard for the snarling dogs, she rushed past them and stumbled through the open doorway. Once outside the building, she gulped in deep breaths and choked on the dust kicked up by the teams being swiftly changed. She clapped a hand over her mouth. She couldn't be sick in front of all these men.

Turning from the wagon yard, Amelia rushed toward the corner of the little building. She saw Mr. Carter signal her, but she waved him away and struck out for the back of the lot.

Amelia saw a small grove of trees about fifty yards distance behind the picket house. She walked swiftly toward it, jerking her skirts up out of the way as she went. If she was going to be sick, she wanted privacy.

Upon reaching the outer edges of the copse, she pushed her way through a thicket of bushes until she was sure no one could see her. When she finally stopped, she closed her eyes and took deep breaths of the sweet night air. After a few moments, her whirling head and flip-flopping stomach steadied.

Amelia drew a shaky sigh of relief, untied the ribbons of her black chip bonnet and removed it. She glanced around her secluded surroundings. Had she come out too far? She listened to the wind as it rustled softly through dark, twisting tree branches drawn starkly against the moon-bright night. It brought the welcome shouts and jingling harnesses to the lonely place. She smiled. Finding her way back to the station shouldn't prove difficult. Lifting her arms, she stretched the kinks from her tight shoulders.

She knew she should be getting back. The stage would be on its way again soon. Oh, but she didn't want to leave yet. It was so wonderful to be out of the stuffy confines of the stagecoach, to feel the cool breeze drift through her hair. She stood still for a moment, soaking in the silence, the undisturbed peace of the hideaway. Then her mouth twisted in resignation, and she reluctantly started back for the dusty stage station.

At the edge of the wood, she paused and leaned against a tree, its bark rough and fragrant. It was so cool here—cool and quiet. The gentle night air was like a healing balm to her bruised spirit. Just a few more moments of this serenity and she would be able to face the coming morning's reunion with the poise Devin would expect from her.

What would his reaction be? she wondered. She had purposely left before he could write to tell her not to come. A lurking suspicion she didn't want to identify had prodded her quick departure. That and an eagerness to get on with her life. She shook her head, freeing her hair from its loosened chignon and her mind from its disturbing thoughts. Soon all her doubts and worries would be laid to rest.

Amelia looked up into the heavens and beheld a sight that erased all concern for Devin or the waiting coach. Overhead, stars burned so bright they seemed to leap out at her. Their number and brilliance dazzled her senses. At the outer corner of her vision she caught an instant of glimmering movement, a mere sensation of sight. She shifted her field of vision to that quadrant of the heavens and didn't dare blink.

Suddenly another streak of silver arced through the heavens and fell toward earth. Then another followed. And another. She gasped with delight. In the same instant, an arm whipped around her and jerked her against a hard, warm body. A rough hand cut off her breath and cry of surprise.

"Don't move."

Amelia didn't. She couldn't. Every muscle in her body turned to stone. She waited, not breathing, not blinking, not believing.

"If I was a Comanche buck, you'd be on your way to hell, lady. Do you know where hell is?"

The low voice rumbled against her ear, sending icy prickles down her neck. The man's stillness demanded an answer. Amelia shook her head slowly.

"Want to find out?" the man asked softly. "I can take you there."

Deadly menace ground through the voice. She frantically shook her head again.

"Then don't wander anywhere alone. It's a fast ride to nowhere you want to go. You understand, lady? I could rip your clothes off and have at it. Then, if I was in a generous mood, I'd pass you around to my *compadres*. If I wasn't, I'd slit you down the middle."

Amelia squeezed her eyes closed, wishing she could shut out the velvety voice speaking the ugly words. Oh, God, what was going to happen to her? She could feel the man's strength in the iron-muscled arm wrapped around her, pushing against the underside of her breasts. The musky scent of tobacco, leather and man swamped her thoughts. With her back pressed against the hard, flat wall of his torso, her head coming just to his shoulder, his heat scorched through her clothing from head to toe. She'd been a fool to come out here alone.

Amelia's eyes widened with fear as she felt the man's arm tighten around her, shifting his grip. Panic jolted through her shocked brain. She twisted desperately against his breath-constricting hold.

Releasing her suddenly, he clamped her delicate wrist in his large hand and whirled her around to face him. "Hold on, lady. I'm not gonna hurt you. Just teach you a lesson. Didn't you notice all the rifles and the guard in the wagon yard? Every man jack of us has been tromping through the bushes searching for you. I never thought we'd find you. Comanches hit the place yesterday."

"Comanches!" Amelia shook to her very bones. Then she glanced warily at the man. He might be lying. He loomed over her like a night-shadowed phantom, reeking power and violence. The moon's ghostly glow highlighted the harsh planes of his face, the pitiless heat of his eyes. Amelia prayed he told the truth. He stared directly at her and she knew he wouldn't bother to lie.

Before she could demand he release her wrist, the tall man lifted his head to shout to the others that he had found her. Amelia caught a glimpse of his hard slash of a mouth, bracketed by deep creases. Her ear still tingled from the touch of his lips. Her insides still quivered from their lurid message. She flushed hot then cold, remembering how this stranger had manhandled her. Now convinced he wouldn't hurt her, her outrage took hold. Just as she had ignored the warning signs in the wagon yard, she failed to heed his danger signals that whispered beware.

"Scare me a little!" she exclaimed, fuming over his insulting treatment. The man gazed down at her with an arrogant half smile. Amelia swung her free hand to strike the affront from his dark face. Instantly his hand caught her wrist.

Shackling her wrists, he glared down at her with amber eyes that flashed dangerously. "You little fool. Just remember how it feels to have a stranger's hands touching you. You were lucky this time. Next time you might not be." His purring voice lowered to a growl. "'Cause, lady, you feel real good."

Amelia tried to jerk free, but he held her tight. She glared up at him. "Let me go! How dare you!" Her lips curled around the words.

"I dare what I damn well please," the stranger drawled, his eyes lingering for a moment on her mouth. He thrust her hands behind her back and held them there with one hand. Never taking his predator's eyes from hers, he hauled her up against him. Before she could cry out, he grabbed a fistful of her hair and kissed her with a savagery that knew no mercy.

Amelia squirmed to escape his punishing kiss, but managed only to intensify the intimate rubbing of her breasts against his chest. He tightened his hold on her hair, forcing her head back and her lips to open under his. When his tongue invaded her mouth, she frantically kicked at his shins, and finally, tried to grind the stacked heel of her shoe into his booted foot. Nothing stopped the searing touch of his tongue to hers or the turbulent emotions stirring deep inside her, emotions too confusing, too frightening to identify.

"Tanner!" Someone shouted in the distance. "Tanner! Where are you? Did you find Mrs. Cummings?"

Ross Tanner raised his head and called back across the field. "Yeah, I found her." He looked down at her, daring her to say anything. Angry defiance sparked from her blue eyes, but she pressed her lips together tightly. He relaxed the hold on her wrists and hair, absently smoothing the long tresses. Still watching her, he raised his voice so the other man could hear. "She'll be right there." One brow lifted in what passed for a smile. "We're looking for her bonnet."

Amelia blinked in surprise. Her bonnet, indeed! She was incredulous that this black-hearted devil would consider offering any excuses for their long detainment in the wood. Why would he care what the other men might assume? She knew it wasn't fear of reprisals. His very arrogance clearly proclaimed he didn't fear anything.

"Her bonnet? Damn it, Tanner. Tell the woman we have a schedule to keep. We already wasted too much time here. Besides, it ain't safe."

"Did you hear the man, Mrs. Cummings? It ain't safe." Ross released her and leaned down to pick up the forgotten bonnet. "The best lessons are the hard ones out here, and they don't come cheap. Don't wander off alone. And never dare a man anything you can't back up." He handed her the hat. "Especially me."

Amelia jerked the bonnet out of his hand. "Don't worry, Mr. Tanner. There won't be any danger of my daring you into one of your primitive demonstrations. I hope never to see you again."

"That's real smart of you, honey." Ross Tanner leaned against a tree, his thumbs hooked in his gun belt. "But you never know, I show up in the most unlikely places."

"I'm sure you do," she said in a derisive tone. "But I warn you, Mr. Tanner, stay away from me." Amelia crammed on her bonnet, and nearly choked herself tying the ribbons under her chin.

"You warn me, huh?"

Amelia silently cursed the clouds that drifted over the moon, cloaking the night and Tanner's expression. Yet she didn't need to see him. The challenge that tempered his deceptively soft drawl was all too clear. Her good sense told her to gather her shredded dignity and leave. This man didn't need the gun strapped to his hip to tell her he was dangerous. Her wrists ached, her lips burned, all the secret places within her felt violated.

No, this is no man to spar at words with, she thought. He didn't waste time or effort with words. The situation certainly warranted retreat, however distasteful it was. Amelia raised her head proudly and declared in a grand manner, "Goodbye, Mr. Tanner." In a whirl of petticoats, she stomped off across the field toward the stage. The cluster of artificial grapes decorating her bonnet clicked softly in time with each step.

"You're a fast learner, Mrs. Cummings," Tanner called after her.

Quiet, hesitant chuckling followed her until she could no longer hear the rusty laughter of a man who rarely smiled.

Damned woman! Who would have thought Cummings would have a woman like that stashed somewhere? Ross Tanner threw the remaining half cup of coffee into the campfire. The fire leaped and sizzled, sending steam twisting into the night. Stowing the tin cup in a pack, he checked his horse and mules, then went back to the fire and folded his lean body onto a bedroll stretched out beside it. He adjusted the wide leather gun belt strapped low on his hips and tied to his thigh, then pulled his Spencer from its deerskin scabbard and settled it beside him. Using his saddle as a pillow, he lay back and stared up at the stars.

Ross didn't see the beauty of the heavens. Without conscious thought he gauged the season of the year, the remainder of the month, the hour of the night revealed by the fiery pinpoints. He thought of a woman, her heart beating furiously against his own pulse, the warm weight of her breasts lying heavily upon his arm. He remembered their firmness rubbing against his chest. She had tasted sweet and good.

Her blue eyes haunted him. Blue eyes clouded with fear but looking up at him with challenge and fire. She should fear him. She needed to fear him. He wanted her. He burned for her. He would ruin her.

A man could take a woman like her, married, respectable, then finish with her and throw her back to her husband. Devin Cummings couldn't stop him. She wouldn't stop him if he took the time to seduce her. And she was worth the time. So why didn't he ride into Santa Angela and get her out of his blood? What would it be like to actually have her under him, her legs wrapped around him, those blue eyes...

Her eyes. They had been soft and tender eyes. Could he destroy the innocence he had seen in them? Ross pondered that a moment. He remembered the soft silkiness of her hair pooled in his hand, that promising fire in her eyes. Dammit, those eyes again. He sighed and shifted on his bedroll. Maybe a little decency still lingered somewhere deep inside him. He was amazed to find it there. If he destroyed her, as he knew taking her would, he would destroy that small spark of honor he still possessed. Honor the war hadn't killed, honor the *comancheros* hadn't stolen.

"No, Mrs. Cummings you're safe from me," he told the night. "Go to Santa Angela and live with your storekeeper. He'll take good care of you. God knows, I don't want to."

Determined to forget the woman and sleep, Ross crossed his arms across his chest and closed his eyes. All he could see against the blackness of his closed lids were the woman's eyes. Eyes the color of a cloudless day on the Llano.

Cursing, Ross sat up, resting his arms on his bent knees. He knew damn well Devin Cummings wouldn't take good care of his pretty wife. Hell, Devin couldn't even take care of himself. He'd played enough poker with the greenhorn to know that. No, Devin wouldn't take care of the possessor of those beautiful blue eyes, but someone else sure as hell would.

Tyson Briggs. Tyson played poker with them, too. The man was smart, ruthless and wanted to be rich. Dangerous qualities in a man. Briggs had been trying to push Devin out of business for months, only the fool didn't know it. Tyson didn't mind cheating, either. Although the man had never dared cheat him, Ross knew he'd pulled some fast ones on Devin. Tyson will want the woman and Tyson doesn't waste time. Time is money.

Wouldn't that be damned stupid? Deal himself out of the game and let Tyson Briggs take the prize. He'd better ride in to Santa Angela and make sure the game stayed fair. Ross smiled, his white teeth flashing against his tanned face. Nothing like a good game of poker when things were getting a little dull.

Chapter Two

"Stay away from Ross Tanner, Mrs. Cummings. He's nothin' but trouble."

Amelia started guiltily and glanced at Mr. Carter, who stood next to her in front of the Concho Station commissary. Quickly she lowered her eyes, not wanting him to see her confusion. He couldn't possibly know what had happened between her and that infuriating man. Could he have seen through the enormous effort she had taken to appear composed? She knew she must have looked a fright. How she had wanted to scream accusations about Tanner, but she hadn't dared. Devin would have been forced to do something about Ross Tanner's insulting treatment. Her heart skipped a beat at the mere thought of the confrontation.

Amelia swallowed hard, though her mouth had gone suddenly dry. She looked up and replied, "I have no doubts about Mr. Tanner's troublemaking abilities. You have no need to warn me about him."

Amelia missed Mr. Carter's answer as Carl Bettles, a passenger who had joined them at Kickapoo Springs, excused himself and walked between them to enter the large stone building behind the pair.

Carter cleared his throat and began again. "A man like that doesn't need encouragement. He takes what he wants."

"Mr. Carter!"

"I'm serious, Mrs. Cummings. I don't have time to wrap this in silk hankies. The stage for El Paso will be here soon, and I've got to be on it." Haywood Carter squared his big felt hat. "You're a damned handsome woman and in these parts that's all it takes. You heard what Bettles said about Tanner."

Amelia nodded. "Something about Tanner selling horses to him for the stage line."

"That wasn't all, either. He just as good as said Tanner was a *comanchero*." At Amelia's questioning look, Mr. Carter tried to think of a way to explain to her just what that meant. "They're like pirates, I guess. You might say pirates of the plains. They steal, they murder, they trade with the Comanches."

"Trade with the Comanches?" Amelia shuddered. She had read about the savagery of the tribe. Who else but savages would trade with them?

"Yeah, they meet with them out there on the Llano. That's where Tanner finds his horses, though they seem to be wild and not stolen livestock."

Amelia recalled all the questions Mr. Carter had asked the horse buyer last night. When Mr. Bettles had commented on them, Mr. Carter had explained it was the newspaperman in him wanting all the answers. Mr. Carter seemed to know a lot about this area and its inhabitants. He could be right about Tanner's interest in her. Tanner had said he could show up in the most unlikely places. Amelia stared vacant-eyed across the busy wagon yard. Would he follow her?

"Mrs. Cummings," Mr. Carter said, trying to reach through that frightened look in her eyes. "Damn! My stage is ready to leave." He grabbed her shoulder and gently shook her. "Mrs. Cummings!" When she blinked and focused on him again, he repeated, "Stay clear of Tanner. He's a dangerous man."

Amelia looked down and nodded. "I'll be with my husband soon. That should end my problems with Mr. Tanner."

Mr. Carter took a breath as if he would like to say more, then shook his head and climbed aboard the stage. He waved to her through the window as the stage rolled out of the wagon yard. "Good luck," he called.

Amelia lifted her hand and slowly waved after him. Good luck, indeed, she thought. I think I'm going to need it.

Amelia stood on the commissary's broad, wooden porch and watched the stage disappear until all that was left was a cloud of dust. Men and women moved briskly in and out of the commissary, the men tipping their hats, the women staring curiously. Spanish and English ebbed and flowed around her in jovial conversations. Like the dust settling over the road, a strange loneliness seeped down to her heart. Devin should be here to meet her. But he wasn't.

At a gentle tug on her skirt, Amelia looked down at a dark-skinned boy with black shaggy hair. When she smiled, he opened his mouth in a wide grin that showed two missing front teeth. "*Señora,* please to help you, *señora.*" He pointed at the baggage stacked next to her.

Amelia glanced up and down the wagon yard and over at the busy warehouses and work sheds, hoping to see Devin. She frowned. Then she looked at the little boy, whose smile had disappeared with her frown. Her brow eased at his fallen expression. Opening her reticule, she burrowed to the bottom for a stray coin and presented it to the child. With her hands, she motioned toward the wall behind her. "Move my things over there, please."

The boy quickly pocketed the coin and dragged the heavy calfskin trunk and two carpetbags over to the wall. He turned and gave her a jaunty salute. "*Adios, señora.*" With excited Spanish bubbling from his mouth, he ran down the steps and joined a group of children playing in the shade of a rock-walled corral.

The children's laughter floated through the crisp morning air. Amelia smiled. Children remained the same everywhere. For a moment, she watched, touching the emptiness inside her like a bruise that never heals. Maybe here, Devin would be more... She refused to finish the thought. That admitted too much. Her mind switched to more practical things. Since Devin wasn't here, she supposed she should freshen up a little. She was hungry, too, after missing last night's supper. Surely the headquarters for the San Antonio to El Paso Mail Company served a presentable breakfast.

Most likely Devin would be here by the time she finished
eating.

Amelia walked out onto the porch an hour later.
Breakfast passed muster and she had managed to wash away
some of the road dust. The water and the meal had made
quite a dent in her dwindling supply of money, though the
discount they charged on her paper currency hadn't helped
her situation, either. Only gold and silver demanded respect out here, she'd found. Amelia hoped Devin would arrive before lunch. She wasn't sure she had enough money
left. Settling herself on her trunk, she folded her hands and
waited.

At lunch, she bought something called jerky and a glass
of water. Visions of ice-cold lemonade and one of Mama's
good home-cooked meals tormented her as she chewed on
the tough, spicy strip of beef and stared at the horizon, expecting Devin at any moment. She should have left the ad-
venturing to her sister Libby. Libby would have known how
to handle Ross Tanner's arrogance. Libby had always
yearned for adventure, while all Amelia had ever wanted
was a loving husband and a home.

She examined each new arrival as they topped the hill on
which the stage station sprawled. Minutes crawled by, until
another hour had passed.

Blast and double blast, where was the man? Amelia
closed her aching eyes against the glaring afternoon sun and
rolled her head back to relieve her stiffened neck. Taking a
deep breath, she once again took up her vigil. Devin had had
plenty of time to receive her letter saying she was coming.
Maybe it had gotten lost. Maybe he was angry she had
come. Still she sat, sweat rolling between her breasts and
down her sides, her hands neatly folded, her shoulders
bravely straight.

"Ma'am?"

Amelia focused her attention on the quiet voice above her.
"Yes."

"I'm Frank Taylor. Head of this outfit." The bearded
man tipped his hat.

Amelia managed a weak smile. "I'm Mrs. Devin Cummings. My husband operates a mercantile in Santa Angela. I'm waiting for him now."

"Ma'am, you're welcome to stay with me and the missus over at the house. We have plenty of room. Maybe your husband will be here later or sometime tomorrow. We could send a message over to Santa Angela with the mail wagon."

Not another day, not another hour, she thought. "Thank you for your kind offer, but I must get to Santa Angela today. Did you say a mail wagon would be going there? It's not far, is it?"

"Well, not in miles, ma'am. You shouldn't go to Santa Angela alone."

"I've traveled all this way alone, Mr. Taylor," Amelia stated. "I can manage the last few miles. I won't remain alone. Some kind of mix-up has delayed my husband or he would be here now." Amelia said the last to reassure herself more than the kindly stage-line manager.

"I suppose you're right," Mr. Taylor reluctantly conceded. "I'll tell the driver to come by here. He'll leave in a few minutes."

"Thank you again."

"Tell the driver to bring you back if need be. My offer of a clean bed is still open."

"I appreciate that, Mr. Taylor, but I'm sure I'll be fine."

Mr. Taylor tipped his hat and stepped off the porch. Two big greyhounds met him as he took long strides across the yard and entered a substantial stone house. Amelia was relieved to see everyone on the Texas frontier didn't live in those dirty picket houses. With Devin's fastidious tastes, she had no doubts he would be living in something suitable.

When the mail wagon pulled up a short while later, Amelia gladly left her perch while the driver loaded her trunk and bags. Then he climbed aboard the buckboard and sat silently, waiting for her to do the same. Amelia shrugged at the man's apparent rudeness. After all, he was old, she thought. She gathered her skirts and carefully climbed to the seat they would share.

Before Amelia could settle herself, the driver slapped his reins across the mule team's broad gray backsides. Amelia lurched back onto the seat and glared at the unaffected driver. When he didn't offer any apologies, Amelia jerked on the sleeves of her jacket and straightened her heavy, prune-colored traveling skirt. If this was an example of western manners, she wasn't impressed.

They passed through the neat, bustling stage station and traveled up the rocky road toward Fort Concho in silence. Finally Amelia turned toward the driver and asked, "How far is it to Santa Angela?"

"No hablo inglés," the old man grunted, a taciturn frown on his worn-out face. He sat hunched over the reins, a straw *sombrero* riddled with holes clamped down tightly on his grizzled, white head and a dirty *serape* draped over his rounded shoulders.

Amelia wasn't sure what he had said, but his tone was clear. She didn't try to start any more conversations.

As they bumped their way down a hill to ford the shallow river, Amelia noted the trees scattered along the bank. At least some vegetation taller than a wagon wheel existed in this barren country, however odd it appeared. Tiny green leaves sprouted from the trees' branches, which were twisted and pulled by the wind to arch in one direction as though frozen in motion. The misshapen trees depressed her. Tree branches should reach toward heaven, not bend to the wind. Yet when the buckboard traveled under them their shade proved a welcome relief from the sun beating down on her.

Amelia wished the old man would talk to her. Another voice might distract the one still whispering inside her, the one she had tried to ignore all day, the one she would never forget. Ross Tanner's voice. She nervously glanced around her as though thoughts of Tanner could conjure him like the night phantom he resembled.

The wagon rattled and jolted along the pitted, rock-filled road that snaked around low hills. In a short time they reached Fort Concho. Amelia was relieved to see a large military establishment spread across a flat plain. Surely such a show of American force ensured safety from outlaws and marauding Indians.

After delivering the post's mail, they passed through the fort and approached another river's shallow ford. Amelia's apprehension grew. Santa Angela couldn't be too much farther.

When they pulled up out of the river and topped the other bank, Amelia made out a random collection of picket houses and rambling adobe buildings. The closer they got, the more appalled Amelia became. Ragged tents and huts made of little more than sticks and mud were scattered about the shabby settlement. A few skinny chickens pecked about in the many vacant town lots. At this time of day, the streets were empty. Amelia was glad of that. The place made her skin crawl. She would be relieved when they left the seedy village behind.

As they rattled down a rutted, narrow road, which passed for a main street, Amelia glanced inside the open doorways of the buildings. Almost all the adobes housed either saloons or, by the look of the women sitting inside, worse. Quickly she averted her face. Please hurry, old man, she pleaded silently.

When he stopped, her heart sank. She had hoped they wouldn't have to make any deliveries here. She fixed her gaze on the end of the short road. No telling what she might see if she dared look toward the picket building next to them. When the taciturn old man slowly crawled off the wagon and reached for her bags, Amelia tried to stop him.

"Santa Angela. You must take me to Santa Angela. Cummings Mercantile." She said the words slowly and with extra volume.

The old man silently pointed a gnarled finger toward the building.

Amelia gave the building a cursory glance, then said. "No. Santa Ang..." She slowly turned her head. A weathered gray sign above the doorway read Cummings Mercantile in faded, cracked letters.

"There must be some mistake, another Cummings Mercantile. This shantytown can't be Santa Angela."

The driver dropped her carpetbags in the dirt by the doorway. "Santa Angela," he announced in a raggedy voice, and climbed back onto the wagon. "You go."

In a daze, Amelia climbed off the wagon. She stood staring openmouthed at the rough building before her. Unlike the other establishments along the road, its door remained shut. A closed silence shrouded the building. Behind her, jangling harnesses and creaking wheels signaled the wagon's departure. Still she stood rooted to the ground, unable to believe this was Devin's Santa Angela, Devin's mercantile.

From the corner of her eye, she caught a glimpse of a man standing in the arched doorway of an adobe next to her. A quick glance at his low-slung gun belt and the interest in his slitted eyes convinced Amelia it wasn't wise to stand out in the street.

She forced her arm up to raise the iron latch on the door. It wasn't locked, so she pushed it open. Its rusty hinges screeched and she felt the sound run down her spine. This is a nightmare. I'll wake up soon, she told herself. Like a sleepwalker, she entered the dark interior.

A woman dressed all in black, her head cradled on her arms, sat sobbing at a table in the corner. Light from a cracked, dirty window shone on her black hair, arranged in a smooth bun at her nape.

Amelia walked slowly across the dirt floor toward the table. Her heart pounded so hard she could hear it drumming in her head, drowning out the sounds of all but the sobbing woman. She felt her chest tighten, tighten until her heart was breaking and she couldn't breathe. She gulped a breath and said, "I am Amelia Cummings. Where is my husband?"

The sobbing abruptly stopped and the woman raised her head. Surprise rounded her dark-lashed brown eyes. The Mexican woman stared at her a long moment, then replied, "*Señora,* I am so sorry. Your husband, he is dead."

Amelia staggered as if the woman had delivered a physical blow to her chest. She stared ahead, seeing nothing. A loud buzzing in her head blocked out all sounds, all thoughts.

With a rustle of black skirts, the Mexican woman hurried around the table and helped Amelia to a chair. "I will get you some water," the woman said before she rushed out of the room.

The buzzing receded, the room came back in focus. Amelia inhaled a deep breath, relieving her burning lungs. Dead. My beautiful Devin, dead. It wasn't possible, yet she knew the woman spoke the truth. The small hope of her and Devin's future, nurtured with her dreams, watered with her tears, shriveled and died, leaving bitter ashes in her soul.

She'd been robbed. Robbed of the chance to make things right, to make Devin love her as much as she loved him. She could have done it. Devin would have wanted her. He had wanted her. He said so in all his letters. This can't be true!

A hand thrust a cup of water under her nose. Amelia took it, clutching it. Face the truth. Devin never sent for me, never wanted me, not really. "No! No! No!" she cried. Abruptly she stood, sending the ladder-back chair crashing backward. She hurled the cup of water against the hard-packed dirt floor and watched the earth suck the water dry. She would never see Devin again, and she couldn't even imagine a clear picture of him.

Amelia looked up to see compassion in the dark woman's liquid eyes. The woman never uttered any of the expected trite phrases or clumsy condolences. Yet Amelia felt her sympathy soothe like a warm balm. Tears began to trickle down her cheeks, then they poured out of her, washing the ashes away with them.

The woman righted the overturned chair and, placing gentle hands on Amelia's shoulders, helped her sit down. Then she stood behind the chair, her hands a comforting warmth on Amelia's shoulders as the young widow sobbed. Finally the small, heaving shoulders stilled; the wracking sobs quieted.

"Here, take this, *señora*," the Mexican woman said, handing Amelia a plain handkerchief. "I will bring you something to drink now."

"Yes, thank you," Amelia said, her voice raspy and low.

When the woman returned, Amelia drank the warm water, too thirsty to notice its unpleasant taste. She put the glass down and, for the first time, studied the woman now seated across the round table from her. Her black hair was pulled severely back from a high brow into its chignon. She had large brown eyes and a thin patrician nose; her lips were a soft dusky rose. An ugly suspicion reared its green-eyed head.

"Who are you, and why are you here in my husband's store?" Amelia demanded.

The woman raised a dark, arched brow, her eyes hardening for a moment. Then she curved her shapely lips into an understanding smile. With a steady gaze, she explained, "I am Dominga Estrada. My husband, Mario, and I worked for *Señor* Cummings. I am happy you have come."

Her suspicions shamed Amelia. Her Devin would never have betrayed her. She nodded and the two women formed an instant understanding. Amelia glanced down at her shaking hands, then looked back at Dominga. "How...how did...it happen?" She breathed a deep sigh of relief at voicing the awful question. She had to know, yet she dreaded hearing the words.

"Two days ago. Shot," Dominga answered softly.

Amelia closed her eyes, the pain too sharp to go on. After a moment, she looked at Dominga, her brows drawn slightly together. "Shot? I don't understand."

Dominga's steady gaze faltered, her eyes slid away to focus on her hands folded on the tabletop. "Someone is shot almost every day in Santa Angela. It is a very bad place."

Amelia could believe that from her own brief observations. The letters. What about Devin's letters? Letters that had fed her dreams. Dreams that had sustained her that long year, that had prodded her to come to Texas. Those dreams cracked slowly, painfully under the weight of a bewildering reality. Something was very wrong, and she didn't think she was going to get any more information from Dominga.

"Is there some kind of sheriff or law officer I can speak to?" she asked.

"The gun is law in Santa Angela," Dominga said, once again meeting Amelia's eyes.

Couldn't the woman answer a simple question? Amelia remembered Fort Concho, all those familiar blue uniforms. "Is there some way I can get to Fort Concho? I'll talk to the authorities there."

Dominga shrugged. "*Sí,* I will ask Mario to bring *Señor* Cummings's, ah . . . your wagon to the front."

The ride back to Fort Concho was little different from that of the earlier ride to Santa Angela. The afternoon sun was still shining relentlessly in the cloudless sky. Dominga's husband, Mario, remained silent, only this time, mercifully so. Yet everything had changed. Devin and her dreams were buried somewhere on this lonely plain.

Amelia didn't look around her as they bumped and rattled down the road to the river's ford. There was nothing to see, nothing to wonder about. Everything was said and done, except the who and the why. She hoped to find those answers at Fort Concho.

When they came up onto the opposite bank, a soft breeze cooled Amelia's face. It carried a fresh, pleasant scent. Amelia looked up and for the first time noticed a long stain of purples and blues spread across the far horizon.

"How far are those mountains, Mario?" she asked, lifting her arm to point. It was odd she hadn't noticed them while driving here from the stage station.

"Those are not mountains, *señora*. It is a storm." Mario lifted his head and sniffed the air. "You can smell the rain. It is not far away."

Amelia drank in the sweet aroma, and somehow, it made her feel better. "Yes. One can smell the moisture. Will it be here soon?"

"Who knows? If God is merciful, he will send us the rain. If not, he will be merciful to someone else and send the rain around us." The man slapped the reins on the mules' rumps and called out to them in soft Spanish.

Amelia glanced at Mario, thinking what a strange outlook the man had, yet she couldn't find fault with his logic.

She had been surprised when Dominga had presented her husband to her. She had expected a young man, someone handsome to complement the good looks of his wife. Instead Mario Estrada was slightly past middle age, if his silver hair and weathered face were any indication. He stood as tall as his short stature would allow, his height being even with Dominga and herself. Yet when Dominga looked at him or he at her, Amelia could see the love they held for each other as plain as if they had said, "I love you." Amelia envied them.

After fording the river once again, they crossed the short distance to the stables and laundresses' huts at the back of the fort's main buildings, then rounded the corner of a long row of barracks and entered the busy quadrangle.

"I will wait for you out here," Mario said, pulling in front of the headquarters building.

"Thank you. I don't know how long this will take."

"No matter." Mario assisted Amelia down, then brought out straw feeding baskets for the mules, which he attached to their harnesses.

Amelia mounted steps to a wooden porch running the length of the two-storied, stone building. She hesitated a moment before opening the door and entering. What would she say? Who would she ask for? Too much had happened in the past few days. She couldn't think straight.

This indecision was getting her nowhere. The corners of her mouth hardened as she turned the brass knob and opened the door. A young orderly sat at a desk in the center of the room. A closed door was situated on each side. One door was labeled Post Commander, the other read Officer of the Day. The baby-faced young soldier glanced at Amelia and, with a surprised look, stood. "C-can I help you, ma'am?"

Amelia twisted the handkerchief she still held. "Yes. I am Mrs. Devin Cummings. I need to speak to someone about my husband's murder." That was easier than she had thought it would be. She must try to hold on to her composure.

The orderly sidestepped toward the Officer of the Day office and nodded. "Y-yes, ma'am. I'll get Captain Douglas. Have a seat on one of those chairs." He indicated a row of straight-backed chairs lining one wall before he knocked on the door and entered the office. He emerged almost immediately. "Captain Douglas will see you now, ma'am."

"Thank you," Amelia murmured. She walked past the orderly, who held the door for her, and entered the small office. The officer stood behind his desk framed by a map of the Department of Texas behind him. He was a serious looking man in his mid-thirties, Amelia guessed. Tall, with his brown hair grown long in the style of General Custer; he sported a handlebar mustache that also resembled the general's. His sympathetic gray eyes met hers as she halted in front of the desk.

"My deepest condolences, Mrs. Cummings. I am Captain Leland Douglas. Won't you have a seat?" After Amelia sat on the edge of a wooden chair before his desk, he said, "How can I help you, Mrs. Cummings?"

Amelia looked at her hands clenched in her lap, then brought her gaze to the captain's. "I want to find out what is being done about my husband's murder."

"Murder?" The captain sat down in his chair and glanced at some papers on his desk. "Who told you he was murdered?"

Amelia protested. "Killed, murdered. What's the difference? He's dead and I want to know what happened and what the authorities are doing about it."

"I'm afraid there is a great deal of difference, ma'am." The captain paused a moment, studying Amelia. "When did you arrive? I didn't know Cummings was married."

For some reason his words hurt. Hadn't Devin ever spoken of her? This officer must not have been an acquaintance of Devin's. "I only arrived today, Captain. And I am tired of everyone answering my questions with questions. What is the army doing to apprehend and punish my husband's murderer?"

Captain Douglas pressed his lips tightly together. He looked again at the papers on his desk, then stabbed Amelia with gray eyes suddenly gone hard. "This isn't easy, Mrs. Cummings. You should know the facts, and damn me, I'm going to tell you."

Amelia sat back, stunned.

"Your husband wasn't murdered." He raised his hand at Amelia's indrawn gasp. "He was killed in a gunfight at the Dos Tigres Cantina."

"No! I don't believe you. Devin wouldn't wear a gun. Why, he wouldn't be seen in some lowly cantina. My father is a close friend of General Sherman. He'll hear of how you are trying to cover your incompetence with this ludicrous tale."

"Believe what you want." The captain waved away her outburst, his cheeks flushing. "I myself have had plenty of drinks with him at the Two Tigers. I wasn't there the night he was killed, but—" he picked up some papers on his desk and tossed them toward her "—I have several eyewitness accounts from people who have no reason to lie. Read for yourself."

Amelia picked up the top sheet with a shaking hand. The paper quivered so badly, she almost couldn't read it. There, in scrawling, almost illegible handwriting, the story of her husband's death unfolded before her unbelieving eyes.

Devin had been killed in an argument over a woman named Carmela. Who was Carmela? What did that matter? What did anything matter now? Slowly she lowered the paper and picked up another. This one, written plainly but signed with a black X at the bottom, said the same thing. Only the fact that Devin was "slobbering drunk" and "blind with jealous rage" and "Devin drew first on Jake" was easier to read.

Amelia gathered the sheets of paper in a neat stack. She didn't need to read the others. Calmly, almost too calmly, she said, "I owe you an apology, sir." She raised her head proudly. "It seems I have been living under a delusion."

"No apology necessary, ma'am," Captain Douglas said quietly. "I'm sorry you had to find out this way." The captain's voice held a note of admiration for the woman sitting across from him.

Amelia stood up to leave. Nothing more would be accomplished here. "I would appreciate it if you could get word to our families of Devin's death. I know there is no telegraph here, but if you could include something in one of your dispatches." Amelia picked up a pencil and wrote her parents' address across a blank paper on the desk.

"As a matter of fact, I had already sent a letter to his parents. I hadn't sent one to you because..." The captain looked uncomfortable.

"Because, as you said, you didn't know he was married."

"Yes." Captain Douglas shuffled papers and rearranged his inkwell.

Amelia turned to leave. She couldn't get out of the office soon enough. Surely her face would shatter at another word. She would not humiliate herself further by such a display. She was almost to the door, when Captain Douglas stopped her with his hand at her elbow.

"Where are you staying? I'll arrange passage for you back to San Antonio."

Amelia didn't look at Captain Douglas. She kept her eyes trained on the door ahead of her. "I'm staying in Santa Angela, Captain. I won't be leaving for a while." She would never tell him she didn't have any money to stay in San Antonio or even the fare to get there. It would take weeks to arrange money from her father, and she just couldn't ask for any more from him. And she wouldn't go begging to that nice Mr. Taylor, the stage-line manager either. She would think of something. Devin must have some money somewhere.

"Mrs. Cummings, I wouldn't advise that. Santa Angela is nothing more than a holdup for whores and gamblers. Someone gets killed over the river almost every week. It's not safe."

"Did you hear the man? It ain't safe." Tanner's mocking voice echoed through her mind. She stiffened her back. "Nevertheless, that's where I'll be. Now if you will release me.'' The man's hand fell away from her. ''Good day, Captain Douglas.''

''My advice, Mrs. Cummings, is leave here and go back home as soon as you can. The frontier can do strange things to people. If it doesn't kill them first,'' he added as she opened the door.

Amelia turned, but didn't look at the captain. She couldn't bear to see the pity she knew would be in his kind gray eyes. ''My most fervent wish is to go home. But I must see to my husband's business.''

''If you won't leave, then at least find yourself a gun and never be without it. I don't want to write to your parents next.''

Chapter Three

Amelia walked swiftly out of the office, giving little attention to the captain's last words. She swept past the orderly without a glance. Everyone must know. Poor Mrs. Cummings. Poor stupid Mrs. Cummings. Her husband killed over a whore. It was too much. Suddenly to find herself a widow, only to learn she was also a trusting fool. "Never again," she whispered.

Mario stood by the wagon smoking a cheroot. Amelia glared down at him from the porch. His hazel eyes didn't waver under her cold, blue stare. Slowly she stepped down the stairs and onto the rocky soil.

"You knew. You knew how Devin died," she accused.

"*Sí, señora,* I knew, as did Dominga."

"Why didn't you tell me?"

"Would you have believed us?"

Amelia dropped her gaze to Mario's scuffed, pointed-toed boots. "No. I wouldn't have believed you. Not then."

"Will you return to the town, *señora?*"

Amelia raised her head and set her shoulders at a determined angle. "Yes. I have no place else to go." Again she thought of Mr. Taylor's offer. It was tempting, but she refused to be anyone's charity case.

"*Bueno.* Let us leave before the storm catches us in the open."

As Mario assisted her onto the wagon seat, Amelia noticed a frantic hush had settled over the fort. Soldiers rushed along the long barracks' porches, fastening doors and shut-

ters. On officers' row, mothers called their children home.
Even the fort's stray dogs scurried for cover. Amelia cast a
worried glance at the sky's hazy, yellow appearance. How
strange, yet almost beautiful, she thought. Fort Concho's
buildings, the grounds, the people and animals, the very air
she breathed had taken on the glow of the suffused light.
With each breath she took a disquieting recklessness grew
inside her.

After they passed the laundresses' huts, Amelia spotted a
small cemetery situated on a hill a short distance behind the
fort. "Mario, take me to the cemetery."

"I will bring you tomorrow, after the storm. We must
hurry back now. The river rises quickly with the rain."

"Take me to the cemetery—now!" Amelia took a calming breath. She hadn't meant to sound so angry. None of
this was this poor man's fault. "I must go, Mario," she said
in a low, urgent voice.

Mario looked at her from beneath his black *sombrero*. He
saw the awful pain shadowing the reckless light in her eyes
and relented. "You will hurry. Yes?"

Amelia nodded. "I won't be long." She looked over at the
hill. "There's little to do or say."

Mario turned the mules off the road and shouted them
into a canter. Amelia hung on to the iron railing with both
hands. The wind pulled at her bonnet, its grapes bouncing
with each teeth-rattling, bone-jarring bump. Just as Amelia
thought every tooth in her head must be cracked, Mario
brought the team to a halt at the bottom of the hill crowned
with rough-hewn tombstones and crooked wooden crosses.

"You must hurry, *señora*. These storms can be very violent," Mario warned.

Amelia didn't wait for Mario to help her. She climbed off
the wagon and trudged up the low, brush-covered hill. Now
that she was actually here, a heavy dread dogged each step.
Yet a rash impatience pushed her up the twisting trail. Once
on top, a blast of gritty wind hit her, stinging her eyes and
snatching her bonnet from her head. She scraped long,
whipping strands of hair away from her face and looked for
Devin's grave. A fresh mound of earth to her right caught

her eye. She stumbled over to investigate. Two boards nailed together to form a cross were buried in the ground at one end of the newly turned earth. Amelia bent to read the crudely carved inscription. Devin Cummings. Killed April 14, 1873.

Amelia straightened and stood over the grave, reading the uneven lettering over and over. Its finality struck a bitter blow to her heart. Most likely, Devin had never truly loved her. All those months of waiting, planning, hoping . . . lost, wasted. Libby was right. Never marry. Never pin your dreams on anyone.

A booming clap of thunder rolled across the sky. Amelia snapped her head up, her dark musings forgotten. Her eyes widened in awe at the spectacle before her. She stood at the bottom of the tallest mountains in the world, or so the towering thunderheads appeared. The wild wind joined her reckless mood and carried her spirit into the clouds rising majestically into the heavens.

Amelia had never seen such clouds. Corals captured from the setting sun set fire to the deep lavender and cobalt blue of the towering mass before her, while silver outlined each of the huge thunderheads. Like jealous monarchs, they stood, their power and might decked in purple, silver and gold.

Birds winged their way before the rolling, heaving clouds as if proclaiming, "Make way, make way." The thought made Amelia smile until lightning veined across the sky in an instant of frenzied heat. The blinding light forced her gaze down to the plain beneath the storm clouds. She pulled in her breath at what she saw. The thunderheads seemed to scrape the earth and march a boiling mass of dirt before them as they sailed across the ground toward her. Thunder cracked again and lightning catapulted its fiery fingers to earth.

"Señora Cummings. We must go," Mario shouted from the bottom of the hill.

Amelia could just see him over the curve of the hill, holding the skittish mules at their heads. She knew she must leave, yet she stayed. The approaching storm quickened her blood, surged through her wounded spirit.

"*Señora,* you must come now," Mario called.

Reluctantly she turned to leave, but glanced back for one more look. Out of the wall of dirt, a horseman galloped. Dust spiraled behind him to join the chasing storm. She eased around and watched the man and black horse racing the cloud kings, her heart racing with them. She knew the rider. Ross Tanner.

Amelia stood braced against the wind, her skirt snapping behind her, waiting. Why she waited she didn't know. Standing over her husband's grave, waiting for a man she should be frightened of, didn't make sense. Nothing made sense anymore.

Thunder crashed and rumbled incessantly and lightning singed the air. Ross topped the hill, now leading his horse. Amelia saw the great stallion's eyes roll with fear, yet he followed the man without hesitation. A few giant drops of rain pounded the earth, hurting when they hit her head, leaving muddy splatters on her skirt. She wouldn't leave the hill, not yet.

Ross crossed the distance between them in long strides. The wind whipped through his straight, light-brown hair, lifting it from his collar. A brown, flat-crowned hat bucked against his back, held by a leather strap that circled his neck over a red neckerchief. His narrowed eyes, fanned by fine lines, traveled over her. Amelia's heart hammered double-time; her breathing grew shallow. A giddy tension tightened inside her.

Ross halted only inches from her. Close enough for Amelia to note the slight curve in his aquiline nose. Close enough to smell his tobacco and his soft, butternut leather jacket. His lean frame blocked out the furious heavens; his scent masked the earth's damp aroma. Like the storm, his leashed power fascinated her.

"Damn it, woman!" he shouted. "Get off this hill. Do you want your brains fried?"

Struggling against Ross's incomprehensible effect on her, Amelia took a small step back. She couldn't think with him standing so close to her. She refused to let him take the upper hand this time. "Don't tell me what to do!" she shouted above the storm's uproar. "Maybe I want my brains fried."

Ross glanced down at the cross beside Amelia, then dismissed it. He pierced her with his dark amber gaze. His low voice took on a derisive tone. "He isn't worth it, honey."

"What would you know about worth unless it could be weighed with gold or silver?"

A jagged spear of lightning sent an instant of light across his angry face. A slight smell of sulfur filled the air. Unconsciously Amelia held her breath.

Like the lightning, Ross's anger lasted a single, white-hot moment. Raising one side of his mouth in a mocking grin that sent her a chilling reminder of the night before, he warned, "Go home, Mrs. Cummings. Before you're struck by lightning."

"I don't need your advice or anyone else's. I can take care of myself."

"Then do it," Ross stated, and mounted his great black stallion. He brought his hat up and squared it on his head. "I sure as hell won't."

Speechless, Amelia watched Ross guide his skittish horse through the cemetery. Her own anger boiled to the top. The gall of the man! "I'd never ask you for help of any kind." She hurled the words at him, though she doubted he heard.

Suddenly a dark shadow engulfed the land. Amelia glanced apprehensively at the storm clouds passing overhead, turning the day to night, the summer to winter. Absently she hugged herself, rubbing her hands up and down her arms to chase away a chill shivering through her. With a guilty start she remembered Mario standing with the frightened mules. Whatever had come over her? she wondered. Whatever it was she couldn't ever let it happen again.

After one last look at Devin's grave, Amelia ran down the hill calling to Mario as she got closer to the wagon, "Let's go." She was surprised to see him putting a shotgun back under the wagon seat. Well, it looked as if she wasn't entirely alone in this hostile country. At least she had two friends, Mario and Dominga.

Amelia climbed onto the wagon just as the sprinkles became a downpour. Rain poured over them in sheets, settling the blowing sand and cleaning the sweat and dust caked on her body.

Amelia could hardly see as Mario lashed at the mules and they raced for the river ford. She hung on for dear life and lifted her face into the rain, reveling in its clean, driving force.

"Mrs. Cummings, come on in." The mercantile's wood-slatted door opened before Amelia ever touched the latch. "Dominga and I were getting worried, weren't we now, Dominga?"

Amelia looked from a big, good-looking man, who seemed to fill the room, to Dominga standing behind the counter. The man smiled broadly at Dominga, but she remained quietly sullen. Amelia suspected something was going on, and felt badly for holding Mario at the cemetery. She hoped Mario put the mules away quickly.

"Let me introduce myself," the bull-shouldered man said in a pleasant voice. "I'm Tyson Briggs. I own the big mercantile down the street. When I heard you'd arrived in town, I wanted to come over and offer my condolences. Devin and I were close friends."

"Thank you, Mr. Briggs," Amelia said, eyeing the man skeptically. Tyson Briggs said all the right things. His broad handsome face was arranged in the right expression of concern. His clothing was neat and presentable, although she found the bright yellow vest he wore under his gray-checked jacket a trifle loud. Amelia couldn't fathom what it was about Tyson Briggs that put her off. Yet she was uncomfortably aware of how her soaked dress clung to her every curve. Gratefully she took the blanket Dominga handed her.

"I see you got caught out in the rain," Briggs said. "I won't keep you long. I thought you might like to get things settled as soon as possible. I can't imagine a lady like yourself wantin' to stay in Santa Angela for very long."

"Your assumption is definitely correct." Amelia caught Dominga's disappointed expression before she focused back on Briggs. "Do you have something to say that could shorten my stay?"

The big man smiled, "You could say that, ma'am. I keep sort of a bank at my store. Devin kept his extra cash there." His face assumed a serious look. "I hate to be the bearer of bad news, but Devin didn't have any left." Tyson shoved his hands in his pockets and raised his brows. "The fact is, ma'am, I have several of his IOUs."

Color drained from Amelia's face. "IOUs? What IOUs?"

Briggs brought his hands from his pockets and held them up in a calming gesture. "Now don't you worry about those. What I'll do is buy this store from you, take care of the little matter of the IOUs, and you'll have plenty of money to take you home." He grabbed the lapels of his jacket and smiled. "I'm willing to give you a thousand dollars and to forget the substantial amount Devin owes me."

"Just how much did Devin owe you, Mr. Briggs?" Amelia clutched the red wool blanket closer. "And why would Devin borrow money from you?"

"Well, Devin and I played a little poker from time to time, you see, and his luck just hadn't been too good lately." He paused, enjoying his joke, then went on at Amelia's frown, "Devin owed me a little over a thousand, Mrs. Cummings."

A thousand dollars! Amelia hadn't known Devin gambled at all. Losing a thousand dollars would require a great deal of gambling most likely. She hadn't even known the man she had married. All this day, one revelation after another had chipped away Devin's identity until the grave on the hill held a stranger. She scraped back the wet hair plastered to her face. She couldn't think of that now. Amelia glanced quickly at Tyson. If she accepted his offer, she would have money to get home and a little extra. She saw Dominga's large brown eyes staring intently at her as if she was trying to tell her something. Perhaps it was best to give this decision more time. She wouldn't give Mr. Briggs an answer yet. She needed to go over the books first. It was tempting, she admitted. The sooner she could leave Santa Angela, the happier she would be.

"I'll let you know in a day or two, Mr. Briggs."

Suddenly the friendly-neighbor smile was gone, the blue-gray eyes sharpened and the shrewd businessman emerged. "It's a good offer, Mrs. Cummings, a damned good offer. With Devin gone, I'd like to get the matter of the IOUs cleared up as soon as possible."

Amelia met his aggressive eyes steadily. "I understand, Mr. Briggs. Now if you will excuse me. I need to change."

A slow smile lightened Tyson's expression. He quirked a brow. "It will be a pleasure doing business with you, Mrs. Cummings. Good day." Staring intently at her, he settled a black hat on his graying, sandy hair and held her gaze a moment longer before he turned to leave.

Amelia collapsed in a nearby chair. She felt completely drained. This had been the longest day of her life, and it still wasn't over. She had to go over Devin's accounts and make a decision soon. Not only did she not want to stay here, she didn't like the idea of owing Tyson Briggs anything, especially money.

"Here, *señora*. I found these things in your trunk." Amelia gratefully accepted the dry clothes Dominga offered her. "Change in the kitchen. There's a fire." Dominga gestured toward the back of the store, where a wide burlap curtain hung from ceiling to floor.

Amelia found a small kitchen area behind the curtain. On the walls of the little kitchen hung wooden and tin cooking utensils. Cooking was done at the small rock hearth. A table and two chairs stood in the center of the room. A door at the rear led outside.

After Amelia changed into her dry clothes and finished a plate of beans, she sat at the table in the store, enjoying a cup of steaming coffee. Her thoughts whirled in a thousand directions. She couldn't seem to concentrate on anything except the burning desire to leave Santa Angela. Briggs's offer sounded better and better. She no longer cared what Dominga had been trying to tell her. She just wanted to go home. It would be easy to accept Briggs's offer, forget the books, forget the store, forget Devin. Dominga brought in a candle and sat it on the table. Amelia sighed heavily, her decision made. "Do you know where Devin kept his accounts?" she asked.

"I'm not sure, *señora*. He slept in that back room over there." She pointed to a closed door to Amelia's left. "Perhaps in there?"

"Would you look? I . . . can't go in there yet."

"Of course."

Dominga returned, carrying a large green ledger. "This is it, I think. I have seen him write in it."

Dominga placed the book in front of Amelia. "Mario is waiting for me outside. I must go. Do you need anything else?"

Amelia looked up and smiled. "No, and thank you, Dominga. Thank you for everything."

Dominga wrapped a black *rebozo* around her head and shoulders. "Will you accept Señor Briggs's offer?" She rested her hands on the back of a chair in front of her and studied Amelia, her face an unsmiling mask.

Amelia was taken back by Dominga's direct question about something she felt was none of the Mexican woman's business. "Why do you ask?"

"It is important, *señora*. To Mario and me. Also, I think to you. Study the book carefully before you decide."

"I will," Amelia said slowly to Dominga's back, wondering what she would find in the books.

Dominga paused at the door and turned to Amelia. "Bar this door after I leave. Very bad people live in Santa Angela." With that warning, Dominga left, closing the door behind her.

The big room that comprised the mercantile loomed around Amelia. The weak pool of light from the candle on the table left the corners dark. Dominga had closed and latched the shutters on the two small windows at each side of the door. They bumped back and forth rhythmically with the wind that seeped around the edges of the warped window frames. In some places, Amelia saw the dark blue of early evening light filter through cracks and holes in the picketed walls. The wind whistled an eerie tune through them and caused the circle of light across the table to waver.

Amelia scanned the room nervously. Her mama's chickens had better protection from marauders than she had. She spotted a large wooden post leaning against the wall by the door. Quickly she got up and shoved the heavy bar through the iron brackets attached to each side of the door.

Sucking on a splinter, she returned to the table, sat down and stared at the oblong book. Her whole future was written in Devin's neat hand for her to read. All she had to do was open it.

Tentatively she lifted the green canvas cover and flipped past the opening pages until a name caught her eye. George L. Hawkins. Her father. That was her father. She smoothed the page and began to read the short columns of figures. Her father had loaned Devin ten thousand dollars to begin the mercantile! Not one entry was made in the payment column.

Amelia looked up from the ledger page at the shadowed room around her. It all made sense now. Papa had somehow convinced Devin to seek his fortune in Texas. Amelia clenched her fists. Would she ever escape her manipulating father? Perhaps he had meant well, but his interference, as much as Devin's weak character, was to blame for her current problems. Yes, and your own stupid impetuous decision to come join him, she admitted to herself.

Still, if Devin had never received that money, they might still be in Ohio. None of this nightmare would have happened. She wouldn't be a widow stranded in some wretched little village of gamblers, murderers and thieves. And she wouldn't owe her papa ten thousand dollars. She could never pay back that amount.

Teardrops splattered the lined page. She didn't know if she could deal with any more disasters. Take Mr. Briggs's money and run, she told herself. Sure, run back to Papa and tell him to forget his ten thousand dollars. Be in debt to him for the rest of her life. Amelia buried her face in her hands. She had to find some way out of this, some way to go home and begin her life again free of any obligations. She refused to start a new life by going back to the old one. She wasn't going to depend on her parents or anyone else ever again.

Amelia scrubbed at her eyes, disgusted with the tears preventing her from reading the next pages. Nothing could be worse than what she had already learned. The next pages might even supply a little hope. Amelia remembered what Dominga had said.

With careful concentration, Amelia studied the pages one by one. The first month's entries were neat and complete, but as time went by they grew messy and sporadic, until they stopped at a date two months old. The last six months' debits columns were far longer than the credits. Devin had been spending money faster than he was being paid. Amelia was appalled at the large amounts the ranchers owed Cummings Mercantile. It seemed everyone between here and San Antonio owed him money.

Amelia slammed the cover closed. Oh, Lord, what was she going to do? She was stuck here among outlaws and savages with no way to go home.

Amelia laid her head down on the table, using her arms as a pillow. She was exhausted, too tired to think, too tired to make decisions, too tired to cry. Her situation was hopeless. She would have to accept Mr. Briggs's offer. At least she could leave Santa Angela. She wasn't cut out for this place any more than Devin had been. Look what it had done to the once gentle man. Changed him, bullied him, taken advantage of his every weakness. What will it do to me?

"Damn you, Tanner. You're bluffin'." A young cowboy, fresh off the trail, slammed his cards down on the table.

"Call me, junior." Ross lazed back in his chair, studying the freckle-faced kid.

The boy tensed. His face reddened under his high-crowned Western hat. His narrow jaw knotted before he spoke. "C-call."

Ross tossed down three kings and two nines, then reached for the large pot, while Tyson Briggs chuckled from his chair across from Ross. The fuming loser exchanged glances with his friend seated across from him. Neither looked to be over twenty.

Suddenly the freckle-faced cowboy stood. He held his arms out, his hands dangling over the double-rigged Colts strapped to his hips. "You're a dirty, rotten cheater!"

The noisy cantina silenced instantly. Revelers scrambled out of range, leaving a wide, open space behind the boy.

Ross sat with his back to the wall, never moving a muscle. He pinned the skinny cowboy with a cold-eyed glare. "You're not only a liar, junior, you're a bad loser. You may think those are harsh words, but they're a sight better than you're a dead liar and a dead loser. Wouldn't you say so, Tyson?" Ross glowered at the boy.

Tyson was calmly shuffling cards. "Just plug him, Tanner, like you did Fast Benny last week. I wanna win some of my money back."

The cowboy's prominent Adam's apple bounced in his throat. He rubbed his fingers together nervously. His freckles stood out bright orange against his pasty face, but he didn't back down. Ross admired him for that. He hoped he wouldn't have to kill the kid.

"Come on, Rayford. Let's get outa here." The young cowpuncher's friend grabbed the boy's arm and pulled him toward the door. Rayford jerked his arm away. "I won't forget this Tanner." Slowly he backed away, then turned and followed his friend out of the cantina.

A jangling piano struck up a lively tune and the motley crowd of soldiers, drifters and professional gamblers took up where they had left off. Mexican girls in bright skirts and shoulder-baring *camisas* swished around the men and bent low over the tables, displaying their ample charms. A sales tactic that worked, considering the traffic out the back door to the adobe next to the Dos Tigres Cantina.

"The kid called you a cheater. You shoulda plugged him." Tyson poured a whiskey for Tanner, then one for himself.

Ross downed the raw spirits, welcoming the burning taste. He wiped his hand across his mouth and poured himself another drink, ignoring Tyson's raised eyebrows. Ross wanted to get drunk, gloriously, numbing drunk. Then he was going to find a woman. A woman with knowing eyes, not guileless blue eyes that made a man think about crazy things. Damn Devin Cummings for getting himself killed! How had the fool managed that? Tyson would know.

"Heard Cummings bought it," Ross said, absently watching two women fighting in the middle of the cantina's dirt floor. They rolled this way and that, revealing bare brown skin and no underwear. A circle of men cheered them on.

"Yeah, couple nights ago. We planted him yesterday. The pretty little widow showed up today. Too bad she missed the funeral. Wonder what she'd a thought of Carmela's wailin' and squallin'?"

God, at least she missed that, Ross thought. "How'd it happen?"

"Jake Baxter, you know that freight hauler fella. Well, ol' Jake and Carmela were conductin' a little business transaction, when Devin dropped by. Seems like Devin didn't understand the nature of Carmela's business. He was loaded up pretty good. Drew on Jake. God, Jake beat him, and he didn't even have his pants on. The whole thing was close to comical."

Ross poured himself another whiskey. The two women screeched and tore at each other's clothing, scratching each other's faces and breasts until blood smeared across their skin. The crowd of men laid bets on which one would win. Ross looked away, habitually scanning the smoky room, before directing his gaze on Tyson. "Yeah, comical." He sipped his whiskey.

"Don't understand why the fool messed with Carmela. If I had a wife like his, I'd had her here warmin' my bed. She'd keep it real warm, too. In fact, I might see just how warm before she leaves."

Ross's expression never changed, but his hand moved to his gun. His fingers curled around the wooden butt, then relaxed. Damn woman. "Where's she stayin'?"

Tyson laughed at the hysterically screaming women. One yowled like a scalded cat when the other, who was straddling her, bit her bared breast. "Twenty dollars on the biter," Briggs yelled.

With no drinks being sold, the bartender and two other men separated the women. Tyson shook his head and brought his attention back to Ross. He jerked a thumb over his shoulder. "Across the street at the store, I suppose. Don't think she'll hang around long. Refined type. Offered her a thousand for the store and said I'd forget the thousand Devin owes me."

"Real generous of you, Tyson. Thought you were in love?"

Tyson leveled his gun-metal eyes at Ross. "Business is business and love is bull, my friend." Tyson cocked a smile. "Isn't that how you play?"

"Depends on the game," Ross said in a soft menacing voice.

A hired gun and an itinerant preacher sat down at the table. The fancy gunman glanced back and forth at the two men, then said, "If Tanner deals, we'll play a hand or two."

Tyson Briggs shuffled the cards, staring at Ross. Then he laughed and fanned the cards on the table in front of Ross. "Ante up, friends. Winner takes all."

"That's the only way I play, Briggs." Ross scooped the cards up and shuffled them expertly. After the preacher cut them, Ross dealt each man a hand of five-card draw. When he drew the queen of hearts into an inside straight, he looked at Briggs. "The only way."

Chapter Four

"Hey, lady! Lady!" Bam! Bam! Bam! "Lady come on out here." Bam! Bam! Bam! "Let ol' Pete get a look at ya."

Amelia woke up instantly, fear slicing through the grogginess of her exhausted sleep. She held her breath and listened.

The loud pounding on her door continued. "Open this here door, or I'll have ta bust it down."

From his slurred commands the man sounded drunk. Maybe if she stayed very quiet the fool would go away.

"I know you're in there, little honey." The door vibrated with more hammering. "Don't rile ol' Pete. I just wanta say how-do."

Amelia tried to swallow, but her mouth was dry. Blood pounded through her head and the dark room seemed devoid of air.

"If you ain't gonna come out here, little honey, I'm gonna hafta come in there." The loud, annoying banging changed to a threatening assault on the door.

Amelia sprang to her feet. From the sounds at the door, the man was throwing his body against the thick wood. The door would hold, she was certain. Just stay calm, she silently told herself. He will go away soon.

The man threw himself against the door with ever strengthening lunges. "You're gettin' me riled now. I can be awful mean when I'm riled."

Dirt rattled around the thick door frame with each new attack. Amelia heard the door plow against the stout wooden post barring the entrance. No one could break through that.

A loud screeching tore through Amelia's calm reassurances. The brackets. My God, the brackets were giving. Panic twisted her insides. The darkness closed around her. No place to hide. No law to save her. She would have to save herself. But how?

The only weapon she could think to use was the chair behind her. She clamped shaking, damp hands to the chair's backrest and lifted it up to her waist. With small, hesitant steps, she approached the door and stood at its side, waiting for the brackets to give way completely and the drunken intruder to burst through the door. If she surprised him, maybe she would have a chance to escape. Her plan fell apart after that. She could think of no place to escape to.

With each screeching protest from the rusty iron nails holding the brackets, Amelia jumped. Then she spied something more alarming. She couldn't take her eyes from the small, widening line of gray, predawn light that grew between the warped door frame to which the brackets were attached and the picket wall. Even if the brackets somehow held, the door would give way frame and all. She lifted the chair a little higher and waited.

"What the hell are you doin', Pete?"

Catching a shaky breath, Amelia bit her lip and listened. She would recognize that mellow drawl anywhere. Amelia blinked her eyes closed and breathed a tentative sigh of relief. If anyone could make the man leave, Ross Tanner could. But would he?

"Go away, Tanner. You got your woman for the night. Now leave me be whilst I get mine."

Surprised to hear a woman's soft voice, Amelia pressed her ear to the wall. She frowned, not understanding the woman's rippling Spanish. A sharp *"Silencio"* from Ross, quieted her.

"Go sleep it off, Pete. You won't find nothin' inside there, but trouble," Ross said. Amelia noted a cold brittle edge to his words. She wondered if the drunk did.

"I ain't sleepin' nothin' off. I'm gonna get me a woman, and if you don't mind your own business I'll have to make ya."

The soft rasp of steel scraped against leather followed. In a heartbeat, Amelia felt the wall shudder from the impact of Pete's body slammed against the door. Something heavy thudded to the ground.

"Now, Tanner, there ain't no need for all this. You know I was just funnin'."

Pete's heavy breathing filtered through the picket wall. Amelia heard each quivering breath, her ear only inches from the two men.

"I'm not laughin', Pete."

Ross's raspy whisper slithered down Amelia's spine, making the hair on her neck stand up.

"I ought to beat the hell out of you for scarin' the lady in there, but I ought to kill you for drawin' on me. I can't decide which I'm in the mood for."

Pete's slurring bravado vanished. "I—I was drunk, Tanner. A drunk fool. Any man'd be a fool to draw on you."

The wood vibrated again as Ross slammed Pete up against the door. The thin crack widened. "The next time you bother this woman, I'll kill you. You got that?"

"I got it, Tanner. Won't nobody bother the woman. I'll tell it around." Pete's words rushed over one another in their hurry to get out of his mouth. Relief flooded his voice.

"See that you do, Pete. Now pick up your gun and get outa here."

Cloth rubbed against the rough wood, then shuffling steps disappeared into the night.

Amelia peered through the inch-wide crack between the wall and door. Ross hadn't moved. Had there been no wall, she could have touched him. He thumbed a match to flaring light and touched it to a long cheroot while watching Pete scurry down the street. His rough-hewn features reflected the flame. A hint of burning sulfur drifted on the air. Amelia thought a guardian angel had never looked so devilish.

Amelia inhaled a breath to tell him thank-you, but the words caught in her throat when a slender young Mexican woman twined her arms around his chest. Ross ignored the woman for a moment longer, staring down the street, then he flipped the cheroot away and hugged her to him.

"How good are you at makin' a man forget?" Ross murmured.

The woman looked up at him, a puzzled expression on her pretty face. *"¿Qué?"*

"Never mind, honey." Ross hung his arm around her shoulders. *"Buenas noches,* Mrs. Cummings," he added, and the pair walked away, the woman giggling at something Ross told her in Spanish.

Amelia caught her breath, then vowed silently to learn Spanish. Disgust jolted through her. She whirled away from the door. Had she gone mad? She wasn't going to learn Spanish. She wasn't going to learn anything about this loathsome place. She was going to leave as soon as possible. And with Mr. Briggs's money, that would be tomorrow. Today, actually, she corrected. Tomorrow was already here.

Dawn wasn't far away. Dominga would arrive in a little while. She would be ready to leave Santa Angela for the safety of the stage station as soon as Mario hitched the wagon. She found some matches and extra candles on a shelf behind the counter. After lighting a candle, she placed it in the tin holder on the table and scanned the room for her trunk. She saw it sitting in a corner by a display table stacked with blankets.

Amelia stepped over wooden crates and discarded straw packing as she picked her way across the room. She unbuckled the leather straps and pushed the top open. Several dresses, skirts and ribbed bodices were folded on one side, while the other was stacked with petticoats, underwear and shoes. She selected a navy-and-white pin-striped day dress with a small white collar topping the tight bodice and white cuffs at the wrists. She supposed the almost black traveling suit drying in the kitchen would be more suitable for a widow, but it was in no shape to wear. The polonaised day dress would have to do. After picking out clean drawers, chemise and stockings, she folded the clothes over one arm and took up the candle to light her way to the kitchen.

Once in the kitchen, Amelia added kindling and wood to the glowing embers in the hearth and changed clothes. She quickly braided her hair and pinned the long, thick rope of dark hair around her head. After lighting a lamp she found on a shelf, she reentered the mercantile's main room. Setting the smoking lamp on the counter, she looked around. An unidentifiable something nagged at the edge of her thoughts. She couldn't seem to get a hold on whatever it was. She was forgetting something.

She hadn't unpacked. Devin hadn't left anything she wanted. Wait. Yes, he had. His ledger. Her father would want to see the ledger. He was due a lot of explanations—about ten thousand of them, she thought. She expected a few herself. Slowly she rounded the corner of the counter and walked over to the table where the ledger still sat. She picked up the book and took it back to the counter, placing it by the lamp. Her fingers brushed over the black lettering written across the canvas cover. Cummings Mercantile–1872. The last year of Devin's life, and she was going to sell it away for next to nothing.

That's what her father would say. She was fully aware, after reviewing the ledger, that Mr. Briggs's offer was practically stealing the place. Why, the ranchers owed her a small fortune according to these records, and the past two months' transactions hadn't been written down. She couldn't be sure just how much money would be pouring in here once the ranchers paid their supply bills. That's what the farmers did at home, she remembered. They paid once a year at harvesttime. The ranchers must do the same here.

Amelia pounded the ledger with her small fist. What choice did she have? She couldn't stay here. Tonight's episode proved that. A woman alone couldn't live here safely. Her father certainly wouldn't expect, nor would he want her to remain in Santa Angela. That was that. She would have to return to her parents' home. She sighed, and her shoulders drooped. So much for her grand notions to determine her own life, with no obligations to anyone.

With nothing else to do, Amelia flipped open the ledger and began to turn the pages slowly. She wondered when the ranchers settled their accounts. The farmers had always paid her papa in the fall, after harvest. The ranchers must have something similar to a harvest, but she didn't see any of the accounts showing payments.

No, she couldn't stay and wait to get her due. If Papa knew she was here alone, he would demand she return home. He wouldn't care about the money. Mama would be horrified to know the true character of Santa Angela. Amelia was sure she was doing the right thing. But it felt so wrong. She had never thought of herself as a coward, and running away from the problems here, giving up all her hopes, was just plain cowardly. She slammed the cover closed.

Amelia paced back and forth before the counter, wrestling with her overwhelming desire to leave Santa Angela and the equally overwhelming feeling of defeat if she did. She had taken hold of her life and come out here to join Devin. His death didn't change that. If she went back now, she knew she would never be able to break away again.

She glanced around the shabby mercantile. Merchandise littered the shelves and tables. The dirt floor crumbled beneath her feet, and stringy roots escaped from the stained canvas tacking covering the sod ceiling. The town outside the mercantile's rickety walls slept in a drunken stupor. The mercantile, such as it was, was her only chance to gain any kind of independence. The decision she made as to its future would forever follow her own.

What price was she willing to pay to receive what she was entitled to? More than that was at stake, she knew, and she had no doubts it would be high. Devin had paid a dear price, indeed.

Amelia started at a soft knock on the front door. After last night, she didn't know who to expect. With a sigh of relief, she recognized Dominga's voice, identifying herself.

"Just a moment," she called, moving quickly to the door and sliding the bar through its brackets.

"*¡Santa Maria!* What happened to the door?" Dominga exclaimed, standing in the portal and examining the damaged door frame.

"A drunk decided to come calling last night. When I wouldn't open the door, he seemed determined to open it himself." Amelia opened the window shutters and busied herself closing her trunk and refastening the straps.

Dominga followed Amelia, pushing her *rebozo* from her head and smoothing a hand over her sleek, pulled back hair. "This *borracho,* what did he do?"

Amelia turned to Dominga and saw concern etched across her handsome features. "Nothing," she said with a reassuring smile. "He only damaged the door. Luckily Mr. Tanner came along and persuaded the man to desist his rude behavior."

"Ah! The persuasion of Señor Tanner is very powerful."

Amelia paused and considered her own unexplainable reactions to Ross Tanner. "Yes," Amelia agreed, "Mr. Tanner certainly has a way with words."

She had to smile at the understatement. An imagined picture of how Pete must have looked when Ross gave him his warning crossed Amelia's mind. She knew she felt safer. Yet somehow, deep inside, something about Ross Tanner frightened her more than his fast gun, more than the cold expression he always wore, more than his outlaw reputation. It was the heat in his eyes whenever they moved over her. She recalled Mr. Carter's warning about the man taking what he wanted.

Amelia shook her head and busied her hands with refolding blankets on the table. She was tired, overwrought from the devastating day and night of her arrival in Santa Angela. She must keep tighter control on her imagination, or she would crumble out here.

Dominga poked her head from behind the kitchen's burlap curtain. "Coffee will be ready soon, *señora.*"

"Good," Amelia answered. "Pour two cups. We need to talk."

A short while later the two women sat in companionable silence sipping hot, fragrant coffee from tin mugs. They had finished a quick breakfast of cornmeal mush that Amelia had found bland but edible.

"I'll be staying in Santa Angela for a while," Amelia suddenly announced, breaking the early-morning quiet.

"You will not take Señor Briggs's money?" Dominga inquired. She didn't look at Amelia, but slowly stirred her coffee.

"The man's a scoundrel. That much is clear. I carefully studied the books, as you suggested. His offer was little more than out and out robbery."

Dominga laid her spoon on the table next to her plate. "Perhaps. A man cannot be blamed for trying his luck."

Amelia looked at Dominga in surprise. "You don't like the man any more than I do."

"No, but I have my reasons." Dominga lifted her eyes to look squarely at Amelia. "Señor Briggs is no fool, and I am glad to learn you are not one, either. But you must be careful when dealing with him. He is a greedy man who takes no chances. It is good you have made a friend of Señor Tanner."

"I have certainly not made friends, as you say, with Mr. Tanner," Amelia insisted. She wished her voice hadn't been so strident. Her statement didn't sound quite as she had meant it.

"You should. He is *mucho hombre*."

"What, pray tell, is *mucho hombre?*" Amelia asked, finding the Spanish words not so difficult to pronounce.

Dominga paused, searching for an English equivalent. "Much a man. *Sí,* he is very much a man." Dominga nodded and took a sip of coffee before she added, "A beautiful woman has a need for such a man in this country."

Amelia colored at Dominga's frank description of Ross Tanner and quickly changed the subject. "As I said, I will be staying for a while. How long depends upon when the ranchers settle their accounts, or if it will be possible to gain a more reasonable offer from Mr. Briggs or someone else."

"If Señor Briggs has made an offer, believe me, no one else will."

"Oh." Amelia arched her brows and sighed. "I see." She wasn't sure she did, but if Dominga believed this, then it was most likely true. "Well then, when do the ranchers harvest their cattle?"

Dominga's mouth pursed in puzzlement. "Harvest the cattle? Ah, your meaning is the roundup. Most have already had a roundup and have driven their cattle to New Mexico or Colorado. They should be back in a short time."

Amelia set her empty mug on the table. Perhaps she wouldn't be required to stay in Santa Angela very long. "Are you speaking of days, weeks, months?"

"*¿Quien sabe?* Who knows? *señora.* They will be here when they are here. It does no good to worry about the day."

"My concern was how long I would have to stay here."

Dominga placed her hand over Amelia's. "It is not important to think on this. You will be here as long as God wills it."

"Yes, I suppose you are right," Amelia conceded. She didn't argue with Dominga's calm patience in God's will, but found it difficult to curb her own desire to make plans and get things done.

Dominga rose and began gathering dishes. "Mario will repair the door today. The hay is too wet for him to cut, so he will most likely stay in Santa Angela."

"Mario cuts hay?" This was news to Amelia. She didn't realize how much Mario had figured in her plans to run the mercantile until she realized he might not be available.

"For the fort. The money helps," Dominga said while rinsing the breakfast dishes in a pail of water sitting on a splintered sideboard.

Amelia picked up a towel and began drying the chipped bowls and bent spoons. Money! Of course. She had completely forgotten about wages. How would she pay the couple for their help? Suddenly an idea occurred to her.

"Dominga...this is rather embarrassing...I won't be able to pay you or Mario for your help. I can offer a place to stay.

I don't want to live in the store by myself, anyway. And there's plenty of food. Of course I'll pay wages when the ranchers' accounts are settled." Amelia held her breath. She didn't know what she would do without the couple's help.

Dominga silently dried her hands on the towel Amelia had discarded on the sideboard and hung it on a hook before she answered. "Señor Devin, he was very good to Mario and me. He gave me work when no one else would. You see, I too had an offer from Señor Briggs. For work, of sorts."

Dominga's eyes dropped and color washed her high cheekbones. Amelia didn't have to ask what the big man's offer was. Humiliation and pain clearly marked Dominga's face.

"That is why I know you will have no more offers for the store." Dominga's lovely face brightened when she raised her eyes to Amelia's. "There is no need for you to share your small home with us. I will work for you, and Mario will help when there is something you and I cannot do. It is enough you are keeping the store open, Señora Cummings."

Tears stung Amelia's eyes. Dominga had given her a wonderful gift. To know Devin had not changed completely, that he had retained some part of the honorable man with whom she had fallen in love. The knowledge went a long way to heal some of the hurt darkening her soul. She quickly blinked the tears back. No time for weeping now.

"First of all, you must begin calling me Amelia. I hope we will be friends." Amelia raised her hand to stop Dominga from saying more. "Second, you and Mario living here with me would be a blessing. Really, I would feel much safer. After last night, I don't think I would ever sleep."

"But you said Señor Tanner..."

"I don't want to depend on Mr. Tanner or anyone else for anything."

"This I understand. It is done. Mario and I will move our things tonight."

"Good." Amelia pulled the burlap curtain back. "Now that that is all settled, let's see about getting this store in shape. And the first thing to go will be this ugly thing."

With a hard jerk, she pulled the burlap down. Dust flew everywhere, and she immediately began to sneeze.

Dominga's rich, throaty laughter filled the room. Soon Amelia's light, musical laughter joined in. Once Amelia started, she couldn't stop. It seemed like an age since she had laughed aloud. Yesterday she thought she would never laugh again.

"Well now, ain't this a pretty sight. Two pretty women fillin' the mornin' with laughter. Why, a man couldn't ask for more."

Amelia turned and stared at the deceptively pleasant face of Tyson Briggs. Immediately a guarded wariness arrested her bright smile. Briggs's early appearance threw her completely off-balance. She needed more time to collect her thoughts on the best way to deal with him. His overwhelming presence was no help. This morning, Briggs wore a sheepskin coat with wide lapels that exaggerated the breadth of his barrel chest and shoulders. His height made him larger than most men, and when his muscled bulk was added, his size was indeed formidable.

"Good morning, Mr. Briggs," Amelia managed to say with a calmness she didn't feel. Inside she quaked at telling the big man no to anything. Her already high estimation of Dominga's character soared. She met his eyes with difficulty, but didn't allow her gaze to slide away. Tyson Briggs's impassive steel-colored eyes held no reflection of his genial smile. An indication, to even Amelia's inexperienced dealings with men, to show no weakness.

"I hope it's a good morning, Mrs. Cummings. Heard you had a little trouble." Briggs motioned back over his shoulder toward the door.

Amelia wasn't surprised he had already heard about her early-morning suitor. He had probably hoped to find her in tears and eager to leave. That he almost had chafed her pride.

"Only a little," she replied while tossing the dusty burlap in a corner and nonchalantly brushing dust from her clothes. She didn't want to give him the satisfaction of knowing how much the episode had frightened her.

Briggs arched his brows in that way he had of friendly arrogance. "Glad to hear it. Yes, sir, glad to hear it." He nodded toward Dominga, who had remained standing behind Amelia. "Dominga can tell you what a rough place Santa Angela is."

"Yes, I have warned her many rattlesnakes live here," Dominga said, her heavy tone indicating her intense dislike for Briggs.

Briggs propped his hands on his hips, pulling his coat back to reveal a scarlet vest under his black suit. He grinned the first genuine smile Amelia had seen since meeting the man. "Now that's the truth of it."

Amelia grew uncomfortable witnessing Tyson Briggs's heated appraisal of Dominga.

With decided familiarity coating his voice Briggs said, "But did you tell her some of us rattle a warning, and some kinda sneak up behind a person with no warning at all."

"Does it matter, *señor?*"

Amelia spun around to see Mario standing in the kitchen. He must have come in the back door while she and Dominga were talking to Mr. Briggs.

"A snake is a snake and should be killed," Mario continued. He slowly walked over to the women and stood beside Amelia, yet in front of his wife. Deadly intent burned in his hazel eyes as they looked up at Tyson Briggs. Amelia knew she had to do something to stop this David and Goliath confrontation, but her brain refused to send speech to her mouth.

A low chuckle rumbled in Tyson's deep chest. His eyes flicked over the much smaller man derisively. "Gotta have snakes to eat the mice."

In that instant that stretches endlessly between life and death, Amelia heard Dominga gasp and saw her lunge for Mario's arm as it reached for the wicked knife sheathed at his belt. As if the women were attached by tangible lines, Amelia moved in perfect timing with Dominga and whirled around, placing her back to Tyson and facing Mario, positioning her body between the two men.

Amelia squeezed her eyes closed and grimaced with the expected pain of the bullet that would surely slam into her back. Miraculously, nothing happened. Time resumed its normal pace. She breathed a sigh of relief and opened her eyes to look into Mario's angry mottled face. She winced under the murderous glance he directed at her before grabbing Dominga's arm and yanking her through the kitchen and out the back door.

Amelia held her breath a frozen moment, then turned slowly to face what she assumed would be the mountain of wrath behind her, considering Mario's bewildering reaction. Instead Tyson held her gaze while he lifted the gun he had drawn close to his ear, pointing it toward the ceiling. He thumbed the hammer closed and cocked a brow and satisfied smile when it clicked into place. In a loose movement, he dropped his arm and holstered the big Colt, which seemed small strapped to his hip.

Tyson Briggs shook his head and heaved his shoulders in an exaggerated sigh. "Shoo! Those Mexes have hot tempers. Always wantin' to pull their damn knives on a man."

Without thinking, Amelia rushed to her friends' defense. "You goaded Mario into that foolish display."

Briggs affected an expression of hurt innocence. "Mrs. Cummings, you witnessed everything. We were talkin' about snakes and mice. Nothin' to get a man all worked up."

"I certainly did see, Mr. Briggs. I saw you push Mario into a situation where you could lawfully kill him. I know a little of what has been going on here." Amelia poked her chin a little higher and glared into Briggs's flinty eyes.

Briggs leaned over and crossed his elbows on the counter, resting his weight on his arms, his face mere inches from her own. "Mrs. Cummings, you don't know nothin' about the goings-on out here. I don't have to worry about the law if I want to kill a man. There's no law here. A man makes his own."

Briggs paused, letting that sink in. And it did, right to the pit of Amelia's churning stomach. She struggled to swallow the hard knot of panic gagging her throat, shutting off her breath.

Satisfied with the reaction he easily read in Amelia's blue eyes, Briggs drew himself to his full height. He reached in his pocket and pulled out a soft leather drawstring bag, opening it with a jerk. Before Amelia's startled eyes, he held the bag high over the counter and poured its shining contents onto the dusty surface. A shower of gold pieces clattered from the bag, bouncing like flat, golden hailstones.

"When you leavin', Mrs. Cummings?"

Amelia pulled her gaze from the scattered coins up to Briggs. His chin was tucked, and he peered at her from beneath his sandy brows. With each pounding beat of her heart, outrage flooded through her.

"Go to the devil, Mr. Briggs!"

"Why, Mrs. Cummings, didn't you know? I already have, and he sent me here."

"You don't frighten me," Amelia lied. She stood rigidly before him, thankful beyond belief for the counter that provided some kind of barrier between them.

"I don't want to frighten you, Mrs. Cummings." A tiny thread of sincerity laced through Briggs's voice. "I want to buy this place so you can go home. You're a fine woman. And fine things tend to get broken out here." Briggs gazed past her, his gray eyes softening into a cloudy day. "The heat, the cold, the sand, that damnable wind." He blinked, his eyes assuming their familiar hard focus. "Sell out and go home before this land grinds you up."

Despite the peek inside Briggs's softer nature, Amelia refused to let go of her defiance and indignation. Nothing else held her up. "I won't, Mr. Briggs. I'd rather die than sell the mercantile to you."

"Those are brave words, Mrs. Cummings, but don't confuse courage with foolishness. We bury fools up on the hill."

Stung by Briggs's insult to Devin, Amelia swiped a broad arc across the counter, hurling the gold coins onto the dirt floor. "Get out!" she gritted. "Get out!"

Their gazes fused. Amelia saw the face she had expected to encounter earlier. She had succeeded where Mario had failed. Tyson Briggs looked ready to explode. The thought of all that strength, all that anger, about to be unleashed on her turned Amelia's bones to butter.

"Señor Briggs!"

Amelia gasped and turned in the direction of the softly accented voice behind her. She watched Dominga's slender, black-clad figure glide around the counter and descend gracefully to the hard-packed earth to gather the scattered coins.

"Your money, *señor.*" Dominga held the coins cupped in her hands, extending her arms upward.

Amelia was amazed by the calm dignity displayed by Dominga. From what wellspring did the woman draw such strength, such courage? Dominga stood before Tyson Briggs, her hands dusty from gathering the coins from the dirt floor, yet she met his gaze steadily until he looked away. Amelia felt somewhat childish after engaging in all her dramatics. From the odd expression on Briggs's face, Amelia wondered what thoughts were going through his wily mind. Whatever they were, it would be best to assist the big man's leave-taking.

With great effort, Amelia gained control of her runaway emotions by emulating Dominga's proud bearing and regal manner. She picked up the leather bag from where Briggs had tossed it on the counter and held it out toward Dominga, then yanked the drawstrings tight after the Mexican woman had filled it with the coins.

"Mr. Briggs, I won't be selling the mercantile just now," Amelia said, handing the heavy bag to Tyson Briggs, who accepted it without a word. "If you will excuse us, Dominga and I have much to do today."

Briggs studied each woman, his expression a stone mask. With a chiseled smile, he said, "Don't take too long to change your mind." He thrust the gold-laden bag into his pocket before turning and walking toward the door.

Amelia clamped her full lips against the tart rejoinder she ached to hurl at his retreating back. Allowing Tyson Briggs to provoke her into another shouting match would accomplish very little. It might even be dangerous, she realized belatedly. She had a lot to learn about living on the frontier. It seemed she already knew plenty about dying.

Chapter Five

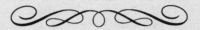

Fire. Fire seared his flesh. Each gasping breath scorched deep into his lungs. He licked dry cracked lips and tasted sweat pouring off his face. He had to get out. Walls. Glittering. Blinding. High walls swallowed him. Trapped him. Get out. Get out.

"Ross."

Someone called. A woman. Where?

"Ross."

On the rim. The woman balanced on the edge. Warn her. "Don't come closer. Don't..." She didn't hear. "Stay away." She wouldn't listen. She wouldn't go away. She beckoned to him.

"Ross," she called. "Ross."

She stood fast against the wind; long dark hair whipped about her face. He wanted to see her face.

"Ross," she called, and motioned to him.

"I can't. The walls. Too high. Go away. Go away." He shouted until his voice cracked. She waited. "You'll fall, too. Stay away."

She leaned closer and held her arms wide. "Come to me," she called.

The woman didn't understand. The walls were too high. The fire too hot. She couldn't help him. She would fall, too.

The wind. The wind would push her into the fire. He had to take her. Climb the walls. He would climb the walls. The walls burned his hands. No air. Dust choked him. Try. Try.

"Ross. Come to me."

*Her voice pulled him closer. He would make it. Just a
little more. He saw her face. Blue eyes. Blue eyes like cool
mountain lakes. He could almost touch her. His foot. He
couldn't pull it up. Something was dragging him down.
What? "Mando! Mando, let go. Let go!"*

Ross Tanner jerked awake. The dream burst into a thousand pieces. He rubbed his hands across his face. His skin
felt hot and wet. God, he had to get outside.

Pushing himself to a sitting position, he staggered to his
feet and immediately grabbed hold of his head. It didn't feel
attached to his body. Not knowing where he was, he hoped
he could find the door—quickly. The only thing he knew for
certain was that he had been lying on a stinking bed in the
hottest damned 'dobe he had ever been in.

Somehow Ross found the low doorway that led outside.
He managed to make it through the door, then collapsed on
all fours in the dirt and emptied his guts. Never again. I'll
never drink rotgut whiskey again. Just the thought of the
kerosene-tasting alcohol heaved up the rest of last night's
efforts to forget Amelia Cummings.

With his stomach wrung dry, Ross grabbed ahold of the
rim of a water barrel next to him and pulled himself to his
feet. Bright sunlight blasted against his sealed eyelids and
pounding red streaks shrieked through his brain. His hair
flashed into flames. He plunged head and shoulders into the
barrel and relished the blessed, cool silence until his lungs
demanded air.

When he lunged up, tittering giggles applauded his per-
formance. His eyes flew open and blinked against the water
pouring down his head. He raked his streaming hair back
for a better look. Five small, ragged Mexican children,
hands clapped over their mouths, stared at him with round
black eyes. It was then he realized he was stark naked.

Ross glared his meanest, fiercest scowl, which sent the
children squealing to their mamas, all of whom grinned
from the doorways of their ramshackle adobes. His day was
going from bad to worse with little hope of getting better.

Cursing all women, he stumbled back into the hut to gather his clothes.

He didn't bother waking the black-haired woman, but flipped a silver dollar on the bed and hoped she had been worth it. After pulling on his pants and boots, Ross left the hut knowing he would never see her or her kind again. Only one woman could put out the fire in his blood.

Was that Ross Tanner? Amelia grabbed hold of the wagon seat and iron rail at her side to steady herself against the jolting. She fixed her gaze on the man walking toward the river she and Mario were about to cross on their way to Fort Concho. The distance between them was far enough that she didn't worry he might notice them, but close enough for her to recognize those flared pants he favored wearing. This morning he wore little else.

She should be ashamed of herself. She was positively gawking at the man. But who was here to know? Only Mario, and he was still so angry at her he hadn't deigned to look her way all morning, much less speak to her. A curiosity in the human form was natural. With that bone thrown to her growling conscience, Amelia calmly took Ross Tanner's inventory.

She began with his darkened hair, swept back to a jagged line along the base of his neck. It appeared wet. She noticed he carried a bundle, presumably the rest of his clothing, under his right arm. His gun belt looped his left shoulder, the holster under his arm, the pistol in easy reach. She wished Mario would slow down. They were overtaking him too quickly. Though she intended to offer her thanks for his help last night, she absolutely refused to speak to a half-naked man, and she was sure he would make the most of an embarrassing situation. At least, embarrassing to her. Ross Tanner exhibited little modesty and no manners.

Certain he heard the wagon rattling behind him by now, Amelia trained her gaze straight ahead. To show the slightest interest in him wouldn't do. No, that wouldn't do at all. Ross never shortened his long stride, nor did he look over his shoulder. Amelia cast quick glances, then longer looks, and finally couldn't pull her eyes away. As the wagon drew nearer, Amelia noticed a rivulet of water trace the deep indentation down the center of his broad back. She followed the tiny stream until it dampened the center of his pants. The long muscles stretching and giving under his smooth, sun-warmed skin fascinated her.

As fascination threatened to become beguilement, Amelia snapped her eyes shut to break the spell. When she opened them, she focused on the shimmering river, yet the spell still held her. A memory floated to her on the gilded rush of the river, an image of a captured cougar displayed by a traveling wild West show that had come through her town. Ross moved like the wild beautiful animal, all muscled elegance and lethal power. They shared the same lazy arrogance. The same potential for danger smoldered in their hunters' eyes. Young and entranced by the lithe beauty of the tawny cat, she had strayed too close. Only the bars had saved her. Now the cougar stalked his prey freely, and she had ventured into his territory.

That unsettling thought yanked her back to reality. She cast a furtive glance in Ross's direction. To her relief, she saw him follow a sharp bend in the river and disappear around a high bank. As the wagon lurched into the river, Amelia heard a distinct splash in the distance, then a man's loud whoop.

"Señor Tanner finds the water cold today, I think," Mario said.

Amelia chanced a glimpse under her bonnet's brim to evaluate Mario's surprising comment. It seemed a stone or two had slipped from his face. "From the sound of things, I must agree," she said.

Amelia waited patiently and hoped he would continue the conversation. Nothing could be gained by ignoring what had happened this morning. She hated the uneasiness between them. However, she was uncertain how to proceed. She didn't want more hard feelings.

Time for talking things out diminished with each plodding mule step. Fort Concho's stables and laundresses' huts came into view as soon as the wagon rocked onto the opposite shore. Amelia couldn't wait any longer. This might be her last opportunity to patch things up. "Mario, I'm sorry about this morning. I don't mean I regret what we did, Dominga and I, I mean I'm sorry if we caused you shame before Mr. Briggs."

Mario burst into laughter. He flung his head back and boisterous, rollicking laughter poured out of him. Amelia stared utterly amazed. "Mario...Mario...calm yourself. Everything will be fine."

Mario bent his head and shook it back and forth. "*Ay, señora,* forgive me, *por favor.*" He looked heavenward and muttered, "*Ay, yi, yi.*" Then he said, "You have much to learn." Still shaking his head and chuckling, he pulled the team to a halt under the scant shade of a wild plum tree that grew along the riverbank. After he tied the reins around the hand break, he heaved a sigh, then said, "I must explain."

"Yes, please do." Amelia straightened her back and raised her chin as she waited for yet another lecture pointing out her vast ignorance.

Mario removed his hat and hooked the chin strap on the knotted reins. He shoved a hand through his short salt-and-pepper hair, then rested his elbows on his knees. He didn't look at her but off into the distance. "*Señora,* you are new to this country and comprehend nothing."

Amelia raised her eyebrows at his blunt summation. She fiddled with her reticule's cord and searched for an answer.

Mario deemed that a statement of fact and continued, "I have lived a long life. This gray hair is my badge of honor. It tells everyone I have survived to earn it." He turned to Amelia. "Do you begin to comprehend."

Amelia studied his fine hazel eyes for an answer, but found only more questions. "I'm afraid I don't."

Mario nodded and focused again on that faraway place in the distance. "You are young," he said, as if that explained it all. "Foolish men do not earn gray hair in this land. They die. A man must be cunning, and he must be brave. He must fight to protect what is his, or another man will take it. My gray hair says I am cunning for I am here. I have a treasure other men want. My Dominga. She is still mine after many years. A cunning man will choose his time to fight. This morning I had chosen mine.'' Mario swung his head around to face her. ''This morning you saved the life of Tyson Briggs. Not mine, as you think.''

Amelia sat back and regarded Mario for a moment. Something didn't make sense. ''Why did Dominga interfere?'' she asked.

''She feared the Anglos' vengeance. A woman's foolishness. With you as my witness, Ross Tanner's gun would have silenced any who caused trouble. Another time will come.'' Mario retrieved his hat and placed it on his head.

''Then you trust Mr. Tanner more than I do,'' Amelia retorted, and turned away to study the feathery new growth on a twisted, spine-covered bush.

Mario worked the knot loose and started them on their way. ''You are young.''

And foolish, Amelia finished for him, although silently. She didn't want to argue with him. Perhaps she did have a lot to learn about living where men took on the characteristics of wild animals, but one thing she had learned without anyone's assistance. If she couldn't trust a father who loved her and a husband who had vowed his love before God, she couldn't trust a rough gunman who regarded her with little more feelings than lust.

Before they reached Fort Concho, Mario hauled the mules to a halt in front of a sprawling rock building. ''Do you want to look around the sutler's place while I see about work?''

Amelia shook her head. ''No, I'll stay here and enjoy the morning sunshine.'' Sweat already pitted her armpits and her hair scratched her scalp under her dark-blue bonnet.

Mario shrugged and jumped down from the wagon. He ran his thumbs under his suspenders, and entered the store through wide double doors. Amelia sat erect, her hands folded in her lap. She directed her curious inspection to the frantic goings-on at a prairie-dog town spread across the plain a short distance to her right. She smiled and thought they looked like busy gossips popping from burrow to burrow. Wondering if any more rain would come, she looked for clouds in the sky and lost herself in its fathomless blue. She sighed and inspected her gloves and thought she must dye them black. She looked and inspected everything but the building next to her. The sutler's store. Devin's grand dream.

At the sound of boots hammering across the sutler's wide, wooden porch, Amelia glanced up, expecting to see Mario. A package-ladened soldier nodded to her and stepped off the side of the porch on his way to the nearby barracks. Her attention caught, Amelia's eyes drank in the solid walls, and covered porch and row of windows. Inside the wide doors, she saw ladies selecting material at a long counter, and a child begging for candy from the large glass jars lined up along the counter. This was what she had expected yesterday.

Quickly she looked away. It did no good to dwell on how things could have been. She must make Cummings Mercantile just as attractive. Customers will cross the river with the right incentive. She shifted on the wagon seat and glanced repeatedly at the store's entrance. Hurry, Mario. I have much to do.

Just as Amelia's patience had run its course, Mario appeared, and they were once again on their way. Amelia fidgeted with the note to her parents she had just pulled from her reticule and wondered exactly how she would tell Captain Douglas she would be staying on in Santa Angela for a while. Her situation wasn't as bad as all that. The power and might of the United States Army counted for something. Troopers came to Santa Angela. They would help her should any problems arise.

As they entered the fort, Amelia's eyes widened at all the activity. The broad parade ground centered between the long row of barracks and the row of officers' quarters resounded with bugle calls and shouted orders. The clarion notes pierced the morning air and mingled with the jingling of harnesses as a long line of dusty cavalry separated into companies.

Passing by the horse soldiers' smartly wheeling lines, Amelia discovered all the troopers to be black men. She had read about the Negro soldiers making a name for themselves in the West. Buffalo soldiers, so the newspapers had named them. A whipping pennant emblazoned with a number nine proclaimed their regiment.

"More trouble," Mario muttered, finally breaking his silence.

Amelia spun around. "Trouble?"

"The black soldiers. They are fierce Indian fighters, but they always bring trouble to Santa Angela when they come to the fort."

"Why is that?"

"Like all soldiers, they go to the cantinas to drink and find women. The Anglos do not like this, and there are many fights," Mario explained.

Amelia glanced back at the men dismounting from their horses, then turned to stare ahead, a dejected droop to her shoulders. Instead of a cause for restraint among the inhabitants, the troops would be just another spark to add to that lawless tinderbox across the river. These Texas Southerners still clung to their tattered Stars and Bars. She had witnessed several angry incidents between the military and citizens while traveling across the state. Most still looked with hatred upon the army's blue uniforms. Put former slaves into that uniform and trouble would no doubt follow.

Amelia slapped the envelope in her palm. Lies. She had filled the letter with lies. She couldn't rewrite it. She couldn't tell her parents the truth. Only one man stood between her and the jackals that fed on the fort's payroll. A man so expert at dealing death he struck fear among the devil's own. A man whose motives she didn't understand—or trust. Papa might deserve such a letter, but poor Mama surely didn't.

The wagon halted in a block of shade in front of headquarters. Mario assisted Amelia to the ground, then climbed back on the wagon and took up the reins. "The men at the sutler's said to talk to the quartermaster. I will return for you in a short time."

"I'll wait for you here. My business shouldn't take long," Amelia said. She climbed up the weathered steps as the wagon rattled on its way. Amelia shook out her navy skirts and straightened the matching bonnet. She was about to turn and step up to the porch, when a sound caught her attention, a faint disturbance of the usual rhythms played by the wind and the fort's activities. Before she could identify the rumble, Amelia's gaze riveted on a rider as he cornered the stables and galloped across the quadrangle. She stumbled backward, up the steps, as he yanked the horse to its haunches in front of the headquarters building. Amelia coughed and waved at the cloud of dust the skidding horse sprayed upon the porch.

The cowboy leaped off his sweating mount and rushed past Amelia in a flurry of pounding boots, clanging spurs and flying white duster tails. He paused in mid-flight and stepped back. "Pardon me, ma'am," he panted, and touched his hat before he continued his charge on the commander's office.

In wonder, Amelia watched the cowboy cross the open door's threshold, then heard him shout, "Comanches! Comanches hit us!"

Amelia jerked her head around and scanned the horizon for the savages she was sure gathered there to charge down upon them to burn and pillage.

Captain Douglas met the young man just inside the door. "Now slow down. What happened and where," he commanded.

Hearing the calm assurance in Captain Douglas's voice and seeing no befeathered savages, Amelia turned to hear the cowboy's explanation.

The sweating man took a big gulp of air and blew it out. "Comanches, sir. They hit us broad daylight, just as we was crossin' the South Concho upriver about ten miles. Stole half the herd. We beat it here with the rest of 'em."

"Dead or wounded?" Captain Douglas snapped.

"Lost two men, sir, but, by damn, we got some of them red devils, too," the cowboy shouted.

"Corporal," Captain Douglas shouted.

A soldier, squinting through round spectacles, hurried out of the office and followed Captain Douglas and the cowboy, who were both rapidly crossing the porch. "Yes, sir," he answered, his pale face flushed with excitement.

Captain Douglas paused beside Amelia and turned to face her. "If you'll wait inside, I'll be with you in a moment."

"Of course, Captain," Amelia replied. Not wanting to miss the excitement, she slowly backed up one more step and remained on the porch to see what happened next.

Captain Douglas started across the parade ground toward the stables with the two men trotting at his heels. "Fetch Lieutenant Bailey. He's overseeing the water detail. Tell him to meet me at the stables. Tell D Troop to saddle up and carry three days' biscuits and ammunition. By damn, we'll catch those bastards this time."

The tall officer stopped abruptly, and the young rider almost plowed into him. The captain turned and the cowboy stepped back. "Tell your boss to take his herd south, down below Santa Angela. The grass is good there. We'll provide a guard while you're camped and an escort when he's ready to move out."

"Yes, sir." The young man turned and started running back to his horse.

"And for God's sake," the captain shouted after him, "cross the North Concho downstream and keep your animals away from the watercress growing along the shore. Doc will shoot every steer if they trample his greens."

"We'll find a good place, sir. Don't you worry." The cowboy practically flew into the saddle and kicked his mount into a full run.

Amelia coughed and choked on the dust kicked up from the horse's flying hooves. A red cloth appeared before her watering eyes. Amelia grabbed it and covered her nose and mouth with its silken folds and musky scent that teased her memory.

"You!" Captain Douglas stabbed the air directly at her. "You stay right where you are. I'm not finished with you yet."

Amelia choked back a cough and peered over the red material, her streaming eyes wide with surprise. Me? she mouthed under the cloth.

What had she done? Then she noticed his accusing eyes were focused someplace over her head. Amelia lowered the red silk and peered over her shoulder. Silver conchos, their leather lacings fluttering in the breeze, met her curious inspection first. As her eyes traveled upward over a leather, Spanish-cut jacket, her heart thudded to a stop.

A lightheaded sensation waved through her. When she met Ross Tanner's whiskey eyes regarding her with lazy interest, her heart pounded wildly, flooding her face with a becoming blush that only caused her more embarrassment. It was hard to look him in the eye after her recent assessment of his bare torso, but somehow she managed. It rankled her unbearably to give the man any indication that she was indeed the simpleminded peabrain he seemed to think she was.

Amelia grew more uncomfortable under Ross's scrutiny. Admitting defeat, she looked away in complete confusion as to what to say or do. If only he wouldn't look at her that way, like . . . well, she didn't know. No one had ever looked at her with such guarded intensity. Cringing inside, she wondered if he had known she had watched him walking to the river. She nervously glanced over her shoulder again and saw his eyes change to a molten gold as they moved over her.

She couldn't just stand here, allowing the man to take liberties. Liberties! Why, he hadn't even touched her. But Ross Tanner didn't need to touch a woman to make her feel his interest. Oh, this was too much. She had to think of something. Something polite. After all, the man had helped her. What did one say to a man like Tanner? His neckerchief. She grabbed the idea as if it were a lifeline.

Amelia turned around and attempted a pleasant smile. "Thank you, Mr. Tanner, for your neckerchief. How kind of you to offer it to me." She held the large square of red silk out to him. The fluid material flowed over her hand and fluttered softly in the wind. She wondered for a moment if he was going to refuse to take it.

Ross looked past the red silk directly at her. "Is this supposed to be a peace offering?"

"Did you intend it to be?" Amelia asked.

A slow smile deepened the creases on either side of his wide mouth. "Maybe." He gently pulled the red silk through her fingers, then tied the scarf around his neck. His eyes never left her.

Amelia stared with amazement at the change in Ross. He was actually trying to be pleasant, even smiling. All of which raised new suspicions in her mind, but she decided to see what he was about. "I assume no more lectures will be forthcoming."

Ross moved around her and slouched a shoulder against the weathered post, his thumbs hooked in his gun belt. Amelia adjusted her stance in order to continue facing him and found he stood closer than was comfortable. He slanted a look upward, then trained his eyes back on her. "I . . . assume . . . there won't be any need for lectures."

Amelia ignored his rather mocking reply. He wasn't going to goad her into any unseemly display. This exchange would remain pleasant. She did, after all, owe him a debt of gratitude. A reminder that prompted her to say, "It was very kind of you to help me last night."

Ross shrugged and looked ill at ease. Then he said, "Catching the next stage out?"

"No. I'll be staying in Santa Angela for a while longer," Amelia replied. She waited bravely for the ax to drop.

"I've already told you what I think about that." He pulled a thin cheroot from his inside coat pocket and, scratching a match on the post, lit it, his hands cupped around the fitful flame.

Unconsciously she let out the breath she had held. "Yes. You made that perfectly clear at the cemetery." Amelia watched him light the cheroot, then narrow his eyes against the smoke as he slowly shook out the match. She couldn't help noticing his hands. He had beautiful hands, tanned and strong with long slender fingers. An artist's hands. The discovery surprised her.

"You know last night was just a taste of what you can expect over the river," Ross said in his low, husky tone.

Amelia nodded and dropped her eyes. Then she recalled his threat to Pete or anyone else who bothered her. "I have a feeling there'll be no more Petes."

"Don't count on that, Mrs. Cummings. More likely somebody will get killed."

Amelia stared at him. "I don't want anyone killed. I..."

"I know you don't, but empty threats don't carry weight with these men. This is no lecture. I'm just telling you the way it is. For whatever damned reason, I put my gun beside you. To some men, having you would be worth the risk. They face death every day for less."

The magnitude of what he said almost crushed her. She hadn't realized ... She looked at Ross, a thousand questions mirrored in her eyes. He stared steadily back at her with a big cat's calm arrogance and revealed nothing. He wanted something. Everyone did. Hadn't she learned that? She knew Ross Tanner would exact his price. She felt trapped. She couldn't let him do this for her. She would tell him to leave town. To go away. "Mr. Tanner, please, you can't—"

"Mrs. Cummings. Is this man bothering you?"

Amelia looked around Tanner's shoulder. Glaring at the man in front of her, Captain Douglas slowly climbed the steps. "No, of course not. We were only...ah..." Her eyes darted from Ross's amused expression to the captain's angry one. Hot color washed over her face.

"Well," Captain Douglas prompted.

Amelia grew annoyed at the captain's brusque questioning. It was none of his business whom she chose to converse with. Besides, he had interrupted at a terrible time. She cleared her throat, then said, "Mr. Tanner and I were merely discussing mutual acquaintances."

"Mrs. Cummings," the captain said, his exasperation more than evident.

At that moment, Ross shrugged away from the post. Blocking Amelia's view of the angry captain, Ross turned to face him. "Let's get our business over with, Douglas."

The cavalry officer paused and searched Tanner's face suspiciously. "All right, Tanner. After you." Captain

Douglas stepped aside and waited for Ross to walk into the building. He turned sharply to Amelia and said, "What can I do for you, Mrs. Cummings?"

"I hoped you would include this note in your dispatches to San Antonio for telegraphing from there. It's to my parents," she replied.

"Of course. Hand it here." He held out his hand.

"Thank you," Amelia said, and gave the captain her message. Obviously this wasn't the time to discuss her decision to remain in Santa Angela until the ranchers paid her.

When she didn't say anything, Captain Douglas said, "Is there anything else?"

"Not today, Captain. Mario will be by in a moment." She glanced at the door Ross had disappeared through. "I'll just wait out here."

"I would suggest you wait at the hospital. It's much cooler." His tone implied a strong suggestion.

"Yes. You're probably right." Amelia had hoped to stay here. She wondered what possible business Ross Tanner could have with the cavalry.

Captain Douglas waited for a moment. "Well then, good day."

"Good day, Captain," she replied, and started across the porch to the side steps. She stopped as soon as she heard the door slam, then moved out of sight of the office's open window. As nonchalantly as possible, she stood on the porch and listened.

It wasn't right to eavesdrop, but she wanted to know about Ross Tanner, and if that meant listening at windows she would. The man intrigued her despite her good sense telling her to avoid all contact with him.

"Your uncle was in here last week. Said he'd lost another three hundred head in a Comanche raid."

Captain Douglas's voice sounded strained.

"That's a damn shame," Ross replied, his indifferent tone revealing far more than his words.

Ignoring Tanner's detached manner, Captain Douglas continued. "You could end it. Just tell us where the

Comanches hide on the Llano. If we could clean them out, they'd be forced to go to the reservation at Fort Sill.''

"You mean what's left of 'em. You're right, Douglas. That would end it.''

"Damn it, Tanner. It would end the senseless killings of Texas ranch families, help the cattle business get Texas back on its feet.''

"Texas can go to hell.''

"What kind of man are you, Tanner?'' the captain asked, contempt edging his voice. "That's your own blood kin fighting for their lives.''

"Blood kin, huh. Don't remind them or me. We like it better that way.''

Amelia frowned. Bitter resentment fairly poisoned the man's voice. What did it take to make a man hate like that? Something terrible.

The voices in the other room grew louder, sharper. Amelia leaned closer.

"I could arrest you. We know you rode with those renegade *comancheros.*"

Amelia held her breath and waited for Tanner's reply. Would he deny it?

"If you know that for a fact, then go ahead and arrest me. Otherwise let well enough alone.''

"That's impossible until you cooperate. Tell us where the *comanchero* leaders sneak off to in New Mexico. Without a market, the damned Comanches would stop raiding.''

Another pause followed. She pictured the two men staring each other down like two tomcats on the same fence.

"Even you aren't that ignorant, Douglas. Comanches live, breathe and die to raid. It's their life. As long as white men settle on their land, they'll burn 'em out. Nothing I can do will change that. If it was me, I'd do the same.''

"I have no doubts about that, Tanner. Just stay out of my sight. And if there's even a hint of trouble, your ass is mine.''

"Is that a promise?''

Amelia heard heavy footsteps approaching.

The captain yanked the door open so hard it banged against the wall. "You're dismissed, Tanner."

Amelia wished she could disappear. But she must wait on Mr. Tanner. She couldn't leave matters the way they were. From where she stood, she couldn't see Captain Douglas. Fortunately he couldn't see her, either. Ross sauntered through the door, his knotted jaw the only indication of the grilling he had just received.

Amelia swallowed and said, "Pardon me, Mr. Tanner, but could I have a word with you?" Directing all her attention toward Ross, Amelia disregarded Captain Douglas's incredulous expression when he looked around the door-jamb.

"Go ahead. Have your say," Ross replied.

"In private, if . . . if you don't mind, please."

Ross raised a brow and said, "Follow me."

Amelia walked past the glowering captain and followed Ross to where he had his horse tied, on the side of a small building next to headquarters. She had to gather her skirts to keep up with his angry strides. This might not be a good time to speak with Mr. Tanner, either, she thought, but it's certainly too late to do anything about that.

"Now what's so damned important?" Ross demanded once they had reached his horse. He crossed his arms and waited for her to begin.

Amelia tried vainly to concentrate on what she wanted to say. With him towering over her, his sharp eyes fixed on her, she lost her train of thought, but not her nerve. She decided to just begin. "We were unable to finish our conversation earlier. I wanted . . . needed . . . that is . . . Mr. Tanner, the truth of the matter is . . . I can't ask you to . . . to . . . be my . . . ah . . . protector, so to speak."

"You didn't ask me."

"That's true, but . . ." She turned to the side and fingered a silver concho on Ross's saddle. "Let me explain. I owe too many people too much already. Mr. Briggs, my . . ."

Ross wrapped his fingers around her upper arm and turned her to face him. "Has Briggs said or done anything to you?"

Amelia stared into eyes that would chasten the Furies. "No, of course not," she hastened to say. "It's just that Devin left some gambling notes owed to him, and it is my responsibility to pay them."

Ross let her go. "Your responsibility?" His brow quirked, then he nodded. "Go ahead."

He wasn't making this any easier. Plunging on, Amelia tried to explain this most delicate matter. "Mr. Tanner, I can't have you threatening the town on my behalf. What will people say?"

"You mean the whores and the other rubbish the wind blows in." The lines fanning Ross's eyes crinkled; his expression softened.

"I'm trying to make you understand. I can't be in your debt. I don't want to owe you anything. I have nothing to give in return."

"I haven't asked for anything, have I? Or is it—" the warm light in his eyes suddenly dimmed "—you're afraid I will."

"Yes. I suppose you could put it that way," she said quietly. An uneasy feeling crept over her.

"I don't see any other way to put it," Ross ground out. "All right." She hadn't wanted this to become another argument, but she wouldn't let him intimidate her into backing down from this issue. She could be as direct as he. It helped having the United States Army at her back, too. "If you must know, Mr. Tanner, I don't trust you."

"It seems to me, lady, trust is one luxury you can't afford. I didn't see any of these trustworthy bluebellies over at your place last night. Most likely you won't, because they have sense enough to stay out of Santa Angela at night. You got nobody but yourself and me. And I don't think you're quite ready to take on a prairie dog, much less—" Ross suddenly stopped and glared down at her. "I won't promise you anything."

"Then go away. Leave town. Go see your *comanchero* friends," she blurted, and immediately knew she had said the wrong thing.

Ross gripped her arms. Fury vibrated through his hands and sent fear coursing through her body. After the first time he had intentionally scared her, she had never been frightened of Ross. Now he petrified her into shocked silence. Her taunt had strayed too near.

Suddenly he released her. She thought she would sag against him; everything solid inside her crumbled. With the same effort she saw Ross exerting, Amelia fought for control.

Ross spun around, and never touching boot to stirrup, he swung up into the saddle in one fluid movement. Amelia never stirred. Her muscles had lost all strength.

Ross held his reins loosely in one hand; the other hung at his side. He looked down at her over the arrogant thrust of his strong jaw. "Pray to God I *don't* leave town, Amelia."

Chapter Six

"Miss, please tell Mrs. Cummings Captain Leland Douglas wishes to speak with her."

Amelia finished hanging the iron skillet on its hook over the counter. She peered over her shoulder and flashed a smile to the man standing below her. "Tell her yourself, Captain."

"Mrs. Cummings. I beg your pardon. I didn't recognize you in those—" Captain Douglas flushed and didn't attempt to finish the sentence.

"These clothes?" Amelia spread wide her coarse nut-brown skirt. "I was quite lucky to barter some sturdy homespun from one of the ranch women."

"How fortunate, indeed," the cavalry captain said with illconcealed discomfort. "Can I help you down from there?" He held a hand up toward Amelia, who was standing on the counter.

"Why, thank you, sir." Amelia placed her rough, chapped hand in his. For a moment his eye caught hers and sympathy softened their gray depths. Amelia's smile never slipped; her gaze remained steady. Captain Douglas's mouth thinned under his sweeping mustache, but he made no comments as he assisted her down. Amelia stepped first to a chair and then to the floor. Replacing the chair in its usual position under the table that centered the room, she smoothed the new red-checkered cloth covering the table and turned to face the captain. "Now, what did you wish to see me about?"

Captain Douglas had removed his hat and he held it by his thigh. "I haven't had a chance to speak with you since you were last at the post. I've been on a scout for two weeks." He looked about the mercantile's interior and nodded. "The place looks good."

Good? Amelia scanned the clean shelves that she and Dominga had scrubbed with lye soap, and the ceiling canvas they had pulled down, repaired, washed and tacked back up because she couldn't afford new cloth. Her gaze took in the neatly arranged merchandise, the canned goods they had dusted, the blankets they had washed and folded, the bolts of material they had stacked, the leather goods they had polished. She inspected the floor and remembered the buckets and buckets of water they had hauled to sprinkle it with until it was as hard as iron. She looked at the sparkling, cracked windows sporting red-checkered curtains they had stayed up nights sewing along with a matching tablecloth and two skirts and blouses for her from the ranchwoman's homespun. "Dominga and I have made a few improvements," she said finally.

"More than a few, I'd say." Captain Douglas proceeded to inspect her as he had the store. His dark brows plunged lower.

Amelia felt like a trooper on parade. She tucked a loose tendril of hair behind her ear and patted the heavy bun at the back of her head to make sure all her pins were in place. When he continued to stare, Amelia asked, "Captain Douglas, is there something wrong?"

His heavy scowl cleared immediately. "Forgive me for staring. I'm being very rude, but there's something different about you."

"Yes, well, one does look different in homespun. It is rather unattractive, but very practical." She lifted the hem slightly. "I didn't want to ruin all my good dresses. As you can see by all the burn marks, I'm not quite adept at cooking at a fireplace yet." She laughed. "I actually caught one skirt on fire while washing blankets."

"Good God, were you hurt?" The scowl reappeared deeper than ever.

"No, no," she assured him, though he still looked doubtful. "Just soaked. Mario and Dominga splashed buckets of water over me. I was rather a comical sight standing in a puddle, my hair streaming down my back and my skirt and petticoats quite scandalously shortened."

From the look on the cavalryman's handsome face, he was about to launch into a subject she didn't want to discuss. She was saved from that unpleasant exchange when two drovers walked into the store. "Excuse me, Captain," she said quickly. "I'll get Dominga to help these young men." Amelia disappeared behind the red-checkered curtain hanging between the kitchen and store.

In a moment, Dominga appeared from behind the curtain and walked over to the counter. "Captain Douglas, Amelia asks if you will join her in the kitchen for coffee."

Captain Douglas nodded toward the curtain. "The kitchen through there."

"Yes. She is waiting." Dominga turned to the drovers, took their supply lists and began filling their orders as the captain stepped into the kitchen.

"Have a seat." From where she worked at the weathered sideboard, Amelia pointed a flour-covered finger at the kitchen table. A colorful bouquet of wildflowers arranged in a tin can stood at the center of the table. Amelia held up dough-covered hands. "You'll have to help yourself. There are cups beside the coffeepot."

Captain Douglas tossed his hat on the scarred tabletop and poured a cup of the fragrant coffee. He hesitated over a second cup and lifted his brows. When Amelia shook her head, he sat down. "By the look of the store, you must be planning to stay for a while," he said, then sipped his coffee.

Sifting a little more flour into the bowl, Amelia replied, "Just until the cattlemen pay off their accounts. Then it's back to Ohio for me."

"You shouldn't have to wait too long. Most of the ranchers took their herds north several months ago. What was left of them, anyway."

Amelia forgot her biscuit dough and looked up. "Do you mean what was left of the ranchers or the herds?" It had never occurred to her she might not be able to collect on her accounts.

"Both," Captain Douglas answered. "Last year was a bad one. Comanches hit the ranches hard. They stole thousands of head and burned out many of the ranches. Many of the families moved out. One of the old-timers who had served out here before the war said this part of Texas was more settled then than it is now. And I believe him."

"But, Captain, my father assured me the Indian problem was under control. General Sherman spoke to him personally."

"This past winter was quiet. Maybe that's what your father meant. There was a large operation last fall when General Sherman ordered Colonel Mackenzie into the field. We found a sizable camp on the Red River and were able to bring captives back to Fort Concho. The bucks have been pretty quiet while we held their women and children."

"I didn't see any Indians at the fort."

"Washington took too much heat. The fools back East don't know what we're facing out here. The result was we sent them to the reservation at Fort Sill several weeks ago. The reservation people do little to control them. Now the people out here will take the heat. That's why I'm glad you won't be staying long. The raids will start again unless we can find their base camp. Those d—" he cleared his throat "—those *comancheros* will have to be stopped from dealing in stolen Texas cattle, too. But that's enough about my problems. Are things going well for you over here?"

Amelia finished mixing the biscuit dough and set the bowl aside. "I suppose they are. I have no complaints." And she didn't. She fell onto her cot in the kitchen every night too tired to worry about tomorrow. Each morning brought a whole list of tasks to be done that day.

"Are you sure you're making the right decision by staying on here?" Captain Douglas watched her over the rim of his cup as he drank his coffee.

Amelia never thought of that question anymore. Mulling it over, she cleaned her hands before sitting down at the table and answering. "No, I'm not. Especially after what you've just told me. I might be waiting here for no good reason. But I'm too busy to fret about it. At least out here I feel as though I'm working toward something. I've never felt that way before." Amelia marveled to hear herself say something so personal to a man she hardly knew. Yet she felt a kinship with Captain Douglas. Perhaps it was his kind gray eyes or the concern he always showed for her. Maybe it was simply the fact they both shared roots in a civilized world. Whatever it was, she liked talking to him.

"Maybe that's the difference I see. You don't look like the lost soul you did when you first arrived."

"That's odd. I still feel like one. I've made so many mistakes and misjudgments since coming here."

"I hope you haven't made the mistake of speaking with Ross Tanner again." He set his tin cup on the table and looked intently at her. "Mrs. Cummings, he's a bad one, no better than a renegade."

"I haven't seen Mr. Tanner since I spoke with him at the post." A sense of unease filled her whenever she thought of that day. An uneasiness that bordered on guilt, for she had never seen such naked pain mirrored in anyone's eyes—or such cold fury.

"He's still hanging around, and I think I know why."

Amelia raised her hand to stop him. "Please, Captain, I appreciate your concern, but have no worries about Ross Tanner. The few times I have had reason to speak with him, we have argued terribly. The man doesn't even like me, and I certainly hold no friendly feelings for him. And greenhorn or not, one doesn't need frontier experience to read the pent-up anger in the man just waiting for a reason to explode. Frankly, I don't ever want to be witness to that."

"Good. I can leave with a much easier mind."

"Have you been sent back East?" This was a blow. She didn't know another soul connected with the army. She would miss Captain Douglas.

"No. Colonel Mackenzie is taking the Fourth farther south next week. Apaches are raiding on the border."

"I see." Amelia lowered her eyes and contemplated her sore hands folded on the table. She didn't want the captain to misread the disappointment she felt. When she looked up she was startled by the odd expression on Captain Douglas's face. It was both sad and disappointed. She didn't know what to say.

Captain Douglas stood abruptly. "I'll be leaving. If you need anything, the man taking my place is Captain Foster. Don't hesitate to call on him."

Amelia rose and offered her hand over the table. Hesitantly the captain took it. She shook his hand and said, "Thank you for all of your help. Hopefully I'll be gone by midsummer, but you have my parents' address. Please keep in touch."

After releasing her hand, Captain Douglas picked up his hat. "I'd like to very much." He turned to leave, then stopped. Without facing her he said, "Mrs. Cummings, I hope you won't take this wrong, your bereavement being so soon. I wanted to tell you before I leave. I admire you very much." Then he ducked through the curtain before Amelia could put two words together to reply.

Amelia took a step toward the swaying material, then stopped. What would she say or do if she stopped him? Absolutely nothing came to mind. She found that altogether aggravating. She always thought of too much to say to Ross Tanner. Amelia returned to her task and beat and tortured the sticky dough into biscuits.

Her night to cook came around too often, she thought while dropping four biscuits into the baking kettle. Too bad it wasn't Dominga's night. Her round, flat tortillas tasted much better than Amelia's rock-hard biscuits. Keeping her face turned away as much as possible from the fireplace, she set the heavy iron pot into the hot coals and piled more coals on its lid. It seemed to take forever to bake enough biscuits for supper, and she couldn't help it if ashes fell on the poorly baked bread. Maybe Dominga wasn't just being kind when she had offered to cook every night.

Lost in her determination to concentrate on the simple preparation of the evening meal instead of the disturbing comparison of her reactions to Captain Douglas and to Ross Tanner, she jumped when Dominga spoke.

"Amelia, Señor Briggs is here." Dominga had parted the curtain just enough for her face to show. Distress lined her smooth brow.

"Come finish this stew." Amelia dried her hands and passed by Dominga as she came into the kitchen. "Don't worry. I have the money to pay him this week." She saw relief flood over Dominga's features. Amelia paused and collected herself before entering the store. She never liked speaking with the big man. He always looked so hungry.

Pushing the checkered material aside, she walked into the room with her head held high. "Mr. Briggs, how good of you to save me the trip to your establishment."

Tyson Briggs turned from his inspection of a wicker basket full of fresh eggs and looked her over. Amelia thought of Captain Douglas's eyes and how different the same color could appear. Mr. Briggs's eyes cut like chipped flint.

"What, no widow's weeds?" he asked.

Amelia flushed despite her efforts not to. As usual, Tyson Briggs struck at his quarry's weakest point. To her way of thinking, she had mourned the Devin she had loved for the past year. She wanted to get on with her life, but her decision had set loose her harping conscience. Finally she answered Briggs's rude question. "What I do and don't do is none of your concern, Mr. Briggs."

Briggs tipped his hat back, then propped his hands on his hips. "I guess not, Mrs. Cummings. I was only thinking of my old friend, Devin."

Amelia's features remained calm. Only the thin line of her mouth revealed her displeasure. She walked to the counter and pulled a metal box from its lower shelf. "I have your money—last week's and this week's." She banged the box on the counter and, taking a small key that hung on a cord at her waist, opened it. She counted out a stack of bills that left very little to lock away. "Twenty-three dollars. I believe that was our agreement. Ten dollars a week plus fifteen percent." She doubted if Devin had borrowed gold, but Briggs had insisted she pay the discount on greenbacks when repaying him.

Tyson ambled over to the counter and picked up the stacked bills. He tapped their edges on the counter, then began counting. "It's all here, except . . ."

Amelia narrowed her eyes. "Except what?" She hated his cat-who-ate-the-cream smile.

"My interest. You missed last week. I'll have to charge you a one percent penalty. That comes to a—"

"I know what it comes to," she said, biting off each word. Amelia banged open the boxlid, counted out a dollar and thirty cents in small change and slammed the coins on the counter.

"Now, Mrs. Cummings, I'm only thinking of you. I know you don't know about business. This is the usual way of doing things. What would people say if they knew I was treating you any differently?"

Amelia wanted to ask him which ones, the whores or other riffraff, as Ross had asked her. Instead she said, "How very considerate of you, Mr. Briggs. Now if you'll excuse me, I'm busy."

"I can see that." Briggs surveyed the store's interior. He hadn't seen it since it had been put back in order. Finally his eyes settled on the basket of eggs. Walking over to the basket, he picked one up, turned to Amelia and held it between his finger and thumb. "Nice eggs."

Amelia held her breath. The eggs were very valuable. They not only brought in customers from Fort Concho, they were expensive, too. She had managed to pay Briggs this week from the egg money. One of the Mexican women who worked at Bismark Farm traded eggs for coffee. She tried not to show her agitation and said, "Thank you." Slowly she closed the lid on the box and shoved it under the counter.

"Yes, sir. Nice eggs. Hard to come by, too."

Amelia breathed a sigh of relief when he gently replaced the egg in the basket. She watched him saunter around the store picking up items, examining them and tossing them on the shelf or table where he had picked them up. His inspection brought him to a window. He raised a corner of the curtain and cocked a brow toward Amelia. "Nice, very nice."

Amelia didn't answer, but followed him with her eyes like a mother cat with new kittens. The man was up to something.

Finally he made his way back to the eggs. "You know, I used to get nice eggs like this, but the Mex who brought them hasn't come around lately."

"Perhaps she found a better deal," Amelia replied.

"Maybe. Then again, she may only think she's found a better deal. A good friend would explain things to her." He shook his head. "Never did think the woman was on the bright side. Well, I can see how busy you are. I'll be seeing you next week."

"Don't bother coming down here. I'll bring the money to you," Amelia replied. "I'd like to see how an experienced and intelligent 'friend' like yourself does business."

Before he passed through the door, Tyson turned and settled his snakeoil-salesman smile. "I'd like that. I sure would. Just don't be late. I'd hate to call in the note."

Amelia spoke with quiet, yet desperate firmness. "You won't be *forced* to do that. I'll have the money."

Briggs tipped his hat. "That's a relief. That sure is a relief." Whistling a gay tune, he turned and walked into the street.

"Goddamn it, Henry! Get this place cleaned up!" Tyson Briggs stormed into the large adobe that housed his mercantile. "Look at this place." He grabbed up a fistful of flour from a ripped open bag and threw it on the floor. Weevils crawled through the splash of white. "Look at that, Henry. Goddamn bugs. Who wants to buy that?"

A short man with a pencil behind his ear and terror stamped on his pasty features poked his head up from behind a long L-shaped counter. "But Mr. Briggs, you said—"

"I don't give a damn what I said. Sift out those weevils." Tyson stood in the center of his store and, like Thor, thundered out lightning-bolt orders.

With his bald head sweating, Henry grabbed his pencil and scribbled on his pad as fast as he could.

Never lessening the strength of his tirade, Tyson began to move about at hurricane force. Rusty cans flew across the room, dirty pots and pans careered off the walls and rotting vegetables splattered the wooden floor. Finally he came to a stop at one of four large, fly-specked windows. "Get these windows clean. And curtains—I want curtains."

"Curtains? Mr. Briggs, I can't sew curtains," Henry squeaked.

"Christ, man, use your head. Hire a woman. In fact, hire two women. Maybe they can get this place to look like something."

"But what?" a voice in a far corner asked.

Tyson Briggs whirled on the offender. When he recognized the man, sunshine broke across his stormy features. "Tanner. What are you doin' hidin' in the corner?"

Ross Tanner casually crossed the room and surveyed the damage. "Hell, I was taking cover." Stepping over the wreckage, he made his way to stand by Tyson. "A man can't even buy his smokes without runnin' into trouble." Ross kicked a soiled corset and shook his head. "What bee flew up your ass?"

Tyson shrugged his bull shoulders. "Just trying to fix up the place a little. No harm in that, is there?"

Ross slanted a glance at Tyson. "You tell me."

Tyson smiled at Ross. "How about a beer?"

"If you're buyin'."

"Let's go." Tyson led the way through an archway into a smaller room that smelled of the whiskey barrels stacked along one wall. Several tables made from boards nailed together to top barrels crowded together in the darkened room. Ross sat down at one of them in the far corner, as was his habit. Tyson pulled up another chair and bellowed, "Henry! Draw us up two beers."

Leaning back in his chair, Ross asked, "You going to tell me what all that was really about?" His eyes appeared deceptively sleepy as they observed Tyson's every movement.

Tyson waited for Henry to serve the beers, then took a long drink. He wiped the foam from his mouth with the back of his hand. "It's that damned Cummings woman. Just got back from her place. Have you been in there?"

Ross thumped his mug on the boards that passed for a tabletop. "No."

Tyson smiled at Ross's answer. "Thought you might have seein's how everybody in town knows they got you to answer to if they bother her. That was a real good move and shoulda worked."

"Worked what? Mrs. Cummings isn't that kind of woman."

"But you're that kind of man."

One deep groove beside Ross's mouth crooked. Time to change the subject, he thought. "What's going on over there that's got you so worked up?"

"Not what I'd like, I'll tell you that. She's got her place all cleaned up, even started takin' some of my business. Why couldn't the woman just take my offer and leave town?"

"Probably because she's not stupid."

"Well, maybe not. But she won't last long. She doesn't have much cash, and she owes me money. Not a good combination." Tyson finished his beer and slammed his mug on the table.

"Doesn't sound good, but then, I never would've thought she'd stay in the first place."

"Henry," Tyson shouted over his shoulder, "bring us another beer." He swung his big head around to Ross. "Hell, I didn't, either. I'll admit I underestimated her. She even talked me into letting her pay on her stupid husband's debt by the week. Said she'd pay up when she got paid. What could I say?"

Ross emptied his mug and exchanged it for a full one from Henry. "Could've said no."

"Henry, dammit, get those two women now." Tyson drank the mug half-empty and watched Henry scurry out the front door. He shifted his bulk toward Ross. "I thought about that. But I knew you wouldn't likely walk out on a good game. And a good game is hard to come by."

"I'll drink to that." Ross lifted his mug in a mock toast and tossed down some of the warm brew. When he set his mug on the table, he caught Tyson watching him. He knew that look from too many nights at the Dos Tigres when big money centered the table between them. He waited.

"How long will you be hanging around Santa Angela?" Tyson asked.

Ross retained his poker face with ease. Tyson always tipped his hand. "I'll be around long enough."

Tyson's lids lowered to a speculative half-mast that failed to shutter the interest gleaming in his icy gray eyes.

"Long enough for what?" Tyson finally asked.

Ross slowly rose to his feet and finished his beer. He returned the empty mug to the table. He liked making Tyson wait. "Long enough," he finally said.

A congested look crossed Tyson's face before he smiled. "Don't go runnin' off. Sit down and have another beer."

Surely Tyson didn't think he could get him drunk on beer. "No, thanks, Tyson."

"Suit yourself." Tyson leaned back in his chair and hooked his arm over its top slat. "Be at the Dos Tigres tonight?" he called after Ross.

"Most likely," Ross answered as he walked through the arched entry into the store. He passed Henry and the two young Mexican girls he was hustling through the door. Ross caught their happy, animated faces fall into pained expressions as they surveyed the damage.

With Henry's piping commands following him into the street, Ross mounted his horse and started him in a slow walk down the road. He was in no hurry to collect his gold from Frank Taylor for the horses he'd sold the stage line. Ross spotted a small figure in homespun, dabbing some kind of mortar mixture at the mercantile's picket walls. He ran his gaze appreciatively over her full breasts and rounded hips, revealed by the lack of petticoats. He thought Amelia Cummings would look like a lady whether in silk or homespun or nothing at all. He spurred his horse into an easy canter. It was time. In fact, it was past time.

''Bring me another beer,'' Tyson shouted. He hadn't left the quiet interior of the taproom.

After Henry scuttled in with another beer, Tyson sat and deliberated on what his next move would be. It was one thing to run a greenhorn woman out of town, but quite another to make an enemy of Ross Tanner. He could just sit easy. The woman wouldn't stay long, anyway.

Hell, he couldn't do that. It just went against the grain to pass up all that money that would be coming in as soon as the ranchers settled their bills. If she had sold out to him, it would have been such a sweet deal. Besides, he needed the cash. Half his accounts had left the area. You couldn't blame the bastards. Comanches had cleaned them out. He supposed her customers would be in the same fix. If he could somehow get control of her accounts, he might be able to hold on long enough to grab that sutler's contract.

Tyson rose from the table and walked over to the arched entry that led into the main room of his store. With his arm held over his head, he leaned against the cool adobe and inspected the activities. Henry was sweeping up and two young Mexican girls were already emptying the shelves. He could always depend on Henry to get things done. It irked Tyson to see how much money the Cummings woman was already costing him. Besides the business she was pulling away, he'd have to pay these new employees. Granted, they worked cheap and one of them didn't look half-bad. If she was friendly, he might even keep her on. But it still rankled.

Tyson sipped at his beer and tried to think how he could turn the situation to his advantage. If only he could figure out what Ross's stake in this was. No way did he want Ross Tanner gunning for him. Maybe he'd made a mistake in not forcing the woman to sell by calling in his note. But he hadn't been able to pass up Ross's challenge that night at the Dos Tigres. Tanner probably knew that, too. So until Ross got tired of the game, he'd have to go easy. If only the

Cummings woman would lift her skirts for Tanner. He'd leave town in a hurry once he got what he wanted. Hell, he didn't know why Tanner hadn't just taken what he wanted already. That had him worried, too.

He sipped absently at his beer. There had to be some way to get his hands on those accounts she had and close that store without forcing Tanner into some kind of showdown. He had taken care of her husband. Surely a frail woman wouldn't be hard to handle. And what a pretty thing she was, too.

Tyson halted the mug of beer halfway to his mouth. He was very still for a moment. "I've been a damn fool," he muttered.

"Did you say something, Mr. Briggs?" Henry inquired.

"I said get this place cleaned up, pronto. You've got a week." Tyson drained his beer and slammed the empty mug on the counter as he crossed the room. When he wiped his hand across his mouth, it seemed to press a devilish smile in its wake. He squared his hat and walked briskly out of the store. One of the young girls crossed herself as he passed.

Chapter Seven

"**Y**ou should have seen his face!" Amelia sat down at the place set for her at the kitchen table. Dominga brought over a plate of tortillas and joined Amelia and Mario, who was already digging into his tough beefsteak.

"Tell us every detail." Dominga passed around the plate of hot tortillas. The coal-oil lamp in the center of the table cast tiny gold stars in her brown eyes and glowed around the trio. From the open back door, a cool evening breeze whispered through the shadowed kitchen, tugging at tendrils of hair at the temples and necks of both women. Crickets chirped outside in rhythmic accompaniment to a twanging piano filling the night air.

Amelia held her fork in front of her like a queen's scepter and launched into her story. "I marched right into his store and said, 'Here's your payment, Mr. Briggs.' He grinned that no-good smile and said—" Amelia ducked her chin and lowered her voice "'—Well, Mrs. Cummings, I'm glad to see you.' I smiled sweetly." She demonstrated a big, white-toothed grin and batted her lashes. "'I'm sure you are,' I said. Then I took out my leather bag and poured two hundred dollars in gold coins onto his counter. Just like he did here." Amelia tossed down her fork and selected a hot tortilla, tore it in two, and used half to scoop up some beans.

"What did he do then?" Dominga asked eagerly. She smiled brightly at Mario, who frowned back at her. Dominga's smile faded slightly before she turned her attention back to Amelia.

Amelia swallowed a bite of her bean-stuffed tortilla, then said, "That's when I wish you could have seen his face. Never have I seen so many shades of apoplexy. His face turned from stark white to beet red, then slid back down the scale to white. I thought he would explode. Instead he calmly counted the coins and put them away. Then the oddest thing happened. He gently took my elbow and led me to one of his windows and asked my opinion on whether green stripes or solid blue would be more attractive material for curtains." Amelia shook her head and cut into her steak.

"Well?" Dominga asked.

"Well, what?" Amelia concentrated on prying apart the charred, stringy beef.

"Which did you tell him?"

"I suggested the green stripe. I told him anything green in this country would be welcome, indeed. Then he laughed and repeated what I'd said to his employees. They all laughed uproariously. That's when I decided to leave. The whole episode was just too strange. He said he would be down soon to ask my advice about tablecloths for his taproom." Amelia laid aside her knife and fork and looked at Mario. Her eyes narrowed. "I'm not sure what he's up to."

"Did you tell him you bought Señora Ortega's chickens?" Mario poked a piece of steak into his mouth.

"Why should I? It's none of his business." Amelia picked up her fork and stabbed the stubborn meat. When she looked up, lamplight played into her eyes, igniting them with blue and gold sparkles. "Besides, I thought it would be wiser to be out of range when he first hears about it."

With a bark of laughter, Mario leaned back and said to Dominga, "I think our little *gringa* is finally learning not to charge into the wolf's den." He pushed his plate out of the way and crossed his arms on the table. "Why did you buy those chickens? Why make trouble for yourself when you will leave soon?"

Amelia pushed the remaining beans around her plate with some leftover tortilla and thought about Mario's questions. She shrugged. "I don't know exactly. I didn't like the way he bullied that old woman." She paused, then looked directly at Mario. "And I didn't like the way he was manipulating me. Thank goodness Frank Dolan paid his account this week."

Dominga spoke up. "Thank God, for He was good to us."

Amelia smiled and agreed. "Yes, thank God. Let's hope He won't let the Comanches steal the cattle I took as partial payment from Dolan. What I'll do with one hundred longhorns, I don't know."

Dominga started to speak, but Amelia held her hand up. "I know," she said. "It does no good to worry about any of that." Dominga nodded and finished her dinner.

Amelia absently put food in her mouth, chewed and swallowed. She said she wouldn't worry over the cattle she now owned, but she didn't say she wouldn't plan. Only she didn't know anything about cattle. She much preferred gold, but she hadn't the heart to turn down Mr. Dolan's offer. Besides, one hundred head of cattle was better than nothing, which is what she had feared she would have had to settle for. The ranchers were in a bad way. Dolan was the first to come in to pay his account. She hoped he wouldn't be the last. She really had no way of knowing. She would just have to be patient. Patient! How she hated that word!

Mario stood and rubbed his hands up and down his trim middle. "I have an early day tomorrow so I am going to bed. With all these grass fires, the haying crew must travel a long distance to find grass to cut." He bent over and kissed Dominga's upturned cheek. *"Buenas noches."*

"Buenas noches," the women chorused. After Mario left the room Dominga turned to Amelia. "Your Spanish is getting better every day."

"I only wish I could speak Spanish as well as you speak English." Amelia poured both of them a fresh cup of coffee. "Did you learn as a child?"

"Yes, I..." Dominga lowered her eyes in a shuttered expression. A tiny frown pulled at the corners of her full mouth, then it vanished. Quickly she looked up at Amelia, her features smoothed of any distress. A brief smile covered her agitation. "Still no letter from your parents?"

Though she was curious about Dominga's sudden change of subject, Amelia thought it best not to comment on it. She answered her question as if she hadn't noticed. "Not after that terse 'Sell out and come home' message Captain Douglas received and sent over last week." Amelia sighed in exasperation. That message was exactly the kind of bullying she was trying to escape. She would be home soon enough, and on her own terms.

"Will they be expecting you?" Dominga asked.

Amelia looked down at the lamp's rocking gold reflection in her coffee. She missed her sister and mother terribly and hated to worry them, but it wouldn't hurt for her papa to stew. "I wrote a long letter explaining things better than I could in the brief note I sent with the army dispatches from San Antonio. I don't know when or if they'll get my letter. Mario said the stage people keep grumbling about something sickening their horses and mules and ruining their schedules." She sipped the strong black brew and looked back at Dominga. "It may be quite a while before I hear from them."

Deep shadows crept into Dominga's eyes and darkened them to a mournful black. She stared past Amelia. "It is hard to live so far from family and home."

Amelia's brows drew together as she studied her friend. She resisted the strong urge to pry into the bleak landscape reflected in Dominga's fixed stare. Lately when she couldn't sleep, she wondered about Mario and Dominga, even invented wild histories for them. They were as out of place in Santa Angela as she was. Not that their past mattered. They had stood by her, helped her. She tried to think of something to bring Dominga out of her dark reverie. Finally she said, "Yes, it is hard, but luckily you have Mario."

The shadows eased away from Dominga's eyes as she focused on Amelia. "What a burro I am! Forgive me, *por favor*. I didn't . . . you are alone, and I . . ."

Amelia reached across the table and clasped Dominga's hand. "Forgive you? What nonsense. Besides, I'm not alone. I have you both.'' A brief instant of guilt attacked Amelia. She realized she hadn't missed Devin as she should, but she didn't know which Devin to miss. The Devin she had married or the Devin she had discovered here.

Dominga squeezed Amelia's hand. "We have each other."

Amelia held the small calloused hand in her own hardened palm. She buried her twinge of conscience. The past was not going to follow her into the future. "I've never had a better friend." The words were spoken from the heart and Amelia flushed slightly and quickly let go of Dominga's hand. Five restrained years of marriage with Devin had left their mark. She found herself changing the subject as quickly as Dominga had earlier. "You look as if you might drop."

Dominga stifled a yawn. "It has been a long day."

"Every day is a long day," Amelia replied, a weariness in her voice she hadn't meant to reveal.

"Are you feeling well? Is the water still making you sick? Look, you hardly touched your dinner." Dominga searched her friend's face for signs of the debilitating stomach cramps Amelia had suffered her first week in Santa Angela.

Amelia lifted her lips in a tired smile. "I'm fine. Don't pay attention to me. I'll be all right with a good night's sleep. Go on to bed."

Dominga picked up their coffee mugs and carried them to the sideboard. "I will if you won't stay up sewing bonnets tonight. We have plenty in stock now."

"Not tonight. I promise."

"Bueno." With quick, efficient movements, Dominga untied her apron and hung it on a peg by the door. She paused a moment, then turned to Amelia. "Do not worry so much. I will light a candle to the Holy Mother."

"Light two. I think we'll need them." Amelia was doubtful another candle could find space around the colorful statuette of Mary Dominga had placed in special reverence in her room.

"I will," Dominga replied. "One for us and one for Ross Tanner." Knowing how Amelia would react to that statement, Dominga whisked through the curtain.

Amelia banged her fist on the table. Ross Tanner! Ross Tanner! Ross Tanner! She was tired to death of hearing about Ross Tanner! Either Mr. Carter or Captain Douglas cursed the man, or Dominga or Mario praised him. Whose opinion should she trust? Her own, she knew. But she didn't know enough about Mr. Tanner, and what she did know frightened her.

Amelia stretched her arms high over her head and yawned. She couldn't stay up all night speculating about Ross Tanner. She had to get some rest. Maybe tonight she was exhausted enough to sleep.

Amelia quickly attacked the dinner dishes. She enjoyed the break from doing dishes when she cooked and she supposed Dominga did, too. She stacked the rinsed plates and cups on a spread towel and dried her hands. After throwing the towel to the sideboard, she examined her hands and wanted to cry. They were ruined. It would take months to soften them after she returned home. She heaved a deep sigh. Well, it couldn't be helped.

Amelia pushed the table next to the curtain. It wasn't much of a barrier, she knew, but it gave her kitchen-turned-bedroom a little more room and some feeling of privacy. She took down her folding cot and bed linens from one of the shelves Mario had added to the tiny kitchen. After she assembled the wood and canvas contraption and made up her narrow bed, she pulled a nightgown from the trunk that doubled as a bureau and extra countertop. Then she blew out the lamp.

With only the faint glow from the fireplace for light, Amelia repeated her nightly routine. She brushed out her hair, removed her clothes and sponged the day's perspiration from her body. Shivering in the drafty room, she quickly donned her white flannel nightgown.

Hot all day, cold all night—what a climate, she thought as she carried a cracked blue porcelain basin of tepid water to her cot, where she set it on the floor. It was only then she sat down on the taut canvas and removed her rolled-down stockings and button-up shoes. She wasn't about to bring any sand from the dirt floor into her bed. She rinsed her feet, patted them dry with her quilt, and, tucking her feet under her, emptied the water onto the floor. Wanting no scorpions to find a cozy home in her shoes, she placed them on a nearby chair where she had laid out clean stockings. Finally she pulled the quilts and sheet over her and scooted down the squeaky cot. With her arms thrown over her head, she stared at the stained canvas ceiling. Her eyes refused to close.

Tonight the kitchen seemed especially confining. Trying to find a more comfortable position, she twisted to her side, but the cot wouldn't cooperate. She shifted to her back again and pulled in a big breath and blew it out. But it did little to release the restless energy that kept her awake.

The eternal wind had chosen this night to tame. She hadn't realized how its assault on the picket walls had buffered the noise outside them. A group of riders thundered down the road and sounded as if they were galloping across the sod roof above her head. She heard each word in a drunk's ribald song as he passed her door. When a gunshot exploded nearby, it was as if the gunman stood next to her bed.

The other noises were irritating nuisances she could ignore. Not the nightly gunshots. She hated the gunshots. They always reminded her of Ross Tanner.

What an enigma the man presented. He was quick-fire temper with a renegade's reputation. Yet... No! She wouldn't think about him. Amelia forced her eyes closed. She had become almost afraid to sleep. Sleep unleashed disturbing dreams her ever wary conscience could not control—dreams that melted the cold anger in Ross's eyes into pools of heated gold, dreams that softened the hard line of his mouth into an enticing smile, dreams that delivered the promise of his sensitive hands into an awakening reality. Her cheeks flushed and her eyes flew open.

How she missed that exhausted stupor that had given her immediate, dreamless sleep those first weeks after her arrival. Then she hadn't heard the gunfire; she hadn't lain awake brooding over Ross Tanner, wondering when he would show up at her door. Could she sleep at all if she didn't know he was out there—somewhere?

Probably not, she admitted. She had gladly given up the comfort of the big bed in the sleeping quarters to Mario and Dominga. Their nearness made it possible to ignore all the creaks and bumps of the night. But she knew it was Tanner that kept the drunks from her door and the rough drifters politely holding their hats in hand when they came into the store. Still, if he might actually kill someone . . . or if he should be killed . . . She swallowed down her panic.

Tanner had been right that day at the fort. She prayed every night he wouldn't leave town. Whenever she heard a gunshot, she paid dearly for that prayer.

Ross snapped the cylinder into place in the Colt .45 he had bought that day. The mustered-out trooper must have been desperate for money to sell this weapon, he thought. He held the revolver in the palm of his hand and admired its precision balance. It was well worth the gold it had cost him.

With a practiced expertise, Ross finished assembling the gun and began polishing it with an oily cloth. A cheroot hung loosely from his lips, curling smoke into his eyes while it drifted toward the thatched ceiling of the small adobe. A low melody from the nearby river and a chorus of crickets eclipsed the town's faraway din.

He set the cloth and pistol down on the small, slapped-together table before him and flipped his cheroot through the adobe's arched doorway. In the distance the cantinas beckoned with their bold lights, promising a good time. For a moment Ross thought of going in to Santa Angela, but the idea didn't appeal to him. Maybe he had stayed in town too long this time. He wouldn't leave, though, not until *she* did. Picking up his holster, he rubbed down the leather with hard, sure strokes. His word meant something—if only to himself.

Ross added extra oil to the rag and gave special attention to the important part of the holster—inside, where the polished metal would slide against the soft smooth finish. Tossing the cloth aside, he holstered the Colt, then pulled it out and shoved it in several times to test the new gun's fit. Perfect. He'd give it a tryout tomorrow.

When Ross thought about tomorrow an uncertain urgency swept through him. It made him pace the room, until he finally settled a shoulder against the door frame and looked out into the night. God, he loved this country. He wanted to be out on the plains, where a man could see the sky swallow the earth in every direction. If trouble was coming his way, he saw it miles before it reached him. He could prepare for it, know how to fight it.

Ross studied the lights of Santa Angela. Trouble waited for him there. Amelia Cummings had been nothing but trouble since the night he had met her. But he wasn't sure what kind. It made him uneasy, careful. Somehow she had drawn him into something he'd never intended or wanted. He didn't know how she'd managed it. He didn't even like her.

After that day at the fort, he had dismissed her into the company of all those respectable ladies, who had tried to force-feed their brand of respectability down his throat, until he had choked on their self-righteousness and hypocrisy. He hadn't wanted their so-called respectability then and he didn't want hers now. He wanted only one thing from Amelia Cummings. And tomorrow he would go about getting it.

Sunrise had been bloodred. Amelia had watched spellbound while the scarlet sphere rose from the edge of the world, its color consuming the earth like an incoming tide. Even the rooster, strutting proudly, had been daunted into a halfhearted crow before scratching back into the coop.

Amelia had quickly scattered feed to the subdued chickens and hurried back into the kitchen, slamming the door behind her. But it was too late. The eerie sunrise had caressed her with its fiery fingers and left its seed of unease growing inside her.

Through the long morning and early afternoon Amelia jumped each time the door opened. She didn't know what to expect, which made the waiting even harder, but she knew the day was marked. When Dominga had ventured a question about her odd behavior, Amelia had snapped an answer. Dominga avoided her the rest of the day. Amelia hardly noticed. She waited.

Amelia had lost count of the number of times she had started over on the column of figures she was adding. Finally, thoroughly disgusted with her inability to concentrate, she threw her pencil down, marking the tablecloth, and crossed her arms with something close to a pout forming on her pretty mouth. If something didn't happen soon, she would burst. Yet she dreaded what that something might be. She almost felt sick.

She glanced around the mercantile. She had to do something. She couldn't sit still. Rising from her seat at the table, she walked behind the counter. With jerky, clumsy movements, she sorted through the collection of odds and ends that had collected during the day. As she turned to restack two cans of peaches on a shelf behind her she knocked the basket of precious eggs onto the earthen floor behind the counter.

For a moment she stared at the yellow yolks and clear egg whites on the dirt floor. She knew it was stupid, but she wanted to cry. She wanted to stamp her foot and bawl great tears over the broken eggs. When she saw Dominga's concerned expression from where she was helping three Spanish-speaking ladies with material, Amelia swallowed back the tears. She raised her arms and tilted her head in an expression of bewilderment, then knelt behind the counter to clean up the mess.

Once hidden behind the counter, Amelia clenched her hands in hard fists to keep from grabbing up the remaining eggs and throwing them against the far wall. She forced herself to relax her grip. She took a deep breath. She was going to get through this crazy day without doing anything she would regret tomorrow.

With surprising calmness, she found some rags next to the shotgun they kept under the counter. After salvaging the unbroken eggs and placing them in another basket, she wrinkled her nose in disgust and began the sticky job of cleaning up the muddy goo.

Amelia heard the door open and for the first time that day she didn't look to see who had entered. When she heard his voice, she knew. The waiting was over. Instead of relief, the knowledge brought more agitation.

"Afternoon, Señora Estrada. Mrs Cummings here today?"

"*Sí*, Señor Tanner. She is behind the counter."

"*Gracias.*"

The soft chink of his spurs crossing the room tightened the tension running through Amelia until it hummed like a guitar string. She darted glances from the sticky rags in both hands, then to the top of the counter. She started to stand, then she knelt. She looked at her hands holding the grimy mess as if they belonged to a stranger. When the spurs stopped in front of the counter, she threw the rags back onto their shelf and stood.

Ross moved down the counter until only its width separated them. He leisurely explored her body with his hooded eyes, not saying a word. He didn't have to say anything. The arrogant possessiveness in his look, in his stance, said it all.

As his intense gaze touched her, a warm sensation tingled across Amelia's frayed nerves. No man had ever looked at her that way. She felt exposed, body and soul. She moved slightly away from him. This was a different Ross Tanner.

Amelia studied the man across from her, trying to discover just what had changed about him. She saw wind, sun, distant horizons, lonely plains in the shadows and angles of his face. Deep lines rayed from his narrowed eyes, which today shone like a flame reflected through whiskey. The same long creases flanked his strong nose and unyielding mouth. He took off his flat-crowned hat and laid it on the rough planking. An act of gentlemanly courtesy she hadn't expected. His straight hair, the color of blowing brown sand, brushed his collar and fell across his brow. Both hands rested on the counter, long fingers splayed. She couldn't see the gun strapped to his hip, but, like a mountain cat's sheathed claws, she knew it was there. He was a man who had come to the frontier, conquered and survived. He was the uncharted western plains, violent and unpredictable. He was the same man she had met a month ago on a star-filled night. Now she owed him a debt. Perhaps he had come to collect.

"What do you want?" she finally asked. Mr. Carter's warning echoed through her brain: "Ross Tanner takes what he wants."

Ross watched Amelia's little pink tongue moisten her lips. A stab of desire hit his gut like a fist he wasn't expecting. If he told her what he really wanted, she'd have reason to be nervous, he thought. With the patience it took to walk down a herd of wild mustangs over miles of prairie, Ross proceeded ever so slowly.

"They said over at the sutler's store you might have some shells for this." His voice, deep and drawling, possessed a deceptive softness that forced Amelia to listen closely to what he said. Ross pulled the Colt from its holster and set it on the slatted wood counter.

"Yes, I—I believe we do." Amelia cleaned her hands with a damp cloth she kept under the counter beside the shotgun. "That's one of the new Colts?"

"Yes, it's a .45 and the shells are a little scarce around here. The army won't sell me ammunition," he answered.

Amelia glanced up at him to see if he was mocking her. His amber eyes seemed to challenge her to mention that day at Fort Concho, but she wasn't about to bring it up.

"How many boxes will you need?" she asked.

"A couple will do."

"Fine. I'll get them for you." Amelia walked down to the end of the counter and picked out two boxes of cartridges from the shelf behind it. She returned and slammed the boxes on the counter in front of Ross. He startled her by grabbing her hands and turning them over, palms facing upward.

"My God, what have you been doing?" Ladies' hands were always soft, not chapped red and riddled with broken blisters.

Amelia jerked her hands from his grasp and clasped them behind her back. "Look around you," she gasped. The tears were there again. She fought them back.

For the first time, Ross took in the store's changes. He had been so focused on Amelia he hadn't noticed the improvements that had disturbed Tyson Briggs. When he brought his attention back to Amelia, he studied her closely. The neat picture he had drawn of her somehow didn't fit.

"You did this yourself. You didn't hire—"

"Hire with what?" Amelia said, her voice raised sharply. "Dominga and I broke our backs—" Amelia suddenly stopped as Dominga brought her customers over to the counter to tally their bill. The other woman looked from Ross to Amelia, her brows raised in surprise. The three buxom matrons cast furtive glances at them while they paid for their purchases and quickly left the store.

Amelia could feel the tension pulling tighter and tighter inside her, until she thought she would snap into pieces. She mustered all her control and said, "Please help Mr. Tanner finish his purchases, Dominga. I'm going to the back."

"Mrs. Cummings," Ross called after her. "Amelia."

Amelia's back stiffened more. She wanted Ross Tanner to go away, to leave her alone. She turned to tell him just that. The words caught in her throat when a young Mexican man burst into the store.

"Señora Estrada! Señora Estrada!" he cried.

That's all Amelia could understand of the rapid Spanish that followed. That and the stricken look on Dominga's face. Amelia looked on in horrified confusion as Dominga ran into her room and ran out wrapping a black *rebozo* around her head. She turned a tear-streaked face to Amelia. "It's Mario. He's been hurt. They have taken him to the hospital at Fort Concho."

"Wait. I'll go with you," Amelia called after her.

"There's no time and only one extra mount," Dominga said over her shoulder. "I'll send word."

Amelia stood in stunned surprise after Dominga had galloped away. Poor Dominga. She'd be all alone. That day she had learned about Devin came crashing down around her.

Amelia grabbed Ross's sleeve. "Take me to the fort," she demanded.

Ross looked down into Amelia's imploring blue eyes. Real concern stamped her features. Could she actually care about Dominga and Mario? He could feel her small hand shaking through his clothing. He felt himself being pulled into the promise of those blue eyes again. To shield himself he remembered those words she had said at the fort. Maybe she was different from his uncle's wife and her friends in some ways, but not when it came to her opinion of him. That's what counted after all. Ross took her hand from his sleeve and held it when she tried to pull away. "I'll..."

"I'll be damned... She's purtier than they said she was over at the cantina."

Suddenly Amelia felt her hand released. Three skinners, the men who accompanied the buffalo hunters and skinned hides from the dead carcasses, stood near the doorway, staring at her. They all wore dirty fringed buckskins and had knives a foot long and three inches wide strapped to their sides. Two stood slightly behind a great bear of a man who sported a high-crowned beaver hat atop his black, shaggy head. His bushy beard and mustache were streaked with gray and glistening with grease. Eyes like wet black stones glittered at her.

The room filled with the stench of raw alcohol, sour sweat and death. The odor grew stronger, nauseating Amelia as the trio stalked toward her. The top-hatted giant leaned on the counter next to Ross. The man on the left, his thin white hair plastered to his skull, giggled crazily. Never taking his watery red-rimmed eyes from Amelia, he placed himself at one end of the counter. The third man, short and stocky, sported two long braids hanging from beneath a black bowler hat. As he limped to the other end of the counter he sized up Ross. Trapped! Amelia's mouth dried, leaving only the metallic taste of fear.

Damnation! Ross cursed. Every sense sharpened, but he stayed still, still as death, revealing nothing. Could he make it to his gun? Why couldn't Amelia have been sensible and left when she should have. He had tried to warn her.

"They said you was alone over here," the big man said. "We thought a handsome woman like you shouldn't spend the evenin' all by her lonesome. Right, Arno?" The beard and mustache gaped, revealing a jack-o'-lantern grin.

The bowler-topped man on her left began to edge around the counter. "Right, Bearpaw," he breathed. One filthy hand caressed the rough boards; the other hovered over the knife strapped to his leg. The shrill giggling of the third man screeched along Amelia's ravaged nerves.

After examining each sweating face, she lost hope of reasoning with the malodorous trio. All thoughts flew from her brain except a prayer for survival. She looked at Ross. Not a flicker of reassurance flashed in his cold amber eyes.

Like the pincers of a scorpion, the two skinners on each side moved closer and her lungs squeezed shut with each step they took. They ignored Ross, who leaned nonchalantly on the counter, the Colt Peacemaker inches from his hand. That dismissal intimidated Amelia most of all. The man and the gun posed no threat to these brutes.

Knowing Ross was there, although he hadn't given her a look or sign, kept her from falling over the precipice into defenseless terror. Amelia knew she had to do something. Her hands were steady as they slowly reached for the shotgun beneath the counter. Better to die fighting than face the fate these animals promised.

Amelia swung the heavy weapon up and aimed it at Arno, who was now only a few feet from her. Bearpaw lunged across the boards and grabbed the sleeve and front of her dress. Her finger tightened on the trigger. A deafening roar numbed her ears. The shotgun's recoil slammed into her shoulder and threw her to the floor; her dress was torn by Bearpaw's huge, meaty hands. A second sharper report followed. Coughing and gagging on the roiling smoke and dust, Amelia struggled to her feet. A wrenching pain tore through her shoulder. Gasping, she leaned on the counter and frantically searched for Ross and her attackers.

Through the thick haze she saw that Arno was out cold, with dirt and sticks of wood from the roof piled around him and filling his hat, which had been knocked off by the downfall. A large iron skillet lay on the floor next to his head. Fearfully she peered over the counter and saw, slumped in a corner, the giggling man, his face frozen in a staring comic mask; blood trickled down his face from a black-edged hole in his forehead.

She quickly looked away from the horror, only to see Bearpaw and Ross circling each other in the center of the room, her neat table and chairs kicked out of the way. The knives clutched in their fists reflected the light from the crimson sunset that blazed through the open windows and door. Bright red flashes and arcs marked each slash and thrust. Somehow Ross managed to keep the giant from cutting him. With a great roar, Bearpaw suddenly rammed Ross with his head, hitting him in the solar plexis. Both men crashed against a long table piled with pots and pans.

Ross felt the air whoosh out of his lungs. His knife went skittering across the floor. Grabbing two pots, the first things he could lay his hands on, he banged them together like cymbals. Only, Bearpaw's head happened to be between them, softening the clang, but providing a satisfactory crunch.

Bearpaw's momentary stun provided Ross with enough time to push the big man off him. He staggered to his feet. God, where was his gun? He couldn't win a knife fight with this monster. No time to look for it now. The bastard was coming at him again. Maybe a chair would slow him down. He had to make time for Amelia to get the hell out of here. "Run, Amelia. Run!" he shouted.

Amelia heard a low groan from the man on the floor. Tearing her anguished gaze from the fight, she looked at the moaning skinner. He was trying to sit up, dirt and twigs falling from his head. She couldn't leave Ross to fight her battle. He'd be killed for certain. She refused to let that happen. Seeing the iron skillet beside the stocky man, she reached down and grabbed the handle with both hands. Without hesitation, she brained the man right between the braids, then smiled as he sank to the floor a second time; then she hauled the heavy skillet onto the counter.

A chair went flying through the air and broke apart as it hit Bearpaw's mammoth shoulders. He roared like his enraged namesake, shaking his great shaggy head, and started for Ross. The pain in her shoulder forgotten and her heart pounding madly, Amelia rucked up her skirts and scrambled onto the counter. She heaved the huge black frying pan over her head and tried to catch Ross's eye. With feet braced and skillet raised she waited her chance.

Ross saw Amelia standing on the counter like some avenging angel, with the skillet wavering over her head. What the hell, they needed a miracle. He launched a keg of nails at the huge skinner, forcing him back toward the counter.

When Bearpaw's rosy pate came within range, Amelia brought the heavy skillet down right on the shiny target with a loud, flat bong. The huge man swayed from side to side like a redwood ready to fall. "Timmm—berrr!" she yelled, and swung again with all her strength. The wild swipe almost pulled her off her precarious perch. The heavy skillet clanged to the floor.

Bent at the waist, Amelia windmilled in a desperate attempt to regain her balance, but the floor came rushing to meet her. Two strong arms caught her and a hard chest cushioned her fall. She and Ross hit the floor the same moment Bearpaw did.

Amelia found herself sprawled in a most unladylike fashion on top of Ross. After a long moment in which they stared at each other, she felt an absurd impulse to laugh. She couldn't stop the smile that crept across her lips or the great lungfuls of laughter that followed. Then Ross laughed, too. When she looked down into his eyes it was as if her dreams had come true. His eyes had softened to a heated gold, his mouth wore an enticing smile and his hands—those strong, sensitive hands holding her arms sent shivers down her spine.

As suddenly as her laughter had started, it stopped. Heat from the long, hard body stretched beneath hers warmed her breasts and belly. His heart pounded against hers.

She watched his laughter slowly fade, the lines and grooves of his face assume their usually harsh symmetry. He knows, she thought; he knows what I'm feeling. She could see it in his eyes, their depths deepening, studying her.

Ross savored Amelia's soft curves pressed against his body. He watched the tumult of emotions tinge her cheeks, soften her lips, widen her eyes in bewilderment. His hands moved slowly to her neck. Her skin was warm and soft and smelled like wildflowers. With gentle fingers he brushed the hollowed curve from shoulder to breast. "You're going to have quite a bruise there," he said, his voice low, caressing.

Sweet fire burned her shoulder. She tried to jerk free, but his strong hands held her close. Something was happening. Something dangerous. More dangerous than the unconscious giant her skillet had brought down. "Please, you have to let me go," she demanded.

"I know," he whispered, "but not now." He couldn't let her go. He wanted to roll her over and rip away the remaining cloth that covered her breasts. He wanted to touch her, to please her.

His raw sexuality was a magnet pulling her down closer to his lips. She could feel his desire harden against her own responding body.

"Mrs. Cummings!" Captain Douglas shouted. "Are you all right? What's going on here?"

Chapter Eight

Ross expected to see mortification burn Amelia's cheeks. Instead he could swear he saw disappointment cross her features before Douglas pulled her away from him. Damn, she was a confusing woman! But he admired her. God how he admired her. Amelia Cummings was one hell of a fighter.

Ross didn't struggle when two burly troopers grabbed him up by the arms and held him between them. No use giving them an excuse to clobber him. By the look on Douglas's face, the bluebelly was hoping he'd try something.

"I warned you, Tanner." Captain Douglas had positioned Amelia behind him, protecting her from the curious stares of the troopers and gathering crowd at the door. With a belligerent lift of his jaw, he said, "I told you I'd be waiting." He gestured with the pistol he held in his hand. "Take him to the fort."

Amelia shoved the captain out of her way. Holding the torn shreds of her bodice close to her chest, she shouted, "Wait! Take your hands off that man."

Captain Douglas grabbed her arm and whirled her around to face him. "What in the hell are you saying? You're in shock. That man—"

"That man saved my life. Have him released this instant." Captain Douglas stared hard into her eyes. Amelia met the thrust of his accusing glare with ironclad determination. "This instant," she repeated.

Captain Douglas's hand dropped from her arm, but his eyes never left hers. He lifted the flap on his holster and returned his service revolver. "Let Tanner go," he ordered in a low, disgruntled voice.

"Now if you're ready to listen, I'll tell you what happened here. These men—" Amelia motioned toward Bearpaw and his smelly companions "—came in here to harm me. If not for Ross Tanner, I'd be worse than dead."

Captain Douglas heaved in a big breath and nodded, much like a schoolboy who had been caught stealing apples. Amelia didn't like hurting him, but she didn't have time to consider the captain's ego. She had to find Dominga. "Please clear this vermin from my store. I'll give you a more detailed statement tomorrow. My friend's husband has been hurt and taken to your hospital and I must go to her."

Captain Douglas gave the order to haul the three skinners outside. Revulsion curled Amelia's lips as she watched the soldiers grab hold of the skinners' legs, one for each of Bearpaw's, and drag them out her door. What if Mr. Tanner hadn't picked this day to walk into the store? she wondered. She closed her eyes against the instant of terror that screamed through her and took a deep breath to regain her composure. She had made it. She had survived. Now it was time to get on with what had to be done.

Walking to the counter, she retrieved the Colt lying on the floor, then crossed the room to Tanner, who hadn't moved from where the soldiers had released him. Holding the gun by its wooden butt, she extended her arm to return it to him. The men standing in the doorway behind Ross scattered.

Ross gingerly took hold of the weapon and holstered it. He had a lot to teach her. More than he had planned when he'd walked into the store earlier.

"Now, Mr. Tanner, I believe I was asking you to take me to the hospital to see about Mario?" Amelia clutched the shredded calico to her breast, much as she did her dignity, and waited for Ross's answer.

"I'd be happy to oblige, ma'am." Ross stared at Douglas over Amelia's head. The implication of Amelia's actions were plain to both men. Ross wondered if Amelia understood. Later. He'd have to think about all this later.

"Thank you. I'll change and we can go." Amelia turned and headed for the kitchen. She was relieved the troopers had removed the dead skinner's body and his unconscious companions. She would see them enough in her nightmares. She couldn't find it within herself to equate the prairie scum to human beings worthy of her pity or sorrow. It was as though Ross had killed a rabid animal.

When Captain Douglas brushed past her without a word, Amelia caught his arm. He turned and looked at her, his head held at a proud angle. "Thank you, Captain, for..."

"For what?"

Amelia was genuinely sorry to hear the clipped disapproval in the captain's voice. But the look of censure in his set features angered her. He had no right to judge her. She hadn't done anything wrong. Amelia raised her jaw to match the captain's. "For what, indeed, Captain."

Captain Douglas touched the brim of his hat in a curt salute. "Good evening, Mrs. Cummings."

Amelia raised her brows at the formal dismissal. She nodded. "Good evening to you, Captain," she said in a voice equally cool.

Amelia watched him stride stiffly out the door and yank it closed after him. A frown marred her smooth forehead. She looked over at Ross, who was gauging her expression with quiet interest. Men! Did everything have to be a contest of some sort? Must they sulk or gloat at every turn? She shrugged away her questions. She didn't have time to ponder the childish antics of grown men who should know better. Perhaps Captain Douglas would be in better spirits tomorrow.

"I'll only be a moment, Mr. Tanner," she stated over her shoulder on her way to the kitchen.

Ross sauntered over to the counter. He pushed the spent cartridge from the Colt's cylinder and let it fall to the countertop, where it tapped a muted tattoo. So they were back to "Mr. Tanner." He looked at the curtain separating the kitchen from the store. Light bloomed behind the thin material. Ross watched Amelia's shadow move back and forth as she undressed. A hunger, sharp and demanding,

gripped him. All he had to do was walk through those curtains and take what he wanted.

Turning away from the beguiling shadow dance, Ross
leaned against the counter and dropped a loaded cartridge
in the cylinder. With shaking fingers he turned it one notch,
then let the hammer drop on the empty slot. For God's sake,
she trusted him. He holstered the gun and focused on the
window in the darkening room. She trusted him.

Amelia had never straddled a horse, but Mario had taken
her team this morning. It was either this or sit in front of
Ross with his arms circled around her, and there'd be none
of that. She hated the knowing deepening of the creases on
Tanner's face when she had balked at his suggestion. His
smile had suspiciously resembled a leer.

She wasn't sure her present position was any improve-
ment. Her last nice calico dress was going to smell all horsey
from trailing over the big black's posterior and her ankles
hung out from beneath the pulled-up curtain of petticoats
and skirt in a shameful manner for all to behold. The worst
of it wasn't the speculative look on Tyson Briggs's face when
they had passed him as he walked down the road toward the
cantina or the giggles of the cantina girls who had become
acquaintances. The worst part of this whole situation was
how she was forced to hold on to Tanner's solid body and
how much she liked it.

After the horrible experience she had just endured and not
knowing what to expect when they reached the hospital,
Amelia was tempted to lay her cheek against Ross's muscled
back. She longed to close her eyes and breathe in the night
wind scented with leather and him. It was reaction, plain
and simple, she knew. She wanted—no, needed—just for a
little while, someone strong to lean against. A man. But not
Ross Tanner. Never Ross Tanner.

Ross twisted around and said over his shoulder, "Hang
on tight now. We're about to ford the river. I'd hate to have
to fish you out of the water."

Amelia felt his body move beneath her hands where they
held his waist. She leaned in closer and slid her hands

toward his middle. The muscles contracted beneath her palms. The sound of rushing water and the river's smell filled her senses. Her thoughts drifted to the day she had watched him walking down the road in front of her. A picture of his muscles moving beneath his tanned smooth skin teased her. Here she sat, holding on to that sculpted back, that leashed-in power.

"You cold?"

"No," Amelia declared, suddenly reminded he could feel her body, as well. "I mean yes. Yes, it is rather chilly this evening." Of course it was a lie. Yet what else could she say? His nearness had some wild, inexplicable effect on her that made her shake from head to toe. She closed her eyes and gritted her teeth. Her hands balled into tight fists. Reaction. That was her problem. But reaction to what?

Chilly? Hell, it was one of the hottest nights Ross could remember. After reaching the far bank, he urged his mount into a smooth canter. Amelia's arms tightened around him, as he'd hoped they would. He regretted seeing the beacon light from atop the hospital's belvedere growing closer. He could ride like this all night. Ross's wide mouth stretched. Well, maybe not exactly like this.

Amelia was relieved when they rounded the end barracks building and entered Fort Concho's compound. This ride couldn't end soon enough. When Ross pulled the horse into a walk, she straightened and grabbed two handfuls of soft leather jacket to steady her seat on the big horse's rump. As they came abreast of a group of troopers lounging along the barrack's long wooden porch, enjoying their evening smokes, Amelia saw the spectacle she and Ross must present reflected in their rapt expressions. She hoped the failing evening light hid her burning cheeks.

She wished harder for nightfall when she spied the looks cut her way from the people gathered along officers' row as she and Ross angled across the parade ground toward the hospital. Matrons rocking gently on their porches laid down their stitchery; young ladies dropped their coquettish smiles and little girls set aside their dollies to stare at them. The light still held true enough for Amelia to distinguish the deep scowls on the faces of the husbands, fathers and swains standing in attendance.

How different these people staring at her made her feel. Their disapproving stares crawled all over her. By merely fording a river, she had crossed from one world into another. This was supposed to be her world, among the educated and the civilized. Yet they made her feel uncomfortable and out of place. It seemed she didn't belong on either side of the river.

Amelia straightened her spine and pulled back her shoulders. These people knew nothing about her. Nor did they want to know anything. Had any of those gentlemen offered her assistance? Had any of their ladies offered her friendship or compassion? No! Some of the more daring had crossed the river to inspect her. Oh she knew what they were doing when they came into the store. Not so long ago she might have done the same thing.

"You, okay?" Ross asked.

Amelia focused on the broad back in front of her. "I'm fine," she answered in a firm, steady voice.

"Good. We're just about there. I'll hang around until you and Señora Estrada are ready to go home. Unless you'd rather I didn't. I'll understand if—"

"Mr. Tanner, are you suggesting that you would leave me stranded here?" Amelia added an imperious note to her question to mask the catch in her voice.

"Hell. I was just—"

"Must you swear so much, Mr. Tanner?"

Ross didn't answer until they reached the hospital's imposing two-storied building, which stood behind the officer's quarters out of the curious porch sitters' view. Swinging his leg over the horse's neck, he slid to the ground, then turned and held his arms up to Amelia to help her dismount.

Amelia followed his example, but with much pulling and tugging of skirts and petticoats until, with her hands resting on his shoulders, she felt the strength of his hands clasp her waist and lift her off the horse. Ross lowered her slowly to the ground, his eyes locked with hers.

She knew she was standing on solid ground, but for the life of her, she couldn't swear to it. Caught up in the warm gold of his eyes and the slightest notion of a smile that played around the corners of his mouth, she felt suspended somewhere between heaven and hell. Surely any involvement with this man promised one or the other, she thought. Perhaps both. At this moment she was willing to take her chances.

"You've become a pretty good bargainer," Ross said. "I'll make you a deal."

Amelia's heart fell to her feet. This was it. The words she had dreaded hearing these past weeks. His price. She pushed against his leather-clad chest and attempted to step back.

Ross held her tight, not giving an inch. "If you'll drop this 'Mr. Tanner' business, I'll cut out the swearin'. At least, I'll try to."

Amelia's eyes fixed on a silver concho that caught the lantern light from the hospital's porch. She couldn't look at him. "I—I don't know. It seems so..."

"Friendly," Ross finished. "It seems so friendly. After you saved my life tonight—"

"I saved your life?" Amelia jerked her gaze to meet his, her eyes wide with incredulity. "You saved—"

Ross placed a long finger against her soft lips, silencing her, and continued as if she hadn't said a word, "With that big frying pan of yours." Ross stepped closer. "After that, I feel real friendly." He traced her lips with the rough pad of his finger.

Glancing up into the building heat in his eyes, she quickly capitulated. "It's a deal. We can be friends. Now, let's shake on it." Anything to get him at arm's length.

One corner of Ross's mouth lifted as he slid his hand from around her waist and stepped back far enough to shake hands. He clasped the small, roughened hand she shoved at him and sealed the bargain. Friendship was a beginning.

Amelia turned and started up the three steps leading to a portico that wrapped around the entire building. She needed distance. Thinking clearly proved impossible whenever Ross Tanner was anywhere near. She had to keep her head. If she didn't, she would be lost. Why? Why him, for heaven's sake?

Before she entered the hospital door, she turned to look at Ross as if seeing him might answer her question. A tall, lean man looked back at her with a predator's eyes and a rogue's boldness. She pressed her fist against her midriff, against the tumult whirling inside her. She had to get away. Leave Santa Angela. She turned and entered the open doorway. Soon. Very soon.

Amelia entered a long entrance hall with what appeared to be a large dispensary room on one side and an office on the other. The overwhelming smell of carbolic chased away any thoughts except those concerning Mario. He must be hurt very badly to be brought here, she thought.

She walked slowly until she reached another hallway that bisected the entrance hall. There she paused and peered left, then right. Large wards lined with neat rows of beds stood at each end of the hallway. She noted some stairs to her right that led to the second story. She was in a quandary as to which way to go. She didn't like the idea of wandering about the hospital alone. Seeing an open doorway across the hall, she ventured in that direction. An orderly looked up quickly from his meal in the deserted dining room.

Amelia stopped in the doorway. "Could you show me to Mario Estrada's bed, please?"

The young white-coated soldier stood and wiped his hand across his mouth. He pointed toward his left. "Doc put the Mex down at the end of that ward, ma'am."

Amelia's mouth tightened. She nodded and turned on her heel without further acknowledgment. It was difficult to listen to a man she respected referred to as "the Mex." Continuing down the hallway past the dining room, she walked under the stairway and entered the ward. Six beds lined the walls. Amelia walked quietly down the center of the wing and halted a short distance from the only occupied bed. From the smell she guessed that the two small rooms at this end of the ward were the water closets.

A candle burning on a small table next to the bed illuminated a bloodied bandage wrapped around Mario's head.

His face appeared pale and still. Dominga knelt by his side. Her head was bowed and her arms were stretched across his chest. She clutched a beautiful ivory rosary.

Amelia's first impulse was to rush to her friend's side. Instead she held her breath until she was satisfied she could actually see the steady rise and fall of Mario's chest beneath the army-issue blanket. Closing her eyes, she breathed her own quick prayer. When she opened them, the scene before her wavered through the tears gathering on her lashes.

Perhaps Devin had lain much like Mario. Or had he died quickly? She hoped he had. No matter what he had done, she couldn't endure thinking of him laid up in pain, dying all alone. Amelia dashed her tears away with a shaking hand. She wouldn't do this. She wouldn't torture herself with these unlikely visions. Dominga needed her.

"Dominga," Amelia called softly.

Dominga turned her tear-ravaged face toward Amelia. When she recognized who had spoken her name, she struggled into the chair next to her and motioned for Amelia to come closer.

"How is he?" Amelia whispered after sitting on the empty bed next to Mario's.

"No need to lower your voice," Dominga said in a hoarse voice Amelia hardly recognized. "He can't hear us."

Amelia darted a worried glance at Mario. "He's not...?"

"No. But he hasn't opened his eyes since it happened."

"What exactly did happen?"

The rosary beads clicked in Dominga's nervous hands. "I—I don't know. They told me they heard a rifle shot and then Mario fell. His head was creased by the bullet."

"But who...?" Before Amelia finished the question she thought of one person who would like Mario out of the way. "Tyson Briggs. He could have hired someone, perhaps."

Dominga shook her head. "No. He is bad, but he is no coward."

"But who else...?"

Dominga reached across the short distance separating them and laid a hand over Amelia's. "There are many."

Pulling her hand back to her lap, she sat up straighter. "We thought no one could find us in this lonely place." She glanced down at her hands nervously fingering the beads. "But we were wrong."

"I don't understand." Amelia leaned forward and tried to see Dominga's face.

Dominga looked up, then around the room. Seeing they were alone, she fixed her gaze on Amelia. "It is a long and ugly story, but I think it is one you should know."

"We have all night," Amelia said quietly.

Amelia listened to Dominga's soft voice telling a tale she wouldn't have believed had it come from anyone else. Back in the fifties, Mario and Dominga had lived in California. Mario owned a rich landholding dating back in his family to the Spanish kings. Dominga's family were neighbors, wealthy in their own right. At an early age, Dominga was betrothed to Mario. Though a large age difference separated them, they grew to love each other as Dominga became old enough to marry. They planned a happy life together among their families and friends.

With the flood of Americans that poured into California at that time came an ambitious sea captain. After meeting Dominga at one of the many parties the *hildagos* liked to give, he wanted to marry her. When he discovered she was betrothed to Mario, he set about ruining the Estradas with phony papers and claims against the Spanish land grants. His wild scheme worked, like many others at that time, and Mario was left penniless. To ensure their own property against such pirating, Dominga's family married her off to the sea captain at the age of fourteen. Mario joined the infamous Joaquin Murietta, and rode against the encroaching *americanos*.

Dominga managed to meet Mario secretly until her husband caught her. He beat her unmercifully, kicking her repeatedly in her distended abdomen until she lost her baby. Mario killed him and they had been on the run ever since.

"We don't know if the law still posts a bounty on Mario's head or if the *americano*'s family has posted one. It doesn't

matter. After a time, someone finds us. Then we run again."
Dominga's proud carriage collapsed. "Only now, God has
decided to take my Mario from me, too."

"You mustn't give up hope," Amelia said. It seemed so
odd for her to be urging hope on Dominga.

"Look at him." Dominga extended her hand in a palm-
upward command, while the silver cross swung gently from
the rosary beads snarled in her fingers. "He will not wake
up." The cross shook. "The doctor said he might never
wake up." Dominga covered her face with her hands and
broke into hard, gut-wrenching sobs.

Amelia knelt beside Dominga and held her while she cried
against her shoulder. She patted her back gently. "Everything will work out. You'll see." Over and over, Amelia repeated the words Dominga had said to her so many times
this past month.

Finally Dominga grew quiet, but she kept a tight hold on
Amelia for several moments. Amelia ignored her painful
knees until Dominga relaxed her hold and straightened. She
handed her a white handkerchief much like the one
Dominga had given her when she had learned of Devin's
death, then she sat back on her heels. Giving her a moment
to dry her tears, she said, "You're exhausted. Mr. Tanner is
waiting to take us back to Santa Angela."

"You go. I can't. Mario might wake up and I want to be
here when he does." Dominga gazed back at her husband.

"I understand." Amelia supposed Dominga wanted to be
here in case he didn't wake up, too. But she was relieved to
hear the note of hope in the other woman's voice. She hated
to think of what would become of her friend if her foundation of faith crumbled.

Amelia placed her hand on the empty bed and pushed
herself to her feet. After enduring the ride over here and the
long cramped position on her knees, her legs protested any
more use with aching stiffness. "I'll see you in the morning."

Dominga nodded her answer.

Amelia had no intention of leaving the hospital. If something should happen to Mario, good or bad, she wanted to be here. She wouldn't be able to sleep, anyway.

As she was about to leave the darkened ward, a shadow suddenly disengaged itself from a black corner under the stairs and approached her. She almost screamed, until she recognized Captain Douglas as he stepped into the light. "My goodness, Captain. You almost frightened me to death." She placed a hand to her pounding heart.

"I'm sorry. I didn't intend to scare you. I wanted to catch you before you joined Tanner. I'd like to talk to you." Captain Douglas spoke in a low, urgent voice.

"Certainly. What is it you wish to say?" Amelia supposed he wanted to apologize for his rudeness earlier in the evening.

"We can talk in here." Captain Douglas cupped her elbow in his hand and led her down the hallway into the office by the entrance, then shut the door.

Scattered papers covered a small desk placed in the center of the room. Shelves of medical books lined one wall, while cases held a variety of steel instruments, porcelain cups and pestles, and bottles in different sizes and colors.

She turned to face the captain, who stood by the door, gazing at her as if she were that Egyptian sphinx creature spouting incomprehensible riddles. Losing patience with his continued silent stares, she asked, "Well, what is it?"

The captain dropped his gaze, then snapped his eyes back to her face. "What in the hell do you think you're doing parading through the post, hanging on to that outlaw?"

Amelia was shocked into silence. She didn't know if she was more surprised at his question or his language. She didn't care for either. "This conversation is finished." She gathered up her skirts and attempted to pass him.

Captain Douglas grabbed her arm. "It's only begun."

Impervious to her cold stare the captain refused to relinquish her arm. "Unhand me. Now."

"You're going to listen to me first."

Amelia wondered how she had ever thought his eyes were a soft gray.

"I warned you that day you came to my office, inquiring about Devin. I told you then that the frontier did strange things to people. Now will you look what's happened to you? You've taken up with a fast-gun no-good, and from what that bounty hunter told me you're living with a murdering Mex and his whore."

Amelia's hand cracked a stinging slap across the captain's cheek. His face went white, leaving the imprint of her hand in bold outline. His hand clamped down on her arm until she clenched her jaws into rigid knots to hold back a cry of pain.

The pain eased from her arm as Captain Douglas slowly opened his hand. So many words jumbled together to hurl at the captain's rigid face, they formed an aching knot in Amelia's throat. She realized, looking at the contempt curling his mouth, that she would be wasting her efforts. She reached past him for the doorknob and pulled the door open. Captain Douglas made no moves to stop her. She brushed by him on her way out.

"I cared for you."

Amelia paused on the other side of the doorjamb. Then, without looking back, she walked briskly away. The man didn't deserve an answer.

Her frustration and indignation evident with each resounding footfall, she strode down the hallway toward the entrance, startling an orderly coming out of the dispensary across the hall. He looked on in astonishment when she abruptly halted, whirled around and retraced her steps.

When Amelia saw Captain Douglas leaving the office, she quickened her pace. When they came abreast of each other, she grabbed his uniform sleeve and pulled him around to face her. Her gaze stabbed into his surprised expression. "Captain Douglas, you comprehend nothing."

She released his sleeve with a disdainful flourish and left him standing with his mouth open, staring after her. She made her way around the corner and down the hall toward the wing where Mario lay. She slowed as she approached the stairs. She desperately needed to be alone. Ross Tanner waited for her on the front steps, but she couldn't face him right now. She had to find some quiet place to think, to make sense of all that had happened today.

On impulse, she climbed the stairs to the upper story of the main building. When she reached the top she found herself in yet another hallway. Slowly she walked down the corridor, aided by the light from one smoking coal-oil lamp attached to the wall. Three doors faced each other on each side of the hall. Not a sound could be heard behind the closed doors. Amelia didn't dare open one, fearing what she might find behind the doors.

Disappointed at not finding a quiet corner to escape to, she started to turn away, until she noticed a ladder attached to the wall near the center of the hallway. She looked up and saw a wooden trapdoor fixed in the plastered ceiling. The belvedere. Of course, the ladder led to the belvedere atop the hospital. Certainly no one would be up there.

Without stopping to examine her madcap scheme, Amelia looked around her, then began to climb the ladder. When she was able to reach the trapdoor, she raised one hand and carefully pushed the square wooden door back on its hinges. After a quick look over her shoulder, she climbed the remaining boards and thrust her head and shoulders into the belvedere. Her long skirts almost tripped her several times, but she managed to push herself to a sitting position and pull her legs on through the opening. She took hold of the rope handle attached to the trapdoor and lowered it slowly and quietly into place. Then she inspected her small hideaway.

A large lantern hung from the low ceiling. Its bright light filled the small room, which she guessed to be about six feet square. Windows provided a view of the countryside in every direction. When she stood up to sit on a three-legged stool in one corner she noticed the ceiling was slightly lower than her own five feet three inches.

Close quarters to be sure, but the little room provided the quiet corner she so desperately needed. It seemed odd, yet a little grand, to sit up here, high above her problems. She didn't know what she could possibly do for Mario and Dominga, but she knew she had to do something. Then there was Ross Tanner. He probably waited for her down below right at this moment, wondering when she would come out of the hospital. She didn't know where that friendship would lead. He still frightened her and she certainly didn't trust him.

With the lantern's light reflecting against the windows, Amelia couldn't see the surrounding countryside clearly. She couldn't pass up this opportunity to view the plains from this vantage point. Unlatching the two windows facing her, she pushed them open. Wind gusted around the little room and extinguished the flame in the lantern. Amelia looked at the floor and waited for her eyes to adjust to the darkness. She blinked several times, then searched frantically for a block of matches. She knew the belvedere served as something like a lighthouse to travelers on the plains. When she couldn't spot any matches, she decided she would inform one of the orderlies the lantern had blown out when she returned to the first floor. Since she was up here now, she might as well enjoy the view. Surely a few moments without the light wouldn't hurt.

When Amelia looked out across the plains her heart leaped into her throat. A fiery ring surrounded Fort Concho. Or so it looked to Amelia. She turned in every direction and saw the same reddish flush glowing in the hills and valleys of the low clouds hanging over the land. Prairie fires. She remembered Mario speaking about them. Never would she have dreamed they covered such a wide area. Though she couldn't see any flames, she could see their movement dance against the heavy lid of dense vapor. The horizon shimmered with their heat.

Directly overhead, inside the ring, the sky appeared shrouded with thick, black veils that occasionally parted to reveal small patches of glittering stars. Otherwise, the night was black save for the inflamed clouds and the scattered lights from Santa Angela.

Amelia crossed her arms on the windowsill and propped her chin on them. Could this be hell, as Tyson Briggs had suggested that day in her store? Amelia closed her eyes against the smoldering heavens that created such dark thoughts. But the wind nagged her with its damp breath, smelling faintly of fire and smoke, until she had to look again.

Amelia sat up straight. "Stuff and nonsense!" she exclaimed to the night. Texas was her ticket to independence and Santa Angela was her ride, though it was a rough one. She could handle it. Every day she learned she could. Let Libby march and wave placards for the suffragettes back in Ohio. Out here on the frontier she worked toward her own goals. Amelia smiled to herself. When she returned home wouldn't Libby be surprised at how her elder sister had changed.

Captain Douglas was correct. She had changed. Thank goodness she had changed. She knew she could come up with some kind of plan to help Dominga and Mario escape this bounty hunter. Amelia refused to consider that Mario might not recover. As for Ross Tanner, she would bring this insane infatuation to a halt and somehow remain his friend. God knows, the man needed a friend.

Amelia leaned over the casement to pull the windows closed. She could face the challenge downstairs now. Yes, she could be Ross Tanner's friend. She would just have to be very careful. Keep her distan—

The trapdoor hitting the wooden floor cracked through her thoughts like a gunshot.

Chapter Nine

"Merciful heavens! It's you!"

Ross Tanner twisted so quickly to face the startled voice he almost lost his footing on the ladder. "What the h—blazes are you doing up here?"

Amelia rode an emotional seesaw between fear and relief. Seen through the resulting haze of light-headed giddiness, she found the odd picture Ross presented to her devastatingly funny. She covered her mouth to stifle the errant giggles that threatened to escape.

Ross's brows gathered in a heavy scowl. "What's so damned, I mean danged funny?"

Amelia dropped her hand to speak, but when she opened her mouth, she couldn't stop the laughter that spilled out. Ross's wide mouth settled into a hard straight line and he began to move farther through the opening in the floor. Amelia's seesaw crashed to solid ground, jarring her back to sensibility. She quickly gathered her wits. "I'm sorry...really. It's just that with the dim reflection of the fires outside lighting your features you look like some devilish jack-in-the-box."

"A what...a jack..." Ross's eyes narrowed. He slowly climbed the last few rungs of the ladder and sat on the edge of the trapdoor's square opening. "I've been called a lot of things in my time, but never some kind of hell-bent toy." He pushed his hat back. "I don't think I like it."

"Well, you needn't be so humorless about it. I certainly meant no insult."

Ross cocked his head to one side. "Maybe you did and maybe you didn't."

"Oh, for heaven's sake." Amelia crossed her arms. "I'm sorry I ever mentioned it." What was wrong with the man, Amelia thought. Didn't he have a sense of humor? It suddenly occurred to her that he most certainly did, and she was being made the brunt of it. She looked away to collect her thoughts. When she turned to issue her own sally, the words melted away under the heated suggestion in his eyes. She read his intentions in the lazy way his gaze slowly moved over her. When his eyes at last met hers, her heart began a slow, hard beat that sent a warm flush to her cheeks. Her little hideaway didn't seem so safe anymore.

He's doing it again, she thought. She wasn't sure exactly what "it" was, but she knew that "it" was dangerous and her only defense against "it" was to keep her distance. This was definitely the time for a hasty farewell. She sprang to her feet but only managed to bang her head on the low ceiling.

"Damn!" she exclaimed against the sharp pain ringing through her head.

"Mrs. Cummings!" Ross raised his brows in an exaggerated expression of surprise.

"Oh, hush!" Amelia squeezed her eyes closed and rubbed the sore place on her head that quickly rose to a tender knot. An irrational irritation followed the pain. If she had been close enough she might have hit him. "This is all your fault. If you hadn't followed me up here..."

"Followed you. Hell, I didn't know you were up here. I came up to relight the lantern. If I had known you were here you can bet I'd have been up sooner."

Amelia grabbed up her reticule. "Well, you needn't have bothered. I was just leaving."

"I don't think so," Ross replied from his new position. He sat with his long frame propped against the far wall. One arm rested on a bent knee, while the other leg stretched in front of him. With the pointed toe of his dusty boot he nudged the trapdoor closed.

Amelia jumped at the solid thunk the square board made as it closed off her exit. Panic raced through her. This was ridiculous, she thought, trying to regain control of herself and the situation. She was leaving and she was leaving right now. She moved forward and grabbed hold of the rope handle, preparing to yank it open. She froze when Ross's warm hand closed around her wrist. She lifted her head and found herself nose to nose with the man she had vowed to keep at a safe distance. This was definitely not a safe distance. No, indeed!

"Mr. Tanner..."

"'Ross.' Remember?" A semblance of a smile deepened the creases bracketing his mouth.

"Yes, well." Amelia didn't know if she had breath to go on. She managed to take in a shaky gulp of air. "Ross, I— I really must be leaving now."

"Not yet, sweetheart. We have some business to finish."

Amelia's heart pounded so hard its drumming seemed to fill the small room. Play dumb was the only reply her scattered thoughts conjured. "Business? What business?" She searched his face with wide-eyed innocence.

Ross hesitated for a brief moment, almost taken in by the clarity of her eyes. Then he remembered how willing and eager they had looked that afternoon before that jackass captain had interrupted them. Finally he tossed aside his hat and whispered, "This business."

Ross clasped the base of her head with his free hand and covered her inviting mouth with his. The swift, hard kiss surprised Amelia's defenses into stunned silence. His warm rough lips caressed hers with an urgent passion that slipped past her guard and stole into the deep, hidden secrets of her dream. All rationality retreated under the full assault of her senses as she reveled in a wonderful freedom from restraint. She tilted her head and explored Ross's lips with her own.

Ross moved closer, bringing her wrist to his neck as they both straightened to their knees. Her small hand crept inside his collar and stroked the sensitive skin beneath his hairline. Ross trailed his hand down the length of her arm

to her ribs. He found the side of her breast and rubbed the
heel of his hand against its soft fullness until the rapid rise
and fall of her breathing rewarded his efforts. He wanted to
gently squeeze her breast, but he dragged his hand from the
tempting softness. Rushing would only frighten her. He
cursed the damn corset that guarded the softness of her
waist before he flattened his hand against the small of her
back to pull her closer. At least he could enjoy her firm
bosom nestled against his chest.

One forgotten bastion of defense prodded Amelia to
brace herself against the pressure at her back. She slipped
her hand inside Ross's jacket and placed it against his chest.
The hammering of his heart beneath her palm slowly tore
down the last fragile walls protecting her from total surrender. She leaned in closer and slid her arm around his
muscled torso to hold his body tight against hers. A pulsing
excitement had spilled over her body. Thinking was
impossible. When Ross raised his head she looked at him
with a hunger of her own.

Ross's pulse trip-hammered when he saw Amelia's
languorous half-closed eyes. Their blue serenity had melted
away, leaving them almost black from the dilation of her
pupils. He had wanted only a kiss, but no power in the
world could make him back away from that invitation. He
ran his tongue over her red swollen lips before closing his
mouth over hers. His tentative hold on any control snapped
when her tongue boldly danced with his. The unexpected
response drove him crazy with wanting her.

Ross plunged both hands over the gentle swell of her
bottom, then squeezed its firm roundness through her thin
calico dress and petticoats. Damn all this clothing, he cursed
a second time. He wanted to feel her skin warm in his hands,
to hold the fullness of her breasts, to see the color and shape
of her nipples, to feel them pout beneath his tongue. Ross
broke the deep kiss to run his lips and tongue over her jaw
and down her neck as he ground his hips against her.

Ross's hard bulge rubbing against her belly shot quicksil-
ver heat straight through Amelia. She gasped with the intense need her body instantly demanded. She tilted her head

to the side to give him better vantage to her tender skin and massaged his broad back, stroking the flexing muscles as his hands moved over her. Prodded by instincts that no lady admitted she possessed, she inched her hand lower, lower until the cold hard steel of his Colt yanked her out of her dreams. Reality rushed in with a vengeance. No love, no home waited with this man. They had to stop. Stop.

"Stop," she said breathlessly. She didn't realize she had spoken until Ross abruptly pulled away from her and clamped his hands firmly to her shoulders.

Ross breathed in rapid, deep breaths. "Stop? What kind of schoolgirl game are you playing? You want it as bad as I do."

Amelia grasped at words like a drowning person reaching for straws. "You're partly right, Ross." She gazed into his eyes, entreating him to understand. She didn't want to hurt him. "You want *it*. I want something far more. Something I don't believe you're willing to give."

Ross searched the blue eyes that had snared his interest with their calm beauty and their honesty. He tried to understand what she had said, but his blood ran too hot. Only one thing was clear. She didn't want him. Not the way he wanted her. He could make her want him. The fever shining in her eyes, the hard points of her nipples pressing against the cotton fabric of her dress told him he could easily make her forget her silly female excuses. But he wouldn't. Not her. Not Amelia.

Ross thrust her away so hard she had to brace herself with her hands to keep from falling backward. He settled against the opposite wall, opened the windows next to him and looked out across the smoldering heavens. "Get out," he said in a flat, hard voice.

When she didn't move, he turned to her with an accusing glare. "If rape is that mysterious something you want, just stick around." While Amelia quickly moved to snatch up the rope handle once again, Ross turned back to stare out the window.

She looked up in time to see him scrape a hand through his hair. The wind played through it as he continued to stare out the window. He looked so lonely. Amelia recalled his conversation with Captain Douglas at Fort Concho. To hear Ross talk so callously about his family and how they hated one another had struck her then as something sad. Now that she knew him better, she thought she understood why he had said such a crude, hurtful thing.

Her hand eased away from the bristly handle. She sat back, her legs folded beneath her, and clasped her hands in her lap. "Coward," she said softly.

"Oh, yeah?" One corner of Ross's mouth lifted in a derisive smirk. "Who's runnin'?"

"Any woman would run if a man claimed he was about to rape her. Who's making me run?"

Ross cut a look her way that convinced Amelia that all she had been warned about him was probably true. With the night's malevolent light defining his craggy features, he appeared totally uncivilized. Yet she didn't reach for the handle. Appearances were often deceiving. She had learned that much.

"I said get out," Ross repeated.

Amelia winced slightly at his low-menacing tone. Leave, her good sense shouted. But she couldn't. She wouldn't leave him like this. "You aren't going to frighten me away," Amelia replied with a steady voice, though her hands had tied knots in her reticule's strings. "You said we were friends. Remember?"

Ross swung his head around to face her. "I don't need a friend, honey. What I need is a woman." He lowered his head slightly and gave her the full impact of tawny eyes on the hunt. "Come over here and I'll show you."

His challenge almost sent Amelia to the trapdoor again, that and the raw hunger he didn't bother to mask. She wouldn't give up, not yet. Perhaps she could show him why he needed a friend. She moved to take a seat by the window next to him. The bravest thing she had ever done, or the most foolish; either way she knew she would get whatever she deserved. She fussed with her skirt and adjusted it around her feet, avoiding the confrontation she knew was coming.

Ross reached out and grasped her hand to stop her fidgeting and make her look at him. It crossed his mind to force her hand between his legs and show her just how much he needed a woman. Instead he rubbed his thumb along her damp, roughened palm and said, "Lady, you're every kind of crazy."

"I don't think so," she whispered.

"You're scared."

Amelia jerked her hand from his easy grasp and grabbed handfuls of her skirt to dry her sweating palms. "I'm nervous."

Ross turned his gaze back to the night outside the windows. "You should be, honey. You sure should be."

Amelia studied his darkened profile against the heat shimmering against the fire-reddened horizon and held her breath. She didn't think it was a good sign he continued to call her 'honey' and 'lady.' He had called his harlot things like that, she remembered. She wished he would say her name. Her heartbeat raced, making her head ache with its mad pounding. Had she made a mistake?

"I'm going to do you a favor. You ought to be more careful who you pick for friends." Ross moved so quickly he caught her completely off guard. He grabbed her upper arm in a grasp that hurt and jerked her around to face the burning sky. "See those fires, honey? Do you see them? Answer me!"

"Yes, yes, I see them." Sudden dread grabbed at her.

"I joined some old friends after the war. We used to ride over from New Mexico and set those fires. Look around you, baby. Sometimes God starts them with a bolt of lightning and sometimes 'ol Scratch starts them with Comanches. We *comancheros* liked to do our part." Ross took hold of her other arm, twisting her around to face him. "You were right. I don't have anything else to give you. It's all been burned away." He let her go then and turned his attention back to the night. Now she knew. Now she would leave.

Amelia absently rubbed her hands along her upper arms. "Then leave this place. Start over someplace new." Her hands grew still. Perhaps he could be...

"I love this land. It's a part of me. Leaving it would be like leaving a part of myself. Maybe the best part."

Sadness fell over Amelia in heavy folds until her shoulders could no longer support its weight. Her gaze dropped to stare at nothing but the pain she felt deep inside her. "I hate it here. The wind blows straight from hell and covers everything with dirt, even the people's souls." Amelia remembered that Bible verse and shivered. "This is a terrible land," she whispered. "A land of whirlwinds." She looked at Ross. "Maybe this is hell."

Ross placed a finger under her chin and gently raised it until their eyes met. "The only hell on earth, Amelia, is the one we carry inside us."

Amelia gazed into the unguarded pain that tarnished the gold of Ross's eyes and wished she could chase away the demons that haunted them. Yet she knew those same eyes filled her with demons she must battle. A battle already lost.

She took his hand from beneath her chin and kissed the open palm, then placed it against her cheek. Ross cupped her chin and moved slowly closer. Amelia closed her eyes, waiting for his kiss, waiting to be carried to that faraway place of white-hot currents where only the moment lived. Her lips formed an inviting pout.

Ross caressed her jaw and marveled at the softness of her skin. He wanted her. God, he wanted her. And she was willing to give him all he wanted. Then he remembered how she had almost given her life for him that day. A realization that kicked him in the guts. She had already told him she wanted more than a toss in the hay. Hell, he liked her too much. More important, he owed her. She was damned lucky he always paid his debts. Ross kissed her forehead, then released her.

Amelia opened her eyes. She watched in disappointed bewilderment as Ross sat back against the wall, one hand resting on his knee; the other, clenched in a fist, lay along his thigh. The lines along his mouth creased deeper into his face. His eyes looked tired and old. Amelia started to rise.

"Don't."

She eased back to her seat on the stool. "Why?"

"You can't understand what I could do to you."

Amelia couldn't stop the blush that crept up her neck and stained her cheeks, but she ventured on bravely. "I'm no young girl, Ross. I was married to Devin five years before he came to Texas."

Ross's hand on his knee closed into a fist, then slowly opened. "That's not what I mean, Amelia. You don't know what I'm capable of doing. When I rode with the *comancheros* I didn't just start range fires, I—"

"I don't care what you did years ago. What's important is that you're here now, not out there." She gestured toward the burning horizon.

"A part of me wants to ride those whirlwinds. You don't want anything to do with that part." Ross scraped away the sweat glistening along his upper lip. "Go. Now."

"I—"

"I said go! God, woman, are you stupid? Get out of here before I do what I'm dying to do. Believe me, in the morning you'll be relieved. And I'll be damned sorry."

"Maybe I would be damned sorry, too," Amelia retorted. She tried vainly to find a clue to what was going on in his head, but his stark features only offered despair.

Ross glanced upward and sighed. Then he turned his attention back to her. His gaze pierced through her. "What do you want, Amelia? Do you want me to push you to your back, throw your skirts over your head, yank your drawers down and climb on you?" Ross's world rocked at the tears springing into Amelia's eyes, but he had to make her understand... make her leave... before he forgot his good intentions. Jesus, good intentions?

"No! I want you to love me."

"Listen! Listen to what I've told you tonight. I can't love you. Understand. I can't. There's nothing inside to love you with."

Amelia scrubbed away the tears cascading down her cheeks. "You're wrong. I know you're wrong."

Ross lunged across the short distance separating them, and dragged her back to sit on his lap. He cradled her against one arm that held her shoulders in anything but a lover's embrace. His fingers dug into the softness of her upper arm while his other hand plunged beneath her skirts to hold her hip in an equally punishing grip.

Amelia pushed against his chest to escape, and felt Ross's hand slide down to her thigh. Each time she moved, his hand inched around the back of her thigh, coming closer and closer until one more wiggle would plunge his fingers between her legs. She stared into the eyes of that caged cougar and knew his threat was very real. She dared not move.

"I'm wrong, huh?"

His voice whispered shivers down her spine, reminding her of the night they had met.

"I was beginning to think you might be wising up from that crazy greenhorn that wandered around Comanche country by herself at night. But I guess you're the same stupid female you were then. I followed you to Santa Angela because I thought you had nice tits and I liked the color of your eyes. I was so hot for you I picked up some whore because I had found rape to be too much trouble. I chased away that drunk at your door because I didn't want him to get something I didn't want to bother with taking. Yesterday I was on my way to collect for all my trouble."

Amelia wept openly now. God, his words slashed her heart to bloody shreds. "Stop. Stop. I don't want to hear any more. Let me go."

"I'll let you go when you understand one thing. I'm not some kind of knight in buckskins like you think. You talk about love when I only want this." Ross hauled her against him in a hard embrace and kissed her.

Amelia's arms were trapped between them. Still she tried to push away. But it was no use. She was helpless to stop the crushing kiss bruising her lips. His hand began a slow exploration of the rounded contours of her bottom over her drawers. Amelia kicked to free herself. He grabbed a hand-ful of delicate cotton and pulled so slowly Amelia could hear each stitch pop from the band tied to her waist. She imme-diately stilled. Ross let go of the cloth and his hand ex-plored her thighs and bottom at will.

Ross's mouth choked her, smothered her. His hands de-filed her. He was punishing her and she deserved it. Why couldn't she learn? Never trust. Never love. Never trust. Never love. Amelia stacked the litany in a wall around her heart until she felt nothing, not even pain.

Ross felt the fight go out of her. Thank God he could let her go. Now she would leave. She would give up her crazy notion of loving him. He didn't want her or need her. Damn it, he didn't! How had he gotten into this mess? Ross set her away from him. "If you ever come near me again, I'll know what you want."

Amelia slowly lifted her gaze and met his eyes. She nod-ded her understanding.

Ross had half expected some kind of sassy retort until he looked into her eyes. For the first time since he had met her, he couldn't read her thoughts in their blue depths. None were there to read. He had taught her the most important thing for surviving in this country. Never show the other players your cards. He had a sudden urge to lean out the window and puke.

"Hey, Tanner!" a voice shouted from in front of the hospital's porch far below them. "I sent somebody to see about ya. You been up there a long time. What's going on?"

Ross sprang to the window. Amelia sat in a dejected heap on the floor.

"Don't bother sending anyone," Ross shouted down. "I'll light the lantern and be right down."

"Private Saunders is already on his way. We thought you might've forgot or something."

Or something, all right, Ross thought. He turned around and saw Amelia staring at him, her face white and her eyes enormous. Ross grabbed hold of the rope handle and opened the trapdoor. He looked through the opening and was relieved to see the hall empty. Good. Maybe he could get her out of here without anyone knowing they had been up here together.

"Come over here. Quick," Ross whispered.

Amelia ignored him. She didn't want to move or think.

"Come on, hurry. Before someone sees you."

"I don't care," Amelia replied softly.

Ross reached her in an instant. He shook her shoulders. "You do care. Do you hear me? You do."

Amelia looked into the eyes that had tormented her with their cold, then hot ambiguity. She saw something flicker in them. Something she had never seen before. Fear, perhaps? Whatever it was, she suddenly knew she did care. She cared very much about not being connected with this man in any way. She pushed his hand away. "I'll go."

Ross moved back to the trapdoor opening. He straddled the square doorway, a knee on one side, his boot braced against the other. "Here, take hold of my hands. There's no time for you to climb down the ladder. I'll lower you through, then you drop to the floor. It's not a long drop."

Ross grabbed hold of her wrists, not giving her any choice but to follow his plan. He lowered her as far as his arms would reach from his awkward position and let her go. He heard her drop to the floor below. "You'll have to run into one of those rooms. Hope the doors aren't locked," he called down to her in a loud whisper.

Ross watched Amelia run to the closest door. When it opened she hurried inside and closed the door softly behind her. From the corner of his eye, he saw a gangly young soldier take the last step on the stairs and enter the hallway. He swung around and got busy lighting the lantern.

While pulling the windows closed, Ross spied Amelia's purse under the little stool. Cursing the bootsteps scraping up the ladder, he grabbed up the black satin bag and crammed it under his jacket.

"I see you finally got the lantern lit. We get in a heap of trouble if the durn thing goes out." The private had climbed the ladder, so only his head showed above the floor.

Ross took one more quick look around. "Get out of the way. I'm coming down."

''About time,'' the soldier grumbled as he stepped slowly down the ladder.

Amelia pressed her ear to the door to listen for retreating footfalls. She could hear a muffled conversation between Ross and the soldier. Why didn't they hurry? She wanted to get away from this place as quickly as possible.

She heard the trapdoor bang into place and then voices growing closer as the two men walked down the hall. One voice was low and drawling. The other lacked the depth of full manhood. When they drew close enough for her to distinguish words, she had no doubts about who said what.

''What kept you up there so long?'' the private asked.

''Well, kid, I guess you could say I got carried away.''

Carried away, indeed! Amelia dug her nails into her palms with tight fists. She waited until she could no longer hear their voices or their boots. Then she slowly opened the door and peered to the left, then to the right. Noting the hallway was quiet, she scurried out the door. She waited in the shadowed corridor, allowing Ross enough time to get the soldier out of the way. She couldn't stop herself from glancing up at the trapdoor. She would never be able to look across the river at the lit belvedere without remembering this night. No matter how many times she looked, she would never understand what had come over her to make her behave as she had, to make her forget what Devin had taught her. One thing was certain. She had to leave Texas. Get away from Ross Tanner. He possessed the power to destroy her and she had begged him to use it.

She couldn't blame anyone but herself. She should have known better than to reach out to a wild thing. That's what Ross was. Untamed. Unpredictable. Lethal. But she knew better now. She would never forget again.

Chapter Ten

"Ma'am . . . ma'am, wake up."

"Just a little longer, Mama," Amelia mumbled, and buried her face deeper into her pillow.

"Ma'am, you got to wake up now."

Amelia blindly pushed away the persistent hand that shook her shoulder. "I'm sleeping in this morning, Mama."

"You can't be sleepin' here and I ain't your mama." The young orderly shook Amelia's shoulder with more determination. "Come on now, ma'am. You gotta wake up."

Amelia couldn't understand why her mother continued to pester her. She was so tired. So— Suddenly a loud boom shattered her dreams of home like fine crystal hit with a high C. Amelia jerked to a sitting position and met her own pale reflection in the panes of a stark window on the opposite wall. It stared back at her with wide-open, frightened eyes. Her in-drawn breath pulled in the harsh odor of carbolic.

"Ma'am."

Amelia jumped with a soft exclamation and twisted her head around to face a white-coated young soldier gazing at her with blue eyes. She pulled the rough wool blanket up to her chin and tried to unscramble the frantic messages her senses rushed to her brain.

"Ma'am, they already fired the cannon. The doc will be here soon. You got to go. Doc won't cotton to his beds bein' used up by females."

"Doctor?" That word gave her wits a good shaking. Finally all the strange images and smells fit together. "Of course. The hospital. This is the hospital."

Relief eased the worried face staring at her so intently. The young man nodded and grinned. "Now, if you'll just straighten up your blanket nobody needs to know you slept here last night."

"Yes...yes, certainly." Amelia threw the scratchy blanket back, and with loud crackling from the straw mattress, she rose to her feet. She stretched her hands high over her head, then rubbed the small of her back. It would never be the same. Surely each roped square that supported the mattress would brand her back forever. But the little bed had felt wonderful last night when the orderly had given her permission to use it. She turned around and quickly put the narrow bed back to rights. "Thank you, Private Saunders."

The private was busy pushing the window open on the other side of the bed. "Not at all, ma'am. You looked plain tuckered out when you came in last night." He turned around to face her. "Hey, how didja know my name?"

Amelia stopped poking hairpins into her gathered straggles of hair. She swallowed hard when she remembered where she had heard his name and his voice. He was the orderly sent up to the belvedere last night. "I suppose I overheard it...sometime."

The young man shrugged. "I guess so. I haven't been here long. Didja see those fires last night?"

"No!" Amelia winced at that emphatic tone. Quickly she turned her attention back to the bed and tugged at invisible wrinkles in the blanket. She pulled in a deep breath and slowly let it out. "No, I didn't." Much better, she thought. "Were there fires?"

"I should say so. The whole sky was lit up. I don't know how you missed seeing such a sight. Were you—"

"When did you say the doctor would be here? I would like to ask him some questions about my friend." Amelia gave the bed one last pat and turned her full attention to the orderly. She smiled her best smile.

"Uh...uh...what didja say?" The private's face flushed, staining his splotchy sunburned cheeks totally red.

"The doctor," Amelia prompted.

"Oh, yeah, the doctor. I almost forgot." Private Saunders glanced up and down the ward, his thin face once again reflecting the tension it had shown earlier. "He'll be here any minute. Will you go get her up?" He motioned toward Dominga several beds down. "I've got to finish cleaning up. The doc can skin a man alive with one look."

"Don't worry about a thing. I'll take care of Mrs. Estrada."

"Good. I'll be in the examination office up front if you need anything." The soldier bobbed his head in a final farewell that tossed sandy hair as coarse as a horse's forelock into his eyes. His flushed cheeks flared crimson as he stabbed his fingers through the troublesome bangs and walked briskly out of the ward.

Amelia heaved a sigh of relief. Thank goodness she had been able to make him think of something other than her whereabouts last night. She was too tired and befuddled to come up with good answers to nosy questions. She couldn't even answer her own questions.

Amelia scraped her hand up the back of her hair and tucked the loose ends into what felt like a bun. Time to get this day started whether she wanted to or not. She looked at Mario, who hadn't changed positions since she had seen him last night. Her gaze moved to Dominga, who was curled in a tight ball on the bed next to his. Her expression was troubled even in sleep. Amelia closed her eyes and sighed wearily. Seeing them like this hurt. What could she do? She felt so frustrated.

She walked to the open window and leaned against the windowsill on her crossed arms. Not a tree or hill interrupted the faraway horizon. The early-morning breeze cooled her face and smelled of wet soil and grass. The heavy skies had thinned to a gossamer gray lace that sailed silently across the heavens. Blaring bugles, shouts and barking dogs spoiled the peaceful picture, but for the first time, she had a glimpse of how this land could appeal to someone. Stop! Amelia banged her fist against the windowsill. She had made a perfect mess of her resolve to keep her distance from Ross Tanner, to simply be his friend. Friend! Ha! What a fool she had been. She might as well befriend a wild cougar.

Amelia recalled her decision to help Mario and Dominga to escape. Probably a worse disaster waited for them if she butted in to help. Whatever had made her so confident last night? She tried to recapture that bright optimism that made all her problems seem solvable up in the belvedere. No. She wouldn't fool herself again. She could thank Mr. Ross Tanner for showing her how really stupid she could be. It would be best to leave well enough alone and get out of Texas.

She whirled away from the window. Straightening her shoulders, she shook out her skirts and plastered a pleasant look on her face. At least she could give Dominga moral support. Quickly, before her false bravado followed her optimism and confidence, she made her way to Dominga's side. She glanced at Mario first, making certain his chest still rose and fell in shallow breaths, then gently shook Dominga.

The second Amelia touched her shoulder, Dominga bolted off the bed and shoved Amelia to the side. "Has something happened?" she asked in a shaky whisper.

Amelia put her arm around Dominga's shoulders. "No, no, dear. He's the same." She gently guided her to the chair by Mario's bed and helped her sit down. Dominga never took her eyes from her husband. "I'm sorry I startled you," Amelia went on in a calm voice. "I thought you would want to be awake when the doctor came."

"Sí, muy gracias." Dominga darted a glance at Amelia before she leaned over and straightened Mario's blanket.

Amelia almost turned away from the utter hopelessness clouding Dominga's eyes. Deep shadows bruised the delicate skin beneath them, emphasizing their dark despair. All purple and black, they reminded Amelia of crushed pansies from her mother's garden. Loose strands of black hair draped Dominga's pale face like mourning crepe. Amelia swallowed down the tears gathering in her throat. "I'll sit here while you go and refresh yourself. I've already made use of the facilities," she lied. Dominga wouldn't be forced to greet the doctor from the water closet door if she could help it, Amelia vowed.

Dominga nodded her reply and, with one more pat of Mario's hand, made her way to the nearby water closet, quietly shutting the door behind her. Amelia sat down in the chair Dominga had just vacated and scanned Mario's features for any sign of hope. His face remained composed and almost bloodless. Yet his lips held a little color. The bandage on his head had been redressed during the night. No new bleeding appeared on it. Surely that was a good sign. His breathing remained constant, but shallow. Amelia glanced up at the entrance to the ward. She hoped the doctor would come soon.

When Dominga returned, Amelia noticed she had raked back the loose hair framing her face into a rough semblance of her usually tightly coiled chignon. Her cheeks showed a slight blush from a cold water cleansing. Something she was sure her own face could use. She dreaded facing the image the cracked mirror would reflect.

She stood and moved to the other side of the bed. "There's been no change," she said to the silent plea in Dominga's eyes.

"Why won't he wake up?" Dominga took up his hand. "*Por favor*, Mario. Wake up," she pleaded.

Amelia wrung her hands and wished there was something she could do. She would find that doctor and bring him here. Something else had to be done. Amelia was about to tell Dominga her plans, when she saw a white-coated figure enter the ward. No mistaking his authoritative stride for that of an orderly's. "Here comes the doctor, Dominga. Maybe he can tell us something."

Both women stood up and eagerly waited for the tall man with thinning red hair to approach them. As he neared Mario's bed, Amelia felt his keen blue eyes brush over her from beneath his fiercely slanted bushy eyebrows. She didn't need a mirror now. She had never been so brusquely dismissed with a glance. The young private had certainly been correct when he described one of the doctor's looks. With thick muttonchops and a full mustache that matched the fiery red of his eyebrows and hair, Amelia recognized a formidable man.

He nodded curtly to both ladies, then leveled his gaze at Amelia. "If I may please." A slight Scottish brogue colored his speech.

Amelia immediately moved out of his way. "Of course, Doctor." When he passed her to take her chair, Amelia caught a faint whiff of bay rum. An aching nostalgia for her father crowded her thoughts for a moment. She stubbornly dismissed it and watched the doctor examine Mario.

After checking Mario's pulse against the big gold watch at his waistcoat, he lifted his patient's eyelids. "Uh-hum," he mumbled.

Amelia and Dominga exchanged quick glances. Did "uh-hum" mean anything? The doctor repeated his noncommittal remark after each probe and prod.

Amelia couldn't wait any longer. "Will he be all right? Why doesn't he wake up?"

The doctor slanted a look at her from beneath his strident eyebrows. Then turned back to his patient. Amelia didn't say another word while he unwrapped the head bandage, poked at the angry wound, then wrapped Mario's head again. That done, he stood and, without a word, walked to a nearby table and washed his hands in a porcelain bowl filled earlier by Private Saunders. Amelia held her tongue, though it was difficult. Dominga remained silent, watching his every move.

Drying his hands on a white towel, he began, "I can't see much change, Señora Estrada. We don't know much about head wounds. I've seen men come to in a few hours, a few days, even after several weeks. I won't give you any false hope. I've seen men never wake up." He tossed the towel back to the table and rolled down his sleeves. "I will say this. His pulse is strong and he doesn't seem to be slipping. All we can do now is wait."

"And pray," Dominga said.

"That's probably the best prescription of all. I'll check on him later today. Go home and rest. We'll take good care of him."

"No. I want to stay with him," Dominga replied. "If that is allowed?" she quickly added.

"It usually isn't, but I think I can make an exception. After all, it is my hospital. I'll send someone in with some food. You eat it, now. You don't want your husband to wake up and have a sick wife on his hands."

A tremulous smile played across Dominga's lips. "No. He wouldn't like that. I will eat. *Gracias.*"

With that settled the doctor turned his scowling attention toward Amelia, who now stood at the end of the bed. "I won't have two women in here. This is an army hospital. You, young woman—" he pointed at Amelia "—come with me."

Amelia started to argue with the doctor, but decided against causing a scene. No use in disturbing Dominga. "I'll be leaving in a minute," she replied, and took some slight pleasure from one raised brow before he nodded and walked briskly from the ward.

"Dominga," she said softly, "Mario is going to make it. One day he told me he was a survivor. He will pull out of this." Amelia pushed total conviction behind each word, though where it came from she didn't know.

Dominga merely nodded and pulled her rosary beads from her pocket.

"I'll bring over some fresh clothing and your hairbrush later."

Dominga nodded and began to move the beads through her fingers, one at a time.

Amelia felt completely closed out, just as she had last night when she had returned to the ward. She had sat and watched Dominga slide the ivory beads through her fingers over and over, silently replaying her evening with Ross with each rotation, until finally the beads halted and brought Amelia's whirling thoughts to rest, as well. The nice young orderly had helped her put Dominga into the next bed. Then she had collapsed in another. She hadn't put up more of an argument with the doctor because she really hadn't wanted to stay. She needed to get back to the store. She had done all she could for now.

After a quick trip to the water closet, Amelia wearily walked down the aisle between the two rows of beds. Sharp pain grabbed her thigh muscles with each step, adding more misery to her battered and bruised spirits. With no one to see her, she pushed and shoved at her tight corset to dislodge the stays that stabbed into her ribs, but her efforts met with little success. She wondered briefly if the stiff whalebone could become permanently embedded in one's skin. Amelia picked up her pace as she entered the main building. She wanted desperately to get back to her little room and take off these sticky, horse-smelling clothes.

As Amelia cornered the bisecting front hallway, she stopped abruptly at seeing the doors that opened into the porch. How in the world was she going to get to Santa Angela? Not with Ross Tanner, that was for sure. She would have to hunt up someone to give her a ride. Her spirits plummeted further at the prospect of asking any of these people for help. Amelia drew up her shoulders. Nothing for it. She would have to find someone going to Santa Angela.

Amelia was almost to the doors, when the doctor's tall form stepped into the hall and blocked her way. "I'd like a word with you."

What now, Amelia thought. She raised her chin ever so slightly. "Yes?"

The doctor signed a paper an orderly brought to him, then turned his full stern-faced attention to Amelia. "I take it you're the merchant lady from across the river. The lady the Estradas live with."

Amelia's spine stiffened a trifle more. "Yes." She refused to volunteer any information.

"I'm assuming you're a friend of theirs. Is that correct?"

"Yes, I am." Amelia wasn't sure where all this was leading, but she wished the doctor would get on with whatever it was he was leading to.

"I don't think Mrs. Estrada is in any shape for me to tell her this, so I'm telling you. You can do whatever you wish with the information. That bounty hunter has already talked to me about Mario. Wanted to know if he'd live, how long he'd be laid up and so forth. I told him Mario couldn't be moved too soon after he came to. It would kill him. The bugger said he didn't care. The reward would pay dead or alive."

Amelia felt the blood drain from her face. "Yes, go on. Surely you have some other purpose for this conversation other than making me ill."

"Just this. I like Mario. He's done work for me around the hospital. If he killed a man, I figure the man needed killing. Should he recover, I'll hold him here as long as I can so he can regain some of his strength. But I can't guarantee how long that will be. This Luke Badger has a legal warrant and he's eager to collect his blood money."

Amelia's opinion of the man changed rapidly. At least this was something in the way of help for her friends. "Thank you, Doctor. Is there something I can do to help?"

"I doubt that there is, lassie. But don't give up hope. I've been battling death for better than twenty-five years, and I've seen hope do some miraculous things."

"Thank you again. I'll keep in mind what you've said."

The doctor patted her arm with one of his big hands. "You do that, lassie." Then as unexpectedly as he had appeared he turned and reentered the examination room, a loud shout for his assistant his last remark.

Continuing on her way, Amelia thought over the doctor's words. Hope. Hope springs eternal. Wasn't that the saying? She feared her spring had run dry.

Amelia was forced to push aside her morbid thoughts when she crossed the threshold into the ashen dawn. She had to find a ride. Perhaps someone at the stables could help her. Bypassing headquarters seemed wise after her last conversation with Captain Douglas.

She had stepped down the steps into the rocky yard, when she noticed a team of mules tied to the hitching post outside the picket fence surrounding the hospital. They looked suspiciously like hers. After further examination, she realized they were her mules and they were hitched to her wagon. She didn't remember seeing them here last night. Maybe she hadn't noticed them. Poor things. Left out here all night. They were probably starving.

She petted each one gently on the nose. "You'll be home very soon," she whispered. They twitched their ears, then one stretched its neck and shook its head. One corner of Amelia's mouth quirked downward. "Even the mules don't think I can manage," she muttered on her way to the wagon seat, "and they couldn't know I've never driven a team of mules."

When she saw it, her breath caught. Her black brocade bag, its long fringe riffling in the fresh breeze, sat on the edge of the wagon seat. Its knotted drawstrings curled around a pistol. Only one person could have put them there. Ross Tanner. She knew instantly the wagon hadn't been here last night. Ross had brought it.

She made a quick inspection of the area around her, but saw only two sleepy soldiers lighting lamps in the headquarters building not far away. He was up to something, she decided. But what? An apology for his barbaric behavior? Hardly. More likely he was trying to confuse her the way he had last night. He would lure her closer with those lazy tawny eyes and house-cat manners. Until she came too close. Then he would leap at her like the wild cat he was and tear her to pieces. He had taught that lesson well. She'd never go near him again.

The river warned Amelia before she ever saw it. Over the jolting rattles of the wagon, she heard its clamoring grow louder as the team drew nearer to the ford. It was no surprise when she finally reached the flooded banks of the Concho.

She pulled the team to a halt with little of the difficulty they had exhibited to her earlier commands. They weren't eager to enter the swollen river, either. She had found driving the mule team to be much like driving her father's matched bays. The mules were just more contrary and harder to handle. Perhaps something in the air out here bred all the creatures that way. At the moment, Amelia couldn't muster up even a small smile at her own joke.

Clouds swathed the sunrise to a muted flush on the eastern horizon that did little to brighten the dawn. Still, the light was sufficient for Amelia to see the line of debris on both banks. The river had gone down. But how much, she couldn't guess.

The smart thing to do would be to turn the team and head back to Fort Concho and wait for the river to go down. For many reasons, that idea didn't appeal to her. She had left too many sticky situations back there to feel comfortable standing about biding her time until the river calmed. She wouldn't exactly be welcomed with open arms, either. Still, being uncomfortable for a few hours had its advantages over drowning.

Amelia glanced around her and measured how much room she had to turn the team. Not much. She gauged the width of the river. It really wasn't *that* wide, she thought. She could see Santa Angela's tattered skirts from where she sat. Turning around now seemed a waste. Besides, she must get back to the store. No telling how much had been stolen. If she waited till noon to return, she might not have any store left.

The mules tossed their heads and stamped their hooves. They were ready to go home and so was she. So what was she waiting for? The good sense to tell her to turn around, that's what, she thought. At that moment a flock of birds shot into the air from their treetop roosts. The mules pricked their ears. Something or someone must be moving about in those trees, Amelia guessed, though she couldn't see anything. She remembered that a man had been found by the river not too long ago with his throat cut.

Her heart bounced inside her chest. She gathered up the reins in two tight fists, and in her best imitation of the mule skinners she had seen she slapped the reins down hard and called, "Haw!"

The broad leather straps yanked Amelia off the buckboard's splintery seat. She gritted her teeth against the pain stinging through her armpits and tightened her grip on the long reins. The mules plunged into the river, splashing water back into her face. She slapped the leather again and called encouragement to the working team. Water rushed past them and rapidly covered the mules' legs as they fought the current to reach the middle of the river. Amelia thanked God when the water reached the mules' bellies and went no farther.

She slapped the reins again and called out to the mules. Water splashed across her feet. She felt the wagon slipping to the side with the turbulent current. "Haw, haw," she called, and urged the team to work harder. At last she noticed the mules' legs emerging from the swirling river. She called to them again and worked the reins until she thought her arms would drop.

Slowly they pulled the wagon up the opposite bank and stopped. Amelia saw their muscles quiver and jerk beneath their gray hides. She collapsed on the wagon seat and felt the muscles along her arms, legs and back do the same. They had made it. Never would she call them dumb mules again. At this moment she wouldn't trade her team for the most beautiful blooded Thoroughbreds in the world.

Not liking this side of the river bank any more than she had liked the other, she gently urged the team into a slow walk. The wagon rattled into town without disturbing its drunken stupor. Not even the dogs stirred as she rolled through its quiet streets.

The two armed men standing at her door stood out like parsons at a bawdy house. They didn't seem disturbed by her scowling stare and merely tipped their hats when she passed by on her way to stable the mules at the rear of the store. At the sight of two more men at her back door, her scowl changed to a worried frown. She pulled the team to a halt by their lean-to and retrieved Ross's pistol from where it had fallen to the floor with her reticule. She dried it with her skirt, then holding it gingerly with one hand climbed down from the wagon. What she would do with the thing she didn't know. But it gave her courage. Something was going on here and she guessed Tyson Briggs was behind it.

He had been acting so strangely lately. Constantly asking for her advice in decorating his store. Going a bit overboard with his compliments. She hadn't been fooled by his civil manners and kind words. Now this. She wouldn't put it past him to use force to keep her out of the store.

"Ma'am? Need some help?"

Amelia whirled around and pointed the gun at one of the men who had walked over from her back door. "What's going on here?" she demanded.

The young cowboy's prominent Adam's apple bobbed in his throat. He raised his hands in a peaceful gesture. "Mr. Briggs asked us to keep watch on the store while you were gone. He said to help you out any way we could. I thought you might need some help with your team there."

Amelia studied the man for a moment. He was very young. Probably not even nineteen. Freckles scattered across his thin face beneath a hat that looked two sizes too big for him. Why, he was just a boy.

Amelia lowered the gun, but kept her gaze glued to the cowboy. She didn't trust anything Tyson Briggs was behind. She stepped away from the team and stayed out of reach. "I could use some help." Bone-weary, she wasn't about to turn down any offers this morning.

"Thought you might, you bein' such a little lady. Name's Rayford Long." He stuck out his hand. Amelia hesitated, then briefly shook it. Rayford's thin face widened in a grin. He jerked a thumb over his shoulder. "That there is my partner, Nate Bigelow."

Amelia's doubts about the two eased somewhat under Rayford's innocuous grin. "Pleased to meet you, Mr. Long."

Rayford began unbuckling the mules' harnesses. "You just take your pretty little self into the house while I wipe down your team. Looks like they had a mighty hard time makin' it across the Concho. I'll give 'em an extra portion of oats."

"Thank you, Rayford. That's very kind." Amelia slipped the gun into her skirt pocket.

"It ain't nothin', ma'am. Some of the boys, they don't like mules, but I kinda have a soft spot for 'em."

"I know what you mean, Mr. Long." While Rayford busied himself unharnessing the mules, Amelia petted their soft noses and said, "I'll bring you each an apple later."

"Yes, ma'am, my ol' daddy's mules loved apples." Rayford hung up one harness and began working on the other. "I used to sneak 'em out to the barn."

Amelia scratched the mules behind their ears. "Do you live far from here?"

"Folks had a place up the Brazos. It ain't there no more. Comanches burned 'em out, killed my ma and pa. I guess them mules ended up feedin' redskins. They don't cotton to mules except maybe to eat 'em." Rayford began wiping down a mule with an old rag he had found on a hook.

Silence hung over the little lean-to. Amelia didn't know what to say. I'm sorry seemed so insufficient. Then an idea occurred to her. "You know, Mr. Long, I'll need some help with these mules. I don't have much experience with them. Would it be too much bother for you to come over in the evening and, you know, feed them and groom them?"

"Heck no, ma'am. I'd be obliged to do that for you."

"I can't pay you much—"

"Pay me! Heck, I don't want no pay. Ma taught me to be a gentleman and help ladies out and all. 'Course, as soon as I can get on at one of the ranches I'll have to be pullin' out."

"Of course. Then it's settled. But I insist on giving you something in return. Perhaps some tobacco." She had noticed all cowboys smoked.

"I wouldn't turn down a little Bull Durham once in a while."

"Sounds fair to me. Shall we shake on it?" Rayford reached under the mule's neck and shook her hand. "Thank you again, Mr. Long."

"It'll be my pleasure, ma'am."

As Amelia walked to the store she heard Rayford's voice talking softly to the mules. Somehow the day didn't seem quite so gray anymore. She smiled brightly when Nate opened the door for her. "You can leave now, Mr. Bigelow.

And tell the men at the front they may leave, also.'' She would discover what Tyson Briggs was up to later.

Nate blushed to the roots of his shaggy brown hair and dipped his head in a silent reply, then shuffled off toward the lean-to. Amelia entered the kitchen and shut the door, then threw the bar into its place. She would have to find some way to lock the doors from the outside. Locking the store up when she was gone had never been a problem with Dominga or Mario always here.

She looked around the darkened kitchen. The fire had burned out, leaving only ashes that puffed into swirls when the wind blew down the chimney. A melancholy moaning was the only sound. She looked at the little table with its three chairs and knew only one would be used from now on. Loneliness unlike any she had ever known crept over her. She heaved a great sigh to remove its weight from her chest, but it settled back heavier than ever. If only Dominga and Mario were simply moving on. If only fate promised them something other than death and defeat.

Hope the doctor had said. Hope, indeed.

Amelia started to unfasten the small buttons of her bodice. Her fingers stilled. Without examining her crazy notion, she walked quietly through the dark store and entered Mario and Dominga's bedroom. There on a tall chest sat the colorful statue of Mary holding a baby Jesus. Candles placed in various holders of tin and cracked pottery were arranged around the statuette. Amelia took up a block of nearby matches and lit every one. A soft glow brightened the soft clay features of the mother and child. The smell of melting wax permeated the air. Amelia didn't question her unusual action. It felt right somehow. It was some small thing she could do for Dominga.

The skinners' stench skulked in the dark corners of the store's gloomy confines. Amelia wrinkled her nose and rubbed her hands up and down the sleeves of the homespun dress she had changed into. The rough material soon chased away the goose bumps that followed the shivering reminder of yesterday's close call. Fresh air, this place needed fresh air. Quickly she rounded the corner of the counter and, stepping carefully over pots and pans and around overturned tables, made her way to the front. Fastening back the shutters on both windows, she opened them wide. For a moment, she closed her eyes and stood breathing in the fresh morning air that washed away the stink of sweat, blood and fear.

Calmer now, she opened her eyes and surveyed the quiet street. She frowned in disgust. Soon teamsters would stir up the dust with their big freight wagons and the cantinas would shake out of their early-morning lethargy and open for business. By heavens, she would, too. She turned to assess the damage when a movement down the street caught her attention. That big man wearing a scarlet vest had to be Tyson Briggs. Whatever was he doing standing there on the street at this hour? His mercantile was in the other direction. He pulled out his pocket watch, then snapped it shut. It looked as though he was waiting for someone.

Amelia stepped back to be sure he couldn't see her and waited with him. He could throw up all the friendly smoke screens he wanted, but she still didn't trust him. In a few moments a tall thin man stepped into the street from the arched doorway of a nearby brothel. He stood very still and scanned the street. When his scrutiny moved to Amelia's window, she stepped back farther into the shadows. Instinctively she didn't want even this man's gaze to touch her. With one more look over his shoulder, the man walked slowly across the road to meet Tyson.

She noted the two men didn't exchange handshakes, the stranger keeping his hands free, never far from the two pistols slung low across his gray striped pants. As he talked to Tyson, the man's eyes were never still. Tyson nodded, then gestured with his arm for the stranger to proceed him up the street. Then he shrugged his great shoulders and led the way to the Dos Tigres across from Amelia.

As they drew closer, Amelia studied the stranger's features. He had a hooked nose and a long face. Short, thin lips gave him the demeanor of a disapproving parson. Dark eyes that missed nothing were sunk into deep hollows. This was no ordinary cowpoke. His pant legs were tucked into knee-high, black leather boots that gleamed with polished care. The matching vest sported a gold watch chain. His gray shirt lay open at the neck, a black string tie fluttering loose beneath its collar.

Just before the two entered the cantina, the stranger stopped and peered across the street. He inspected the mercantile for a moment, then picked out Amelia. The cold shadow of death lurked within those black eyes. She crossed her arms and grabbed her elbows as if a chill wind had blown through the window. The man nodded and followed Tyson into the cantina.

Amelia knew without a doubt the identity of the stranger. The bounty hunter. What had the doctor said his name was? Luke something. Luke Badger. Tyson Briggs and Luke Badger. Amelia sighed and shook her head. It would take more than candles to save Mario.

Chapter Eleven

Tyson Briggs swatted at the fly buzzing lazy circles in front of his eyes. He pulled at his collar. The muggy morning promised a hot, miserable day. "Maria," he called, signaling to a girl sitting quietly in a dark corner of the cantina. "Get these plates cleared away and bring us a round of beers."

"No beer. Water." Luke Badger glanced around the Dos Tigres before settling his black gaze on the cantina's open doorway.

"Suit yourself. Bring him some water," he instructed Maria when she arrived with two brimming mugs. She started to take away one beer, but Tyson shook his head and tapped a finger on the table next to the mug in front of him. Amber liquid sloshed over the mug's side as she hastily set the yeasty brew where Tyson had instructed. With quick, jerky motions, she gathered the egg-and grease-smeared plates and hurried away.

Tyson didn't blame her. One go-around with the bastard next to him had already cost her a black eye and split lip. Tyson cut a quick perusal over Badger. He didn't like sitting in with the bounty hunter, either, but he was a new player in the game. A new player changed the fall of the cards. So far, the hand he'd been playing wouldn't win a piss pot.

"How about a hand or two of poker?" Tyson suggested. He pulled a worn deck of cards from his coat pocket and thumbed the deck next to his ear. The blurred rippling brought a crooked smile to his lips. Nothing like a game of poker to get to know a man, he thought.

"Don't gamble," Badger replied, his voice dry and sharp, like a steel blade run through sand. He never spared a glance at Tyson. The open doorway remained his target.

Tyson frowned and shoved the deck back in his pocket. He shifted his weight to see what was so damned interesting. The cantina's open doorway provided a perfect view of the mercantile across the street. He wasn't surprised to see Amelia Cummings bustling back and forth inside her store. He looked over at Badger, but couldn't read anything in his black eyes. Damned Indian. He'd like to take a knife to that long black hair Badger tied back with that prissy red ribbon. Craziest damned thing he ever saw. Wore fancy white man's clothes, but kept his hair long like some redskin. Probably a half-breed. Likely a mean combination. From the stories he was hearing, Luke Badger was meaner than most.

"Who does that woman belong to?" Badger asked suddenly.

Tyson sat back and took a long drink from his mug. He didn't like the direction in which this conversation was moving. He set the mug down and paused a moment. How could this work into his plans? He wasn't sure, but he couldn't think of any reason to lie. "She don't exactly belong to anybody. She's a widow." He started to tell about Tanner, but decided against that. He didn't want his poker *compadre* drilled in the back. Besides, he didn't know anything for sure. Last night, when they rode off together, he thought Ross might have drawn a winning hand. But apparently he had counted on the queen and lost his bet. Amelia had returned alone this morning.

The bounty hunter merely nodded. He lifted the glass of water to his lips and sipped, never taking his eyes from Amelia.

What a cold son of a bitch. Didn't drink, didn't play cards. Couldn't trust a man like that. Tyson decided at that moment to get rid of this pecker. He didn't hold with how Badger treated women, either. One thing to use a woman, but damn it, a man didn't abuse them. Still, no use dealin' the cards unless he thought he could draw a better hand. Maybe he could dig some information out of Badger. "Heard they got Estrada out at the fort's hospital. Too bad you missed."

Badger drew his hand into a tight fist. Slowly he pulled his attention from Amelia's door and looked at Tyson. "Too bad the army guards the hay cutters, or I could have taken him."

"Take him now. What's the difference? Dead or alive, right?"

"Difference?" Badger shrugged. "The man is already dead. Now or next week. That is the only difference. I will still take his head to California."

Tyson took a long pull from his beer mug to chase away the aftertaste of Badger's last statement. Talking about heads right after breakfast just wasn't civilized. He wiped his hand across his mouth and asked, "Why cool your heels in this sand pit?" He hoped he discovered something to use soon or he might be forced to give it up until later.

"The army in its wisdom protects the murderer for now." Badger's thin lips disappeared in a smile. "They can't for long. But—" Badger resumed his scrutiny of Amelia's mercantile "—patience holds its own rewards."

The only reward the bastard would likely find over there was a headache or a kick in the balls. Tyson kept a leash on his tongue and continued carefully. A flickering of an idea was beginning to form. "Some think so. Now me, cold, hard cash beats out any other rewards, especially the kind that can be picked up anywhere."

"I am a good hunter, Mr. Briggs. A good hunter never loses the trail of his prey, no matter how many side tracks he may take. My prey is always gold."

"It's been my experience if the hunter hesitates, the prey escapes." Tyson watched him, waiting for his response, hoping it would be the right one.

Badger turned to face him. "If you speak of Mario Estrada, I see no problem. The man's half-dead already."

Tyson saw his chance and took it. "Do you know that for sure?"

"The doctor told me he couldn't be moved. He wanted the man to die in peace."

Tyson watched the bounty hunter's black eyes get all fired up. He loved it when just the right card fell his way. He paused to relish the moment, then he played his hand. "The same doctor who won't let you see him? The same doctor that has the army all riled up against you?"

Luke Badger pounded the table with his fist. "I will kill them all."

"The whole post?" Tyson shook his head. "Not likely. I have a better idea."

Ross Tanner eased back into the cool swirling water of the stream. After his long hot ride, he couldn't have found a better camping spot. Soft white sand tickled against his naked thighs and back as it gave way to his weight. He flexed his hard buttock muscles and rocked his shoulders to mold the sand to match his body's deep contours. He sighed his satisfaction and folded his arms behind his head, then closed his eyes against the white bursts of sunshine that filtered through the thick awning of tree branches overhead.

The stream was shallow under his shoulders, but deepened gradually so the current washed over his legs and belly. Mentally he marked the place just above his head where his Colt and rifle rested on a grassy bank. He lay very still and listened to the birds, the wind in the trees, and the water. If riders approached he knew he would feel their vibrations before he heard anything. He was safe here. Alone and safe.

It had been a long ride into the plains, but it had been worth it. Since early this morning when he had seen that Amelia had made it safely across the Concho, he had ridden hard and fast. It had taken an hour to walk his stallion down and rub him dry. He didn't like what he had done to his horse. He didn't like a lot of things he had done lately. Amelia Cummings could take credit for that. The woman had somehow managed to dig up his conscience. He had liked it dead and buried. He had no use for a conscience out here. A conscience could get a man killed.

Still her eyes haunted him. Love me, they had pleaded. Like hell. Love was for fools who believed in fairy tales and happy endings. She should thank him for showing her how life was. Winners and losers. Winners took and losers gave. He should have taken her offer and bedded her. Then he could move on. Keep moving, that was the important thing. When you stopped, things got clouded up. Life got complicated. Too many attachments to pull you down. To hurt you.

Stop thinking of her, damn it. He had ridden all the way out here to get away from her. And he would. Ross concentrated on the chatter of the trees and the laughter of the water. After a while, their quiet company relaxed the tight muscles in his shoulders. Soon his thoughts flowed with the soft water that eddied around his body.

The earth. The sky. This was life. No lies. No promises. Only survival. He understood survival. She didn't. A filthy curse fell from his lips. He couldn't leave her there alone. Abruptly he rose from the water and shook the moisture from his hair. With both hands, he scraped his wet hair back and stepped onto the bank.

Long, angry strides took him past the shade from the trees along the stream's bank to the hot plain beyond. He stood, feet wide apart, hands braced on his lean hips, and scanned the beckoning western horizon. Ride on to the west, the hot wind urged as it pushed against him, drying his body in moments. The horizon's call was strong, but he turned and faced east. East, to the Conchos. To Santa Angela. To Amelia.

Somehow that woman had tied a tether to him. No matter how far he rode, she pulled him back. He thought he had cut it last night, but it was still there, stronger than ever. He could no more deny its pull than the Gulf tides could deny the power of the moon. In a day or two he would go back to Santa Angela and this time he would finish it.

But first, other business had to be attended to. Ross cursed the delay, yet he had no choice in the matter. Lives lay in the balance.

Long afternoon shadows shaded the front of the mercantile. Amelia sat down gratefully at the gingham-covered table in the center of the store and lifted her face to the slight breeze the open door provided. The clouds had cleared by noon, leaving the sun to blaze down through the humid air they had left behind. She pulled out a handkerchief and mopped at her face. Pushing at the damp curly tendrils of hair framing her face, she opened the ledger.

For a brief moment the numbers swam on the page. She blinked her eyes to focus on the neat columns. When she returned to Ohio, she would sink into her soft feather bed and sleep a week, but now she had work to do. Much more pleasant work than the drudgery she had done all day repairing the damage to the store and its inventory. Recording the payments made today could hardly be called work at all. With each figure she added, she imagined herself closer to Ohio.

Two ranchers had paid their sizable accounts today and given her important information. Several of her customers had taken their herds on to Colorado to get better prices. Those men would be returning later, but at least she knew they were coming. Unless, of course, they lost their herds before they arrived in Colorado. That happened too frequently. Then there were those who never made it back to their families in Texas, poor souls. She had heard about some of those unfortunate ranchers, too, and had sadly crossed their names from the ledger. She wouldn't belabor widows and orphans for payment, or the defeated men who had come in promising payment next year.

When she had completed the bookkeeping she understood the incredible gamble these men chose when they settled on the frontier. Fortunes were indeed being made. Not a little of which had come her way. When she returned home she would be able to live very comfortably. Most important for now, she could pay Tyson Briggs his money and remove that threat to her peace of mind. Whatever that was.

Amelia tossed down her pen and rubbed her hands across her eyes. She couldn't remember feeling at peace since Devin had taken himself off to Texas. Events had overtaken her and spun around her faster and faster until she felt caught in the whirlwinds that dreadful Bible verse had foretold. Soon she would escape. Soon.

Picking up her pen, she turned to the last page of the ledger. She used this page to keep track of the growing number of longhorns she owned. A task growing increasingly more difficult. She owned over three hundred head and they were scattered over the plains between here and San Antonio on different ranches. With the Comanches increasing their raids just as Captain Douglas had predicted, she worried about her property. For all she knew, her cattle were on their way to the far reaches of the Llano Estacado being traded for guns with the *comancheros*.

She smiled and remembered telling just that to Dominga. Dominga had told her, as she had many times before, not to worry. That it did no good. It had seemed funny at the time. She had planned on giving the cattle to Mario and Dominga, and the store, too, when she left. It would have been a good start for them and small repayment for all they had done for her. Now all that was finished. If Mario survived the head wound, he would only die later. Fate would be kinder if he died now. Immediately Amelia regretted the thought. It was disloyal and heartless, yet...

Amelia closed the book. Realities, that's what counted, what she had to face. But she didn't like it. Reality decreed she could do little for the friends who had done so much for her. Sending fresh clothing to Dominga and taking her away from this place when everything finished just wasn't enough. Frustration ate at Amelia constantly. She wanted to throw something. Scream at someone. Cry. Yes, cry. Cry for Mario and his stolen life. Cry for Dominga, who would be broken without him. Cry for herself and the love she had to give that no one wanted. She gathered up her pen and receipts. She wouldn't cry. She refused to waste the tears.

After putting away the ledger and boxing up the receipts, she picked up the heavy pail of water waiting on the counter. Thank goodness she had only two more tasks to finish and she could call it a day. She lugged the dripping wooden bucket to a far corner and sprinkled water on the dirt floor with a dipper that had holes punched in its bottom. With a slow sidestep, she covered the area to the opposite corner. Dipping and sloshing water about, she zigzagged across the dusty floor, dampening it until gradually only the front of the store remained dry.

She paused for a moment, setting the bucket on the table, to massage her aching shoulder. Ross had been right. An ugly splash of purple and yellow marked the spot where the shotgun had recoiled against her body. She looked down at the scuffed surface and loosened clods of earth at her feet and realized she stood at the very spot he had said it. Memories of that encounter and those following it blasted against her senses with the shotgun's bruising force.

She groped for a chair and collapsed. Her numbness had finally worn away and now revealed a terrible pain. She tried to work up a searing, healing anger, but that proved only to exacerbate the wound. She couldn't be angry with Ross, only herself. Ross had never deceived her, never masqueraded as anything but himself. A dangerous man who promised her nothing. Amelia rested her forehead in her hand. The man had even warned her, for heaven's sake. Still she had ignored her own good sense and followed her heart. A singularly stupid thing for her to have done. Her heart's inability to choose an appropriate recipient for her love had been proven without a doubt.

Like a penance for salvation, she closed her eyes and relived last night, when the heavens had smoldered with the violence of the land and she had begged Ross Tanner to love her. Love her or make love to her? She had never questioned the difference. But to a man like Ross, the difference was very real. He had been most explicit in that explanation. Now that difference was plain to her, as well. She must learn to regulate the act of love to a simple act of fornication. Convince herself that that was all she hungered for from Ross Tanner because that was all she would ever get from him.

Perhaps love had nothing to do with her feelings for Ross Tanner. He surely generated different emotions than Devin had. From the first time she had met Ross, he had released something wild inside her. Once awakened it had stalked her. Once tantalized it had consumed her. Full, raging desire had rampaged through her blood, demanding, seeking, making an utter fool out of her.

She couldn't deny that. But she wouldn't deny that something else drew her to Ross. Something almost sad. His loneliness called to her with a haunting serenade that filled her with an overwhelming need. A need to... She groped for the right word and smiled ruefully when she thought of it. Comfort. Yes, to comfort him, make him laugh, soften those hard amber eyes, care for him, care about him. She sensed he was as inexperienced with a caring relationship as she was to living on the frontier. Perhaps loving someone in that way frightened him as much as living out here frightened her.

None of that mattered, of course. He had made it plain he didn't want her to come close enough to show him. He *was* a coward. But so was she. She wouldn't risk the price he demanded on the outside chance she could teach him all the ways to love. Perhaps he didn't have a heart to reach. He seemed thoroughly convinced he didn't. If Ross proved himself right, she would be left in ruins. She wondered if, possibly, he was aware of the same thing and that's why he...

Her eyes snapped open. Don't do that to yourself, Amelia. Forget how his kiss had stopped the moon, the earth and the stars. Forget how his voice stroked that wild thing inside her until she wanted nothing else but to feel his hands stroke her body, as well. Forget everything, but his violence, his power to destroy. Then she might survive. Then she might make it back to Ohio with her heart only bruised and her soul intact.

Enough of this woolgathering, or she would never finish the floor and take care of that hole in the ceiling. She clenched her jaw against the pain in her shoulder and grabbed the bucket's handle. Quickly she started sprinkling water on the floor, gradually backing her way toward the front. She didn't know what she would fix for dinner. Something fast. What was there to cook? She'd just open up a can and make an early night of— Suddenly, from out of nowhere, a hard body blocked her progress out the door.

She cried out her surprise and dropped the bucket, sloshing water over her shoes. A big hand reached out and wrapped around her arm to steady her. She rolled her eyes toward heaven. Please God, not again.

"Mrs. Cummings. You all right?"

Pricked with a pinpoint of disappointment, Amelia said sharply, "I will be when you release me, Mr. Briggs."

Instantly her arm was released. "Thank you." She picked up the bucket, cursing under her breath about another mess to clean up, and walked briskly into the store. She knew Tyson Briggs followed her inside. He never came by without a reason. She suspected this time he would be expecting her bottom-of-the-heart thanks for watching the store in her absence. She tossed the bucket behind the counter with a clattering racket. She didn't know whether to give him his thanks quickly so he would leave or make him wait for it.

Slamming her hand on the counter, she turned around. "What can I do for you today, Mr. Briggs?" Immediately she regretted her words. Tyson Briggs stood hat in hand, holding a string of catfish. She had the awful feeling he meant them as a gift for her. She looked at the slick gray fish, then at him.

"I thought you might need something for supper tonight, seeing's how Mario is all busted up." He held the fish out to her like the class naughty boy offering an apple to the teacher.

Amelia couldn't refuse them. "Thank you, Mr. Briggs, but—" how could she not take his fish "—but I don't know how to clean them," she added in a rush.

"I can take care of that. First off, how about giving me that bucket to put 'em in?"

"Of course," she said weakly. Amelia rounded the corner of the counter and picked up the bucket. Now she felt compelled to make amends somehow. The man had been uncommonly polite lately and he *had* done her a favor last night. She brought the bucket to him and said, "Forgive me for sounding so sharp when you came in."

Tyson took the bucket and dropped the fish inside it. "Forget it. You've had a rough time of it lately. Anybody'd be a little testy."

Amelia smiled. "That's kind of you, Mr. Briggs. Still, there are no excuses for poor manners. You very kindly posted guards at the mercantile last night and you deserved thanks, not a sharp tongue. I insist you help me eat all those fish." Her smile never slipped, but she blinked, wondering what had made her say that.

Tyson gazed at Amelia for a moment as if considering the invitation, then a slow smile curled his mouth into a look that would have prompted Ross to fold his cards immediately. "I'd be happy to join you for supper."

Amazed by the change in Tyson's demeanor, Amelia halfheartedly returned his smile. "That's...wonderful," she said. "Why don't you clean the fish while I patch that hole in the ceiling."

"I have a better idea. I hate cleanin' fish. I'll get one of the girls at my store to clean 'em, and I'll stay and help you out."

"Oh, no, Mr. Briggs. You've done enough already." Amelia didn't know what to think about this Tyson Briggs. She almost wished for the brash bully to return. She had learned what to expect from him. With this Tyson Briggs, she didn't know what was coming next.

"No, no. I insist. After all, you are alone here. You might fall." Tyson turned without further comment from her and shouted for a boy in the street. "Take these back to my store and have somebody clean 'em. *Andale.*"

Tyson returned to the center of the store and pulled his gray-and-black checked coat back with his hands propped on his hips. "Well, now." He nodded toward the roots hanging from the hole in the canvas sheeting. "That won't take long to fix. Where's your patching?"

Amelia retrieved a two foot by two foot square of canvas from a shelf behind the counter. "I was going to use this."

"Looks good to me. Mind if I take off my coat?"

Amelia's brows shot up. "Why, no, Mr. Briggs. Go right ahead."

Tyson shrugged off his jacket and exchanged it for the piece of canvas. "Where's your hammer and some flathead nails. Those'll probably work best."

"Just a moment." Amelia neatly folded Tyson's immense coat and placed it on the end of the counter. Finding the hammer and required nails quickly, she set them on the counter.

Tyson picked up the hammer and put some nails in the pocket of his scarlet vest. A chair met his needs to reach the ceiling. "This the famous skillet?" He gave the large iron pan hanging in front of the damaged ceiling a knock with the hammer.

Amelia laughed. "You heard about the skillet?"

"Who hasn't?" Tyson began tacking up the canvas. "Mighty brave thing you did." He looked down at her. "You're a lot tougher than you look, Mrs. Cummings."

"Mr. Briggs! I'll take that to mean you don't think the Texas frontier will grind me up." Amelia stacked her last can of peaches on a shelf and looked over her shoulder at Tyson. Would he remember making that remark to her?

Tyson glanced down at her and said, "It will, Mrs. Cummings. It will." He began hammering again. "It just might take a little longer." He finished the last corner with a definitive ping. "That's all." Tyson stepped down from the chair and pulled the remaining nails from his vest. After placing them on the counter with the hammer, he shrugged back into his coat. "I take it you don't believe me."

"On the contrary. I believe you to be absolutely right. That's why I won't be staying any longer than I have to. You'll be happy to know I can repay Devin's IOUs."

Tyson suddenly grew still. "Business been that good?"

Amelia turned to busy herself with straightening canned goods. She didn't want him to see the triumph shine on her face. "It hasn't been bad. I suppose the ranchers on your accounts are beginning to trickle in, too."

A short telling silence followed.

"You bet," Tyson exclaimed a little too heartily.

Very interesting, she thought. She schooled her features in a noncommittal expression and turned to find Tyson regarding her closely. "That's good to hear. With the Indian trouble increasing, I'm relieved most of the ranchers haven't been wiped out."

"Not yet," Tyson said softly, almost to himself. Quickly he recovered and poked a thumb over his shoulder. "Well, what do you think?"

Amelia made a mental note of his quick change of subject before she answered. "A very nice job, Mr. Briggs. Thank you again."

"Happy to lend a hand. I guess with Mario gone, you're gonna need some help around here."

Amelia's face fell. She didn't like to think about Mario's impossible situation. "I hadn't thought of it really."

"Yeah, too bad about Mario. Terrible way to go."

"He's not dead yet, for heaven's sake," Amelia protested. "He's tough and hanging in there." Amelia grimaced at her choice of words. She didn't like associating the word "hang" with Mario at all.

Tyson closed the distance between them and placed his hand on her shoulder. "Mrs. Cummings...Amelia. Fate would have dealt a kinder hand if Mario died quietly in the hospital."

Amelia turned away sharply and scrubbed away an errant tear. "I know," she said quietly. "A trip back to California to face some trumped-up trial will only prolong the inevitable I'm afraid."

Tyson pulled her around to face him. His eyes caught hers with their direct intensity. "That bastard won't take him to trial. He'll take him about a mile away from the fort, then kill him. Then he'll whack off his head and take that to

California. Mario's wanted dead or alive. All Badger needs is proof.''

Amelia searched Tyson's flinty gray eyes for some evidence of deception. They revealed nothing. But she believed him. She had seen him talk to the bounty hunter this morning. Tyson had no reason to lie. Her gaze slid away from the cold, hard truth projected by Tyson's solemn features.

Tyson lightly squeezed her shoulder before removing his hand. ''I'm sorry. Truly I am.''

Amelia detected none of the usual mockery that spiced all of Tyson's speech. She believed he was sorry, and that made the truth even more terrible. She nodded silently and walked away.

''I guess you won't be wanting any company for supper,'' Tyson stated quietly.

Amelia pulled her chin up. ''Not at all, Mr. Briggs. Company right now would be welcome.''

''Even mine?''

She turned around, a small smile playing at the corners of her mouth. His question had echoed her very thought. ''Even yours, Mr. Briggs.''

''Let's drop this 'Mr.' and 'Mrs.' thing. We're neighbors.''

''I see no harm in that . . . Tyson.''

Tyson smiled his winning smile. ''Good. How about I go see about those fish and you rustle us up some cornbread to go with it. I haven't had a good pan of corn bread since I left Missouri.''

Amelia followed Tyson to the front door. ''I'll do my best, but I don't guarantee the results. I still haven't mastered cooking on a hearth.''

Tyson put on his hat. ''It'll beat those damned tortillas.''

Amelia shook her head as she took up the heavy post that barred the door. ''Don't count on it.''

Tyson stepped into the street and looked back at her. ''Damn the corn bread. I'll enjoy the company.''

Amelia smiled and didn't repeat her last statement, as she wanted to. Instead she said, ''Go around to the kitchen door when you come back. I'm closing up." She heard Tyson say "Sure thing" as she closed the door and slid the post through the brackets. The new reinforcements Mario had added to the frame caught her eye. She ran her fingers over the boards and nails.

"Sorry the corn bread crumbled so." Amelia poured fresh coffee for herself and Tyson, then took her seat at the table dwarfed by the size of the man sitting across from her. Tyson's tall broad frame filled her little kitchen. That and the smell of fish.

"It might not have been exactly like Momma used to make, but it was mighty good. In fact, I haven't had a meal like this since I left home, and that was a long, long time ago." Tyson watched her over the brim of his cup as he drank his coffee.

"Crumbly corn bread doesn't deserve such outlandish lies," Amelia replied.

Tyson smiled easily. "Maybe not, but that catfish did. My momma never did a better job. 'Course, the fish we had tonight couldn't compare to what I used to catch out of the muddy Missouri." He sat back and rubbed his hand over his thighs. "My, my, me and my five brothers ate so many of those big cats I'm surprised we didn't grow feelers." Tyson wiggled his index fingers under his nose to look like the spiny whiskers on a catfish and opened his eyes wide like the bugged eyes of a fish.

Amelia laughed at the spectacle. "You'd be a record catch for sure."

Tyson lowered his hands to the table and clasped them together. He leaned forward and looked at Amelia with steady gray eyes. "You really think so?"

The smile froze on Amelia's face. "What do you mean?"

"You think I'd be a good catch?"

The smile melted. "You're not up to something fishy, are you, Tyson?" Amelia replied in an attempt to recapture the banter they had enjoyed throughout the meal. This couldn't be what she was afraid it was going to be.

"I couldn't be more serious, Amelia." Tyson held his hand up. "Before you say anything let me finish. I'm nothin' like what Devin was, refined and all. I was raised on one worn-out farm after another until finally my pa just gave up one day and died out in the middle of a rocky field. My momma and I fed my little brothers with whatever we could find. I wasn't lyin' about all the catfish we ate. In fact, tonight was the first time I could bring myself to eat it again. With you sharin' it with me, it made a good meal."

"Tyson—"

"Just let me finish. I was raised hard and rough and that's what I am. But I learned to survive, to work hard and to appreciate fine things when they came my way. I'd be good to you. You're a fine lady and I appreciate that. You would always be something special to me. Do you understand?"

Amelia studied the earnest gray eyes leveled at her. The only time she had seen them completely naked was when he had spoken to Dominga. "Yes, I think I do. But you don't love me and I surely don't love you."

"Love? What the hell does love have to do with anything? This is business. A good deal will last longer than any kind of yearning to rub bellies, though I would make that good for you, too. We'll need sons and daughters with the same fiery spirit and brains we could give 'em to take over the empire we'll build. With your daddy's influence with General Sherman, that sutler's contract would be right here in my back pocket in no time. Money, land, cattle, power would follow just like bees to the honeycomb."

Amelia gave Tyson a puzzled look. "My father's influence...where...how—"

"Devin was always braggin' about that. I'll never figure how he could squander a fine woman and a sure thing." Tyson looked up, arching his brows, and sighed in disgust. He shook his head, then focused his attention back to her. "I'll guarantee you a good life, the best I can give. That's a promise I'll keep. It's the smart thing to do."

Amelia stood abruptly. She had to bring all this to a stop. "Tyson, I can't marry you. I'm not even sure I like you.

And even if I did, I don't want to live my life out here. I hate Texas. This whole marriage idea is impossible."

Tyson stood, also, towering over her. "No, it isn't because it's a good deal," he replied. "Hear me out. I don't expect you to go into this thing because you love me or like me or because you don't have a choice. When you hear the rest of the deal, I think you'll agree we can do business."

Amelia propped her hands on her hips and glared up at Tyson. "Well, let's hear it so we can finish this ridiculous conversation."

A look of pure pleasure lit Tyson's features. "Marry me and I'll guarantee the bounty hunter leaves for California with the gold Mario's head would buy and Mario and Dominga can disappear to parts unknown."

Chapter Twelve

Amelia sank slowly to her chair. "Say that again. Forgive me if I can't quite grasp your tender marriage proposal combined with this sudden concern for the Estradas."

Tyson took her hand in his engulfing grip and pulled her to her feet. "It's simple. You hold Mario's life in the palm of your little hand here." He held her hand higher. "All you have to do is—" he placed her hand in his waiting palm and curled his strong fingers around it "—give it to me in marriage. In return, I'll take care of the bounty hunter. For the record, I don't give a damn about Mario. I need your accounts and connections and—" he stepped closer and said in a low, intimate tone "—I want you."

Amelia pulled her hand from Tyson's grasp. "In that order, I suppose?"

Tyson tilted his head and cocked his brow in that infuriating fashion. "Don't tell me you care."

"Hardly," she answered calmly. "But if I'm to consider this business deal, as you prefer to call it, I prefer the term blackmail, then I'll need to know your terms exactly."

"Do you have a choice?"

"Yes, by heavens, I do. I must choose whether to trust you."

A slow smile stole over Tyson's features clear to his cold eyes. He nodded approvingly. "I knew you were smart. Smart and spirited. And a beauty to boot. I wouldn't ruin a good mare and I'll use a gentle hand with you. I want this partnership between us to work. I wouldn't start it out on a lie.''

''Just a strong twist to the arm.''

Tyson shrugged and his mouth rose in his favorite snake-oil-salesman smile. ''What fate provides . . .''

''You'll use,'' Amelia finished for him.

''Exactly.'' Suddenly the mocking smile vanished. ''Amelia, I'll treat you square.''

Amelia believed him. He would gain nothing and lose everything by going back on his word. Otherwise she wouldn't have believed him if he had sworn on his mother's Bible. ''Just how much am I going to cost you? I hope it hurts.''

''It'll take all I have here and probably some of yours. I've convinced the bastard to give me until day after tomorrow to gather up the three thousand dollars in gold he wants. Otherwise he's going to take Mario from the army. He's got the legal papers. He said he can void them some way. I didn't ask how. I didn't want to know.''

''He's probably lying.''

''Probably, but if he is lying, the Estradas will have time to get lost again. At least there's a chance he isn't. The only chance the Estradas have.''

Amelia didn't bat an eye under Tyson's hard scrutiny. She looked straight at him and lied, ''It's a deal.''

Tyson grabbed her up and kissed her soundly on her mouth, a kiss she suffered in limp surrender. He released her with a jaundiced look and retrieved his hat from the hook by the back door. ''That'll get better. You'll see.'' He shoved on his hat. ''We'll be good together.''

Amelia's cheeks colored at his blunt appraisal. The mere thought of the man touching her immediately drained the color from her skin. ''When will all this take place?''

''You have a thousand in gold?''

Amelia nodded.

''Have it ready by midmorning Thursday. The son of a bitch is usually finished beatin' up his whore by then.''

Amelia's face grew paler, but she nodded her agreement. She hoped Tyson would think her sensibilities had been insulted rather than guessing the real reason for her pallor. He mustn't guess what she was planning.

"I'll go get the preacher tomorrow and be back early Thursday morning."

"I'll be ready." Amelia surprised herself with her steady voice. The deception was becoming easier by the minute. She shut the door quietly after Tyson left, hardly able to suppress the excitement stealing over her long enough to see him out the door. The thump of the cross bar dropping in place released her pent-up frustration like the snapping of a watch spring wound too tightly. Whirling around the kitchen, she washed up the stacked dishes on the sideboard, banked the fire and took down her bed things. Only then did she slow enough to think of the practicalities of the notion that possessed her.

Taking an andiron from the hearth, she pried up one of the flat flagstones in front of the fireplace. Nestled in a deep hole beneath it lay a large canvas bag. She wrestled it out with a grunt and hefted it to the table, where she poured out its glittering contents. She knew to a dime how much money was gathered in the bag, but she needed to see it, recount it, stack the coins into neat rows. Did she have a thousand to throw in? Ha! More like six thousand, Mr. Tyson Briggs. She didn't need him to pay off this bounty hunter. She could save Mario herself without resorting to a marriage with that big bully. Thank God. She couldn't imagine a worse fate. Now all she needed to work out was how, where and when.

It was simple really. Exchange three thousand dollars for the warrant the man carried. She was certain the army wouldn't release Mario without a warrant. Not if that red-headed doctor had anything to do with it, and she was sure he would. That took care of the how. And tonight was the when. She needed to move before Tyson pulled anything and she couldn't let Dominga spend any more days and nights worrying about her Mario. Yes, tonight. That still left the where. A problem, indeed. She looked into the fireplace at the smoldering coals buried beneath the ashes. Where did one find a bounty hunter in Santa Angela in the middle of the night?

Amelia began counting out a thousand dollars in gold coins. She would give him the rest after the Estradas escaped. After shoving the remainder in the canvas bag, she hugged it to her chest and slowly returned to the fireplace. Surely it could be no great secret where a man like that could be found in such a small place. She recalled what he looked like and paused for a moment at the hearth. Heat from the fire brushed against her face or she might have shivered. Think, Amelia. Is this the right thing to do? Quickly she poked the bag back in its hiding place and pushed the rock over the hole. She knew it was the only thing to do. She couldn't marry Tyson Briggs.

Standing, Amelia brushed her hands together to rid them of sand. She could do this. After all, she wasn't a frightened little greenhorn anymore. She had learned a thing or two. She reached up on the mantel and took down Ross's revolver and examined it carefully. Too bad she hadn't learned how to use this thing properly. Actually, what was there to know? One simply pointed it at one's target, pulled back this lever on the top and used one's index finger to operate the trigger. At close range one couldn't miss. Besides, she was certain if she brandished it in an expert manner she wouldn't need to fire it. She thrust the pistol into her skirt pocket. Its weight tugging at her waistband gave her extra confidence.

Now how to find this bounty hunter. Amelia paced the small space from the door to the hearth and back again; the pistol bumping a comforting rhythm against her thigh. She would ask someone. Simple. But whom to ask wasn't so simple. She had never poked her nose past her door after dark until last night. Riding with Ross Tanner hardly prepared her for a door-to-door search for a bounty hunter.

Her pacing grew slower and slower until she finally sat down. Frustrated tears gathered in a hard knot in her throat. She couldn't let this one little problem stop her. Mario's life was at stake and she just couldn't marry Tyson Briggs!

"Hey, mules, how are you this pretty spring night?"

Suddenly Amelia looked up. A relieved smile eased the worry lines from her brow. Rayford Long. He could tell her what she needed to know. If she asked in the right way, he'd never know what she was about and neither would Tyson.

Amelia blew out the coal-oil lamp on the table and sat back down in her chair. Fear and excitement waged an unsettling battle in her stomach. Alone, with nothing but darkness and the throbbing rhythms of a Spanish guitar from a nearby cantina for company, the battle settled into a low hard knot of anxiety.

A gunshot cracked close by and Amelia snapped to attention faster than a private caught sitting in the general's chair. Like thread cut from a spool, she collapsed back on the chair, holding her hand over her heart, as if that would slow its frantic beating. She took a deep breath. She had to get hold of her runaway nerves. She couldn't possibly face the man in this condition.

Amelia took deep breaths and her heart finally slowed to a reasonable gallop. Without its thundering in her ears she could hear herself think, which was enough call for alarm. Would this plan of hers just add to the long list of stupid things she had done since her arrival in Santa Angela? Had she really thought this through? Her hand went unconsciously to the revolver in her pocket. She stroked its hard metal through the soft homespun of her skirt. Perhaps she was risking Mario's only chance to survive because she couldn't bring herself to marry Tyson Briggs. No, that would be the easy thing to do. Let some man take care of her problems. This was the hard way, the better way. She could take care of her own problems.

With that resolve putting starch back into her backbone, she gathered up one of Dominga's black *rebozos* and tossed it around her head. She would look just like any other Mexican woman until she reached this Luke Badger. Then she would begin negotiations. A man like that understood one thing—gold. Amelia stood and tied the soft leather bag to her waist. Cupping the gold coins in her palm, she tested their weight, causing the coins to chink their cold metallic song. She spoke this man's language. Her mission would succeed. It had to.

Amelia swallowed down the lump of fear that threatened to choke her and, carefully lifting the cross bar from its brackets on the back door, opened it. She winced at the rusty hinges' long, drawn-out creak. She had no way of knowing if Tyson would have her watched. Poking her head through the small opening, she peered into the cool spring night. She didn't see anything unusual, but she waited a moment to see if anything happened. Nothing.

With a tentative step outside, she passed through the door, but didn't close it. She held her breath and waited again. Nothing.

She pulled the door closed with a backhanded maneuver, while her gaze darted from a rustling bush to a rolling tin can to the soft swishing of a mule's tail in the lean-to. Still nothing.

Most of Santa Angela's nightlife commotion seemed to originate on the street in front of the store. If Rayford was correct, Luke Badger rented a small adobe located on a road two vacant town lots behind her store and down toward the edge of town. She wasn't familiar with that part of town, but thought it was generally quiet. Most likely no one would see her. Instead of taking comfort from that tonight, she grew more uneasy. What was she waiting for? At last she could do something. Do it! Quickly she looked left and right, then crossed the expanse of yard between the store and the lean-to.

She edged around the building until she faced the dark empty lots behind the lean-to. The large black squares of other residences and closed businesses rose from the dark ground in silhouette against the night sky, as sparsely numbered and as widely spread as gravestones on the new side of a cemetery. In some, golden squares of light flickered in their windows like the eyes of a jack-o'-lantern on All Hallow's Eve. Leaning away from the splintery wood of the mules' rickety home, she made out one lonely light on the edge of town in the adobe Rayford had mentioned. Good. The bounty hunter hadn't left his lair for the shabby delights of Oak Street. Instead of sending a message to her feet to get moving, that knowledge stuck her shoes to the rocky soil as if it were quicksand.

Amelia leaned back against the thin, splintery wood and bit her lower lip. She closed her eyes and chanted under her breath, "This is crazy, this is crazy, this is crazy." Finally she opened her eyes and looked across what now appeared to be an endless wasteland stretching toward the tiny light. It was as though the scrub- and trash-strewn earth flowed before her eyes like the flooded river she had crossed that morning. Torrents of water didn't threaten to drown her, only fear.

To make matters worse, Luke Badger's dark image stirred through her brain like a slick black adder crawling across her flesh. She tried to wipe his memory from her mind with the shaking hand she used to brush away the cold sweat from her brow. But it lingered there, rank and sooty.

She wanted to fling herself back into her cozy kitchen and bury her head under her pillow. She wanted to leave Texas tomorrow. She had enough money. After all, money wasn't everything. Oh, heavens, she was scared. Gathering Dominga's *rebozo* in her hands she buried her face in its softness. Dust, a subtle rose scent, and just the faintest hint of candle wax tickled her nose and her conscience. No, money wasn't everything, but friendship was. She tossed the fringed edges over her shoulders. At least it was to Dominga and it was to her. She wouldn't desert Dominga and Mario. She pushed away from the lean-to and plunged into the unknown depths that threatened to swallow her. She could only hope the outcome would be successful.

Walking swiftly across the open ground with her head bowed and her direction as accurate as migrating birds, she yanked impatiently at her skirt and petticoats when they snagged on thorn bushes. The heavy bag of gold at her waist kept even time with the gun in her pocket. Both brought a measure of comfort with each nudge against her thighs. She peered from beneath the black folds of wool surrounding her face, hoping she wouldn't see anyone, yet wishing she weren't so alone. Only the moon and stars accompanied her, and they looked cold and distant.

Before the chilled sweat covering her skin had a chance to dry in the soft night breeze, she found herself in front of the adobe's closed wooden door. Her hand rose to knock despite the primal will to survive screaming inside her head, run! run! run! She could smell her fear and knew this animal inside would, too. Still she knocked softly against the rough wood.

Each worm hole, each splinter, each gouge and cut of the battered door became her sole focus, her universe, until it ripped away into eternity, sucking her breath with its flight. She stared dead center at a pearl-handled Colt pointed straight at her head. She lifted her gaze from the round black void at the pistol's end to confront the same deadly emptiness in Luke Badger's deep-set black eyes.

Her mouth gone as dry as the desert, she had difficulty swallowing down the choking lump of fear that seemed to have taken up permanent residence in her throat. With noticeable effort she finally managed a weak "I'd like to talk with you, Mr. Badger."

Only a slight half blink of one eye indicated Badger heard her. Then, with the force of a striking rattlesnake, he grabbed a fistful of her bodice, jerked her inside and slammed her back into the wall next to the door. He kicked the door closed with a bang that sounded to Amelia as if it were a million miles away. This wasn't happening to her. This was someone else with a fist pushing between her breasts so hard she could hardly breathe. This was someone else with a cold, hard revolver's barrel digging into her temple.

She stared up into a face that was all taut brown skin and prominent bones. And eyes. Eyes that had burst into life like black coals in a firepit. At that moment Tyson's words came floating into her brain from where she had stuffed them under disbelief: "The son of a bitch is usually finished beatin' up his whore by then."

She was no whore, by heaven, and the sooner he learned this the better off she would be. Ladies were simply not treated in this manner. "Unhand me this instant," she said in her most commanding tone. "I am Mrs. Cummings and I have business with you."

His dry, rustling laugh poured ice water down Amelia's spine. It was like listening to dead leaves scratch across a smooth marble gravestone. A wild urge to close her eyes and start praying overwhelmed her, but she didn't dare. She glued her eyes to his in a desperate hope he would think she was only half as scared as she was.

"In good time," he finally answered. "All in good time."

His words flowed over her with the cold breath of an opened crypt. The man was crazy and so was she for coming here, but now she had to put up a good front. For herself and for her friends. "A good time would be now," Amelia replied firmly.

"Not so fast, my spitting little kitten."

Badger removed his fist from her chest and Amelia took a deep breath to fill her starving lungs. Immediately his hand reached under the black shawl and closed around one of her breasts. In blind reaction, Amelia struck at his hand.

Badger jabbed the pistol into her temple. "Don't scratch, little kitten."

Amelia forced her hand to her side and suffered his touch on her body.

Badger roughly massaged one breast, then the other. "Nice, very nice."

Amelia inched her hand toward the pocket holding Ross's pistol, waiting for her chance. If she went for it now, she knew he'd kill her. And while that idea didn't compare too badly with the other things he would do, she couldn't sacrifice Mario's life.

With one last painful squeeze to her breast, Badger trailed his hand over her belly and cupped her between her legs. He smiled at Amelia's gasp. Then his hand traveled over her body quickly.

Too late, Amelia realized his purpose in this degrading exploration of her person. He was searching her. Their hands reached her pocket at the same moment. His, a heartbeat faster, closed around the pistol first.

He pulled the gun from her pocket and held it before her face. "Ah, the little kitten has sharp claws. That's not so nice. She will have to be punished."

His words rang like a death knell in Amelia's brain. Valiantly she fought the strong current of fear that threatened to drag her down into the drowning depths of hopelessness. Panting from the struggle to keep her head clear, she said, "I've brought a thousand dollars in gold to buy Mario Estrada's life. You can have the other two thousand when you give me your warrant and they leave town."

Ross's pistol dropped with a flat thunk to the earthen floor. Amelia blinked at the short burst of ripping material as Badger jerked the leather bag of coins from her waistband.

He dangled the bag before her eyes, then shook it, jingling the coins inside it. "Tyson Briggs has promised me the same. What is your bid?"

"You'll get nothing from him. Tyson won't pay you unless I marry him and I won't."

"I think you would, little kitten. I think you would do anything to save that stinking Mex."

Amelia scrambled quickly for anything to say that would convince this monster to deal with her. "Gold. I can pay you more gold."

"Interesting," he replied.

"Move that gun from my head and we'll talk terms." Amelia wondered if she had said the right thing. With his hands busy holding the gun and gold, he couldn't put them on her.

"The little kitten is still spitting. I like that." Badger holstered his pistol. He took up the edge of the shawl with two fingers and slowly opened it. "What else do you have to offer?"

Amelia jerked the shawl from his fingers. "Nothing."

Badger dug his fingers into the soft flesh of her upper arm and yanked her around to stand beside him as he turned to face a table in a dark corner of the small adobe. "See that big jar there by my saddle? Estrada's head will be in that jar in two days. Look at it good, little kitten. Imagine his eyes staring at you from inside the jar."

Gorge heaved into Amelia's throat at the sight of the filthy jar. She tried to pull away, but Badger held her tight. "Let me go!" she cried.

"So demanding, little kitten." Badger shoved her away so hard she almost lost her balance. He tossed the bag onto the table next to the heinous jar, then strode after her. He pushed her again. "So, you have nothing more to offer."

Amelia staggered away from him. "I'm leaving." She grabbed a chair and pushed it at him.

"When I say so." Badger kicked the chair out of the way and followed her around the room. Then he pushed her. "And I haven't said so. What else do you have to offer?" Reaching for the *rebozo,* he yanked it away from her and threw it to the floor.

Amelia had no recourse except to keep backing away from his long strides. "Nothing," she stated in a desperate breath while trying to stay out of his reach.

"Nothing?" Badger asked. He grabbed a handful of her bodice and yanked hard, sending tiny buttons flying across the room. "You aren't thinking, little kitten."

Amelia whirled around and made a mad dash for the door. She screamed when he grabbed her sleeve and jerked her up next to him.

"Not leaving so soon, little kitten? We have business to discuss. Don't you want to bargain for your stinking friend?" He ground his erection obscenely against her buttocks. "What price will you pay, little kitten?"

Amelia jerked and twisted like a frenzied wild mustang ridden for the first time. She kicked backward against his shins and jabbed her elbows into his ribs. Determined to free herself from his groping hands, she flung her head backward, catching his chin with a hard blow. Her head felt as if an anvil had fallen on it, but Badger's grunt of pain was music to her ears. The second his arm loosened, she tore free.

Freedom lasted a single gulping breath. Badger clamped his hand to her shoulder in a bruising grip and spun her around to face him. Rage smeared his face with crimson streaks; his eyes glittered with pleasure as he raised his hand. Amelia raised her arms to ward off the blow she knew was coming, but too late. Badger struck her across the face with the back of his hand. The force of the blow sent her reeling toward the floor. Ringing, whirling pain dragged her toward a floating darkness, but Ross's gun crunched into her ribs. Never was pain so welcome. She grabbed the gun and rolled over, fanning the lever back before she extended her arm toward the looming black hulk that was Badger.

"Put your hands on your head," Amelia commanded between panted breaths. "Now! You son of a bitch."

Badger slowly complied.

"If you blink, I'll kill you," she said as she struggled to her feet.

"Your hand is shaking so badly you'll miss."

"Do you feel lucky tonight?"

"Perhaps not, little kitten. But your luck isn't so good, either." Badger smoothed a hand over his slicked-back hair. "The price for Mario's head just went up. In fact, it doubled. When you bring the rest of the gold tomorrow night, if you can, bring with it a better attitude. That's my price—I'll accept no other."

An urge to kill consumed Amelia. Restraining it sickened her. She wasn't sure she'd hit him, and if she missed, there'd be no bargain. She wouldn't chance that. She backed toward the door.

Amelia held the gun on Badger while she fumbled with the door latch behind her. She didn't bother to comment on Badger's demand. She had no doubts he knew her answer.

"Pull your claws in, little kitten. I'll not touch you again tonight. Tonight and tomorrow think of all the ways you can please me. I'm very hard to please, little kitten."

"You're nothing but a savage," Amelia bit out.

Badger's head rocked back as if she'd struck him. His nostrils flared. "You'll pay for that, little kitten. You'll pay."

* * *

Honeysuckle. White lace curtains gently lift and fall against the window that fills the room with fresh morning light. The deep feather mattress covered in crisp white sheets smelled of sunshine. Mama sings below and the mouth-watering aroma of frying bacon and hot coffee drifts up the stairs. Home. Home at last. Safe.

The cool, smooth wooden floors and soft carpet of faded roses feel good beneath her bare feet, and the carved oak wardrobe waxed to a shiny patina overflows with dresses of every shade and style. Choosing just one is so difficult. Swishing petticoats, rustling silk dress, kid slippers.

Lace curtains tickle her face and arms and the wooden window ledge feels warm beneath hands. Birds sing in the tree outside the window, whose branches reach toward heaven and don't bend to the wind. Gingerbread houses, green lawns, white picket fences, yellow jonquils and red tulips.

A man dressed in black walks down the sidewalk. Bootsteps ring in the quiet morning, coming closer and closer. Her gate swings open and pops closed. The man looks up, his black eyes blazing at her. Luke Badger! The honeysuckle vines quiver and shake on the trellis below the window.

Run! Run! Wild roses spring from her carpet and grab at her skirts, scratching her skin. The crystal doorknob slippery in her hand. Pull harder, harder. Open! Open! A laughing Luke Badger is climbing in her window, chinking spurs behind her. Closer, closer. The door opens. Dominga stands on the other side and cradles a jar in her arms. Inside, Mario's hazel eyes stare at her in a frozen glare.

Amelia screamed until her vocal chords refused to vibrate. She sucked in deep, wracking breaths and frantically searched the kitchen for familiar objects. "A dream. Only a dream," she whispered.

Saying the words didn't work. They didn't chase away the tremors that rippled from her soul to every inch of her body. She turned up the lamp. Still the terror of her dream lurked in shadows. After a moment her breathing returned to normal, much in the same way it had after her panicked run across the fields to her kitchen. Yet the terror remained.

Irrationally, Amelia left her chair and checked the bar across the back door. She knew it was in place. She had checked it five times before finally falling into a chair and crying herself into an exhausted sleep. She leaned against the door, her arms folded around her midriff, and rocked her forehead on its rough surface. What was she going to do? What could she do?

Turning from the door, she paced the kitchen as if it were a cage and she a wild thing newly captured. The dream told her what she already knew. She was trapped. Trapped between Badger's demands and the Estradas' desperate needs. If only she could relive these past hours and somehow undo what she had done. But she couldn't. Badger's price had to be paid, no matter what it cost her.

Every alternative led to Mario's head in that jar. Except one. His death. God forgive her for even thinking of that release. She was left with no others. If she tried to kill Badger, she would probably miss. She couldn't run to Tyson now. Even if she could persuade him to help her out of this mess, Badger wouldn't cooperate with Tyson any longer.

She had been selfish and cowardly in not accepting Tyson's offer. She had placed Mario in terrible jeopardy by going through with her foolhardy plan. At the time, it had seemed the right thing to do. She sighed heavily. Her plans always seemed the right thing to do and yet they always got her into trouble.

Trouble? This was disaster. This was hell. There was no escape. Either she submitted to that horrible man or Mario would be killed.

Suddenly she wished Ross Tanner hadn't left town.

Chapter Thirteen

The cock's crow announced the passing of night into day. To Amelia, the raucous call only marked so much sand that had sifted through the hourglass Luke Badger had set her to watch. Supposedly time remained a constant. Yet time had charged through the night like a steam locomotive behind schedule. She supposed it was time to jump on board.

With a major effort she pushed herself to her feet, then stomped them on the floor and bent her knees to relieve the tingling of renewed circulation in her legs. Stumbling from the table to the counter, she lifted a dipper from its hook, scooped up water from a bucket and drank as if she could drown the squirrels racing in her stomach. The tepid water only made her feel slightly ill. She sloshed more into a tin pan and splashed her face.

She winced when her palm touched her jaw. Prodding gently with her fingers, she traced a painful circle from jaw to cheekbone. After drying her face and hands, she fished a mirror from her trunk and examined her face. A faint bruise covered the area. She'd been lucky. It could have been worse. She tossed the mirror back into its nest of little used petticoats. How would she look tomorrow?

Amelia had no illusions about Luke Badger. He had made her aware of something vile and ugly. People existed who actually took pleasure, carnal pleasure, from hurting others. She had seen it in Badger's eyes. A gleam that went beyond cruelty heated those cold black eyes. She felt sick—sick and scared. Scared she wouldn't be able to force herself to go through with what she must do.

She changed dresses and put on a clean apron. Combing out her hair, she braided it neatly and pinned it up in a new style she had found easier to keep. Somehow, going through her daily routine brought her a little peace. She scooped some chicken feed into her apron and went out to greet the day.

Perversely the sunrise painted the eastern horizon in gorgeous yellows and pinks. Amelia regarded the gaudy display with frank disappointment. She wanted the day to mourn with her, to grieve for the passing of her youth, her innocence, her capacity to hope for a better tomorrow.

Smarting at the betrayal, she forged ahead and scattered the feed in a desultory manner. Usually she found the chickens humorous with their bobbing heads and clucking complaints. She had even named them. This morning they were just chickens. Likely they would remain just chickens after tonight's ordeal.

Flapping her apron, she emptied it of any remaining grain. At least the chickens would be happy. Amelia turned and dragged her feet toward the back door as though she carried the world on her shoulders. Unable to go any farther, she sat down on the upturned wash kettle. The store could just wait. With her shoulders bowed and her hands clasped loosely in her lap, Amelia lost herself in the sunrise. She closed her eyes and memorized each brilliant color, each subtle blending of one hue to the next. She knew it would never look so beautiful again.

"*¡Santa Maria!* What happened to your face?"

"Dominga!" Amelia jumped up and rushed over to Dominga, who was giving instructions in Spanish to the man accompanying her. She gave him her horse's reins and he led her mount away. Amelia noted fatigue marked her friend's face with new lines. She touched her own and wondered.

Dominga turned a worried frown to Amelia. "Who did that to your face?"

Amelia's hand covered the bruise. "No one. I—I fell yesterday while patching the ceiling. Tell me, how is Mario?"

Amelia held her breath. She couldn't answer any more questions. Not this morning.

Dominga's brows drew together as she studied Amelia for a moment. Then her face brightened so much it rivaled the dawn for glory. "He lives, Amelia." She hugged Amelia tightly, then stepped back to tell her the rest of her news. "He woke up about an hour ago. He is still groggy, but he is demanding food. The doctor said that was a good sign. He expects Mario to recover completely."

"That's wonderful, Dominga." That news produced a powerful relief that washed away great stains of stubborn guilt from her conscience.

Amelia didn't have much time to breathe easier, for suddenly Dominga's bright facade crumbled and revealed her pain-ravaged soul. Her courage to endure, her strength to believe, her very essence drained from her body before Amelia's eyes until only a shrunken shell of the woman remained.

"Amelia," she sobbed. Her fist clutched at her chest as if a knife had stabbed her in the heart. "Amelia, he will kill him."

Amelia gathered the other woman to her bosom and held her while great sobs tore from her throat. At that moment, she would have wrestled the Devil himself for Mario's head. She clasped Dominga's shoulders gently and held her at arm's length. "Come inside, Dominga. Let's have some coffee. I have something to tell you."

With a shaking hand held to her mouth, Dominga nodded her agreement and followed her into the kitchen. Amelia motioned for her to take a seat while she quickly prepared the coffee. She wasn't sure what she would tell Dominga. Not the truth, that much was certain. Tell her simply that hope existed for Mario, she thought. That would be enough.

Amelia sat down across from Dominga and enfolded her clasped hands in her own. "I think I've found a way to get rid of this bounty hunter."

Dominga's chin jerked up. "You have seen Señor Tanner, too?"

Caught completely off guard, Amelia blurted, "He's here in Santa Angela?"

Dominga blinked her confusion. "Of course he is. He stopped by the hospital just before I left. I thought that was what you meant. Señor Tanner, perhaps, could persuade this bounty hunter to leave. He has been a good friend to us and to you."

Hardly that, Amelia thought, but she saw an advantage to lay a smoke screen. She fabricated quickly. "Well, he's—he's a part of my plan. The bounty hunter is only interested in the reward for Mario." Inside, Amelia lamented, if only that were true. "Yesterday a whole parade of customers came in to pay their accounts. I couldn't believe it. Now I have more than enough gold to pay Mario's—" she paused a moment to conjure up a believable amount "—thousand dollar reward. Mr. Tanner can take this money to Luke Badger and that will be the end of it." She even managed a smile.

Dominga abruptly stood up and walked about the room. She turned to Amelia. "Do you really think it will work?"

Amelia swallowed hard, but she didn't bat an eye. "Yes, Dominga. I do."

Retracing the steps Amelia had paced last night, Dominga walked up and down the little room. "A thousand dollars. So much. How can we repay you?"

"Under the circumstances, that's hardly important. But if it makes you feel better, much of that is wages I owe you."

"I don't need anything to make me feel better. I would do anything to save my Mario. I would crawl on my knees and beg…beg…Tyson Briggs for the money. I was thinking of Mario. His pride takes over his brains at times."

"We just won't tell Mario."

Dominga paused and looked at Amelia. "Lie to him?"

"Sometimes it is necessary, Dominga"

"Of course you are right." Dominga retrieved the pot of coffee from the fire and poured them each a cup before she sat down. "When will all of this take place?" She brushed the tears from her cheeks.

"I'll talk with Mr. Tanner later today. It will all be over tonight. We can bring Mario home tomorrow."

Dominga smiled a sad, faraway smile. "Home?" She looked around the tiny kitchen. "Yes, in the past weeks this has been home. More than any place in a long, long time. But, Amelia, we must leave as soon as possible. If this bounty hunter found us, others will follow. Even if others didn't follow, I wouldn't trust Tyson Briggs not to lead them here. He hates Mario. We should have left long ago."

Amelia sipped her coffee to give herself time to get her voice under control. Fortified somewhat by the strong brew, she said, "Of course you must leave. I won't be here much longer myself. Almost all my accounts have returned."

"See, didn't I tell you? There was no need to worry. I thought my time with Mario was over. But because of you, we have been given more. Mere words are not worthy of my feelings for you. Truly, you are my friend."

"If I am, it's because you have shown me how to be a friend. Without you and Mario staying here, risking discovery with each passing day, I would not have survived."

"You are kind to say that, but what you say is not true. Inside—" Dominga placed her fist against her heart "—you are strong. Like the live oak, your roots go deep. They anchor you against the wind."

Amelia was deeply moved. "Thank you," she said softly. She only wished Dominga's statement was true. She felt more like the tumbleweeds she had seen rolling about. The wind sent them on an endless trek toward nothing.

Dominga took one last drink of coffee and stood. "I must change and return to the hospital. Mario will worry if I don't return soon."

"Won't you eat some breakfast?" Amelia asked.

"*Gracias,* but no. When all of this is over I will feast for days." Dominga slipped through the curtain into the mercantile.

Amelia slowly took the cups to the counter and rinsed them. When all of this was over? It would never be over for her. Dominga's news about Ross came into her mind, but she dismissed it immediately. She couldn't ask him to risk his life to save her from Badger's depravity.

"Is this where you fell yesterday?" Dominga called from inside the store.

Amelia tossed aside the dish towel and entered the mercantile. Dominga had opened the shutters and morning light streamed through them, lifting some of the gloom in the larger room. Dominga stood by the counter and looked up at the patched ceiling canvas.

"Yes. Can you imagine? I was standing on the counter and lost my balance. I hit the side of the table."

"Aye, that must have hurt. What happened to the ceiling?" Dominga inquired. She scanned the room, her mouth set in a curious frown. "You've redone some of the displays and shelves, too?"

"After you left for the hospital we had a pretty wild time around here," Amelia explained. She leaned her elbows on the counter and told Dominga about the tussle with the buffalo skinners.

Dominga laughed behind her hand. "I can see you swinging that skillet around. That is surely the most expert use you have found yet for a skillet."

"More insults about my cooking!"

Both women laughed at Amelia's sally. It was good to laugh with Dominga again. Somehow the laughter lifted Amelia's spirits like the rays of sunshine that poured into the dark mercantile. It planted a small seed of hope that grew inside her like a weed. She wanted to laugh again tomorrow and the next day and the next. She hated herself for her weakness, but she knew at that moment she could not make herself go through with Badger's demands. It was simply too horrifying to imagine. But she couldn't desert Mario, either. That left Ross Tanner.

"You said there were two," Dominga managed to say at last.

Amelia pulled her attention back to Dominga. "Two what? Oh, you mean the buffalo skinners. Yes, two were left."

Dominga's face sobered. "I wonder if they could be the two men who escaped from the jail last night. A group of men were gathered around there this morning when I rode by. There was much excitement. I heard them talking."

Amelia eased back and gripped the edge of the counter. "I didn't know Santa Angela had a jail." She hadn't had time to wonder where those two prairie scum had been taken. She had assumed to the post.

"Some call it a jail. It is only a very small stone building at the edge of town. Those two dug out like dogs."

Amelia glanced quickly at the door. All she could manage was a weak little "Oh."

"Don't be frightened. If they have any brains, they will be halfway to the border by now."

Amelia worked up a reassuring smile. "Of course." Dominga had enough on her mind without worrying about her. She wouldn't waste time worrying over where those awful men were, either. Her real problems were frightening enough without conjuring up trouble that so far hadn't happened. She could only solve one problem at a time. So far, her problem-solving record wasn't very good. Surely it couldn't get worse. Absently she knocked on the wooden countertop.

"Señor Tanner has returned, *señora*."

Amelia closed her eyes and sighed. "Thank God," she whispered. She gave a coin to the small Mexican boy who waited expectantly at her back door.

"*Muchas gracias,*" he said. An appreciative smile stretched across his dirty face.

"*De nada,*" Amelia replied. She returned the boy's smile and said, "You have done good work today. Come back tomorrow and I'll have some more jobs for you."

The boy ran off shouting like a wild Indian. For a moment Amelia watched the young boy kicking up puffs of dust with his bare feet as he ran. A familiar melancholy settled over her like a sad, worn-out ball gown that had been beautiful when first worn. She never could throw away her dream of having children. She shook out the illusive need, held it close for a moment and then tucked it to the back of her mind.

Amelia closed the back door and barred it. The mercantile was already closed for the day. She had tried to stay busy to keep her mind from dwelling on the fast-approaching night. Customers had come in and gossiped about the Estradas, the buffalo skinners' escape and the price of cattle. It had been next to impossible to behave normally, but somehow she had. Once, Luke Badger had stopped in front of the cantina across the street and watched her. When she had noticed him, he had touched the brim of his hat. She wasn't sure how long he had remained standing there in the sun. She only knew she had flown about the store like a trapped bird until she noticed he had disappeared.

As the day had worn on and the little boy she had sent to scout out Ross's location hadn't returned, she had grown more desperate. Finding Ross became her most important objective. Now that she knew where he was she acted quickly. She didn't know how long he would stay in one place and the top of her hourglass was almost empty.

Without wasting time on recriminations or doubts, Amelia dislodged her stash of gold and counted out five thousand dollars. Only change remained. As she scraped her last chance for a ticket home into a cut-down flour sack, she mentally tallied the remaining accounts to be paid. After she sold the cattle, she still could go home and live comfortably for a while, even after she paid Papa his money. My, but there was money to be made out here. She hoped she survived long enough to make it.

After tying the top of the flour sack closed, she placed both sacks back in her hiding place. She couldn't travel around Santa Angela in broad daylight with five thousand dollars in gold even if she could carry it. Ross could stop by here on his way to see Luke Badger tonight.

While changing clothes, her conscience poked and prodded at her. This just wasn't right. Finally she thought of an iron lid to clamp it quiet. Hadn't she saved his life? Her conscience was too strong to remain under irons. Hadn't he saved hers just as well? No matter how much trouble her conscience gave her, it was nothing compared to her pride. She couldn't help reliving those scenes at the cemetery when she had vowed never to ask Ross for any help. How those words haunted her. In just moments, she would virtually crawl to him. She could tell her conscience Ross Tanner would make her pay and make her pay dearly. No such salves existed for her smarting pride. Pride was a difficult thing to willingly sacrifice, but sacrifice it she would. She shoved on her gloves, grabbed up her reticule and plumped up her bustle. It was time to go.

Amelia made a dismissive wave toward the mules swishing their tails in the lean-to. Too much time and bother were required to harness them. Ross's adobe wasn't far, only a short walk out of town to a place by the river.

The late-afternoon sun slanted tall shadows halfway into the road in front of her mercantile. Amelia walked through the shade into the sunlight that cast its unmerciful glare on the debauched faces of the buildings across the street. All was quiet at the Dos Tigres as she rounded its corner and continued her journey out of town down the side street next to the cantina. She walked swiftly to the end of the row of straggly picket buildings and sun-scorched adobes. Nodding to a few passersby who tipped their hats, she kept her eyes trained straight ahead and hoped Tyson hadn't returned with the preacher. She wasn't ready to confront him yet with what she had done.

It took all of her strength to walk down the gauntlet of curious faces. Her progress and destination would be carefully watched and fully reported. She wouldn't have to tell Tyson their "engagement" was off. Thankfully, Luke Badger didn't appear from any of the dark doorways she passed.

After waiting for a freight wagon to pass, Amelia crossed the last road in town and walked past a small stone building. She saw a mound of fresh earth along the building's foundation. This must be the jail. Unexpectedly she remembered the back door to the mercantile had been open when she'd run home last night. At the time she had been too disturbed to think much about it. After a quick search through the store she had dismissed it. What if...

No. The wind had blown the door open. Nothing had been disturbed. Those animals would have wrecked the place. She increased her pace just the same.

Once out in the open country behind the town, Amelia noticed the land looked somehow different, cleaner. If not for her final destination, the little jaunt would have been pleasant.

As she walked across the plain, she held her hand next to her face to shade the sun that threatened to blind her left eye. She was extremely relieved when, in a short while, the bright ball of fire slipped behind the trees along the Concho. At the same time, she begrudged the time that was slipping away with the light. An urge to run the remaining distance to Tanner's adobe lasted an instant. No matter how little time was left, she couldn't force herself to hurry toward a confrontation with Ross Tanner. The last one still hurt too much.

Instead of the straight bead she had walked last night, she slowed her pace and studied the terrain she had never really seen. Bouncing in the high seat of a wagon hardly afforded one the best view of a land overwhelmed by its infinite dome of blue, blue sky.

Splashes of wildflowers covered the browns of the earth like dabbles of paint on an artist's palette. From tiny stars to fluttery buttercups the blooms danced and flirted with the wind. Though their spiky leaves or thorny stems proclaimed them to be hardy desert plants, Amelia thought she had never seen a more beautiful display. She wondered how long the fragile blooms lasted.

After glancing up quickly to confirm her direction, she returned her gaze to the ground. It was easier to look at wildflowers than to watch the adobe cabin grow larger and larger. The growing murmur of the river and whisper of the trees gauged the closing gap between her and Ross Tanner quite well. Finally she had to look up. From the short distance that now separated them, she saw Ross was bare to the waist and seemed to be shaving with the help of a mirror hung next to the door.

Amelia slowed considerably more at the sight of his long, smooth back muscles stretching beneath his tanned skin. Her palms itched annoyingly beneath their prim white gloves. She pinched the material at one wrist and jerked the glove tighter against her skin. She repeated the procedure on the other glove, then came to a halt several feet behind Ross.

Shifting her weight from one foot to the other, Amelia fumbled for something to say. She opened her mouth, but nothing came out. She snapped it shut before she could say something stupid. Why hadn't she rehearsed her speech before she got here instead of gawking at wildflowers? She knew very well why. She loathed coming here and asking Ross to help her. But she hated even more setting eyes again on Luke Badger.

Think! Think! Words rolled to her tongue like tree sap in cold weather. Good...day...afternoon. I have a...a...job for you. No. I'd like to hire your gun. NO!

Finally Ross saved her the trouble. "All gloved and bustled. I'd say Miss Amelia has come calling."

Ross didn't bother to turn around to address her. Amelia surmised he had watched her approach in the mirror. He must have seen her fidget and hesitate. That made everything worse somehow. She wanted to poke her chin in the air and stomp back to Santa Angela, but under the circumstances that sop to her sensibilities would be not only foolish, but dangerous. She choked down her pride and said in a straightforward manner, "I have something to ask you."

Ross turned and wiped the remaining soapsuds from his face with a towel that draped his shoulders. "You don't have to ask. I told you the other night I'd know what you want."

A full frontal view of a half-naked man was as shocking as Ross's words. Married life hadn't prepared her at all for a broad, muscled chest covered in a thick mat of dark hair. She realized at that moment Devin had only been a boy. She jerked her attention from where it had wandered down a trail of hair that disappeared into the very low waistband of Ross's pants. His eyes appraised her arrogantly, stealing any coherent thoughts she might have gathered. "I . . . I . . . that is . . . you . . . you—"

"Well, spit it out." Ross pulled the towel from his shoulders and tossed it behind him.

Amelia forced herself not to give ground when he sauntered toward her with his deceiving loose-limbed grace. She began breathing again when he stopped next to a tree a few feet in front of her. He leaned his bare shoulder into its rough bark and hooked his thumbs into his gun belt, which tugged his tight pants lower. His expression rivaled the adobe walls for blankness and gave Amelia not a clue what he was thinking except that he wasn't overjoyed to see her. In fact, he looked downright hostile. What had she expected? Though it was difficult to keep her eyes trained on his hateful expression she didn't dare lower them. If he was going to be so disagreeable, then she would hurry and get this whole terrible business over with.

"I—" Amelia swallowed down the infuriating lump that threatened to spill tears down her face. "I need you to deliver something. Something important."

"I'm no delivery boy, Amelia."

"I know that, of course. I need—" Amelia drew in a deep breath "—I need someone with your expertise."

"Expertise?" Ross studied her through cold amber eyes. "Just what kind of expert are you needing?"

"I suppose you'll make me spell it out. I need someone who is good with a gun to deliver something important to Luke Badger."

"That the bounty hunter after Mario?"

"Yes. Will you do it?"

"Not until I know exactly what's going on. I know you must be in some kind of harebrained trouble or you wouldn't be standing here now."

Amelia clenched her hands into tight little fists. Oh, it was hard to stand here and listen to this. "It wasn't harebrained. I had good intentions—"

"God save me from a virtuous woman with good intentions."

"Would you just listen? If you don't want to do this I'll . . ." Amelia heaved a sigh. "Just listen."

"All right. Let's hear it."

"Well, you know what terrible trouble Mario is in. I wanted to help, but there just didn't seem to be any way. Then Tyson Briggs offered to buy off the bounty hunter if I married him—"

"Marry him?" Ross shrugged away from the tree.

"Yes. He wants my accounts and my connections is the way I believe he put it."

"That all? Never mind. Go on."

"So I thought why couldn't I pay off the bounty hunter."

"Naturally you marched over alone to this cold-blooded son of a bitch's place with your money and your good intentions."

Amelia looked down and nodded. She couldn't look at the derision on his face. It had been a stupid thing to do. Now she must stand here and ask this man for help when she had vowed she never would, when she had stated so clearly on too many occasions she could take care of herself, when she had suffered through all his lectures and ungentlemanly demonstrations. Pride, when swallowed, left a bitter aftertaste and an upset stomach.

Ross touched her gently on the cheek. "He do this?"

Amelia quickly lifted her gaze to meet his. "No," she stated firmly. "I fell off the counter when I repaired the ceiling." Her gaze didn't falter under the disbelief that narrowed his eyes. This situation was humiliating enough without Ross knowing the full extent of her stupidity.

Ross shoved his hands in his pockets and tugged his gaze from Amelia's blue eyes to focus on the same open beauty of the sky above her. It was all he could do not to shake the life from her. My God, when he thought what could have happened—might have happened. He inspected her face again and mentally compared it to Maria's at the Dos Tigres. The white-hot rage building inside him cooled to a controllable slow burn. How long it remained under control depended on the next few hours. "It sounds like you've been busy, busy, busy."

His mocking tone threw fuel on Amelia's temper. "Yes, Mr. Tanner, while you were off sulking I was working hard at helping my friends."

"I guess it's a good thing I stopped...sulking and showed up to bale your ass out of the trouble you worked so hard to get yourself into."

"Just never mind." She whirled away from him, hating the tears that stung her eyes. "I'll...I'll think of something else."

She took two steps before Ross wrapped her upper arm in his unyielding fingers and whipped her around to face him. "And just what would that be?"

Amelia looked at the ground and shook her head. "I don't know," she said quietly.

Ross pulled her against his bare chest. For some reason her all-too-apparent reluctance to ask him for help hurt. It didn't matter to Ross that he couldn't blame her. Hitting back was too important. "Tell me Amelia. Tell me how much you want me to help you."

Amelia curled her hands into tight fists and turned her head away from the clean musky scent that clung to his hard chest. She focused on the tree's gnarled roots that had been uncovered by the wind. She couldn't answer him. The words stuck in her throat in a hard painful knot.

Ross held her against him, ignoring her halfhearted attempts to get away. "Cat got your tongue, *querida?* Don't have words to thank me enough for putting my life on the line to save you from—what is it you ladies call it—a fate worse than death?"

Amelia's gaze snapped up to meet his. "I never said—"

"You didn't have to. Not a man alive would pass up the chance you gave Badger."

"All right!" Amelia grew still and closed her eyes. She tried to resist Ross's power to intensify her every emotion whether it be anger or desire. She took a deep, shaking breath and asked, "Will you help me?"

"Look at me, dammit." He thought he would drown in the deep pools of the tear-soaked blue eyes that opened at his demand. "Do you understand that if I do what you ask somebody's likely to get killed?"

Amelia nodded.

"You remember when you told me you didn't want to owe me anything, you didn't have anything to give me in return for protecting you?"

"Yes, I . . . I remember," she said softly. She knew what he was going to say next.

Ross pulled her closer against him until he could feel the rise and fall of her every breath brush against his skin. "I want you, Amelia," he declared in a hoarse whisper. "I want you more than what little honor I have left. I'd do anything to have you."

Amelia looked up and lost the battle she hadn't really wanted to fight. Her anger melted into warm, heavy desire. She wanted him to kiss her senseless the way he had in the belvedere, only today she couldn't stop him and she was glad.

Ross cupped her bruised jaw in his palm and traced her full lower lip with his thumb. "I'd do anything but lie to you, Amelia. You can forget your great sacrifice. Mario died this afternoon. I was just on the way to the funeral."

Amelia stared up at him completely dumbfounded. "Dead? But I saw Dominga early this morning. She said—"

"I'm not sure what happened. It was sudden. I'm sure you left before word could get to you."

"Oh, God, no!" Her voice broke. "Poor Dominga." Suddenly Ross's embrace became a warm haven. All the frustrations, all the worries, all the fear poured out of her in gasping sobs. She leaned her head against the solid wall of Ross's chest and cried for her friends. She hurt as if the news had been about one of her family, and she realized Mario and Dominga had been more than friends. They had been mother, father, sister and brother to her in this vast, wild land.

Ross held her close and rested his head against her sweet-smelling crown of braids. He closed his eyes and regretted to his core the hot tears that rolled down his chest.

Chapter Fourteen

Amelia climbed the stairs to the second floor of the hospital as if they were the stairs to a hangman's scaffold. Dominga's tortured sobs added chains and shackles to each step she took. As she climbed higher, the awful wails grew louder, until Amelia feared she couldn't lift her foot to the next step. Ross's hand at her elbow was a rock she could lean against and did. She didn't know what she would say to Dominga. She supposed nothing. She would have to be strong enough to be a rock for the other woman to lean against. At the moment, she didn't feel as if she could support a feather.

As they walked down the narrow hall, Dominga's sobs broke into groaning pleas for her Mario. Ross stopped at a closed door. Their eyes met in silent sympathy for the devastated woman inside as he leaned past Amelia to open it. She straightened her shoulders and walked inside the small barren cubicle, hesitating a moment at the sight that confronted her. Ross placed his hand gently at her waist and helped her move toward Dominga.

"Dominga, Amelia's here," he said in a gentle voice Amelia had never heard addressed to herself.

Dominga turned red swollen eyes from the uncovered coffin set upon a long bare table in the center of the room and looked at Amelia. "God" she managed between convulsive breaths. "God...has taken...my Mario."

Amelia walked swiftly to Dominga and took her in her arms and held her. She remembered the day Dominga had done the same for her. She had needed a strong shoulder to cry on. She could return some of the strength Mario had so freely given her. She refused to look at Mario's corpse in the simple pine box. She didn't want to remember him pale and lifeless. In the years to come she wanted her thoughts of Mario to be of his wise hazel eyes filled with laughter at life and love for his Dominga.

"Amelia, why don't you help her out to the wagon? I'll get someone to carry the coffin downstairs."

Amelia nodded and shifted around so that one of her arms cradled Dominga's heaving shoulders and the other held Dominga's arm at her waist. They walked slowly out the door and through the hospital until they reached her wagon, waiting in the early-evening gloom. She helped Dominga climb onto the wagon's seat, then pulled herself up onto the driver's side. It was only appropriate that she drive Mario on his last ride.

As she waited for Mario's casket to be brought down, she wondered again at the untimely hour for a funeral. When she had asked Ross about it, he had mumbled something about the heat. She thought it an odd frontier custom, but let it go. She noticed the heavy silence that lay upon the fort's activities. Only a few soldiers stirred along the barracks and no one sat on the porches on officers' row. A funeral procession, no matter how small, was not exactly a spring night's entertainment.

Then she saw him. Luke Badger sat on his horse with one leg crooked around the saddle horn. He waited by the headquarters building like a huge buzzard on its roost. An instant of cold fear tightened inside her, but then it passed. She leveled hate-filled eyes at him, which only brought a smile to his thin lips. She refused to notice him any longer.

She heard scuffling footsteps crossing the hospital's porch and held Dominga's hand. The casket thumped heavily in the back of the wagon and scraped across the wood. Dominga's sobs escalated to keening wails. Amelia pulled the poor grieving woman to her and hugged her tight. Thank God Ross had had sense enough to lay in supplies when he had hitched up her wagon and brought it to her. He was right about sending Dominga on her way after Mario was buried. He had voiced concern over how Tyson was going to react to all that had happened, and he didn't think Dominga should be left to bear the brunt of his reprisals.

Amelia didn't like to think about her contribution to Tyson's anger. Inside the supplies, she had hidden the gold she had left. It should have been used to help keep Mario alive, but now Dominga needed all the help she could give her.

At Ross's signal, she unclasped Dominga's arms from her shoulders and gently slapped the reins on the mules' backs. The wagon moved forward toward the bright evening star that had just risen. Ross rode his stallion in the front and, bringing up the rear, was Luke Badger, who wheeled his horse about to follow them. Amelia cast an uncertain glance at Ross, but he ignored the bounty hunter's presence. She followed his lead.

As they slowly made their way out of the fort's quadrangle, Dominga's cries echoed over the empty parade ground. Amelia gripped the reins tighter to still her shaking hands and swallowed down her own tears. She had known Dominga would take Mario's death hard, but this terrible wailing couldn't be good for her.

After passing the last stable, Amelia noticed small lights dancing on the cemetery's hill. It was an eerie sight set against the horizon's early-evening mother-of-pearl luster. As they drew closer to the cemetery she discovered the lights to be torches held by people waiting on the hill for them. A small crowd had gathered for Mario's graveside services.

Amelia halted the wagon near six men who waited for them at the bottom of the hill. She recognized some of them as hay cutters who had worked with Mario. They gathered at the wagon, then stepped back when Badger rode up and dismounted. He approached the wagon in long, quick strides.

Amelia turned to Ross, who had reined his horse in a tight circle and started toward Badger. As he passed her she caught the deadly intent in his eyes.

Dominga suddenly screamed, "N-o-o!"

Amelia twisted toward her friend and followed Dominga's horrified gaze to the large wicked knife in Badger's hand. Ross swung from his saddle and caught Badger's wrist. "You've got Doc's death certificate. The courts will give you your blood money with that."

Badger jerked his wrist from Ross's grasp. He looked around at the men who had gathered around them, their rifles aimed at his heart. He cursed viciously, then cast his vulture's eyes at Amelia. "Too bad you will never know the pleasure of my weapon, *putita.*"

Ross smashed a fist into his ugly, leering smile. The bounty hunter crashed to the ground, his mouth a bloody mess. The downed man went for his gun. A warning screamed in Amelia's brain, but before the words could reach her throat, a gunshot exploded. Badger's gun went flying through the air and Badger grabbed his wrist.

"Ride out of here. Now."

Ross's words were little more than the wind blowing from atop the hill. But Badger scrambled to his feet and leaped upon his horse. He rode a short distance away and stopped.

Amelia glanced at Ross, but he only watched the bounty hunter a moment, then signaled to the men to go ahead with the proceedings. Two of them covered the open casket with a thin pine board. With ringing blows of metal on metal, they hammered nails into the coffin's lid. Then they slid the casket from the back of the wagon. Dominga wailed even louder. Amelia was relieved when some ladies approached to help Dominga from the wagon. She climbed down and ran to catch up with them as they followed the casket up the hill. No one talked. Many of the women cried quietly into the folds of their black *rebozos*.

The little procession gathered at the top of the hill. Torchlight wavered over the fresh mound of earth piled next to the hole that was filled with shadows. The stench of burning pitch fouled the fresh evening breeze that carried a hint of faraway rain. Amelia looked up at the faint stars just beginning to appear. Not a feather of a cloud marred the vast sky. She supposed God had been merciful someplace else.

Amelia stood beside Dominga, and though she had stopped crying, Amelia virtually held her up. Amelia welcomed Ross's warm presence at her side. The district's priest was too far away to fetch at short notice, so an elderly man had been appointed to say a few words. The words were in Spanish and Amelia couldn't understand them, but she supposed they were sufficiently moving, because Dominga broke into sobbing tears again. She blinked away the tears that gathered in her own eyes.

Her heart ached with each memory she conjured of Mario. She almost smiled as she recalled the day he had driven her to Fort Concho and they had stopped under a tree. How he had surprised her. She remembered the day of the storm when she had stood on this very hill and argued with Ross. Mario had waited for her, ready to help her. He had been quite a man. She slanted a look at Badger, who persisted in hanging about. She supposed he wouldn't be satisfied until he had witnessed Mario's actual burial.

Almost as soon as it began the ceremony was over. People began to file past Dominga, muttering their condolences. She rallied enough to receive them, but Amelia saw the emptiness in her eyes. Finally only the six pallbearers were left on the hill with her, Ross, Dominga and Badger. Using ropes, the men lowered the casket into the black hole in the earth. Amelia couldn't shake the feeling that this was somehow not right. Surely they could have waited until morning. Poor Dominga. The burial would have been much easier to bear in daylight, she thought. But perhaps it was a Mexican custom she wasn't aware of. Certainly there were many of those.

Amelia followed Dominga's gesture and threw a handful of dirt onto the casket. The six pallbearers grabbed up spades and began shoveling dirt into the hole. Amelia winced with each thudding fall of earth.

"Come on, Dominga. Let's leave now," Amelia urged. She wanted to spare Dominga some of the pain.

"No, I must stay until it's finished." Dominga glanced up at Badger, who stood at a distance. Then looked down at the coffin.

By now the earth fell softly inside the hole. It would be filled soon. Amelia couldn't wait to get off this hill. At last she saw Badger turn and leave. Then she heard hoofbeats as he rode away. Ross nodded toward one of the men, and at his signal, the man took off running down the hill. In a moment Amelia heard a second horse start off, but much slower than Badger's.

Suddenly Dominga picked up the spade the man had left and began digging at the grave. In a strong voice she commanded, "Hurry and dig him up."

Amelia stared in a horrified stupor as Dominga scooped out shovelfuls of earth from the nearly full grave. She reached a blind imploring hand toward Ross and gasped, "My God, she's gone mad. Ross, stop her!"

Ross pushed past her and grabbed Dominga. "Give me the shovel, Señora Estrada. You'll just get in the way. The men can uncover Mario faster if you stay back."

"*Sí,* you are right," Dominga answered and she stepped back. "But, hurry, hurry, *por favor.* The doctor said the air will not last long."

Amelia took in the feverish digging of the men and Dominga's words, but her brain couldn't make sense of what was taking place. She turned a bewildered look to Ross. "What's happening? Tell me what's happening!" she demanded. "Has everyone gone mad, or have I?"

Ross gave her a brief glance, then began giving instructions to the grave diggers. His odd behavior confused Amelia more. No matter what had gone between them, Ross had always been able to face her. She stepped over to Dominga and grabbed her arm. "Tell me!"

Dominga never took her eyes from the diminishing level of dirt in the grave as she answered Amelia. "Mario is in a deep, deep sleep. Señor Tanner convinced the doctor to give Mario a sleeping potion made from wild hops. It was so strong he would look dead to Luke Badger. It was his only chance and Mario took it. I just hope it didn't kill him."

Amelia's hand dropped from Dominga's sleeve. Pure, undiluted anger spilled through the overwhelming joy of knowing Mario was actually alive. She stomped over the uneven ground to Ross's side. "You vile, despicable man! Making me believe Mario was dead. How cruel! You should have told me, dammit."

"I couldn't take the chance. Those damned eyes of yours tell the world whatever comes into that beautiful head of yours."

"I beg your pardon. I can—"

"Señor Tanner, we need your help to pull up the casket," one of the men called out. Another man lay on the ground and leaned waist-deep inside the purposely shallow hole to retrieve ropes left intact under the heavy pine box. Amelia pushed her hurt feelings to the side for a moment and held her breath as Ross and three other men strained at the ropes. Two other men grabbed the casket's handles as it emerged from the earth. They all wrestled it to the side. Dominga handed Ross a crowbar. Amelia shivered at the macabre scene, made more dreadful by the weirdly dancing shadows cast by the windblown torches.

Amelia jumped at the nails' first screeching release. She blinked at each new protest as Ross pried open the lid. He shoved it to the side and while one of the men lifted Mario at the knees, Ross lifted his shoulders. "Easy, easy," he cautioned.

Slowly, carefully, they eased Mario out of the rough pine box and placed him on the newly turned earth next to his grave. Amelia could detect no sign of life in the limp, unconscious man. She prayed he hadn't suffocated while buried alive. My God, buried alive! Amelia marveled at Mario's courage.

Dominga produced a mirror from a pocket and held it under Mario's nose. Amelia held her breath while urging Mario to breathe. When the small glass fogged faintly, a collective sigh joined the wind's whisper.

"*Gracias a Dios,*" Dominga cried, and hugged her husband's body.

Amelia glanced over at Ross and saw him take off his hat and rub the sweat off his brow with his sleeves. Another brave man, she thought. She appreciated how difficult it must have been to take his plan to Mario. What a chance he had taken, too. But it had worked, and she admired his willingness to go through with such a dangerous plan. Mario's trail would end at this spot forever. The gamble had been well worth the risk.

She stood back, not able to completely share in the little group's joy. She was elated that Mario had escaped the clutches of that snake Luke Badger, but she was hurt they hadn't trusted her. How could Dominga not trust her? Amelia's gaze fell on Ross as he clasped Dominga's shoulders and prompted her to rise. This was Ross's production. He had chosen to leave her in the dark, she was certain.

"Amelia, spread a blanket in the back of the wagon," Ross directed. "I've got to get them out of here. I don't trust Badger. He may circle around at any time." Ross's sharp eyes scanned the plains. "I don't want to have to kill the bastard. He's got to reach California with news of Mario's death."

Without a word Amelia turned and made her way down the hill to the wagon. She searched out some blankets and made a small pallet on the wagon bed. Rolling up some spare clothing, she made a makeshift pillow. By the time she had finished, Ross and another man had carried Mario to the wagon. Quickly she jumped off the end and backed out of the way. The men lifted Mario onto the pallet, then Ross gave Dominga a hand while she climbed up beside her husband. Dominga covered Mario with another blanket and settled herself against the wagon's side.

More and more, Amelia felt like a spectator to this drama. When Ross walked around the wagon toward the front she hurried forward and stopped him. "Wait. Where are you taking them?"

"To some friends. Say your goodbyes because you'll likely never see Dominga again."

He started to leave, but Amelia grabbed a handful of leather sleeve. "Friends. What friends? Not those *comancheros!*"

"Stay out of it. You can't understand."

"You can't put me off this time. These are my friends. I would have done anything for them," she said in a low urgent whisper.

"Dammit, Amelia. We don't have time to argue. Say goodbye or don't. We're leaving." Ross pulled his sleeve loose and turned toward the wagon seat.

Amelia rushed in front of him and placed her hand on the railing as if she were about to climb onto the seat herself. A maneuver that effectively blocked Ross. "I'm going with you," she stated with calm determination. She wasn't about to be left out again.

Ross tried to stare her down with his deadliest glare. She didn't budge, but glared right back at him. "I'm going."

Ross looked up at the stars and sighed his exasperation. Then he pinned her with an intensity she didn't dare argue with. "Fine. Go. But when we meet those men out on the plain, keep your mouth shut. Understand."

Amelia nodded mutely, then climbed to the seat and took up the reins.

"Move over," Ross ordered four hours later as he swung up onto the wagon's seat. He held back a smile at Amelia's sigh of relief. This had to be the longest she had ever driven a team, yet not a word of complaint had come his way. She deserved credit for that. Taking up the reins, he turned his head and said over his shoulder, "Hold on to Mario, Dominga. We've got a rough ride down into this draw. It'll be rocky."

Dominga rested Mario's head in her lap and smoothed his hair back from his forehead. "I am ready, Señor Tanner."

"How's he doin'?" Ross asked.

"He came around a few hours ago, but now he is sleeping again. But he is breathing more deeply," she answered.

Amelia turned and smiled down at her friend. "I should say." She glanced back at Ross. "Haven't you heard his snores?"

"Guess I've been riding too far ahead." Ross looked at Amelia, then turned his attention to the team. He should have made her stay in Santa Angela. Her nearness was a distraction he couldn't afford tonight. "Hang on, ladies," he called, and started the wagon on its descent into the shallow, but wide dry bed.

"Why are you taking us down here?" Amelia asked in a voice that carried over the rattling wagon.

"Can't have the army's patrols shadowing us. We aren't that far from the North Concho."

"I'm not sure about this, Ross. Mario and Dominga going off with these outlaws doesn't seem right."

Dominga spoke up from the back of the wagon. "If Señor Tanner trusts these men, then so do I."

"There are worse men to trust," Ross added. He heard Amelia's in-drawn breath and crooked up one corner of his mouth with satisfaction. She had something to settle with him and she might as well know it.

Ross concentrated his energies into guiding the mules around several twists and turns, rather than thinking of that afternoon. He looked from side to side and gauged the height of the ravine's walls. This was as good a place as any, he thought, and pulled the team to a halt. The draw was deep enough now that the wagon's large bulk wouldn't catch some sleepy trooper's notice. The moon shined bright enough tonight for a blind man to see for miles. With not a tree in sight this ditch would have to do. Mando knew where to look. He had probably already spotted them, but he'd wait until he made sure nobody had followed them.

Ross set the brake and wrapped the reins around the long handle. He lit a cheroot, then leaned forward, resting his elbows on his knees.

Amelia broke the suddenly too quiet silence. "Where are your . . . friends?" she asked with a noticeable hesitation.

"They'll be along."

Amelia twisted around on the seat and peered into the moon-bright darkness all around them. "Will they find us down in this ditch?"

Ross sensed the nervousness in her voice. He couldn't blame her. "Most likely already have."

"They must hang about the countryside all the time, then." Amelia pulled her shawl tighter and continued looking this way and that.

"Why do you say that?"

"How else would you know they could be contacted?"

Ross drew on the cheroot, pulling the burning smoke deep into his lungs. He blew it out slowly before he answered. "The fires."

Amelia suddenly grew still. "Oh," she replied in a small voice.

A telling silence followed until Dominga spoke up. "Will we travel much more tonight?"

"Mando will want to take you farther into the Llano. Probably won't stop until you get to Mucha Que tomorrow. Then he'll take you north to the Yellow Houses and over to Puerta de Luna. You'll be in New Mexico then and can rest. When Mario's on his feet, you won't have a long trip to Santa Fe."

"In all our travels we have never been to New Mexico," Dominga said.

"You'll like it. Once you get past the Llano it's a beautiful place. You can travel from snows in the mountains to desert heat in no time at all."

"It sounds wonderful," Dominga answered with a sigh. "Why do you stay in Texas?"

Ross rubbed out the cheroot's glowing butt on the sole of his boot, then flipped it to the ground. He looked back over his shoulder at Amelia and after pausing a moment said, "Damned if I know."

"Damned if you don't know," Mario said in a weak voice. The three turned surprised faces on Mario, who smiled briefly at their startled expressions.

"Mario, you son of a gun, I'm glad you finally decided to join us," Ross said.

"You must rest, *mi corazon*," Dominga cautioned like a mother to her child.

Amelia added her admonitions to Dominga's. "Yes, Mario you—"

"Hush, you women. We men have things to discuss."

The two women looked at each other in amazement, then smiled. To hear Mario's teasing was music to their ears.

"*Ay*, Tanner, these women want to make an old man of me."

"No, no, *mi torro*," Dominga crooned. "I want you well rested. I have missed you." With such an endearment, her meaning could hardly be missed. Mario inched his hand toward hers and held it.

Ross regarded Amelia's all too apparent embarrassment with interest. She blushed like a schoolgirl. He had a sudden picture of what her marriage to a fool like Cummings must have been like. A woman with her fire deserved better. She deserved a man with a sure hand and a strong back. But she sure as hell deserved more than that, more than he was willing to give.

"Did everything go as planned?" Mario asked.

Ross allowed himself a moment longer to watch Amelia, then answered Mario. "Yeah, Badger hung around until we buried you, then he rode toward El Paso. You won't have any more trouble from him. The men were reburying your casket when we left."

"*Bueno*. I am now a dead man," Mario said with satisfaction.

"Mario!" both women chorused.

"Can't you keep your women quiet, *mi hermano?* They will have Mackenzie and all his cavalry swooping down on us."

Ross twisted around to see Mando mounted on a gray dappled horse. Damn, I must be getting careless, Ross thought. He hadn't heard Mando's approach at all. Then Mando was good.

Ross ignored Amelia's quick gasp. He glanced up at the star-studded heavens. "Right on time."

"Of course. When my long-lost brother asks a favor, I hurry to comply." Mando smiled wickedly and kneed his horse closer to the wagon. "Aren't you going to introduce me?"

Ross's gut tightened. The brittle shine in Mando's black eyes meant one thing. He had been drinking. He was unpredictable when he was like this. "These are the people I told Paco about." Ross poked his thumb over his shoulder. "The Estradas."

"And the most beautiful *gringa?*" Mando asked, nodding at Amelia.

Ross didn't like Mando's sarcastic tone or that teeth-baring smile of his. He switched quickly to rapid Spanish. "She's with me, Mando. Don't start anything." Ross cursed the white buffalo hunters who had murdered Don Alphonso and left Mando with a soul-consuming hatred for all Anglos. He waited uneasily for Mando's next move.

Mando gave a long, low whistle. At the signal, a small group of mounted men bristling with ammunition belts, rifles and pistols picked their way from around a far bend in the arroyo and gathered behind Mando. He nodded toward the wagon. Silently they surrounded it, causing Ross's stallion to dance nervously where he was tied to the tailgate.

Ross felt Amelia sidle closer to him. Thank God she had enough sense not to say a word.

Mando answered in Spanish. "Start something? What do you think I would start? Would I order my men to drag your woman from the wagon and carry her off to sell. Isn't that what the *tejanos* think I would do? What you must think, too, since you have chosen their side?"

Ross shifted on the seat. "Cut this shit, Mando. I haven't chosen any side."

"Haven't you, my brother?" Mando looked directly at Amelia.

Ross flinched openly at the pain in Mando's voice. When he answered him, he couldn't restrain it from his own. "If I had stayed, one of us would have killed the other."

Mando narrowed his eyes and stared at Ross. Finally he said, "You are killing me now with your words. Despite our different blood, we are not so different. You belong out here with me."

Under Mando's wounding glare, Ross dropped his gaze to study his boots. Mando was right. Part of him hungered for the plains, hungered for the hunt, for the danger.

Mando's anger was his anger. Deserting Mando and the anger hurt too much.

"Ross, is there a problem?"

Amelia's quiet voice startled him and he turned to look at her. Her calm, blue eyes held his for a moment. One moment in which reason returned. Mando had poisoned himself with anger. Ross didn't want to die with him. "There's no problem. Not now," he replied. Then he turned his attention to Mando. "We can't change the way we are or what we believe. Let's part remembering the old days, the good days."

Mando's hands tightened on his reins, making the gray prance and rear. He looked at Ross until sadness dampened the fires that burned in his eyes. "They *were* good days, weren't they?"

Ross relaxed. It was over. "Yes, Mando. The best."

"I will take good care of your friends."

"I know that."

"I will even provide a horse for your *gringa.*" Mando raised his hand and snapped his fingers. In a moment an extra mount was brought to the wagon.

"Thanks, Mando." Ross turned to Amelia and said in a voice that reached only her ears, "Say your goodbyes quickly and let's get the hell out of here."

Amelia shifted around so she could face Dominga and Mario. "No words can describe how I feel. I can't express my thanks."

Dominga replied, "You don't have to say anything. Your friendship was enough. You will be in my prayers every day."

"Dominga . . . I . . ."

"It's time, Amelia," Ross said quietly.

"Yes, yes, I know." Amelia leaned over to whisper in Dominga's ear. "Your wages are hidden in the sack of flour."

Dominga looked at Amelia, her surprise evident in her round brown eyes. "Wages?" she whispered.

"Come on, Amelia." Ross had jumped down from the wagon and waited to help her down from the seat. She nodded her answer quickly and extended her hand to Ross, who helped her to the ground.

One of Mando's men climbed to the seat from the other side and took up the reins to the team. Amelia called out after them as the wagon pulled away, "Take good care of those mules!"

"We will," Dominga promised.

Ross placed his arm around Amelia's shoulders as she covered her face with her hands and cried. He envied her her tears.

Chapter Fifteen

The last rattling reminder of Mario and Dominga's escape disappeared into the night. Amelia dried her eyes with the tattered remains of the white gloves she had donned that afternoon. She missed the Estradas already. Yet she couldn't be sad they were gone. She hoped they found the peace they deserved.

The warm weight of Ross's arm circling her shoulders brought home the full realization of what he had done for her and her friends this day. Her anger at not being included in the funeral charade simply wasn't there any more. A deep gratitude had taken its place. She tried to think of something to say that would convey her thanks. Then she remembered what he had said that afternoon, what he had told her in the belvedere. Ross wouldn't want a simple thank-you. He didn't deserve one, either, she admitted. She knew what he would expect when she had walked across that field today. What had happened between then and now didn't change things. She had asked him to endanger himself so that she wouldn't have to face Luke Badger herself. Suddenly the arm around her shoulders grew too heavy for her to bear.

Amelia stepped away from Ross. Her hands fluttered to her hair and smoothed back dark tendrils that had escaped the braid crowning her head. She glanced at Ross through the crook in her arm. "We should be going. We have a long ride back." Then she busied her hands straightening her skirts and pulling at her sleeves.

Ross quirked his brow at Amelia's sudden skittishness, then turned to check his saddle and do some rearranging. "Not that far tonight. I know a place we can camp." He didn't have to see her reaction to that bit of news.

Amelia spun around to face him. "We aren't riding back to Santa Angela tonight?" She tried to sound calm, but failed miserably.

Ross ruffled his horse's mane, then turned to her. "It's almost midnight now. We'd have four hours of riding ahead of us if we didn't stop."

"I'm not tired," she rushed to assure him.

Ross studied the shadows under her eyes, the droop to her shoulders, the anxious frown between her brows. She was about to drop but she would rather ride all night than be alone with him. He hadn't realized how much he had valued her trust until he had lost it. Lost it, hell. Crushed it was more like it. Ross cursed under his breath. She was lucky he had. "Get on your horse, Amelia," he commanded.

"But—"

"Look, I'm stoppin' tonight just like I planned. You're the one who insisted on comin' out here. You'll have to do things my way."

That's exactly what she feared most. But he was right. He hadn't dragged her out here. Perhaps her fears were totally unfounded. "You don't have to snap at me. I'll do things *your* way."

"Good, now mount up." Ross swung up into his saddle and regarded Amelia with an impatient frown.

Amelia hurried over to the sorry-looking horse the *comancheros* had provided for her. He twisted his head around and looked at her when she took hold of the saddle horn. His lopsided ears quirked and he pawed the ground, then he snorted. "Oh, hush," she muttered.

Thank goodness, this nag isn't as big as Ross's brute, she thought. Amelia put one hand around the saddle horn and the other took hold of the cantle, then she tried to place her foot in the stirrup, but her polonaised skirt proved unsuitable for mounting horses. The horse shied away, pulling her off balance. She caught herself from falling on her face by grabbing a looped rope tied on the saddle.

"Take hold of his reins and the saddle horn."

"I know what to do," she retorted over her shoulder. Amelia picked out the knotted reins from the horse's mane and tried again. She jerked her skirts up over her knees and stuck her foot in the stirrup. This time the horse skittered around and Amelia hopped on one foot after him. "Whoa, boy," she called. "Whoa." Suddenly she felt Ross's hands at her waist. She was tossed into the saddle before she could utter a protest. "I could have done it," she snapped down at him.

Ross handed her the reins she had dropped. "I know. We've been through this. You can take care of yourself."

Amelia grew very still and fixed her gaze on Ross. She had been waiting for this. She wouldn't play cat-and-mouse games with him anymore. "Tell me, Ross. Tell me now. I asked you to use your gun for me today. Name your price."

Ross stood by her horse and admired the fire in her eyes. "My God, Amelia. Not many men have called my bet like that."

"Is that supposed to be a compliment?"

"Yes," he stated simply.

Outwardly Amelia shrugged off his reply, but she held her shoulders a little straighter. "Let's get this over with and out of the way. I pay my debts."

Ross studied her for a moment as he thought over her statement. The wind picked up long tendrils of dark hair and whirled them around her face. Moonlight cast its magic spell over the challenging tilt of her chin, the proud thrust of her full bosom. He read defiance in her eyes and something else, something he couldn't identify, but it wasn't fear. Ross knew what he wanted from her. "You. I want you. Tonight."

Amelia looked away and nodded. She composed her face into a noncommittal look of disdain and listened to the faint ring of Ross's spurs as he walked to his horse. She hoped the silver moonlight masked her complete loss of color. The creak of leather told her he had mounted. She looked straight ahead and waited for the big black to walk past her, then she kicked her horse into motion, following Ross at a short distance through the draw.

Ross's broad back claimed Amelia's full attention. She shouldn't have been surprised, she thought. You didn't ask a man to walk into a loaded gun without expecting to give him something in return. Ross wanted one thing from her. Too bad he didn't want more.

They rode out of the arroyo into a world of moonlight and wind. Amelia scanned the silver expanse of land that spread without interruption into the stars. Dear God, what empty, lonely country. In that moment, her future spread before her much like the land.

Uncomfortable with where her thoughts were leading, she forced herself to look at something else, think of something else. When she looked up, the heavens lured her into their sparkling depths. Stars so huge and brilliant she thought she could reach up and touch them sparkled among the tiniest pinpricks that surely existed only in her imagination. It was like looking into eternity. The sensation was fascinating, exciting, and perhaps a little frightening, too. Amelia lowered her gaze to Ross. Like loving Ross Tanner. She had about as much chance of flying into the stars as she did in reaching him.

"We'll camp here for the night," Ross called over his shoulder.

Amelia guided her horse farther into the wooded area where Ross had led them. The past two hours had seemed like minutes. When Ross halted his horse, Amelia reined in hers some distance away. She watched him swing down from the saddle with his lithe grace and couldn't stop herself from dropping her gaze to fidget with the reins. I pay my debts, indeed! Where had she gotten the brass to say that? She looked up and saw Ross approaching her. She could certainly use some of it now.

Amelia didn't waste any more time wondering where her courage had gone and scrambled off the horse before Ross could touch her. She slid her foot out of the stirrup as soon as she felt solid ground under her other foot and let go of the saddle. Her legs buckled under her weight. Two strong arms caught her from behind just before she hit the ground.

"Steady now. You aren't used to riding that long." Ross clasped her upper arms and led her away from the horse.

Aware of the intimacies they would soon share, Amelia felt an instant of panic at Ross's nearness. His hands on her arms felt too warm, too close. As soon as she could stand on her own, she pushed one of his hands from her arm, then stepped away from him. "I'm fine now, thank you." She distanced them with several more steps, then looked over her shoulder at Ross. He wore that crooked knowing smile on his wide mouth. She crossed her arms and looked away.

"There's a nice little stream not far from that fallen tree in front of you. Wash up, if you want. I'll take care of the horses and build us a fire."

Without answering, Amelia strode off in the direction Ross had mentioned. A little privacy would be welcome. She stepped over the remains of the tree and found the wide but shallow stream. She paused and looked back at Ross. He was tying the horses near the dead tree. "Will it be safe to go downstream?" This was such a wild, deserted place, she thought.

Ross unbuckled the cinch on his horse and heaved the saddle off the animal's back. He dropped it on the ground, then nodded. "Should be, but don't go far." He turned to the other horse.

Amelia followed the dark water around a bend and found some likely bushes that would afford enough privacy to take care of urgent business. That taken care of, she returned to the grassy bank and sat down. Ross could just wait a while. Amelia peeled off what was left of her gloves and tossed them aside. She tried to feel sorry for herself, but couldn't muster up enough self-pity. After all, if not for Ross, she could be spending the evening with Luke Badger or honeymooning with Tyson Briggs, though she supposed her scheme had spoiled all of Tyson's plans.

She picked up a rock and threw it into the water. The resulting fountain of silvery drops brought a smile to her lips, then it collapsed much like the rock's splash. She should have been honest with Tyson. Perhaps if she had... What was the use of should-haves? They were a waste of time. At least this night would end with the dawn. Amelia stood up and brushed off her skirts. She didn't believe that for a minute.

Amelia gazed back down the path she had just taken and girded up her courage. After she took the first step, taking the next wasn't so hard. Soon she saw the fire burning brightly through the trees. She paused just before she entered the clearing. Ross stood by the fire, its flames casting harsh light and shadow over his tall frame as he stared into it. A sudden picture of the *comanchero* leader flashed in Amelia's mind. They both carried the same proud bearing, the same aura of lethal power.

"Come here, Amelia."

Amelia tensed. How had he known she was standing here in the shadows? He looked up and caught her in his steady gaze. Amelia's heart pounded inside her chest. She brushed her palms along her skirt, then walked toward the fire.

As Amelia drew nearer, Ross took off his hat and tossed it on the blankets he had spread near the fire. He unbuckled his gun belt, then leaned over and hooked it over his saddle, which sat at one edge of the blankets. Amelia watched these preparations with growing alarm. By the time she reached the campfire, her pace had slowed to the speed of winter molasses. Ross reached out a hand and clasped one of hers. Amelia didn't resist the gentle pull that brought her closer.

Uncurling each finger from her tight fist, Ross lifted her palm to his mouth and placed a soft kiss in its center, then held her hand close to his heart. "You're a fever inside me, Amelia. I only know one cure. I've fought this thing since the first night I met you. I can't fight it any longer."

Amelia looked directly into the heat that simmered in Ross's eyes. "You don't have to, Ross. I'll give you what you want—the way you want it. No vows of love attached. No obligations."

Ross pulled her captured hand to his neck, then circled her waist and hugged her to his long, hard body. "You feel so good next to me," he whispered, then he kissed her.

Amelia stood stiff and restrained; her free arm hung at her side. She vowed to control her response. No more visits to that wild, free place only Ross could take her. The trip home was too painful. His warm lips moved against hers, then his tongue demanded entry. Reluctantly she opened her mouth and tasted his kiss. His tongue met, then dallied with hers. Anticipation curled deep inside her like faraway thunder. Slowly, almost unwillingly, she smoothed her palm over the soft leather of his jacket to rest at his shoulder.

After a soft kiss to the corner of her mouth, Ross lifted his head. "Turn around," he said.

Amelia gave him a suspicious glance, then dropped her arms and turned her back to him. Focusing on repairing her defenses, she hardly noticed his fingers searching along the thick braid wrapped around her head until it fell heavily down her back. She tried to twist around, but Ross caught her shoulders.

"Be still," he murmured against her ear.

Relaxing her guard very little, Amelia eased around once again. Her fingers grabbed handfuls of polonaised skirt. To keep from running, she focused on a broken branch that jutted upward from the large tree trunk that glowed silver with moonlight. From the small tugs on her hair, Amelia realized Ross was unbraiding its heavy weight. His fingers worked up her back and sent shivery currents along her spine. She closed her eyes and tilted her head forward when he reached her neck. Then his long fingers burrowed under the freed waves and massaged her scalp. Amelia pressed her lips tightly together and forced back a moan of pleasure. His strong hands glided to her shoulders, where he pressed lazy circles with his thumbs just under the base of her neck.

"Relax, *querida,*" he said in a raspy whisper.

His velvety command sent a tingling rush through Amelia. She wiggled her toes and bunched the wad of skirt in each hand tighter. She retrenched to block this unexpected, yet tantalizing assault on her senses. "Please, Ross.

Get this over with." She grimaced at the breathless quality of her voice.

"No way, darlin'. I'm not a wasteful man." He lifted her hair and kissed her nape. "Now turn around and look at me."

Amelia obeyed and gazed up at him with all the trepidation that unsettled her. "Ross, I—"

"Amelia, I know you don't trust me, and I can't blame you." He caressed the high curve of her cheekbone with the back of his hand. "But I won't hurt you. I can give you great pleasure. Do you understand?"

Amelia drew her brows together in a perplexed frown and shook her head.

"I'm not surprised." Ross wove his fingers beneath her hair and cradled her head. "But, you will, *querida*. I promise." He slowly lowered his head and covered her mouth in a deep, lover's kiss that proved he could deliver.

Ross finished the kiss with a low moan. "You're right, Amelia. Time to get on with this."

Amelia opened her eyes and found Ross shrugging out of his jacket. He dropped it to the ground. His neckerchief quickly joined the small pile. Her eyes grew round when he jerked his buff-colored shirt from his pants and pulled it over his head. When it landed with his other clothing she managed to find her voice. "What are you doing?"

"What does it look like? I'm takin' my clothes off. You better hurry if you want to save that dress." He started on his pants buttons.

Amelia spun around, but quickly fumbled with her own dress buttons that ran down the front. She hadn't considered this. No, she hadn't. She gathered up the material and pulled the dress over her head, then shook it out and neatly folded it before placing it alongside the saddles. The thump of Ross's boots hitting the ground added urgency to her already shaking fingers as she tugged at her petticoat tapes. She had never undressed in front of Devin in five years of marriage, for heaven's sake. She stepped out of her petticoat and tossed it by her dress. A shiver ran through her despite the fire that burned brightly nearby.

One more piece of clothing hit the ground somewhere behind her. Amelia stopped fluttering at her corset lacings and stared ahead at nothing. His pants, she thought. Instantly she gave her lacings her full attention and snarled them into a tight knot. She plucked and picked but the knot only tangled worse.

"Got a problem?"

Amelia lifted her head in surprise at how near Ross's voice sounded. Then she jerked harder on the knotted strings, which didn't help at all. "I can't get this knot out."

"I'll take care of that."

"It will only take a moment. Really."

Ross turned her around. "I don't want to wait."

Amelia gasped when she saw the knife flash between her breasts and slide down the strings holding her corset together. Ross pulled it off her and threw it into the fire.

"You don't need that damned thing."

Amelia looked in amazement at her hated corset bursting into flames. Good riddance, she thought. She folded her arms across her chest and looked down at her shoes. She looked everywhere except at Ross. She had never seen a man completely nude. She and Devin had kept their nightshirts on and the lamps off. Married or not, she wasn't ready for this.

"Do you need some more help?" Ross asked with a hint of humor tracing his voice.

"I can manage," she retorted. Amelia sat down to take off her shoes and stockings, then stared into the fire as she removed her chemise and drawers. She laid back stiffly and looked up at the thick canopy of tree limbs that allowed only an occasional star to peek through. "I . . . I'm ready now."

Ross lay down on his side next to her and rested his head on his propped up arm. She felt the heat of the campfire on one side and Ross's heat on her other. She didn't know which warmed her more.

Ross made her look at him by nudging her chin with his index finger. "Ready, *querida?* I don't think so."

"Ross?" Her eyes finished her question.

"You'll know when you're ready and so will I. Now touch me," Ross said in a soft drawl that caressed her as if he had touched her.

Amelia hesitated and studied his face as firelight flickered over the sharp angles of his features and into the gold swirls of his eyes—steady eyes that had never lied—eyes that told her plainly how much he wanted her. No man had ever looked at her with such desire, not even her husband. His heated gaze stirred that latent animal inside her she had worked so hard to keep leashed. She tore her gaze from his and focused on the fire's smoldering reflection playing across his broad chest. She admitted she wanted to touch him and did with a feather-light sweep of her hand. She heard the catch of his breathing and looked up to see his eyes tightly closed as if he were in pain. He raised the hand that lay on the blanket between them, then lowered it.

Amelia realized he was holding himself in check and wondered why. She wished he would simply pounce on her and get it over with. That's how Devin had done it. The experience was slightly painful, but at least it was brief. Finally she asked, "What are you waiting for?"

Ross opened his eyes. "For you," he replied, and combed his fingers through her hair.

Amelia understood then what he wanted. He wanted her to let go the way she had in the belvedere, the way she did whenever he touched her. "Your price is too high, Ross." She caught something like regret pass through his eyes. She swallowed back tears for what could have been. "I'm sorry," she said softly.

Ross picked up a dark strand of hair from her shoulder and rubbed its silkiness between his fingers while he searched her eyes. "Maybe...I am, too, *querida*."

Ross moved over her then and placed his thigh between hers. He kissed her long and hard. Amelia fought the urge to wrap her arms around his muscled back, to feel his satin skin beneath her palms. She lay quietly detached. It took more will than anything ever had.

His hand slid over breast, her ribs, then her stomach, and she froze her thoughts on the night in the belvedere. His hand dipped between her legs and Amelia caught her bottom lip with her teeth to stop herself from pushing her hips into his caressing fingers. When one finger began a slow exploration inside her, Amelia couldn't control melting around it, yet she never moved. Not even when he moved his finger in an imitation of what was to come and she heard her own wetness. She closed her eyes tighter and remembered the awful pain of that fiery night, how he had shredded her heart with his ugly words. No matter what his reasons, Ross would never love her. She couldn't betray herself by giving in to his kind of loving.

Amelia heard a soft curse, then Ross moved his big body between her legs. She spread her thighs to accommodate him. She felt the tip of his shaft move against her moist cleft, then ease its hot firmness inside her, filling her completely. Her eyes snapped open. He slowly withdrew, then plunged back inside her. She was lost.

Amelia moaned from deep in her throat. She grabbed up handfuls of scratchy blanket and met his next thrust, then his next. A spiraling heat ignited deep within her womanhood. Planting her feet on each side of him, she arched her hips in a rhythmic circular motion that communicated the winding flame inside her.

"Put your arms around me, Amelia." His voice was low and hoarse.

She dug her nails into his shoulders. "Ross," she panted. "Oh, Ross."

"I know, *querida*. Hang on now." Ross wrapped his arms around her waist and pulled her up to straddle him as he sat back on his heels. She gasped as he penetrated her deeper still. With his hands on her bottom, he set the rhythm of their mating. Amelia looked into his eyes with wonder at the storm building inside her with each stroke of his hard length. The wind kicked up and swirled her long hair around Ross and her, lifting the silken curtain away from her breasts. Amelia leaned forward and brushed their sensitive tips against the rough hair on Ross's chest.

"Let me taste them," Ross panted in her ear.

Amelia arched her back, offering her breasts without hesitation. He pulled her hips into him and halted their delicious rhythm. Ross kissed each puckered nipple, then flicked them with his warm, raspy tongue. Amelia squirmed.

"Be still, baby. Please be still," he groaned. Then he caught one dusky tip with his lips and pulled it and circled its hard tip with his tongue. The other one received the same treatment until both nipples pouted swollen and wet.

Amelia inhaled long quivering breaths that swamped her senses. She had never experienced anything like this. She hadn't known how a man could make a woman feel. She wanted something more. Ross pulled her nipple into his mouth and suckled it with strong tugs that sent the fire stabbing into her groin. "Yes, Ross, yes," she cried. She moved her hands up and down the corded muscles holding her to him. "The other one. Now the other one," she panted. She couldn't believe what she was saying, yet she couldn't stop. Ross had taken her into the storm and she could only ride the wind.

A sharp tug on her other nipple pulled a groan from deep inside her. She moved her hips and moaned again. Ross clasped her closer to him and kissed her neck, the pulse behind her ear. Then she set her own shuddering tempo that swayed her breasts against the coarse hair on his chest. That burning tension deep inside her twisted tighter and demanded the stroking touch of his hard shaft. She raced toward the edge and the race consumed her, body and soul. Ross tilted his head back and squeezed her bottom hard. Through a haze she saw him lick the sweat from his upper lip as he watched her through half-closed eyes. She kissed him and tasted his essence on his tongue. She pushed against him harder and harder—faster and faster. Then she found the abyss and stopped in shuttering disbelief. Ross pushed her to her back and rode her with his own frenzy. She tossed her head from side to side and moaned with each of Ross's hard thrusts until she plunged over the edge.

Ross collapsed on top of her. Amelia dropped her arms from around his chest and lay perfectly still. Her brain, her body were utterly numb. Reason slowly dragged her from the clouds. So that's what it's like to be struck by lightning, she thought. Then she hit the hard ground of full realization. And it hurt. How could she be so carried away by someone who didn't love her, who had promised her nothing but a brief passionate encounter?

Ross caught his breath at last. My God, he thought, my God. Amelia had been more than he had anticipated. What a little wildcat! He propped himself on his elbows and saw tears flowing across her flushed cheeks, gleaming in the firelight. Pain like he'd never experienced pierced his heart.

Ross rolled off her and sat up to stare into the flames. He had known not to mess with her. He had know what a man like him could do to her. "Hell, Mando was right. I belong out there on the plains with him."

He hadn't realized he had spoken aloud until he felt a light touch on his shoulder.

"That's not true, Ross. You aren't like him. I won't let you say that."

Her quiet voice only served to make him feel more guilty, an uncomfortable emotion he took great care to avoid. "Whether you let me say it or not, it's true, Amelia. My aunt and uncle had the right of it. They always said I didn't belong with decent folks after living so long in New Mexico."

"Is that where you knew Mando?"

Ross watched flames swirl around a log. Around and around they went. "Mando's father raised me."

"How did that come about?"

Ross gazed at the spirals of fire slowly consuming the wood. He had never told anyone about Don Alphonso, about the fire in the valley. He didn't know if he could say the words.

"I'll understand if you don't want to tell me—if the memory is too painful."

Ross sighed. Here she was trying to be kind, for Christ's sake, and he had hurt her. He'd never forget those tears. For the first time in his life, Ross felt the need to explain himself. He reached over and picked up two striped woolen blankets and tossed one to Amelia. "You'll need this." He wrapped the other one around himself and sat cross-legged by the fire.

Amelia drew her blanket around her shoulders then sat down beside Ross. She joined his study of the fire. Maybe if she sat very quietly he would connect the confusing pieces of the picture she was trying to construct.

"Don Alphonso Carlos Madrid Enrique Fierro was a hell of a man," Ross began. "He was a *cibolero*. That's a kind of buffalo hunter. Only in New Mexico a man hunted with a steel lance and trained horse that would race death with him. It was quite a sight, let me tell you. Don Alphonso loved the pure sport of it. Anyway, the New Mexicans had somehow made peace with the Comanches. I can't think of another people who have. Which is why he found me living in a Comanche camp. The band had attacked the wagon train taking my family to Texas. They killed my father and took me and my mother off to a valley on the Llano Estacado. They call it the Valley of Tears. That's where the Indians separate the mamas from their children. Mine didn't go for that idea." Ross bit at his lip. "They killed her. I'll never forget how she fought them." He turned and looked at Amelia. "You'd do the same. I can see that."

Amelia forced her tears to the back of her throat. "Thank you."

Ross turned his attention back to the fire. He wanted to get this over. "Don Alphonso traded some bread and blankets for me and took me home to New Mexico. I was about five, I guess. He taught Mando and me everything he knew about the plains and that was considerable. His family had been in New Mexico for generations. When I was about fifteen, he was showing us how to train our horses so we could join his *ciboleros*. My uncle rides in and wants to take me back to Texas. It took ten years for him to trace me down. I don't know why he bothered. Likely some kind of guilt. He had talked my father into coming to Texas."

Ross shifted and jerked the blanket up around his ears. "I cried and fought until Don Alphonso boxed my ears and said a man belonged to his family. I went quiet then. I wish he had told my family I belonged with them. They didn't cotton to me much. Worked hard to civilize me, but I didn't take to their ways. Things rocked along until the war started in '61. Me and my cousin, Francis, the only one of the bunch that didn't treat me like dirt, joined up with Hood's Texas Brigade. Not many of us came back. Francis died at Andersonville.''

Amelia lowered her head. She had read about the shameful Confederate prison.

''I went back to Texas to tell his folks.'' Ross shook his head with a bark of bitter laughter. ''His mother screamed it should have been me. I turned my horse around and never went back.''

Amelia wanted to touch him, hold him, but she remained still and quiet. Ross being the closed man he was, she doubted he'd ever spoken of this to another soul. Whether he admitted to needing a friend or not, she was gratified to discover he had decided to tell her.

Ross picked up a stick and threw it into the fire. She needed to hear the rest of it, he thought, and he needed to tell it. He understood that now. ''I went back to New Mexico after my...hero's homecoming. I found Mando wild with hatred and riding with the *comancheros*. His father had been killed by white buffalo hunters. They had come across Don Alphonso somewhere up in Kansas and told him to butcher his horse if he wanted meat, so some other men with him say. They ended up killin' him and his horse. Dammit, they died like cattle, not hunters.''

Amelia heard the fury edge Ross's voice with a deep and brutal anger. This was the bitterness that froze the indifferent glint in his eyes, that hardened his wide mouth into an implacable straight line, that left his heart divided. No wonder he didn't trust anyone—least of all himself.

Ross looked away from the fire and gave her his full attention. ''I guess I went a little crazy, too. I joined up with Mando and stayed in New Mexico until a few years ago. Too bad I ever left, huh?''

''Yes, too bad. I could have spent tonight with Luke Badger. That is, if I had lasted until tonight. If some drunk hadn't taken me, those buffalo skinners would have killed me. Ross Tanner, you aren't half the bad man you'd like me to think you are.''

"I'm not, huh? That's why when you were in trouble and asked me for help I made you pay for it."

Amelia gathered her blanket around her and stood. "I asked you to face death incarnate for me, Ross. The only regret I have is that Luke Badger got away with my thousand dollars. Though considering the circumstances, I think that a cheap price, indeed." She spun around, then lay down, leaving Ross to think on that.

Ross twisted around and said, "You're some kind of woman, Amelia."

"I'm a cold woman right now. Come here and keep me warm." She hadn't thought it possible to reach Ross Tanner or the stars. But when Ross joined her under the blankets he proved her wrong on both counts.

Chapter Sixteen

Cold edged into Amelia's deep, dreamless sleep. Its insidious fingers crept through her dark warm contentment, pulling her toward awareness. She shivered and snuggled deeper into the blankets that smelled of Ross. Seeking the comfort of his warm smooth skin, she wiggled over an inch or two. A chilly emptiness jerked her fully awake. Amelia sat up instantly, holding the rough blanket to her naked breasts. "Ross!"

"Good morning, sleepyhead." Fully dressed down to his Colt, Ross walked toward the fire and poured her a cup of coffee.

Amelia closed her eyes to take a shaky breath. He hadn't left her. She greeted him with a hesitant smile and accepted the tin cup he held out to her. She sipped the hot, fragrant brew. "Mmm," she murmured. "That's wonderful. I'm so cold."

One corner of Ross's mouth eased upward. His eyes raked over her. "As much as I'd like to warm you up again, we need to get a move on."

"I wasn't issuing an invitation," Amelia insisted. The man was positively leering at her. Despite the early-dawn cold, she felt warmth creep up her neck to her cheeks.

Ross squatted beside her. "Now don't go getting embarrassed. I didn't mean anything." He gave her a kiss. "You're beautiful when you blush. Never stop."

"It's silly and childish to blush so."

"No, it's not. Your blushes are kinda rosy and warm and, well...innocent."

Amelia rolled her eyes and laughed. "Ross, after last night, how can you say that?"

Ross's expression suddenly grew earnest. "Don't ever think that." He traced the graceful line of her cheekbone and jaw. "What you gave me was good and clean."

"Ross...I..." Amelia had trouble getting past the gathered emotions clogging her throat.

Ross saw he had embarrassed her again. He hadn't meant to get her tensed up. "Put your clothes on, lady. The sun will be up soon and you'll be wishing we'd started earlier." He kissed her again. "I'll saddle the horses."

Amelia fumbled for her scattered undergarments, minus the charred corset, which would remain abandoned forever by the campfire. She smiled imagining what other travelers stopping for water might think if they saw it. She found her drawers in a tangled snarl at the bottom of the bedroll and her chemise lay crumpled in the dirt close by. This rummaging for undergarments was an altogether new experience. Ross Tanner was a wonderful initiator of new experiences.

"You probably need this," Ross stated. He held out his red silk neckerchief. "I thought you might want to...you know...clean up."

Instead of being embarrassed, Amelia welcomed his thoughtfulness with a smile. "Thank you," she said, and took the cloth. Her brows raised to find the wet silk warm. Apparently, Ross had even heated water for her. What surprises this man presented. She wondered what others would come her way this day.

"When do you suppose we'll reach Santa Angela?" Amelia leaned over the saddle horn and raised her bottom from the hard leather. She bunched and poked at her skirts, trying to make herself more comfortable, then eased back down and winced. Thin cotton drawers and no sidesaddle proved a poor combination.

"About midmorning. You worried?"

Amelia gazed beyond the horizon into the sunrise that stained the thin clouds overhead with reds and golds. All her worries could be explained in two words. Tyson Briggs. She was sure he knew by now what had happened. He would be waving Devin's debt in her face and she no longer had the money to pay it. His revenge should be well thought out by now.

"Well?" Ross prompted.

Amelia pulled her gaze from the eastern horizon and focused on Ross riding companionably beside her. "No..." the corners of her mouth rose briefly, she looked away. "Maybe a little."

"The talk will die down—"

"I don't care about that."

"Then what's the problem. Maybe I can help."

Amelia opened her mouth, then closed it, exhaling a long breath. This was Devin's mess and hers. She couldn't bother Ross with it.

"It's just business."

Ross studied her strained expression, but didn't press for more information. He understood, but he wanted to keep her talking. "So how's the mercantile doing?"

"Very well. In fact, I'll have enough money to go home soon. I gave what I had to Dominga, true, but after I sell the cattle I've accumulated and if my other accounts continue to come in I'll recover that and more."

"Go home?" Somehow that idea didn't sit too well. "So you won't stay in Texas?"

"No." Amelia didn't like this conversation. It touched on a subject she hadn't resolved herself. How could she think of any future that included Ross Tanner that didn't include Texas? Had she really considered a future with Ross? Not in Texas, she admitted.

Ross studied her a moment. He recognized the indecision forming a tiny frown between her eyes. He had a chance. "Do you think you could go back to giving tea parties and sewing samplers?"

Amelia flashed an indignant frown at Ross. "I might open a business there."

"Making hats? Running a boarding house?"

"I'll find something else," she insisted.

"*They* won't let you, Amelia."

"They?"

"You know who I'm talking about. All those pompous, fat old men who run things, their suspicious fat wives who tell them how, their sons who will consider you fair game, their daughters who will kindly think you eccentric, but untouchable."

"That's not true!"

"It is true and you know it. How many people from Fort Concho would you call friends?"

None, Amelia reluctantly admitted to herself. Ross was right. All those placards Libby painted were for a reason. Amelia sighed. She was no sign painter. "Well, then I'll go to tea parties and sew samplers."

"And look for another husband." Ross tried to keep the anger from his voice, but the mere thought of Amelia married to someone else rankled.

"I'll never find another..." She looked away. "I won't marry again."

"Then you'll end up somebody's old Aunt Amelia. What a waste. You're a doer, a fighter. Don't go back to that stale life. Stay here in Texas and grow with it."

"A doer? All I'll manage to do is bungle things and get myself or someone else killed."

"You don't bungle things. You try, Amelia. You take chances. Take another chance. Marry me." Ross surprised himself with his proposal, though he never let it show. His fear of her refusal never surfaced, either.

"What!" Amelia turned startled eyes to Ross, who looked at her intently.

"Marry me, Amelia," he said quietly. He looked away. "I wouldn't blame you if you—"

Amelia reined her horse to a halt. "I couldn't marry a finer man. I wouldn't have survived out here if you hadn't been the kind of man you are. A man who doesn't lie, a man who stands by what he says...an honorable man, Ross. If I refuse your proposal it would be for other reasons."

Ross turned his horse and leveled his eyes on her. "Like what?"

What, indeed, Amelia thought. Wasn't this the answer to all her dreams? A husband. A home. A home in Texas? "If I married anyone it would be you. I . . . I love you." There. She'd said it.

"But?" Ross voiced the question still unanswered.

"Ross, I don't think I could ever be happy living on the frontier."

"What about when you came to Texas?"

"That was before I knew how it would really be to live here. The dust, the heat, the wind. The day-to-day struggle to simply survive."

"Give it time, Amelia. The beauty of this land isn't easy to find, but once you see it, no other country will do."

"I'm sure you're right." Amelia fumbled with her reins. "Ross . . . I . . ." She didn't know how to explain this without hurting him. "The violence, Ross. I don't know if I can live with the violence."

Ross looked out over the rugged terrain. "Are you talking about the land or me?"

Ross had always been honest with her. He deserved her honesty, as well. "Both," she answered quietly.

"I can't do anything about that, Amelia. But you can."

Amelia lifted her head and looked at him. "How?"

"By staying here. It's a strong woman that takes the wildness out of place or a man." He fixed his gaze on her. "You're that kind of woman, Amelia."

"How can you say that? I've already told you. I've messed up anything I tried to do."

"If trying to change things instead of standing back and watching things change you is bungling, then that's exactly what I need. In fact, I could use more of your bungling. You've given me something, Amelia. Hell, I can't put it into words. If we weren't on these horses, I'd show you."

Amelia was grateful they were riding. If he touched her, kissed her, she knew she couldn't think things through. No matter what Ross said, there would be no more rushing willy-nilly into things. Every instinct told her to say yes, but

those same instincts had proven themselves completely un-
reliable. No, she had to consider every possibility from now
on. "Ross, I'm so confused right now. Let me think about
this. Nothing can be harmed in that."

"I understand. I don't like it, but I understand. I'll wait,
but don't make me wait long."

Above the next low rise, Amelia spied thin wisps of smoke
climbing into the late-morning air. They had reached Santa
Angela sooner than she'd expected, or maybe her dread of
the coming confrontation with Tyson Briggs was so great,
it had warped her conception of passing time.

Ross slowed his horse yet again to the pace Amelia set. He
glanced at her and wondered what this reluctance to reach
Santa Angela was about. For the past hour she had hardly
spoken to him and had slowed their pace so much he could
have gotten off his horse and walked faster to Santa Angela.
Something was eating at her. "Amelia, what's wrong?"

"I'm sorry Ross. I haven't been very good company. It's
just...well..." Maybe she should tell him. He ought to be
warned of what they might be riding into. "Ross, Tyson
Briggs is going to be furious with me. I've messed up all his
plans and now you and I..."

"Tyson won't cause any trouble with me. If he causes
trouble with you, he's causing trouble with me. He knows
that."

"Ross, this is my problem. I don't want you to get in-
volved."

"It's a little late for that, Amelia."

"I suppose it is, but I don't want trouble for anyone."

"A woman like you is going to cause trouble, but it's
nothing I can't handle."

Amelia didn't draw any reassurance from Ross's statement. By the time they reached the outskirts of town, her
apprehension had grown into full-scale fear. Tyson Briggs
was capable of anything. She inspected each doorway, window and alley as they ambled slowly through the dusty
streets. The people she saw inspected her as closely. One or
two even waved. She nodded briefly in their direction, but

stayed on guard. She glanced once at Ross and noticed he scanned the streets with equal interest. He expected trouble, too.

The little lean-to behind her store never looked so good . . . or so empty. She missed her mules. The contrary pair had become more than animals to her. Drawing closer, she was surprised to see Rayford walk out of the hut. "What are doing here, Rayford?" she asked in a surprised but kind voice.

The lanky boy darted black looks between her and Ross. Finally his eyes narrowed on Ross. "I came to feed the mules this morning and they weren't here. I was worried about ya and hung around. I was fixin' to go tell Mr. Briggs to gather up a search party."

"Thank you, Rayford. I appreciate your concern, but as you see I'm home safe and sound. I won't be needing you to care for the mules any longer. I . . . I . . ." She looked over at Ross, then back to Rayford. "I gave them to my friend, Dominga. Poor woman, she needed a way to get to San Antonio."

"Miss Amelia, you're too nice. You gotta watch people out here. There's a lot of bad ones." Rayford continued to stare holes into Ross.

"I'll remember that, Rayford. Now if you'll excuse Mr. Tanner and I. We're very tired and I have to see about the store."

"I just bet you are," the young cowboy spit out.

"Watch it, junior," Ross said with a quiet menace edging his voice. He didn't want to hurt this kid, but nobody talked to Amelia that way.

"Sure . . . *Mr.* Tanner." Rayford turned his back on them and walked away in long angry strides. The two pistols on his skinny hips gave him the appearance of the back end of a bony longhorn.

Ross lifted Amelia from her saddle. "That kid's headed for trouble." Ross's hands caressed her waist, but he scowled at the corner where Rayford had disappeared.

Amelia placed her palms on his chest and looked up at him. "He's just young."

"He's not likely to get old with that chip on his shoulder."

Amelia raised her brows and tilted her chin. "Recognize someone?"

Ross laughed and kissed her on the nose. "Maybe so."

"Well now. How cozy."

Amelia whirled around and saw Tyson Briggs standing a short distance behind them. His hands drew back his coat, revealing the bright yellow vest that spanned his wide chest. He smiled at them with his derisive manner at full attack. Amelia dropped her hands and pulled away from Ross. "Mr. Briggs—"

"It's 'mister' now? I thought we had decided on 'Tyson' and 'Amelia.' "

"Under the circumstances—"

"Just what would those circumstances be, *Mrs. Cummings?*" Tyson smiled wider at the distress plainly visible in Amelia's pained expression. She better be worried.

"Lay off, Tyson."

Amelia saw the color rise in Tyson's face. He reminded her of the day she had dumped those gold coins on his counter. She watched him struggle to control his fury, just as he had then.

Tyson shifted the cold steel in his eyes to Ross. "So that's the way the cards have fallen."

Ross placed a possessive arm around Amelia's shoulders. "I told you I always played to win."

Tyson tilted his head back at an arrogant angle and crooked a smile. "I guess it's time to count my losses and find another game."

"It appears that way."

"Good luck, *amigo.*" He cut his eyes to Amelia. "You're gonna need it." Tyson turned on his heel and walked away.

Despite the warmth of Ross's nearness, Amelia shivered. Ross pulled her tighter against him and she looked up with a brave little smile. It faded with her hopes of a peaceful settlement to this situation. If Ross ever looked at her the way he looked at Tyson's retreating figure, she would start making her peace with God.

She placed her hand against his stubbled cheek. "Ross."

He pulled his attention from Tyson as the big man rounded the corner to the alley and looked at her. His tight expression eased into a soft, caressing perusal. "You're beautiful," he said, then pulled her around into his full embrace.

Amelia grabbed up fistfuls of his jacket. "Ross, don't put me off with compliments."

"I wouldn't do a thing like that." Ross kissed the corner of her mouth, then the small indentation behind her ear.

"Ross, you're trying to distract me," Amelia breathed. "And you're doing a marvelous job."

"Good," he said against her neck.

Amelia closed her eyes and steeled herself against the havoc his lips and tongue were creating with her thought processes. She managed to push a small distance between them. "Ross, please, I don't want any bloodshed over this."

"I won't start anything. Does that make you feel any better?"

"Not really. I—"

"Does this?" Ross captured her mouth in a deep, hungry kiss.

Amelia's arguments melted like snowflakes on a hot stove. She slid her arms around his neck and raised up on her toes to meld her body to his. How could she think of leaving him when he made her feel so free, so alive?

"You remember this—" Ross kissed her earlobe "—when you're thinking about leaving." He stood back and pushed a loose curl behind her ear. "All this trouble will pass with time, but you and I need each other always. Say yes."

Amelia looked into his eyes. They still reminded her of a mountain cat's, all dark, swirling golds filled with mystery, independence and a beautiful wildness. But the indifference that had always tempered them had been replaced with love. Love for her. That was enough. "Yes, Ross. I'll marry you."

Ross wrapped his arms tightly around her. He closed his eyes and rested his cheek against the soft crown of her head. The chance she might have said no filled him with such pain it frightened him. He hadn't known until that moment how much he wanted her or how much he needed her. He placed his hands on her shoulders and said, "I'll love you till the day I die."

Amelia hugged him around the chest. "Don't say that. Don't ever say that. Don't even talk of dying."

"I won't be dying soon, *querida*. At last I've found something to live for." Ross placed his hands at her waist and stepped out of her embrace. "What's this? Tears, and on your wedding day?"

"Wedding day?"

"I'm not giving you any time to back out. I saw one of the traveling preachers when we rode through town. I guess Tyson's wedding plans won't go to waste."

"Ross, how can you joke about it?"

"Serves the bastard right for trying to force you into marriage. God! When I think about that."

"Ross, no trouble."

"Already bossin' me around, huh?"

"I mean it."

"Hell, I wouldn't make trouble on my wedding day." Ross brushed her lips with a gentle kiss. "Go get fancied up. After I take care of some other business, I'll come by and get you."

"What other business?" Amelia looked down from the sudden change in Ross's expression. "I'm sorry. I didn't mean to sound like some shrewish wife."

"I know you didn't. Now, go on and change. I'll take care of your horse."

Back in his mercantile's dark taproom Tyson finished his fourth beer. "That damned meddlesome woman," he mumbled, and hammered the mug on the table signaling for another. The new girl he had kept on rushed in with a brimming mug and scurried away. The interruption didn't cause a ripple in Tyson's black thoughts. "She can't double-cross me," he muttered. Tyson lifted the beer and poured it down his throat. He didn't bother to wipe away the spill down his vest.

"Mr. Briggs," Henry called softly from the doorway.

"Get out of here. Can't you see I'm thinking," Tyson bellowed.

Henry cleared his throat. "Mr. Briggs, Charlie Hudson is waiting to see you. I told him you didn't want to talk to nobody, but he said it was real important."

"Charlie Hudson." Tyson narrowed his eyes. "Send him in." Probably bringing his deed over, Tyson thought. At least something was going right.

A small bowlegged man with shaggy gray hair walked briskly into the taproom. He tossed a bag of gold coins on the table. "Here's what I owe ya."

Tyson stood, not bothering to cover the look of surprise on his face. "Where'd you get that?"

"I sold the ranch to Ross Tanner for a fair price, you bastard. Now give me a receipt so I can leave."

Tyson glared down at the little man. "Henry," he shouted. "Write out a paid in full on Hudson's account."

Charlie Hudson shoved on his hat and stalked back into the store. Tyson stood in motionless fury, watching the rancher receive his receipt. Unable to contain his rage any longer, he sent the makeshift table and gold crashing against a wall. Damn it, he didn't want to use his ace in the hole, but he had to. He couldn't lose everything. Tanner would discover the game wasn't over yet.

Tyson kicked a chair out of his way and, in two angry strides, cleared the archway and charged into the store like an angry bull. "Henry! Get that Rayford kid over here, pronto!"

Amelia rested her head against the high back of the copper hip bath. Lavender scented steam caressed her face and curled the tendrils of hair that had escaped from the pile pinned to her crown. Thank goodness for the one luxury Devin had managed to possess. She had tried to sell it, but no one in Santa Angela seemed interested in a copper hip bath. She supposed everyone jumped in the river to bathe, or simply didn't. Whatever the reason, at this moment she was inordinately overjoyed that no one had bought it.

Her body ached. Not her legs. Not her bottom. Not her back. Her whole body. She tried to bring her thighs together so she could search for her scented soap, but found it impossible. She pushed them together with her hands, then searched on each side. Sidesaddles definitely had their points of favor.

As she smoothed the creamy soap over her skin, she heard a knock on the bolted front door. Ross would come around to the back and call for her. It must be a customer. Go away, she thought. A great deal of work had gone in to this bath and she was going to enjoy it. Couldn't the person read the sign that said the store was closed? She shook her head and sighed at the next hard pounding. Apparently not. She put the loud knocking out of her mind and tried to relax. Whoever it was would go away soon.

After washing away all the trail dust, Amelia leaned back and let the fragrant hot water do its magic on her sore muscles. She couldn't believe this was actually her wedding day, after all. Ross was a complicated, hot-tempered, arrogant man. Everything Devin wasn't. Strange how she had chosen two completely different men. Strange until she realized she had chosen one when she was a young inexperienced girl and the other when she was a woman who knew what she wanted. She looked forward to life with Ross Tanner. He stripped away her stuffiness the way she peeled off starched petticoats. Yes, life with Ross would be exciting and full.

"She ain't here."

Amelia's eyes popped open. She sat up in the tub and listened. The voice came so clearly through the thin picket wall next to the alley, she could hear every word without straining.

"Why'd you go see her? What's she got to do with this?"

"I wanted to make sure she stayed the hell away from him this afternoon. I don't want her to get hurt."

Amelia's brows drew together. That was Rayford's voice.

"What do you care?"

"She's a nice lady, that's why."

"She's Ross Tanner's whore and everyone knows it."

"Don't you say that about her. Don't you say it."

"Simmer down, Rayford. Ross Tanner won't matter anymore after we get rid of him."

"Dirty *comanchero* scum. Probably sold the guns to the Comanches that killed my ma and pa. He deserves to be shot down like a dog in the road. He'll be coming out of the Dos Tigres soon if the plan goes right. We can surprise him from here."

Amelia scrambled out of the tub. She didn't bother to dry herself, but grabbed the first dress she could lay hands on. Her wedding dress. She fumbled with buttons and ties on the navy alpaca Mother Hubbard, then looked for her shoes. She shoved gritty feet inside her slippers. She had to get to Ross before it was too late. He could be leaving the Dos Tigres any moment.

Amelia tore through the curtain and raced to the front of the mercantile. Gasping for breath through the tight constriction in her chest, she fumbled the stubborn bar through the brackets and threw it to the floor. After jerking the door open so hard it crashed against the wall and made the shutters rattle, she gathered up handfuls of skirt and ran across the street. Those boys would see her warn Ross and know their plan wouldn't work. They would run away and no one would get hurt.

With only a few more steps to the cantina's doorway, Amelia saw Ross approaching the opening. "Ross!" she screamed.

Ross lunged through the door and shoved Amelia to the ground. A gunshot exploded from the mercantile. A woman screamed behind her. She heard a moaning sigh. But her eyes were trained on Ross. His gun was drawn before he hit the ground. He fired, then rolled away from her and fired again. Then silence.

As Ross rose slowly to his feet, Amelia inhaled a deep breath that smelled of dust and gunpowder. A woman wept behind her.

"Are you hurt?" Ross's voice was tight and hoarse as he reloaded his pistol, then with a quick look around, holstered it.

Amelia shook her head. Ross pulled her to her feet and held her tight against him. Amelia felt the tremors run through his body.

"My God, I thought you had been shot," he said against her ear.

Amelia looked across the street and saw Rayford's body sprawled faceup across his young friend's. Blood poured from his chest and darkened the soil at her doorstep. He must have run after her, she thought. Several men gathered around the pair and shook their heads. She knew the two were dead.

"*¡Madre de Dios!*" a woman's voice cried. "She is dead."

Amelia pushed away from Ross and looked behind her. A bullet had caught one of the cantina girls in the neck. She lay across the doorway with her hair spread in a black fan on the dirt. The girl's dead eyes stared at her. Amelia covered her mouth. Nausea boiled inside her. She pushed blindly away from Ross and ran toward her store.

The cowboys' bodies blocked her way. She stopped in the middle of the road and swallowed down the bile that burned the back of her throat. Then she walked slowly toward them. Rayford had no one to mourn him except her. She didn't even know his friend. She wondered if somewhere a mother waited to hear from him. Tears filled her eyes as she watched four men gather up the lifeless bodies and carry them down the road to the undertaker's.

She felt Ross's presence behind her before the warm strength of his hands touched her arms. His beautiful hands that had caressed her body, that had made her wild for him, that had killed these boys. Suddenly all the warmth in her body flowed out of her like Rayford's life's blood. She began to shiver from the chill.

"Amelia, look at me."

"Ross, they were so young. Only boys."

"For God's sake, one of them killed that girl. They wanted to kill me. What else could I do?"

"Nothing, Ross," she said, her voice ragged with unshed tears. "This land made those boys carry guns before they had the wisdom to make the right choices. Now they'll never grow up.''

"Amelia," Ross whispered.

Amelia closed her ears to the pain she heard in Ross's voice. She couldn't look back. No, she didn't want to see his eyes. "Ross, I can't marry you. I can't live with you. I can't live out here. I thought I could, but I'm not strong enough."

She felt the strength go out of his hands, then they slid away. While Amelia watched drifts of sand blow across the blood pooled at her doorway, she strained to hear the last soft chink of Ross's spurs as he walked away. Nothing was left for her now. Nothing but the mercantile.

Forcing herself to step over the stained earth at her door, she entered the store. A moment passed while she waited for her vision to adjust to the dim interior, then she surveyed its bareness. Her gaze took in the sparsely stocked shelves that proved how successfully she had achieved her goal to sell out and leave.

Her shoulders drooped and her feet shuffled over the dirt floor as she made her way to the counter. She leaned against it and studied her broken nails. At least she had managed the mercantile well, if not her life, she thought. Her brows gathered in a frown with sudden suspicion. Perhaps too well, by someone's estimation? No. Not even he would... Her brow cleared and her chin came up. Of course he would. The whole horrible scene played through her mind. The blood. The loss. The pain. Anger slowly filled the emptiness inside her. She whirled around and glared at the Dos Tigres, where she knew Tyson must have sat to watch his little drama played out. Through a throat so thick with unshed tears no voice was left to her, she rasped, "Damn you, Tyson Briggs."

Chapter Seventeen

"**I** guess you never know how a hand is going to play out," Tyson Briggs muttered. He gathered up the money from the table where he and Tanner had sat just minutes before. With a flick of his big finger he turned over Tanner's hand and whistled softly at the three deuces Tanner had been holding. Beat his two pair all to hell. The fireworks had started just at the right time.

He pocketed the greenbacks and flipped a tip to the girl who had brought them beers. As he walked through the bar, Tyson congratulated himself on the conciliatory game he had suggested to Tanner and estimated how much he had made. One good thing he hadn't planned on. This wouldn't be his last game with Tanner. A good player was hard to find and he hadn't liked placing Tanner in a no-win situation. No, he couldn't complain on how his ace in the hole had won him this game.

A commotion at the cantina's entrance brought Tyson to a halt just inside the doorway. He watched a young man pick up the dead girl and carry her outside, while a black-clad old woman trailed behind him weeping and raising her hands to heaven. Tyson shook his head. Too bad about the girl, he thought. She'd been a pretty little thing.

Stepping into the road, Tyson stopped and surveyed the area. The sad little parade turned a corner and death's visit to Oak Street wasn't even a memory. Silence fell on the road like the lengthening shadows that brought shade, but little relief. Tyson tensed and jerked his attention to a tin can that bumped and tumbled along the road. He relaxed when he noted the only other movement was a stray dog trotting past, sniffing at the air. Tyson glanced up at the hazy afternoon sun. Damned wind was kicking up again, he thought.

Holding on to the brim of his hat, Tyson started across the street toward the mercantile. From what he had seen and heard earlier, Amelia should be ready to deal now. With Tanner out of the way at last, he could move in and finish things. Maybe his luck was changing.

Amelia sat at her kitchen table and stared at the soapy gray scum that had gathered on her bathwater. Her thoughts swirled and circled like the patterns designed by the dusty drafts that skidded across the water's surface. She tried to find a focus, a place to begin. But the pain of losing Ross cut into her every attempt.

The front door banged open and she sprang to her feet. Her heart rushed blood to her numb fingers and heat chased away the chill that had gripped her since the shootings. She walked slowly to the curtain and pulled it aside. Disappointment rocked through her at greeting Tyson Briggs's mocking face. "Oh, it's you," she said.

"You were expecting someone else?" Tyson cocked his brow.

Amelia briefly closed her eyes. She *had* expected someone else. Suddenly a long, lonely future stretched ahead of her of expecting to see Ross Tanner behind ever knock at the door. She brushed a shaking hand over her face as if to push aside that dark picture. "What do you want, Tyson?" she said with a sigh.

Tyson hooked his thumbs in his vest pockets and tilted his chin at an arrogant angle. "It's time we settled our business."

"Not now, Tyson." She turned away. She could hardly stand to look at the man. She certainly wouldn't talk to him.

"Dominga here?"

Amelia crumpled the curtain in her hand, then released it. She turned and faced him. The calculation on his face sent a tickle along her scalp. She'd better talk to him before he made more trouble. She fixed her expression in what she hoped was purely uninformative and walked into the store. Ross was wrong. She could lie when necessary.

Preferring something big and solid between her and Tyson Briggs, she remained behind the counter. Looking at him squarely, she said, "You know she isn't."

"I suppose I did. I'm worried about her. San Antonio is a long trip from here."

Amelia hid her anger behind lowered lids and a frown. If she had needed any proof of Tyson's hand in all this, he had just given it to her. She had told only Rayford that story. She fought back the accusations she longed to hurl at him. He would only deny them and cause her or Dominga more trouble. Tyson would be made to pay someday, but not by her. She couldn't afford the luxury. Using every ounce of control she possessed, Amelia met his cool gaze without a blink. "Another family went with her." She fabricated a story as she went. "I asked Ross for help and he made the arrangements for her before Mario's funeral. She wanted to go someplace and start afresh."

"I heard about that funeral. Seemed mighty odd to me."

Amelia shrugged. "It seemed that way to me at first, but under the circumstances..." She would let Tyson draw his own conclusions. She couldn't think of any at the moment.

"Yeah, things couldn't have been too pleasant with Luke Badger hanging around."

Amelia colored despite herself and ran her finger along the counter. "No, it wasn't."

"Mario dyin' like he did messed things up pretty good. I come back with a preacher and find you tangled up with Ross Tanner. Strange how a hand will play out."

Amelia snapped her gaze up to Tyson's. "That depends on who's dealing the cards."

Tyson moved closer to the counter and propped himself on his elbows as he leaned against it. His massive shoulders eased forward. "I didn't know you knew anything about poker."

Amelia lifted her chin a fraction. "I don't, of course. I know in all games of chance someone controls the odds."

"You know, Ross was right about one thing. He knew you were a player from the beginning. Ross made his mistake when he didn't figure on you folding a winning hand."

Amelia gripped the edge of the counter. "Tyson, life isn't one big poker game."

"Yes, it is, honey. You just gotta figure out if you're going to play in the big games, the little games, or just watch." Tyson pushed away and, placing his big hands along the counter directly in front of her, he leaned forward and said, "Game's over. Time to cash in your chips."

Amelia narrowed her eyes. "What are you saying?"

"I mean it's time you decided to cut your losses and go home. Look for a game you can handle."

Amelia twisted away from Tyson. A game she could handle, indeed! She examined the nearly empty shelves behind her. She hadn't done so badly. Then she heaved a long sigh of resignation and turned back. "I can't go home." She hated telling him her circumstances, but he might as well know the truth. Maybe he would leave her alone. "I'm broke."

"Broke? I know your business has been good. You had money to help pay off that bounty hunter. What happened?"

She crossed her arms. "That's not important."

"You gave it all to Dominga." Tyson stood back and looked at her with open astonishment. "You did, didn't you?"

"It's none of your business."

Tyson shook his head. "Honey, you never loan your winnings to another player. Never."

"I'm not sorry. Some value friendship more than gold." Amelia paused a moment to let that sink in, but she didn't see any change across Tyson's impassive face. Why had she wasted the breath, she wondered. She would speak in terms he understood. "Besides, I have more accounts that will be coming in if you're worried about the money I owe you from Devin's IOU."

"You might find out what I learned in that game. Don't count on how the next card will turn. Meantime, you're stuck here. Tanner's gone. Dominga and Mario are gone. So much for friendship. There's just you and those buffalo skinners out there somewhere." At Amelia's in-drawn breath, he continued. "Oh, yes, talk is they've been seen and they weren't headed south to Mexico. Now, I've always said you're a smart woman. Sell out to me and get out of here. I'll give you the same deal I did before. My gold is your best friend—your only friend."

Amelia uncrossed her arms and placed her hands on the counter so Tyson couldn't see how they shook. "You're only trying to frighten me to make me sell."

Tyson shrugged. "You'll have to decide if I'm bluffin' or not. The stakes are high. Going home in style or joining Devin up there on the hill. I'm calling you, Amelia."

Her hands curled into tight fists. "I . . . I . . . Let me think about it tonight. I'll let you know in the morning."

Tyson's shrewd gray eyes jabbed into her, then they softened. Hell, he did admire the woman. She was the only fine thing that this godforsaken country hadn't burned up, ground up, or blown away. "Sounds fair," he finally agreed.

Tyson was about to leave, when he realized he couldn't turn away from those blue eyes of hers. For the first time in his life real regret hit him where he least expected it—somewhere around his heart. He shook his head to clear it and looked away. He couldn't explain what had come over him. Bad tamales or something. One thing was certain. Those skinners gave him an uneasy feeling. "Let me see that scattergun you've got under there," he said gruffly.

"What on earth for?" she demanded.

A heavy sigh of exasperation was Tyson's first reply. When she continued to stare up at him with defiance stamped on her pretty face, he said, "I'm going to show you something that might save your life, dammit."

Amelia arched one brow with skepticism but reached under the counter and pulled out the shotgun. She placed it on the wood before Tyson. A tiny frown formed between her eyes when he picked it up and broke the chamber open.

"Just as I thought." Tyson picked out the cartridges and gave them to Amelia. "You want to load this thing with blue whistlers."

"With what?"

"Blue whistlers. Give me that box marked with the double zeros."

Amelia turned and found the box Tyson pointed to. She pushed it across the counter to him. "What's the difference?"

Tyson opened the box and took out two loads of buckshot. He thumbed them into the shotgun's chamber and closed the breech. Handing the weapon back to Amelia, he said, "Let's just say the old-timers call this load dead medicine."

Amelia didn't know what to say. She hated thanking him, but a bit of gratitude seemed in order. Her hands gripped the barrel and stock. "I suppose I should say thank-you."

Tyson pulled his brows up. "Just a friendly reminder to think about when you're alone tonight and decidin' what to tell me tomorrow."

"Just the same, thank you, Tyson." Amelia searched his broad handsome features for some clue to explain his interest in her safety. She found nothing save his usual arrogant smirk that passed for a smile. "I don't understand you. I know you had something to do with the deaths of those young people today, yet..." She shook her head. "I don't know, Tyson."

"Amelia, I didn't kill that kid, and neither did Tanner. I might of stirred him up a bit and Tanner pulled the trigger, but that kid was on his way to the undertaker the day he strapped on those pistols of his. He was a fool. And I told you where fools end up sooner or later." Tyson jerked his head in Fort Concho's general direction. "Up on the hill.

The bad part of all this is they take others with 'em, sometimes."

"He was just a boy. If he hadn't lived out here—"

"Amelia, a fool is a fool no matter where he lives. The frontier has a way of stripping off the civilized layers and leaving just the man—" he nodded toward her "—or the woman," he added. "You find out real quick who you are out here. Before you start trying to understand me, you better start understanding yourself."

Amelia dropped her gaze to the shotgun in her hands. She was preparing to kill someone to defend herself. She had attempted to use it before. What was the difference between what she was ready to do, had tried to do, from what Ross had done today...what Ross had been forced to do every day of his life? Defend himself. She couldn't blame him because he was so very good at it.

Amelia put the shotgun away under the counter. Some part of her brain registered Tyson's departure, but she didn't acknowledge his leaving. She concentrated on discovering what really had happened that day. Walking through the curtain, she sat down at her kitchen table and tried once again to untangle her emotions from the facts.

Ross Tanner loved her, had never deceived her, had never used her. Since the first time they had met, he had protected her...even from himself. Yet she had turned her back on him when he had finally let down his guard enough to allow another person close to him. She didn't deserve his kind of love. The kind that lasted, that didn't wither under the hot sun or blow away with the wind. He deserved a love that was like those trees down by the river. Their limbs might bend with the wind, but they stayed rooted in the soil.

She had tried to tell him she was a bungler, an impulsive goosebrain that always made bad situations worse. He hadn't believed her. Maybe he did now.

Amelia pushed away from the table. This kind of thinking wasn't going to help her make her decision. She took off the blue alpaca dress and changed into her homespun garments. After carefully folding the dress, she opened her trunk and placed it on top of her belongings. She ran her hand over its fine cloth. This should have been her wedding dress, she thought. When she returned home she would put it away in that old cedar chest in the attic alongside her first wedding gown.

A deep regret and sadness brought tears to her eyes. Tonight, instead of packing her dreams away in some old trunk she could have been spending it in Ross's arms and living her dreams. Dreams. Amelia shook her head and closed the lid on the trunk. What had dreams ever gotten her but trouble?

Dreams of building a home with Devin had brought her to the frontier in the first place. She sat down on the trunk and looked around the small room. Her home. Wind buffeted the walls with gritty gusts that sent dirt sifting through the many cracks. Muddy puddles around the copper tub collected ashes that puffed from the hearth at regular intervals. Drab, gray, dirty. Her gaze stopped on the gay red-checkered curtain. She remembered the day she and Dominga had put it up and a sad little smile played around her mouth. She had done a good job with the mercantile. Hard work and persistence had made it a success. Her smile drooped to one side. At least she had done one thing right.

She spied Dominga's apron hanging on its hook next to the curtain. A wistful feeling came over her. If Dominga were here, what would she tell her to do? Amelia knew in an instant. Amelia looked down at her calloused hands. Dominga had been wrong about her, too. She wasn't like those trees with their deep roots. She didn't stand against the wind. Not when it counted.

Ross and Dominga saw her much differently from the way she saw herself. They had believed in her. Amelia curled her fingers into fists. Perhaps it was time to believe in herself. If she could travel to the ends of the world for Devin, she could damn well stay here for Ross.

The stakes in this game were higher than Tyson thought. Her life didn't mean a thing without Ross to share it. She wouldn't let Tyson or the threat of those skinners send her running. No more running. She would stay and hope that Ross would believe in her more than she had in herself. Amelia hit her thighs with her fists. He *would* come back for her. Glancing up at the shadows gathering in the evening gloom, she just hoped he wouldn't take too long.

Her decision made, Amelia lit the lamp on the table and began cleaning up the mess. After emptying buckets of water into the back lot, she dragged the copper tub to the door and tipped it on its side. A faint lavender fragrance drifted up to her as the last of the bathwater sloshed into the dirt. With the wind grabbing at her skirts, she wrestled the awkward vat out the door and turned it upside down to dry. She doubted anyone would steal it. Bathtubs didn't seem in high demand in Santa Angela.

But, chickens were. Amelia placed her hands on her hips and frowned at her empty chicken pen. Every last chicken was gone down to their feathers which the wind had joined with the thieves and stolen. Nothing was safe out here save bathtubs, she thought with disgust, and turned on her heel to return to the kitchen. She stopped in midstride. The entire back wall of the mercantile was bathed in a bright red. She turned slowly toward the horizon and watched the sun die in a wash of crimson. She had seen such a display before today. Only the sun had been rising that day. The day the buffalo skinners had come.

With a quick look over each shoulder, Amelia hurried into the kitchen and slammed the back door. She didn't draw a breath until the bar had been fit into its slots. A muffled noise from the front of the store lodged that breath somewhere between her lungs and throat. One hand clutched the material at her neck and she froze, then listened. The wind beat against the picket walls with hard gusts that filled the silence with rattles and low whistlings. Her breath eased through her in a heavy sigh. The wind, of course. She had better check the front door and make sure the shutters were locked. She moved with muscles so stiff they cramped, but managed to take up the lamp from the table. Her hand shook so, she thought she might loose the glass chimney.

After placing the lamp back on the table, Amelia spread her hands on the tabletop and drew in long, deep breaths. She had Tyson Briggs with his fantastic tale of returning buffalo skinners to thank for this panic. She was reacting exactly the way he had intended. Furious anger chased away her flutters. Tyson Briggs was not going to win this game.

Picking up the lamp once again, Amelia jerked the curtain to the floor and walked into the main room. She held the lamp out before her and followed its weak glow around the room, hesitating a moment on the closed door of the living quarters, then moving on. The slight trembling of her upraised arm gradually stilled.

While castigating herself in angry mumbles for allowing Tyson to get to her, she sat the lamp on the counter, then rounded its far end on her way to check the door and windows. In midgrumble she stopped and lifted her head. Something smelled rotten. She sniffed the air like a doe sensing danger, but the odor was so faint she couldn't identify its source. She checked the pickle barrel, a side of salted-down bacon, even the sacks of beans stacked in a corner. She couldn't locate anything gone bad. She sniffed the air again and tried to identify the foul odor. Now she couldn't smell it. She shrugged. Whatever it was, it must be outside. Peculiar odors flourished in Santa Angela.

Quickly she checked the locks on the creaking shutters, then frowned at seeing the door unbarred. She should have locked up in here first. She must be more careful in the future. She lifted the thick post and settled it to its place.

With one more glance around, Amelia walked briskly toward the counter and rounded its corner. She paused. A whisper of sourness in the air wrinkled her nose. Slowly she circled the counter, but she stopped again. Something was definitely going bad. One more quick search produced no culprit. It must be something outside. Tomorrow she would check the alley, since the smell, though slight, seemed to be

stronger from this area. Nothing was going to make her un-
bar those doors after dark.

She started to pick up the lamp, but changed her mind.
Leaving it burning wouldn't hurt, she thought. After all,
those skinners were loose somewhere. The light might help
her sleep better. Then she remembered something else that
would be of better assistance to a restful night. She picked
up the shotgun from under the counter and took it back into
the kitchen. It wasn't exactly the sleeping partner she preferred, but it would be welcome until Ross replaced it.

Ross picked up the charred remnant of Amelia's corset.
A stray, unwanted memory of how her eyes had gotten all
big and surprised when he had cut the damn thing off her
tugged a crooked smile to his lips. It lasted as long as the
vision. His mouth tightened into its usual hard line and he
tossed the scorched and battered contraption into the
campfire he had laid in last night's ashes and stepped back
from the smoke and sparks that spewed toward the tree-
tops. He watched the hungry flames consume the tatters
until only the stays glowed red-hot like his memories of her.
Ross twisted away from the fire and sought out his bed for
the night.

He made quick work of laying out his bedroll, then he
stretched out on it. Amelia's soft scent lingered on the wooly
material and tangled his thoughts into erotic knots. He
jerked into a sitting position, then, with a heavy sigh, he
settled back on the blankets. He couldn't escape her. Why
try?

Ross gazed into the night sky that was revealed in frag-
mented patterns through the wind-tossed branches above
him. He let his thoughts ride on the trailing veils of clouds
that slid over the stars. They took him back to the night he
had first met her. He had thought her a fool needing a good
shake into reality. Now, without really understanding why,
he saw the beauty of the heavens she had seen. He ached to
tell her that.

That wasn't likely, he thought, and it was his own damn fault. Ross sat up abruptly and dug a cheroot out of his saddlebags. He lit it with a burning stick from the campfire, then propped himself against his saddle to smoke. Tyson Briggs was a son of a bitch who cheated at cards. He had known that. He should have been ready for some kind of low-down trick. But he hadn't expected a bushwhacking.

Maybe he'd ride into town and kill the bastard. Ross dragged in a lungful of the bitter tobacco smoke and slowly exhaled, then watched the wind carry the curls of smoke into the night. Hell, he wasn't going to kill Tyson Briggs. When you've befriended a hungry dog you couldn't kill it for biting you.

Tyson had somehow rigged that showdown, but he'd only made it happen sooner than it would have anyway. That kid would have come for him sooner or later. He had seen it in the kid's eyes that afternoon. The poker game had started it. Amelia had finished it. Amelia. Ross took a drag on the cheroot again. Amelia was finished with him. Tyson had brought on that showdown, too. Hell, it would have come along sooner or later, too. But, dammit, later might have made a difference.

Ross flicked the cheroot into the fire and stared into the flames that licked at the darkness. Who was he kidding? Violence sickened her and he was...well...he was a violent man. Had to be. This was a violent land.

Ross pulled his gaze away from the fire and scanned the plains beyond the small stand of trees. Instead of the peace he had always drawn from the never ending distances, he saw only loneliness. A vast, forever kind of loneliness. He could hate her for the emptiness he had never seen.

But he loved her. Would always love her.

Ross rose to his feet and cursed his own stupidity to the four winds. Nothing changed. The torment was still there, deep inside him where only Amelia could reach. He brushed a hand over his face. Only one thing to do, and it wasn't run.

He was tired of running. If she wouldn't have him out here, he'd take her East.

He turned away from the fire and walked out into the open where he could see the stars. The wind tossed his hat to his back, where it tugged on the leather strap at his neck. He braced his legs and closed his eyes. The wind blew across the plain and carried music to his soul. He listened, absorbing its alluring rhythms; he breathed deeply, pulling its earthy fragrance into his memory. He lowered his head and slowly turned away.

Ross returned to his camp with long, determined strides and packed up his gear. He would reach Santa Angela before dawn, then wait. His plan ended there. He wasn't sure what he would be waiting for. Forgiveness? No. He'd done what he had to do no matter how much he had hated killing those cowboys. Acceptance? Ross shook his head. He had never waited for that. Maybe he should have. Ross paused to think over that idea, then gave the cinch on his saddle one last tug. The past didn't matter anymore. That was the thing about Amelia. She made a man look at where he was going, not where he had been. He wanted to tell her that, too.

Ross reached for the stirrup he had tossed over the saddle's seat. Instantly he grew still. Something was wrong. Something tingled at the back of his mind, dark and dangerous, yet unidentifiable. He listened carefully to the sounds of the night, but found nothing unusual. Slowly he pulled the stirrup into place, then turned from his quiet mount and searched the darkness. He saw nothing that would trigger that sixth sense that had kept him alive. Yet he knew it wasn't something outside, but something inside himself that warned him. Some detail past remembering or...

The unease grew into an urgency that clawed at his gut like fear. Suddenly the few short hours it would take to reach Santa Angela stretched into eternity. Ross swung into the

saddle of his big stallion and touched his spurs into the
black's satin flanks. The horse sprang into a gallop. Ross
didn't know what demon chased him, but he knew he
couldn't let it catch him.

Chapter Eighteen

Amelia opened her eyes wide and grasped the shotgun lying beside her on the cot. She listened. All was quiet…even the wind. She lay as still as the silence. Her gaze crept along the walls and floor and through the opening into the mercantile, but the darkness smothered everything. That's what had awakened her. The darkness. The lamp she had left on the counter must have blown out, she thought.

Holding the shotgun close to her body, she sat up, listened again, then rose to her feet. She inhaled a breath for courage and wrinkled her nose. A faint whiff of rancid grease soured the darkness. Her brows drew together. She sniffed again, then shook her head and frowned. Whatever she had smelled earlier had gotten worse. Much worse. A side of bacon she had forgotten must have gone bad.

Walking slowly through the kitchen with one hand feeling the darkness in front of her, she found a chair, side-stepped the table and walked into the mercantile. The nauseous odor slapped her in the face. She stopped abruptly. *My heavens, this place smells like a slaughterhouse in August.* She had to find whatever it was and throw it out. From the quiet outside, she estimated the time to be just before dawn. No one would be sober enough to stand, much less bother her.

Amelia set the shotgun down on the counter and searched the shelf behind her for a block of matches. She brushed a hand across her aching nose. The smell was so strong in here, it was painful. With increased urgency, she groped along the splintery shelf until she found the matches. Quickly she broke one from the wooden block, then turned and struck the match on the counter. Lifting the glass chimney, she touched the tiny flame to the wick.

Light bloomed around her. The muscles along her neck eased. After replacing the globe, she lifted the lamp and pivoted slowly, illuminating the dark room as she turned. That awful smell had to come from somewhere. It was worse than bad bacon, worse than anything she had ever smelled except . . . she stopped when the light reached the open door into the living quarters . . . the skinners! Had they hidden in the bedroom and waited until the town slept? Faster than her next thought, a huge shadow in the corner next to the door leaped out at her.

Amelia screamed and smashed the lamp to the ground. The checkered curtain burst into flames that raced up the picket wall beside it. She screamed again as the flames flared against the grinning leers of Bearpaw and Arno.

Tiny fires flickered in their black eyes and their sweaty faces glowed with reflected heat as Arno's grin slackened into a black hole of surprise and Bearpaw roared his frustration. Unable to tear her eyes from the two men, who looked more devil than human, Amelia stumbled backward and swung her arm wildly along the counter. The shotgun. Where was the shotgun? In her panic, she knocked the weapon to the floor on the other side. She almost collapsed under the fear that swamped her. She was lost.

"Arno, grab the bitch!" Bearpaw bellowed at last.

Like the demon from hell he resembled, Arno plunged through the fire and grabbed Amelia around the waist. Before she could do more than scratch his face, he tossed her up on the counter. Bearpaw wrapped his arms around her chest and yanked her against him, almost knocking the breath from her lungs. Amelia cried out in pain and fear.

As Bearpaw pulled her toward the door, Amelia kicked her legs wildly and scratched at his huge hands clasped together beneath her breasts. She opened her mouth to scream, but inhaled a lungful of scorching smoke. Coughing, choking, fighting for air, Amelia twisted and squirmed in a frenzied attempt to loosen Bearpaw's death grip around her chest. She bucked her head backward but hit his chest, not his chin. Bearpaw laughed and tightened his hold.

Amelia hated the weakness that stole through her muscles. Her brain screamed commands that her body no longer obeyed. She felt her strength flow from her, taking her will to escape with it. Dying. This was dying.

From somewhere above her she heard Bearpaw shout to Arno to forget about the cash box and come on. Through eyes almost blinded by tears and smoke she watched Arno struggle to stand on the counter. Heat waves snaked his black silhouette against the flaming backdrop of completely engulfed shelves. Fire rippled over his head and crawled along the canvas ceiling toward her. Bearpaw's hold on her shifted. Amelia gulped as much air as possible into her starving lungs.

"I got the door open," Bearpaw shouted. "Come... uhh... uhh... ugh."

Suddenly the iron band around her chest vanished. Amelia fell forward to her hands and knees and gasped for air. Holding a hand to her aching throat, she looked over her shoulder, wondering what or who had given her a reprieve. She saw two hands pulling a rifle barrel against Bearpaw's massive neck. A man behind the stinking giant was hauling him out the door into the street. Ross! Ross had come back!

A staccato of loud explosions jerked her attention to the front of the store. Dear God, the ammunition boxes! The fire had reached her supply. She saw Arno fling his arms wide and fall backwards into the crackling flames. Amelia buried her face in the crook of her elbow, but she couldn't block out his screams echoing through the popping ammunition. The stench of burning flesh rolled toward her in a black pall of smoke.

Coughing and gagging, Amelia backed away from the horror. Then she remembered the shotgun. She had to reach the shotgun. Ross couldn't hold on to Bearpaw long. Forcing herself to crawl forward into the fetid heat, she searched the hot earthen floor. Each inch forward was like crawling into an oven. Her hands and face burned and the air became impossible to breathe. But she had to keep going. Surely the shotgun was just a little farther.

Ducking her head, she eased closer to the popping ammunition, the crackling, hissing flames and Arno's silence. Her hands raced over the floor until at last her fingers touched, then snapped back from the hot metal barrel of the weapon. Quickly she wrapped her homespun skirt around her hands, then pulled the heavy weapon toward her.

Dragging the shotgun, Amelia twisted away from the growing inferno and crawled in the direction of the door until blessed cool air caressed her face. Using the gun as a cane, she struggled to her feet, then leaned against the door frame and breathed in the sweet air. She blinked her watering eyes and tried to see what was happening outside, but could determine little more than two men scuffling. She brushed a sleeve across her eyes, then saw a broad knife blade flashing in a fiery arc downward that ended in a sickening thud. A low, animal groan followed.

Amelia froze and waited. Bearpaw shook like a giant grizzly and roared. The man behind him slumped to the ground. She stared at the fallen man, then shook her head in total disbelief. "No," she whispered. Seconds ticked by, counted by heartbeats that roared in her ears. Finally one thought broke through the pounding silence. Ross was dead. "No-o-o!" she wailed, and bent double as if the broad blade had ripped through her.

Bearpaw turned his crazed eyes on her. Amelia caught his movement and slowly straightened. She freed her hands of the skirt material. He roared again and charged. Amelia brought up the shotgun and fired both barrels. Bearpaw's chest exploded before her astonished eyes as the recoil sent her reeling back into the mercantile. A table broke her fall, then flipped on top of her as she hit the ground. Partially stunned, she heard a loud grinding, as if the sound came from far away. Before she could react more than to place her hands against the pressing wood, a heavy beam and a large portion of sod ceiling collapsed on the upturned table. Pain shot through her hands and arms.

Amelia coughed the dust from her strained lungs. Surely the dirt had smothered the closest flames. If that were the case, she might have time to escape.

Straining to breathe through the dust and smoke, she shoved at the heavy tabletop. It wouldn't budge. She paused to catch her breath. The flames crackled and popped all around her as they ate the walls' dry wood. The tabletop pushed down on her, hardly allowing space to breathe and none to move. Panic almost stole away her sanity. Then she thought of Ross. He couldn't be dead. He couldn't! She had to free herself. Using the last ounce of her strength, she struggled to slide from beneath the table, but made little progress. It was all she could do to keep the weight from crushing her face.

With her breath tearing from her throat in short, painful gasps, Amelia turned her head to the side and watched flaming bits of canvas drift to the floor. She realized only a matter of minutes spared her from the hungry flames. Surely someone would come. She screamed and screamed until no sound came from her throat. She didn't want to die. Not like this. Dear God, not like this. Ross was dead or he would help her. She could depend on Ross. Oh, Ross, she had been such a fool.

Amelia sucked at the air that was getting thinner by the second. All she had wanted was to make a home for herself with someone who loved her. She had turned away so much more than that. Tyson was right. Fools found their homes on cemetery hill.

Ross noticed a rosy glow bloom on the horizon. The fist of anxiety that gripped his gut twisted until he hurt. Nothin' but a small prairie fire, he told himself as he wiped away the beads of sweat from his upper lip. He swallowed down the nausea that crawled up his throat, and forced his hands to remain calm on the reins. His foam-flecked stallion needed a steady walk after the run he had given him. Ross willed the small blossom of color to spread. It only grew brighter. He could no longer fool himself. Something was on fire in Santa Angela.

The moment Ross finished the thought, he topped the hill that had hidden the flames from his view. From this distance he couldn't distinguish which building was on fire, but he knew. A cold blast of fear sent his spurs digging into his flagging stallion's flanks.

The stallion gave him all he had left and they raced down the rise, quickly closing the short distance into town. Horse and rider tilted around a corner and charged down Oak Street. The stench of smoke and burning flesh hit them halfway to the fire. With a wild scream, the stallion reared and pawed the air. Ross threw himself from the saddle and ran toward the mercantile. He refused to think of what he might find.

Heat from the flames that lit both sides of the road closed around him. He couldn't take his eyes from the smoke and cinders that rose above the raging fire and whirled away into the night. Images of the valley far out on the plains flashed before him like a nightmare. Not Amelia, he thought. God, not Amelia.

Ross tucked his chin and ran harder. Through the shower of sparks in front of the mercantile, he made out a man dragging himself with one arm toward the burning building. He drew close enough to recognize him. Tyson Briggs! Recognition pulled his panicked thoughts into instant focus. He knew what had happened, what had triggered his unease, what had sat at the back of his mind like an unloaded gun. The buffalo skinners!

Amelia had needed him and he had run away from her. No, not from her. From himself. He had to save her. If not... The territory beyond that point was so black and horrible, he refused to enter it.

People gathering in the cantinas' doorways whirled from his view. He caught up with several other men who ran toward the mercantile, then passed them. Ross reached Tyson first. He knelt on one knee beside him. Tyson would know where he could find Amelia, which direction the skinners had taken her, if she was... No! Not that. Panting heavily, Ross carefully assisted the big man to his back. "Tyson..." He took in the bowie knife thrust to the hilt into Tyson's side. "My God, Tyson...what...where's—"

Tyson twisted his hand in Ross's jacket and pulled him down closer. "Ross, thank God," he gasped. "Amelia's inside." His cold gray eyes locked with Ross's. The ice within them melted with a single tear that trickled from the corner of his eye and disappeared in his wet sandy-gray curls. "I tried—" his face crumpled in a hard grimace "—tried to help her." Then all the fight drained out of him. He loosened his grasp and his hand dropped limply to his side.

"I'll get her out," Ross vowed. Tyson closed his eyes as Ross quickly stood and started for the mercantile. Restraining hands grabbed his arms. One man planted himself directly in his path. "You can't go in there!" the man shouted, so as to be heard over the crackling flames and exploding glass behind him. "The walls are gonna fall in any minute."

"Get the hell out of my way," Ross growled. He twisted free and slugged the man to the ground, then ran toward the mercantile. "Drag Tyson away from this heat," he shouted over his shoulder.

Throwing an arm up to protect his face, he charged into the black swirling smoke. His body caught on something soft that threw him to the floor. A body. Quickly exploring its size and shape, he knew it was Bearpaw and not Amelia. He rose to his knees and began feeling his way farther inside. He tried to keep his eyes open to see, but they burned so badly he couldn't. He'd find Amelia or die in here with her. Suddenly he thought he heard his name. He stopped and listened.

"Ross!"

Amelia's voice sounded hoarse and muffled, but Ross was relieved to hear its strength. She sounded very close. Straining to see, he searched the area next to him. His hand touched a piece of rough material. He grabbed it, but the cloth wouldn't lift more than a few inches.

"Ross!" Amelia shouted again. "I'm trapped. That's my skirt."

"Hang on," he shouted. "We'll get out of this." Somehow, he thought. He rose to his knees and, using his hands and squinting his stinging eyes, he made out a beam that had fallen across a table. From the direction of her voice, he realized Amelia was caught under the debris.

Ross took hold of the large, smoldering log and hefted it off the table. Then he grabbed the edge of the table and lifted it high enough for Amelia to scramble from beneath it. As soon as he saw she was safely free, he let the table drop, then scooped Amelia up in his arms. He dodged and darted through the burning drapes of canvas and ran into the street.

The waiting crowd of onlookers cheered and surged around the pair. Ross didn't know which hurt worse, the slaps on his back or the smoke burning his lungs. His hold tightened on Amelia as he turned down the many offers to take her from his arms. He stumbled forward, away from the heat and smell of death, until the smoke in his lungs forced him to his knees. He settled Amelia on the rocky dirt and collapsed beside her.

"Just give us some air," Ross commanded between coughs. The crowd backed away, then began to edge over to Tyson. Ross accepted a tin cup of water from a Mexican woman and gave it to Amelia, who struggled beside him to clear her lungs. "How's Tyson?" he asked the woman.

"Muy malo," the woman replied with a slow shake of her head.

Amelia lowered the cup from her lips and gave the remaining water to Ross. She drew a shaky hand over her mouth. "Tyson?" she said, frowning her puzzlement. Her eyes rounded with a sudden picture of an arc of fiery light on a knife blade and a body falling to the ground. She turned sharply toward Ross. "I thought Bearpaw had stabbed you."

Ross looked up at the woman. "Go see what you can do for Tyson." The woman nodded and hurried away, leaving Amelia and Ross alone on the road. Ross turned his attention to Amelia. "Why? I had run away one more time."

Amelia looked at Ross and gazed into the dark, tortured eyes of a wounded animal. She saw something other than pain and remorse. She saw a plea for help. She knew what she needed to say. "I knew you would come back. I always knew you would come to me."

Something twisted inside Ross, something more pleasure than pain, but the pain was there. She believed in him. Trusted him. He pulled her hard into his arms and held her. The smoke couldn't cover the tangy essence of fear that clung to her hair. Pictures of the horror she had faced alone shook through him. "I'd ride into Hell for you, *querida*." His voice was harsh and broken. "Never doubt it."

Amelia pushed away just enough to see his face. "I never doubted you, Ross. Only myself."

Ross took her hands from where they rested against his chest. He held them palm open before her eyes. "I'd never doubt a woman with hands like these." He kissed each dirty, calloused palm, then gathered her hands against his chest. "I'd never doubt a woman who with these small hands built something from nothing."

Amelia curled her fingers around a silver concho on his jacket. "You were always there to help me."

Ross pulled her head against his shoulder. "Damn, Amelia. Only you could call what I was doing help. My intentions—"

"Intentions!" Amelia pulled away and looked at him.

Ross blinked at the contempt hardening Amelia's usually soft blue eyes. "I—"

"Don't speak to me of intentions." Amelia rested her head against Ross's chest. "Devin had good intentions and little else. My father had good intentions, too. Intentions are nothing but empty promises and I've had my fill of those. Actions, Ross. Your actions have always been honorable."

Ross smoothed a hand over her loose hair. "A lot of people would disagree with you."

Amelia lifted her head and stated firmly, "Those people are either stupid fools busily blurting intentions or blinding themselves with prejudice." She smoothed her hand over his temple to the sharp angle of his jaw. "You had your reasons for anything you've done in the past. A man doesn't change that much."

"Where you're concerned he can." Ross rose to his feet and helped Amelia to hers. He circled his arm around her shoulders and directed his attention to the small group standing over Tyson. "How do you feel now?"

Amelia's gaze followed Ross's. "I can walk."

As Ross started toward the wounded man, Amelia caught his arm. None of this made sense. "Why did he do it?"

He studied her a moment, then shook his head. "I doubt if even he knows why." Ross shrugged away his own puzzlement and looked at Tyson. "Probably saw his chance to cheat the devil before his last hand was played."

Amelia smiled a little at that notion. She hooked her arm through Ross's. "Take me to him."

They walked toward the quietly murmuring group surrounding Tyson. The men parted a path so that Amelia and Ross could reach his side.

She fell to her knees beside the prone man. Ross knelt beside her. "Tyson," she whispered. She saw the bowie knife stuck into his side and tears streamed through the grime on her face. "Tyson," she cried.

Tyson's eyes fluttered open. "I see...Ross got you... out," he said between shallow, ragged breaths.

"Ross and your dead medicine," Amelia replied. "And that only because you helped me escape from Bearpaw."

Tyson's mouth curled into a weak attempt at his mocking smile. "They'll be...buryin' me...up on the hill...now, honey."

"Don't say that." She took a wet cloth that Henry handed to her and wiped the sweat from Tyson's broad forehead. "You told me only fools are buried up there. You're no fool, Tyson Briggs. You're the brave man who saved my life."

Tyson closed his eyes. Slowly, with great effort, he lifted one bloody hand and caught Amelia's as she bathed his face. "You make . . . a man . . . do . . . crazy things."

Amelia moved her hand to his chest, then slid it from beneath his wide palm. She turned her head and caught Ross's hand. He slowly shook his head. She had never felt so helpless. "Somebody do something!" she cried.

"There ain't . . . nothin' . . . anybody can do," Tyson gasped, "once . . . the cards . . . are on the table." He gathered up his last ounce of strength and grabbed Ross's arm. His eyes shone dimly with a little of his wily humor. "Winner take all, Tanner." Air rattled through his lungs. "Winner take all," he breathed. Then his hand dropped and his massive chest sank with his last breath.

Ross closed Tyson's eyelids. *"Vaya con Dios, mi amigo."*

Amelia picked up Tyson's broad hand from the ground at his side and placed it over the other one on his chest. "Surely he did cheat the devil."

Ross laid his hand on Amelia's shoulder. "I wouldn't be surprised. He was a player." He rose to his feet. "Henry, will you make the arrangements?"

The little man nodded his bald head vigorously, "Oh, yes, sir. Do you know if he had any family?"

Ross shook his head.

"That settles that. You men carry Mr. Briggs to the undertaker's, then come on over to my mercantile. I'm buying."

Amelia struggled to her feet and was about to launch into a long speech about respect for the dead, then she caught herself. These people cared for nothing but gold or silver. She had thought the same of Ross once, but he had proven her wrong. She looked up at him. "Take me away from here. Someplace where I can't smell smoke or the stench of greed."

Ross turned one hard look at Henry, who had the wisdom to drop his gaze and fidget with the loose tail of his nightshirt, then Ross slid his hand to Amelia's waist.

"Come on," he said quietly.

They pushed past the curiosity seekers and walked down the road. Ross spotted his horse grazing a small distance past the last adobe on Oak Street. He headed toward the stallion.

They walked slowly, silently, lost in their own thoughts. As soon as the air smelled cleaner and they had walked beyond the fire's glow, Ross stopped and pulled Amelia around to face him. "I'm taking you East. You're right. This is no place to live, only somewhere to die."

Amelia closed her eyes and clung to Ross. East. Back to civilization. Back to safety. Back to— Suddenly a picture of that caged cougar and his haunted, restless eyes came to her mind. She tilted her head up and looked into Ross's beautiful untamed eyes. She couldn't cage him. "You belong out here and I belong with you. We'll stay."

Ross rubbed his thumb across her wet cheekbone. "This is no place for a lady to live."

Amelia turned and rested her head against his shoulder. She looked past the ramshackle town toward the river. The wind-bent trees stood darkly against the dawn's rich gold, crimson and coral. "You told me it could be, Ross, and I believe you. You told me I could make a difference here and I will. We'll rebuild the mercantile, only bigger and better, and with my cattle—"

"And my land," Ross added.

Amelia tossed him a surprised look, then snuggled her cheek against his shoulder and watched rays of gold shoot into the heavens as the sun peeked over the horizon. "As I was saying, we'll rebuild the mercantile, and with my cattle, your land and shall we say, experience, we'll build an empire for our children."

Ross hugged Amelia to him and watched the sun rise. "Got it all planned, do you?" This is what he had feared from the first day he had met her.

Amelia tilted her head back and caught Ross's distant expression. A tiny frown formed across her smooth brow.

He looked down at her and the corner of his wide mouth lifted ever so slightly. "All right, Amelia. No more running."

Amelia relaxed against his side and smiled. "No more running, indeed."

* * * * *

LEGACY of LOVE

Coming next month

CORINNA'S CAUSE
Joanna Makepeace

England/Barbados 1685

Corinna had only just discovered her love for her cousin Oliver, when Sir Lionel Summers arrived to honour the betrothal formed in their childhood. Announcing she meant to marry Oliver instead, Corinna was aghast when her father flatly refused permission, and family secrets had to be revealed...

Lionel, determined to have what he had long desired, insisted their marriage went ahead, but when Oliver became caught up in the Monmouth Rebellion, Lionel knew he had to act, even though a wrong move could cost him Corinna!

COUNTRY MOUSE
Petra Nash

Regency - Dorset

Miss Anne Winterborne was content to keep house for her brother in his country rectory, but their peaceful existence was disrupted when their sister Arabella, young and beautiful, was returned in disgrace from relatives in London. Worse, she was followed by Lord Delamere, supposed architect of Arabella's downfall!

Anne was furious, and determined to keep Delamere at bay, only to be thoroughly disconcerted by the kindness of this urbane sophisticated man! Full of conflicting feelings, Anne couldn't see her way clear at all!

LEGACY of LOVE

Coming next month

PRIVATE PARADISE
Lucy Elliot

New York 1883

Lena Taber had learned a hard lesson amid the poverty and squalor of New York's teeming Lower East Side—not to want what she could never have. And Gilbert Brigham, the young society doctor who had opened his country cottage to the children in her care, could surely never belong to a poor immigrant's daughter.

The countryside was working wonders on her tenement-bred charges, but Lena knew these few precious weeks could bring her nothing but grief. She simply could not stop wanting a man—and a world—that must surely be forever beyond her reach.

THE ABDUCTION
Patricia Potter

Scotland 1550

Proud clan leader Elsbeth Ker longed for peace, but her stubborn English neighbours would have none of it—especially since the mysterious Alexander had returned to lead the Carey clan. Now the crofters had been burned out, and the outraged Kers demanded revenge. But when Elsbeth faced her enemy, what she saw in his steel-grey eyes gave her pause...

Alex Carey was ready for the task of ending the clan feuds, until the lovely leader of the Scottish Kers saw fit to kidnap him—from his very bath! It was time for Alex to come up with a new border truce...one that included the Lady Elsbeth.

FOUR
HISTORICAL ROMANCES
&
TWO
FREE GIFTS!